praise for
The Vanishing Moon

"Abounds in passion and wonder . . . Steinbeck's *The Grapes of Wrath* may have led us to expect that we know what it's like to be forced out of your home during the Depression, but nothing I have read prepared me for Coulson's patient reimagining of the Tollmans' life."　　　　*—The San Diego Union-Tribune*

"Heralds the arrival of an intriguing talent . . . Achieves the quiet beauty of William Maxwell's finest work—generous, episodic, elegiac but not sentimental."　　　　*—The Nation*

"A beautifully told story about family bonds, love, loss, and the power of memory over our lives. This is Joseph Coulson's first novel, and I hope not his last."　　　　*—The Bloomsbury Review*

"Will remind readers of classic authors like Steinbeck and Zola, or perhaps such contemporary masters of wounded male pride and self-doubt as Raymond Carver and Russell Banks."　　　　*—The Buffalo News*

"Wrenching enough to be a page-turner, yet genuine enough to make a profound impression . . . One of the best first novels I've read."　　　　*—The Pacific Sun*

The Vanishing Moon

Joseph Coulson

The
Vanishing
Moon

A NOVEL

a harvest book
harcourt, inc.
Orlando   Austin   New York   San Diego   Toronto   London

for Christine—
who makes all things possible

www.HarcourtBooks.com

First published by Archipelago Books, 2004

Library of Congress Cataloging-in-Publication Data
Coulson, Joseph.
The vanishing moon/Joseph Coulson.—1st Harvest ed.
p.   cm.—(A Harvest book)
ISBN 0-15-603018-7
1. Working class families—Fiction. 2. Middle West—Fiction.
3. Depressions—Fiction.   I. Title.
PS3553.O827V36   2005
813'.54—dc22   2004052608

Text set in Fairfield Light

Printed in the United States of America
First Harvest edition 2005

A C E G I K J H F D B

The moon from any window is one part
whoever's looking.

The part I can't see
is everything my sister keeps to herself.

—Li-Young Lee

BOOK ONE

Stephen

THE SUMMER of 1931 was a season of dying trees. Had we talked to any of the farmers who lived nearby, we would've understood that this blight wasn't a curse or an omen, simply the habit of a beetle and the fungus it carried. But in the particular stand of woods where we lived there was no talk of Dutch elm disease, nor any of the other plagues that preyed on bark and leaves. Instead, we took the dying trees as a personal insult, an emblem of our lives: the house in Cleveland deserted, Father out of work, and Mother going blind. The trees became a permanent feature of our landscape; stark, implacable teachers instructing us in broken dreams, admonishing us, despite the promise of better times, that most of what we hoped for in life was impossible, that to believe otherwise was impractical, even dangerous. Most things that die wither away or we put them underground, but trees stay standing, rows of barren trunks that creak and moan until the onslaught of rain and snow finally brings them down. Trees return slowly to the earth, and so the stubborn shadows of their dissolution darkened our childhood games.

Everyone we knew told us not to climb in dying trees, but Phil went up anyway, ignoring the brittle limbs, cursing when a tree refused to hold his weight. Defiance was his will. When Miss Dossin told him to stay in out of the rain at recess, he went out without his slicker. When Mother complained that too much reading was clouding her eyesight, he gathered all her books and burned them. When we lived in Cleveland, he raised rabbits, and when a rabbit got sick and died, he kept the carcass in our room until Father forced him to bury it. In those days my brother broke rules and crossed boundaries. He gave no ground. He pushed against everything, even death.

WE HEARD the story over and over again, first from Lethea, the midwife, and then from my mother, until every detail became part of the family history. Lethea said that my brother and his twin sister were conceived under a full moon. "Men spring from the sun," she said, "and women from the earth. But the gift of twins, when twins are man and woman, comes from the moon, because the moon partakes of both the sun and the earth." My mother couldn't remember if she conceived her first two children beneath a full moon, but she said that Lethea possessed a time-tested wisdom, and that we'd do well to listen to anything she had to say.

What my mother remembered was that the month of June in 1915 was unseasonably hot; scant afternoon showers provided nothing more than an evening steam bath, and her twin-filled belly felt overripe, ready to burst. "Twins mean good luck," said Lethea. "Twice the light for a dark world." But my mother knew that something was wrong. The days of kicking and turning had just begun when, in a rare moment of peace, she felt something inside her drop like a stone. Her heart had fluttered and she experienced a sudden shortness of breath. Nothing more had occurred, but when the labor pains began, she felt it again, something hard turning inside her.

Lethea arrived at dusk. The contractions came at regular intervals but the twins were stubborn. "Unwilling," said Lethea.

"Ornery and unwilling." She put a thin piece of wood between my mother's teeth, but took it away when it cracked and splintered, drawing blood.

Lethea talked and prayed and rubbed my mother's legs and feet. My mother screamed and wept and pushed. And then my brother dropped his head and shoulders into Lethea's waiting hands, and when Lethea cut him free, he wailed to tell the world of something he had seen.

And then came my sister with less struggle, smaller, the umbilical cord around her neck. Lethea covered the child with a towel, but my mother felt the truth, she felt it when the stone dropped inside her, and now she felt its hardness pass from her body. "Philip was born of tragedy," Mother said. "At the moment of his awakening, he lost his second self."

I WAS BORN eighteen months later, without struggle or tragedy, on a winter night noteworthy only for its calm. I was the second surviving child of what would soon be four children. My sister, Margie, followed me, and then Myron.

We lived in a rented house on a street named Joy, and my first memories go back to the room I shared with Phil and his pets. He kept turtles, frogs, fish, butterflies, grasshoppers, mice, and rabbits. I liked the rabbits because they were fast and mischievous, jumping off the twin beds and hiding behind the closet door.

Phil looked after his rabbits like a missionary after his flock; he tended the sick, cleaned cages, and provided fresh food with an evangelical fervor. Some of the rabbits were sold as house pets to families uptown. Others ran away or we gave them away. In winter most of the rabbits stayed in the attic, but during hot summer months they moved under the back porch where the ground was cool and the latticework kept them safe.

Being younger, I failed to understand the full measure of Phil's devotion. My mind couldn't grasp the fierceness of his loyalty. I didn't even know that it was blood when Phil ran crying into the house, hands and face smeared, shirt and trousers stained. I thought it was berry juice. Or maybe the red across his forehead was rage. That would explain his tearing into Father's closet and taking the rifle that we were told never to touch.

I followed him outside and we crawled under the back porch. It was mossy and dark, but I could see the broken lattice and a pile of bloody fur, and then another, larger this time, and then more piles, some with something half-chewed still moving. Phil crawled from pile to pile, cursing loud enough for the neighbors to hear, laying his hand on whatever remained until he was certain that it was dead. He would not let me help him. He would not let me touch anything living or dead. When we came back into the sunlight, we didn't speak. Phil sat down next to the broken lattice, the rifle on his lap.

When Mother and Father came home, I told them what had happened. Father went out the back door with a resolute expression on his face, but he came back into the house without his rifle. Phil refused his dinner that night. He refused to sleep. He stayed out all night waiting for whatever it was that had done the killing. He waited three nights, but it never came back.

"It killed 'em for fun," he said.

Then he sold the cages, burned five or six bags of wood shavings, and handed Mother the eyedropper and water bottles. By October, he gave away or set free every creature in our bedroom. I pleaded for the frogs and whined about the turtles for almost a week. "Forget it," said Phil. "And don't ask me again."

———

THE WINTER months were slow with only people in the house, and Mother noticed the change. "It feels empty," she said. "Less trouble, I suppose, but empty."

My mother was an expert seamstress commissioned by uptown families to hem curtains or embroider tablecloths. That winter, though, the demand for her skills dwindled until in February her one order was a christening blanket for a neighbor down the street. In that same month my father brought home less money. "Customers won't come out," he said. "Streets are bad. All the ruts are frozen."

We hoped that spring would bring opportunities for work, and when the snow finally melted, Phil and I made the usual rounds, looking to rake winter-killed grass from the big lawns, but we found no employers. And then the unimaginable happened. Fred's Radio & Repair, the shop where my father worked, shut its doors. Father made the announcement at dinner. Even Phil, the least naïve among us, was caught off guard. "But you told us," said Phil, "that everyone needs the shop and always will." Father made no reply. He looked at Mother, and then at the floor. Fred's Radio & Repair was the cornerstone of our world; its collapse suggested that the strongest foundations were vulnerable.

What followed was the first of several visits from the man my father referred to only as the landlord. Mother sold everything of value, including the silver candlesticks that came as a wedding gift from Grandmother. She sold our console radio. My father refused to leave the house for several days; he moved silently from room to room, his face pale and helpless, as if he were a condemned man.

Then, after a blur of packing and hasty farewells, Cleveland became the place my family hailed from, a memory of better days that we cherished and embellished over time.

We moved into a large tent on a half-acre lot that Father bought for twenty-five dollars. The lot was seventeen miles from Cleveland in a place called Mayfield. We had to clear trees and build an outhouse, live without electricity and running water, but the property bordered a meadow, and it sat on the high side of the Chagrin River.

MAYFIELD was the first great adventure of my life, exploring the woods with Phil, running barefoot across the meadow that dropped down to the river. On the border between the meadow and woods stood a line of scruffy bushes heavy with giant blackberries. Our fingers turned dark red, then purple, picking the sticky fruit. The abundance was overwhelming. We ate while we picked, until stomach cramps made us stop.

Phil and I would stay well away from the tent, keeping it out of sight, returning only when wind drove the rain in our faces or when mosquitoes rose up from the river at dusk. I didn't think about Mother and Father, their struggles or fears. I left them alone to take care of Margie and Myron. I gave them time to plan the family's return to Cleveland. My mind, filled with the mystery and wonder of the woods, didn't anticipate the coming seasons, the shorter days, and the inescapable dangers of living without money. Phil knew something about these things, and depending on his mood, he sheltered me or taught me, tried to explain that the world was both arbitrary and just, a contradiction that to his mind made perfect sense.

We made up all sorts of outdoor games, and our unrivaled favorite was the weekly ambush of the bakery wagon. We sat next to the dirt road and listened for the first echoes of the trotting horse. "Jesus, if we only had a nickel," said Phil.

"You say that every time."

His eyebrows came together.

We crouched in the tall grass as the horse and driver rolled by, and then we bolted into the road, running behind the wagon to get the delicious smells. The air danced and swirled, wrapping us in eddies of fresh bread, butter, cinnamon, raisins, and doughnuts. The smells were stronger, even sweeter, as we got closer to the wagon. I imagined myself a bandit then, plundering the wagon's payload of ruby red jelly and golden cakes. Phil and I ran until we were out of breath.

"Next week," I said. "Let's bring Myron."

"He's not fast enough," said Phil.

"I could pull 'im."

"You'd bite the dust. You'd break your arm and he'd break a tooth. Then I'd be stuck carrying both of you back to the tent."

"You always spoil stuff."

"I do not."

"You do! You always spoil my fun. You never do anything I wanna do."

"That's not true," said Phil, cracking his knuckles. "We went swimming yesterday."

"It doesn't matter. Most of the time we do what you want."

"That's because I'm older."

"Yeah, I know, I know. Older and smarter."

"You're not stupid," said Phil. "It's just that some of your ideas are stupid."

"Why?"

"Because half the time you miss what's right in front of your face."

"I see plenty."

"You see those trees?"

"Which ones?"

Phil pointed. "That stretch we walked through to get here."

"What about 'em?"

"They're all dying. Some of 'em are dead."

"They are not."

"For Christ's sake. Look! Can't you see the green turning yellow? Some of 'em are standing without half their leaves! Who ever heard of leaves going yellow—or leaves falling by the bushel—this time of year?"

"Maybe those cold nights we had—"

"It hasn't been that cold."

"Well, maybe they're just old."

"Some of those trees aren't much taller than you or me. I say there's something after them. And whatever it is doesn't make a sound. It's not like at night when you wake up and hear things—like a ticking or a rustling, sometimes a snarl. Something quiet is after those trees."

When we were kids, my brother talked to me, the edge in his voice already sharp, and he frequently described a world that I did not want to accept. At the same time, his ability to see what others overlooked bound me to him. It gave him a strange power over the people he loved, and it gave me the wisdom to know that any story involving me was really my brother's story.

Phil was the first to see those dying trees, and the truth of their dying loomed larger the longer my family lived on that half-acre lot. He was the first to see that Father was an affable fool, that we would be lucky to escape the army surplus tent that Mother called our temporary home. And he was the first to see that Mother was going blind.

MY MOTHER cast a spell over men and boys. At church socials in Cleveland her dance card was the first one filled, and I remember her laughter, her blushing face, and the lush folds of her skirt swirling as she danced with Father, his friends, and sometimes Phil or me. Her body was lean and muscular, almost masculine, but still voluptuous in its movements and generosity. Every action conveyed confidence, what my father called good, old-fashioned, Midwestern self-reliance. There was a purity about her, a promise that her body and soul were safe haven, a place of healing, a sanctuary where sons and lovers could drop their defenses and perhaps show themselves to be something more than men. Maybe it was the long hair that she wore well past middle age. Maybe it was the way she turned her head, the way she curved her slim hand toward her breast or drew her legs up, sitting by the fire, and let her bronze hair stream about her knees. Maybe it was the grief of the girl in her eyes. Men loved her with a poetic passion; she stirred a tenderness in them that living forced them to forget.

Phil was my mother's first child, and he laid claim to the largest part of her heart. Not even Margie, with her piercing blue eyes and a limitless capacity for unqualified love, could displace my brother's privilege. I thought for a long time that my stillborn sister formed the bond between Phil and my mother; but I began to see that of all the children, Phil was the least like my father, and this was the wellspring of my mother's affection. She adored Phil's stubbornness and determination, and so she held him closer, doted on him, tried to temper his strength with a love for kindness and beauty.

My mother adored flowers, pressing roses and lilies and fleabane and sow thistle between sheets of soft ivory paper. She sewed the sheets together, using thick cardboard for covers, and when we packed the house in Cleveland, she gave the book to Phil.

"Why'd she give it to you?" asked Margie.

"She can't see the flowers anymore," said Phil.

"Sure she can," I said.

"She told me," said Phil, "that the littlest ones go fuzzy around the edges."

"Will you let me look at the book sometimes?" asked Margie.

"Sure," said Phil.

And he did. Anytime Margie wanted to see the book Phil sat down with her and turned the heavy pages, trying to name the different flowers that Mother knew so well. We all found wildflowers when we lived in the woods, and we gave them to Phil and he sorted and pressed them.

One afternoon Mother tried to see what we had found, squinting through her thick glasses, until Phil closed the book in frustration. "Don't you dare think of it," she said then, her face sharp with disapproval.

Phil handed me the book, and my mother's words took me back to a day in Cleveland, a day with the first smell of autumn in the air, a day filled with waiting for my mother, waiting for the news she would bring from the doctor who forced bright beams of light into her brown eyes, who made her read a strange and shrinking alphabet on distant charts. She came home at dusk saying that the doctor discovered what was wrong. "It's eye strain," she lied. "Your mother is just tired. The doctor says that if I do less reading it'll probably clear up."

Phil took her at her word and ran through the house picking up her books and magazines. Her reading material amounted to a large box of old novels, copies of *The Saturday Evening Post,* and a few yellowed newspapers, and when Phil came running down the steps, he tripped, tumbling in a waterfall of white pages to the foot of the stairs.

Father slammed the refrigerator. "What in God's name is that boy up to?"

"Philip," said Mother. "Come here this instant."

Phil picked himself up and collected the contents of the box.

"Philip, those are my things. Put them back where you found them."

Phil kicked open the front door. Mother jumped to her feet and followed him outside. We were all outside by the time Phil dumped the books at the curb.

"I'm telling you, Jessie," Father said, "that boy's a hellion."

"Pick up those books right now," said Mother.

Instead, Phil took a small bottle from his pocket and poured its liquid on the books. Mother, seeing the match, tried to grab his arm, but it was too late. She pulled him back from the burst of flames.

Father took off his belt. "I'll teach you to burn your mother's property." But Mother held him off, protecting Phil with her body.

"Jessie, you're spoiling the boy," yelled Father, waiting for her to step aside.

"It's his way."

"I know. He shows no respect."

"He's trying to help."

"You call this help? Pretty soon the whole damn neighborhood'll be out here. It's crazy—"

"It's not! It's what the doctor said."

Father stopped short, lowering the hand that held his belt. Margie started crying and buried her face in my mother's blouse. Phil never said a word. He just stood there watching the pages curl and float upward, the red sparks rising into darkness.

—————

THE BURNING of my mother's library turned out to be a practical matter, since the recovery period for eye strain went on longer than anyone imagined, and because the tent provided no space or protection for books. But the tent's limitations seemed a small matter once my mother worked her magic.

The children's bedroom consisted of four cots separated from the main living area by Grandmother's sideboard and china cabinet. The long sofa, Grandmother's cedar trunk, and the kitchen table and chairs crowded the middle of the tent, and toward the rear was the wood-burning stove that provided heat and cooked our meals. Mother and Father's narrow room was on the other side of Grandmother's armoire and a rickety chest of drawers, where Father put two cots close together.

On hot days the air in the tent was heavy and our clothes and skin began to smell like damp canvas. But even in summer the nights were often cold and wet, the dew making the tent sag, and we were thankful for the dry heat of the wood stove. During rainy days we watched for seam leaks, setting out pots and pans. We tried to ignore the maddening howl of wind, and we prayed that stakes and ropes would keep the roof in place.

If we needed anything during stretches of bad weather it was privacy. I felt on those endless days of confinement the first stirrings of resentment. I longed to escape the watchful gaze of Mother and Father, to rebel against the petty tyrannies of my brothers and sister.

Time dragged under the steady drone of rain. Father slept most of the time, while the rest of us shivered in our blankets, talking when we could think of something to say, feeling uneasy and cramped. Boredom was a subtle taskmaster, weighing us down, making us restless, instructing us in the cruelties of impatience. When Myron hit Margie, or Phil and I started fighting, Mother would always intervene, scolding us for our failure, our lack of imagination. Then she would distract us by telling a story or singing a song. On days when she felt tired, she would pull out the *Sears Roebuck* catalog, the only book that survived Phil's rampage, and we entertained ourselves for hours, reading about electric trains and bicycles, making lists of all the items we would buy. At the top of Phil's list were a bowie knife and a pair of high-top boots. I wanted a black cowboy hat and a pair of chaps. We read our lists to Mother, and she folded them carefully and put them in Grandmother's cedar trunk, saying "Maybe someday, when we're rich."

When the sun returned it brought freedom, and life everywhere began again. Wagons lumbered down the muddy road, delivering ice and baked goods to the big farms. Trucks carried eggs and milk to the markets in Cleveland. We heard tractors and harvesters rumbling early in the morning, buzz saws downing trees, and the voices of men barking orders, shouting over the machinery.

About two miles down the road and masked by a row of evergreen trees was an abandoned construction site. A developer before the crash had dreamt of building an entire suburb between the farms, but he gave up after he dug four holes and poured the basement floors and walls. Rain and runoff collected in these deep, concrete bowls, sometimes as much as two or three feet, forming shallow pools that in the landscape of our games became oceans, lakes, ponds, and moats. It would've been a desolate place if not for a band of noisy ducks that, winding their way up from the river, made for themselves a giant birdbath. Margie loved the ducks, and Phil and I held Margie's hands as we walked on the narrow tops of the basement walls, following a mother and her young, throwing a few crusts of bread into the water. Then Margie thought Myron should see the ducks, so it became a routine that after heavy rain the four of us would hike down the road to watch the birds bathing and splashing. Margie played mother to Myron, holding his hand and explaining the situation. "The ducks waddle up from the river," she said, "because they like a change of scenery."

"Ma-Ma-Margie," said Myron. "I want a du—a du—" Myron closed his eyes. "A duck."

"We can't take a little one away from its mother," said Margie.

"But she won't m-m-miss just one."

"Do you think Mother would miss you?"

Myron nodded.

"Well what makes you think it's any different for a duck?"

Myron shrugged.

Margie turned and lunged toward Myron, pretending to push him off the wall and into the water.

"What are you doing?" screamed Myron.

"I'm scaring you. You're stuttering too much. You need to concentrate more."

"L-L-Leave—"

"See," said Margie. "Now relax."

"L-L-Leave me alone," said Myron.

We knew that Myron stopped stuttering when he was surprised or scared, so we often sneaked up on him or exploded paper bags behind his back. We thought the right jolt at the right moment would cure his stuttering forever.

"Cut it out you two," said Phil. "Or we'll go back. And remember, don't tell Mom and Dad we came here."

Keeping a secret was a challenge for Margie and Myron, but they never let on about our trips to the construction site. We knew that Mother would make us promise to keep off the narrow walls, to stay away from the concrete pits whether they were empty or filled with water. She knew about the well at Carson's Bend and made it off-limits even before we pitched the tent. So the aborted suburb became our secret place; we understood its dangers and wanted to explore its recesses with impunity.

There were other dangers and secrets in the woods, and we knew that looking out for each other was our only salvation. We never went as far as the Mayfield landfill; its stench was a warning that turned us away. We imagined bizarre diseases. We imagined insanity. And there was the dried-up well at Carson's Bend where years ago a farmer filling his bucket brought up an eyeball from the bloated corpse of a boy. Phil and I stopped once at the well, a circle of stone covered with thick planks, and I pictured something dark living at the bottom of the cold, waterless shaft. But more than anything else we were afraid of an old man who lived in a black shack on the other side of the river. We called him Wormwood. We heard the word first from Grandmother when she talked about the high-priced caskets that undertakers waiting for her to die wanted to sell her. "We all end up in wormwood," she said. The old man, who was our closest neighbor, walked with a stiff back and always wore a black hat, a long, black coat, and the look of a criminal caught unexpectedly in the act of a grave sin.

"Look at that wormy face," said Phil. "Old Wormwood is up to no good."

I took Phil's lead. "He must eat nails for supper," I said.

THE DOG DAYS ran toward September, and we became children of the outdoors, moving half-naked through the woods. On the hottest days we swam in the Chagrin, and on one of those days old

Wormwood came down to the river's edge and watched us for a long time. He finally took off his shoes and socks and, sitting on a long, flat stone, put his feet in the water.

I swam toward Phil. "Let's get upstream."

"This is the best spot," said Margie.

"We'll swallow toejam if we stay here," I said.

"You're sick," said Margie. She turned toward Wormwood. "Do you really think he kidnaps little kids and cuts off their heads and keeps them in his cabin?"

"How little?" asked Myron.

"I told you before," said Phil. "He doesn't keep any heads."

"I won't use that rock after he's been there," I said.

"Maybe he's p-p-planning to c-c-come in after us."

"He can't swim," said Phil.

"That's a good thing," I said. "He'd turn the river black if he got in all the way."

"Do you think he ever takes a bath?" asked Margie.

"Once a year," I said.

"He's l-l-lucky."

We laughed, and Phil dunked Myron from behind.

Long, dark weeds like tentacles wrapped around Margie's arm and waist. "Look out," I said. "Old Wormwood's got you!" Margie screamed and whirled in the water to escape the weeds. "You see," I said. "If Wormwood keeps his feet in much longer, we'll choke."

"He's weird," said Margie.

"He wants something," said Phil.

And as the words left Phil's mouth I saw what it was. Margie stood thigh-deep in the cool stream, squeezing water from her long hair, and the soaked T-shirt tied just beneath her breasts did nothing to conceal her hard nipples. For the first time I saw Margie's breasts, large breasts for a girl who was just thirteen, and the sudden revelation of her womanhood was not wasted on Wormwood. He knelt on the rock, transfixed by the vision of my sister rising out of the water. His body was rigid, too rigid, the posture of a supplicant, and so when his lips began to move I knew that prayer and not the mutterings of a madman rose up from him like poetry. I thought I heard him asking for God's help, praying for divine intervention, begging God for just a glimpse of Margie drying herself, peeling the wet shorts and T-shirt from her body. I knew what Wormwood wanted. I looked at Phil and he too was staring at Wormwood, seeing the desire in Wormwood's face.

"Margie, come 'ere," yelled Phil.

Margie dove toward us.

"He's looking—" I said.

"I know," said Phil, cutting me off.

Margie surfaced with a mouthful of water and shot it in Phil's face. "Do you need me to save you from drowning?"

"Let's get Myron and head back," said Phil.

"Already? Let's wait for Wormwood to leave. Then we can sit on the rock for a while."

"No. I don't think so."

"Why not?"

"Don't ask me why, Margie," said Phil. "Let's just go."

"Yeah. There's not much sun today," I said.

"What do you mean?" asked Margie.

"Too many clouds."

Margie looked at the sky. "You're both crazy. I'm going to wait until Wormwood leaves."

Phil and I stayed near Margie, and I watched Wormwood's eyes follow her through the water, and I guessed that on days when we used the rock for sunning ourselves that he had been somewhere nearby.

I used my body to block Wormwood's view, and once he tried to look around me, craning his neck and leaning over so far that he almost fell in the water. Margie finally got tired of waiting, and the four of us climbed the bank on our side of the river.

"At least he stays over there," said Phil. We waited for Margie to finish dressing.

I knew no one we could tell, not Father or Mother, and certainly not Margie. We had no words to explain the thing that lived in Wormwood's gaze. But as the dog days drew sweat, and Margie's skin turned a glowing bronze, Phil and I watched for Wormwood at the river and in the woods, beneath stones and in the shadows of giant trees, at all the edges of our world.

SEPTEMBER broke the heat and my dream of an endless summer. We enrolled at Mayfield School, despite the fact that we had no mailing address or telephone, and the Registrar, who was Todd Lincoln's mother, said, "This is all highly irregular." She said it more than once, and she shook her head while my mother assured her that our current situation was temporary.

We didn't see Todd Lincoln's mother very often after that. She came to school two or three times in a semester to help Miss Dossin with official paperwork. But Todd, of course, was in school from the first day, and he ran around the schoolyard pointing at us and saying our names, telling everyone that we were the new kids who lived in the tent. Some of the kids asked us what it was like, and in their voices was a sense of wonder. We were, after all, living the kind of outdoor adventure that their parents would never allow. But most of the kids looked at us like we were from another country, or they laughed and felt superior, luxuriating in the knowledge that we were worse off than they.

"Where do you get your water?" asked Todd.

"From a well on Mr. Johnson's property," said Margie. "He said we could use it for as long as we need to."

"You drink the water out of Johnson's old well?"

"We boil it first."

"What if someone went and pissed in that well."

"C'mon, Margie, " I said. "I guess Todd goes around pissing in wells."

Todd looked at Margie. "Where do *you* go to the bathroom?"

"In your shoe," I said.

"I'm telling Miss Dossin you said that," said Todd.

"Go ahead," said Phil, materializing out of the air, twisting Todd's arm, whispering in his ear. "If you do, I'll hurt you." Phil let his breath settle in Todd's ear, and then he let him go. Todd ran to the company of his friends and pretended that nothing had happened. He tried not to look at Phil.

POWER IN THE schoolyard shifted on a daily basis, but the indefatigable master of the schoolhouse was Miss Dossin, teaching all of her students, grades three through twelve, in one room. She was kind and beautiful, stern and demanding.

"Mr. Lincoln, take off your cap."

"My mother lets me wear my cap in the house, Miss Dossin."

"Your mother runs your house. I run this classroom. I will not ask you again."

I believe that Phil's considerable affection for Miss Dossin began at the moment Todd Lincoln took off his cap and slumped in his chair. Miss Dossin often demonstrated the expediency of being painfully direct, but she also exercised the art of discretion. She knew that my family lived in a tent, but she never said anything about it. She showed her concern for us by never asking for a mailing address or telephone number. She understood that the four of us had to stick together. She encouraged us to share each other's triumphs and failures, and she allowed us to shield each other against the teasing and practical jokes of our classmates.

On the third day of school, Miss Dossin called on Myron and asked him to read aloud. Myron shrank behind Felda Lane.

"Let's look alive, Mr. Tollman. Pick up your book and read the first paragraph of chapter one."

Margie raised her hand. "I'd like to read, Miss Dossin."

"Did I call on you, young lady?"

Margie lowered her eyes and shook her head.

"I thought not. I believe I did call on your brother."

Myron looked at Phil, taking a long time to open the book. Phil cracked his knuckles and everyone around him started giggling.

"Philip Tollman, I'm not impressed by your bone cracking demonstration. If you continue to practice that disgusting habit, your knuckles will grow bigger than boulders. And don't think for a moment that your little diversion will save your brother from reading. Myron, please stand."

The situation was hopeless. Myron pulled himself out of his desk and opened the book. "Sir I-I-Isaac New-New-Newton—" Then laughter buried the rest of the sentence.

"Children! Children!" Miss Dossin regained control. "Myron, do you always stutter?"

"Yes, Miss Daw-Daw-Dossin."

The laughter began again, but Miss Dossin cut it off. "Anyone who thinks that Myron's stutter is funny will deal with me after school."

No one laughed at Myron in the presence of Miss Dossin after that. But her authority, inviolable as it was, couldn't protect Myron outside the schoolhouse. His stuttering was a soft spot in the family armor, further evidence of our inferiority. Todd Lincoln led the assault with a barrage of consonants exploding from his lips. He sprayed saliva and tied his tongue in knots for the entertainment of his friends.

"Hey, sh-sh-shit for brains," said Todd, looking to see if Phil was anywhere nearby. "How abow-bow-bout a speech?"

Todd's friends joined the fun. "Speech! Speech! C'mon Moron, give us the Gettysburg Address."

Phil sometimes broke it up; other times it was Margie or me. I know that Myron took more than we knew about.

"Come 'ere Moron," said Felda.

"His name is Myron," said Margie.

"That's what I said."

Margie's face turned red. "You said Moron."

"That's right," said Felda. "I said his name."

ALL THIS was bad enough, but then I had to make things worse. I had to give Todd and his friends—as if they needed convincing—more proof that the Tollmans were trash.

I woke on the first day of October with cramps and nausea. It felt like the flu, but I knew it was the fish from the night before. Phil and I had each caught one, but mine hardly struggled. It just went limp on the line. I hadn't thought much about it until I woke up with my stomach turning.

Mother felt my forehead and face, and since I had no fever, she said I should go to school. I went. I started sweating by midmorning.

"Your face is green," said Margie.

I looked at my reflection in the glass but could see no color. Miss Dossin asked me twice if I needed to go to the outhouse. I shook my head, trying to control the stomach cramps that came in unexpected waves. I was grateful when Miss Dossin assigned my grade an hour of reading; she came by my desk and rubbed the back of my neck and told me not to read. "Put your head down and rest," she said. I closed my eyes and the rustling and whispering in the room lulled me to sleep.

It was lunchtime soon, and the room filled with the smell of peanut butter, pickles, warm cheese, and milk. Then, without much warning, something warm shot up into my throat and vomit flooded my desk. It ran down the back of Cory Weiner, dripping off my hands in long, sticky strings. After that I heard my name. It was Miss Dossin's voice. She stood above the scene looking at my puke, calling it my name. "Stephen," she said. "Oh, Stephen."

I ran away from the screams and laughter and found the relative safety of the outhouse, leaving Miss Dossin and Phil to clean up the mess. My stomach felt better after I washed my face and cleaned my shirt, but Miss Dossin said that I should leave. Phil told me later that the smell was awful, so bad that Miss Dossin decided to conduct afternoon lessons in the yard.

Turning the schoolhouse into a vomitory changed my position in the established social hierarchy; I fell from town peasant to town fool, assuming the mantle of scapegoat and giving Myron a much needed reprieve. My classmates made me the sole recipient of their invectives. They called me pukey, puke-head, puke-brain, puke-face, puke-breath, puke-shit, puke-prick, and just plain puke. When I walked into the coatroom, most of the kids held their noses. When I stood in line for the outhouse, the kids closest to me started gagging. I enjoyed a status usually reserved for the elderly or the insane.

I had to take it. I couldn't blame anyone else for what had happened, and some of the kids felt sorry for me and said that it would all be forgotten by Thanksgiving. But Cory Weiner always took the long way around me and never spoke to me again.

After a while I fancied myself a martyr, accepting the role of scapegoat as a service to Myron. But just when I began to fill myself with pride, I noticed my classmates again fixing their sights on Myron.

"Did you teach Moron your little trick?" someone asked.

"Moron's just like his big brother," said Felda.

"He doesn't know whether to stutter or puke first," said Todd.

"Get Moron over here," someone said. "Ask him if he stutters when he pukes."

My days as an object of ridicule were numbered. I was glad for relief, but sorry that my replacement was Myron. "Time," Lethea said, "purifies the most desecrated ground." I held those strange words in my mind while the weeks of October moved forward, changing the landscape with a new season, filling the woods with a firestorm of leaves.

I REMEMBER my mother squinting at the maples, not knowing it would be her last autumn of color. Phil and I, Margie and Myron too, rolled in the leaves, red and yellow covering our bodies like tongues of flame. We showered each other with oak leaves, fragile and pale, and with elm leaves, the last children of dying trees. We ran, making a swishing sound as the leaves swirled upward and fluttered. We flung ourselves into piles of leaves, sometimes face down, breathing the smoky dust of tree bark, covering ourselves with October's deep blanket.

Phil picked up leaves of different shapes and sizes and pressed them with the flowers in Mother's book. When he found out that red was Miss Dossin's favorite color, he collected all the different shades of red that he could find and made a bouquet of leaves. Then he stayed after school one day so he could give it to Miss Dossin when no one would see him.

"Did she like it?" I asked.

"You don't see it, do you?"

"You could've ditched it before you got back here." I looked out through the door of the tent; Mom and Dad were nowhere in sight. "What did she say?"

"She said 'Thank you.'"

"Oh, c'mon. She must've said more than that."

"She did."

"But you won't tell me."

"No."

"Why not?"

Phil took a deep breath. "Because things between a man and woman are private."

"Since when are you a man?"

"Since he fell in love," said Margie, coming out from behind Grandmother's china cabinet.

"Love?!"

"That's right," Margie exclaimed. "He's in love with Miss Dossin."

"You don't know what you're talking about," said Phil, turning away.

I was old enough to understand the attraction. A figure like Miss Dossin already lived in my waking dreams. I wanted to know what my brother felt.

"I'm gonna tell Mom you have a crush on Miss Dossin," I said.

"Shut up."

"I will. I'll tell her unless you tell me and Margie what Miss Dossin said."

"You would, you little puke."

It was the first and only time he used my schoolhouse name.

"You won't be Mom's favorite anymore if she knows you're in love with Miss Dossin."

Phil sprang on me and pinned my shoulders to the cot. He raised his open hand and I braced for the blow. Then Margie caught his arm and he froze, looking at her and then at me. I was scared. I wondered why he stopped. But the look on his face told me not to say a word. It was a strange expression, mixing anger and sadness. Phil let go of me and rushed out of the tent.

"Why did you say that about Mom?" asked Margie.

"What about me?" asked Mother, coming into the tent.

"Oh, nothing," said Margie.

I closed my eyes and thought of Miss Dossin, the girls at school, the picture of Aunt Frances in her sleeveless gown, the world of women that seemed suddenly so exotic and remote.

By Halloween my name came back. Having worn me out as a target, Todd again set his sights on Myron, intending to make up for lost time.

Everyone said that Todd saw his chance when Miss Dossin pulled Myron aside and asked him to stay after school. But it started well before that. Todd was no different than most boys. In him was the need, the sharp longing, to corner a living thing and render it helpless. Setting the trap excited him. He enjoyed each step, the design and the execution. I could picture it all as if I'd been there myself.

I imagined the conversations between Todd and his two cronies, imitating Myron's struggle to speak and laughing to hide their own fears, their own inarticulate terror. I constructed the sequence of events: the meeting in Todd's barn to think of something that would mark Myron forever as a moron, an idiot, a fool who found it impossible to make the simplest sounds. I heard their first moans of exhilaration as the plan took shape. The boys relished their exquisite preparations, breaking into the Church of St. Blaise and cutting a thin wire from a high octave of the piano. Then passing the piano wire between themselves, keeping it warm in their pockets, until the day that Miss Dossin asked Myron to stay after school so she could help him form words, form phrases without faltering and falling into frustration. So they waited for him between the schoolhouse and the woods, waited until his lesson was over, until pride rose to his throat because he managed a full sentence without stuttering. They waited until Myron was close to the well at Carson's Bend, and then they forced him to the ground and Todd's friends, big boys with strong Midwestern shoulders, squeezed Myron's jaw until the pain made him open his mouth, and they held his mouth open while Todd tried to grab Myron's tongue, failing at first, the pink tip slipping between his fingers, but then Myron stuck out his tongue, believing Todd's promise that if he did they would let him go, and Todd gently wrapped the wire around the tongue while the other boys made jokes about Myron being tongue-tied for real. Todd wound the wire three times around the tongue and pulled gently, oh so gently, and then Myron gagged and a faint line of blood ran down the wire, and the boys released his jaw and left him to find his way home.

When Myron got to the tent he could barely speak; his tongue was swollen and still bleeding. Mother stuffed gauze in Myron's mouth to soak up the blood, but she couldn't see well enough to clean the wound. Father did the work. "There's only one cut," he said. "On the side of his tongue. And thank God it's not very deep."

Mother and Father went to school the next day and talked to

Miss Dossin about Todd Lincoln and his friends. The punishment involved an apology to Myron, a promise to never touch him again, and a two-week suspension.

PHIL DID NOTHING for a long time. He waited until Myron's tongue was better. He waited until Todd and his friends felt that all was forgotten, until they felt safe. And when he was certain that the boys expected no recrimination, he clipped my father's hunting knife to his belt and walked through the twilight to Todd's barn, with me close behind.

We surprised the boys, bursting in through the closed doors. Todd made a run for the hayloft ladder, but Phil tackled him and pulled my father's knife out of its sheath and held it to Todd's throat. Todd's friends had the idea to jump Phil, but when they saw the knife, they backed away.

"Keep going," said Phil. "Good. That's far enough. Now don't move. If you move, I'll cut his throat."

Phil nodded to me and I closed the doors. Todd made no sound beneath the knife.

"Your friends can't help you this time," said Phil.

I looked at Todd's friends, and when I looked back at Todd, he was off the floor. Phil held him from behind, squeezing Todd's elbows together with one arm and holding the knife in front of Todd's ashen face.

"If you stick out your tongue, I promise I'll let you go."

Todd began to cry. "Don't hurt me," he screamed.

Phil choked off Todd's air with the back of his hand. "I won't." Phil loosened his hold. "But I want you to taste my knife."

"You're crazy."

"That's right. But not like you. Not crazy enough to wrap wire around a small boy's tongue. My brother never asked to stutter—but he was cursed by God and then by you." Phil squeezed Todd's arms until something cracked.

Todd's tongue touched the knife, and Phil drew the blade across it, ever so gently, until it bled. Todd collapsed to his knees, crying and swallowing blood. Phil put the knife in its sheath. "Todd, if you tell anyone that I did this to you, or if your friends tell anyone, I'll kill you."

Phil and I walked out into the darkness, and when the barn was no longer in sight, I asked him if he meant what he said about killing Todd. He gave me no answer, and his silence made me feel empty and absolutely alone.

chapter two

FRED'S RADIO & REPAIR was once a burgeoning store on Lorain Avenue in west Cleveland. New and rebuilt radios filled the window display, and just inside the front door was a baroque, mahogany console that customers talked about in the same breath with caviar and fine china. The service counter ran the width of the shop. Behind it was a Dutch door that opened into a back room lined with workbenches and shelves, schematics and scribbled diagrams. Strewn on the workbenches were wire and tools, the guts of radios under repair. Shelves held rows of vacuum tubes stacked precariously; other shelves threatened to collapse beneath boxes of dusty transformers. Open drawers overflowed with switches and knobs, volume controls, tuners, faceplates, and grill-cloth; Fred called the back room his radio junkyard, and the odors of solder and pipe tobacco made it smell like a holy place. Customers breathed this strange incense, taking comfort in the reverential atmosphere of the shop, transacting their business in whispers. Fred's Radio & Repair was a sacred store in the new religion of Electronics.

Fred had been dead for two years. He left the shop to his son who loved radios but had little interest in how they worked and even less interest in doing repairs. Eddie Tollman knew this about Fred's son; he knew it long before Fred started coughing up blood and staying home for several days at a time. Fred routinely allowed his son to botch the most basic repairs; then Fred would give the radio to Eddie, saying, "Save it. The customer, by Christ, can't know we made it worse." Eddie always corrected the damage, believing that Fred's sullen, incompetent son would eventually drift into another line of work. Eddie imagined himself and Fred as partners; he thought that someday the shop would be called Fred & Ed's Radio & Repair.

Eddie talked about his future partnership with no one except his wife. He made her the sole partner of his imagination, playing out, through years of failure, a frantic succession of schemes, like a man running out of time.

Always, even in the first days of courtship, he watched for Jessica's approval; he recognized in her what he wanted for himself, a strength of character that refused to shrink from the world. He believed that loving her would reveal to him the secrets of her power, as if he could reinvent himself by imitating the vigor of her life.

Eddie married Jessica, much to his own surprise, to save himself from a smallness of soul, a paralyzing dread of complicated emotional commitments, a slow and steady withdrawal from life that was the hereditary disease of his family. For this Eddie was grateful, but he was not always convinced of his salvation. When he spoke to Jessica about Fred's Radio & Repair his voice had in it a note of pleading. Beneath the excitement of his words was another voice, softer but with the same urgency, saying 'You know what I was, you see what I am: change me, change me.'

"I know he'll make me an offer," said Eddie. "Even though we haven't talked about a partnership. Not directly."

"Fred's a fair man," said Jessica. "Maybe you should bring it up."

Eddie almost swaggered, swaying in the wind of his grandiose musings. Later, he blamed Jessica for encouraging him, for allowing him to use the best part of his heart in the service of an illusion.

As it happened, no momentous actions or words marked the passing of Eddie's dream. He reported for work at the usual time the day after Fred's funeral. Fred's son, finding liberty in his show of grief, came in a few minutes before lunch. "Mornin', Eddie," he said. "The bank called. They say I'm the boss now. They had a slew of papers for me to sign."

Eddie looked at the floor and feigned indifference. Like a man being told about the death of a stranger, Eddie scratched his head. Then he went back to the open radio on his bench.

Only work kept him from hating Fred. Eddie relished the thin line of smoke that rose up from a strand of melting solder; he liked the weight of the soldering gun in his hand.

Eddie possessed healing powers, or so said his customers; he earned the appellation 'Doc' from regulars, welcoming the affection that his handiwork engendered. Eddie understood that people needed and loved him in proportion to the need and love they felt for their radios. They brought broken, silent boxes to Fred's Radio & Repair, setting them on the counter like dead children, and when they returned, the boxes sang, humming along as if nothing had ever been wrong. Without Fred, Eddie did most of the repairs. He did each one with care and precision. He loved the work because it was the only thing he did well.

Eddie's calling had been obvious to no one, especially himself. The son of Swedish immigrants who farmed and built furniture, Eddie first fancied himself a carpenter, but he hung crooked doors, and once, as a favor to the parish priests, he built a porch that looked as if it were running away from the rectory. Putting aside his hammer and nails, Eddie worked as an orderly in a hospital run by the Sisters of Saint Joseph. He moved patients, delivered meals, and emptied bedpans. He approached most of his chores at the hospital with a genial resentment; gradually, the smell of vomit, urine, and death drove him away.

In 1917, two years after his first son was born, Eddie tried to enlist in the army, hoping to serve as an ambulance driver. But with one leg shorter than the other, the military rejected his application. He worked as a truck driver, meat packer, carnival barker, and shoe salesman. He failed to distinguish himself in any of these occupations. He painted houses one summer, but he lost the job when a rung on his ladder broke; Eddie slipped, tipping his full gallon, and a long, falling tongue of white paint licked the homeowner's Model T. After that, he mopped floors and cleaned toilets at the Beresford Hotel, a job that provided a close-up look at flappers and the company of millionaires. He admired the plush carpet and the crystal chandeliers in the lobby, and so, like a butler allowed to live in the master's mansion, he was ready to settle in for life. All this changed when the handyman at the hotel introduced Eddie to the inner workings of radio.

Eddie had cleaned the mezzanine lounge hundreds of times, and so it surprised him when the power cord for the tabletop radio wrapped itself around his foot. He carried the lifeless box to the hotel handyman, begging him not to report the accident, and when Eddie saw the radio come back to life, he was hooked. He read everything about radios that he could find. He listened to the latest models on display at Chatterton's Department Store. He searched yard sales for crystal sets that barely worked; he tinkered and experimented and always repaired them.

Eddie Tollman was thirty-one years old, a father of four, a peripatetic laborer with a dreary employment record and a late-blooming talent. Then he found Fred's Radio & Repair.

FRED NEEDED help. He opened the store in 1924 in the face of ridicule from relatives and friends who believed that radio was nothing more than a passing novelty. By 1926, five million American households owned radios and listened daily; Fred's business quadrupled, and his extended family and social circle called him a pioneer, a visionary entrepreneur of the radio boom. Fred planned from the beginning to make his son a journeyman who would work to build and then carry forward a successful family business. This vision of a dynasty was not to be. Fred's son, Harvey, possessed only a modicum of business sense, very little mechanical aptitude, and even less ambition. He worked in the shop because he respected his father; the prospect of finding a job that better used his talents never occurred to him. In the comfort of his father's shadow, Harvey made very few decisions; he showed no interest in accounting and never concerned himself with competition and overhead. He worked on radios, making no effort to achieve technical mastery, and he was content, even happy; the hint of glamour that surrounded the new medium satisfied him and made him feel important in the world.

Harvey talked to customers as if it were his brains powering the shop, and when repairs were needed, he assured hapless owners that he would attend to the problem himself. When Fred took radios away from him, afraid that his son would make them irreparable, Harvey complained that the old man was a perfectionist, a demanding overseer who trusted no one with his business reputation. Before long, the situation in the shop became a stalemate. Fred loved his son but wondered how he could be related to someone so different from himself. Harvey displayed a son's love and respect, but his father made him feel inadequate. Resentment stirred not far beneath the surface of his filial piety.

Eddie stopped at Fred's Radio & Repair on a frigid day in the gray winter of 1926. His pale eyes watered in the heated shop, and he snuffled through his runny nose. He told Fred that he could fix almost any radio, but when he rattled off the litany of his employment, Fred was not impressed. Harvey suggested that he look for a job somewhere else. Eddie understood the situation and turned toward the door, but Fred motioned for him to stay. Eddie speculated later that day that Fred felt desperate for another man's company. Maybe Fred needed a buffer between himself and Harvey. Maybe the radios piling up around the shop looked darker and more threatening on that winter afternoon. So while Harvey glad-handed a prospective customer, Fred surprised Eddie by taking him in the back and telling him to sit at Harvey's workbench.

"Try one of these," said Fred. "They've all been opened, but I've had no time for a look-see."

"I'll take the Crosley," said Eddie.

"Fine. Fine," said Fred. "You live far?"

"Over on Joy."

"Family?"

"Yeah. Wife and four little ones."

"Harvey's my only kid."

Eddie worked on the silent box, checking connections and tubes with systematic purpose. He tried to answer Fred's questions, but he found it more and more difficult as the radio absorbed him. Eddie nodded and shrugged, almost oblivious to Fred and Harvey, and finally isolated the problem. It took Eddie less than twenty minutes to repair and close the radio.

"I'd be a fool if I didn't take you on," said Fred.

"You've got plenty of work," said Eddie.

"I do. And I recognize money in the bank." The two men shook hands, and Eddie's career—his vocation—began.

Eddie enjoyed three miraculous years working with Fred and

ignoring Harvey. Radio became a household necessity, and the public hungered for information and products. As a team of two technicians and one salesman, the three men achieved a level of success rarely accomplished by small businesses on the west side of Cleveland, and they managed to make Fred's Radio & Repair a neighborhood landmark.

Eddie hardly believed his good fortune. To Jessica he confessed, with an uncommon air of solemnity, that he no longer felt like a boy. "I like the way people treat me at the shop," he said.

"I know," said Jessica.

"You do?"

"You've never been so happy."

"Not at work anyway."

"Not anywhere."

"I suppose you're right."

"There's something else. What is it?"

"I'm bringing home a radio tomorrow."

"Can we afford it?"

"It's free. Like a dream come true. Like magic."

"Who's the magician?"

"Fred. He took it as a trade-in—a console—even though it wasn't working. He rewired it and replaced parts until he was fed up. Last week he told me that if I could fix it I could have it. I got it working today. It's a beautiful thing."

"You deserve it," said Jessica.

"I just want to get it home," said Eddie. "Before Fred changes his mind."

Fred made good on his promise of the radio, and the shop threesome made good on an unlikely chemistry, an avuncular charm, that gradually gave the store a family feel. But somewhere in the middle of Eddie's third year the miracles stopped. Fred started complaining about stomach pains. No one thought anything of it at the time. Harvey told his old man to stay home. "I'll take care of the shop," he said. "Don't worry." When Fred did come into work he looked pale and drawn, and he finally told Eddie that he was spitting up blood. Fred reluctantly took himself to a doctor just before Christmas; the doctor opened his obstinate patient with a scalpel and found stomach cancer. Fred died six months later.

It was only a few weeks after the funeral that Harvey began taking money out of the cash register. "Now don't go worrying yourself," said Harvey. "You know this money's mine." He started counting. "You think I'm gonna blow this dough on some cheap broad. Or drink it up until I'm deaf, dumb, and blind."

"The thought crossed my mind," said Eddie. "But I figure you're paying the rent."

"Wrong again, Doc. You and Dad always had one thing in common—work, work, work. Well, not me. I plan to retire. I'm not going to die here like my old man. I don't ask much from life. Just a little nest egg to tide me over. I'm gonna take this money and invest it in the stock market. Wall Street's on a roll. I know at least a half-dozen guys my age who've made easy money. If you had any brains, you'd ride it too."

"I don't have much in the way of savings."

"You won't lose. It's a sure thing. Look, if I do as well as I think I'm gonna do, I'll cut you in for a few bucks."

"Thanks," said Eddie. "I'll take my paycheck."

"Whatever you say, Doc. But if we play our cards right, this store and the stock market could make us both rich."

Harvey invested more than fifty percent of the store's profits; he lost it all in the October crash.

Fear swept through Cleveland like a grass fire. Banks closed and soup kitchens opened. Small businesses collapsed in a flurry of pink slips and delinquent bills. Locked doors and soaped windows became the ubiquitous emblems of failure, but Fred's Radio & Repair managed to stay open. The shop survived at first on a backlog of service orders. Then Eddie and Harvey earned meager fees from three commercial accounts, repairing and replacing radios in two luxury hotels and an office building. The two of them tried to ignore their diminishing returns. They went about what little business they had hoping that the 'wonder of radio' would shelter them from the economic storm.

Eddie walked to work under the brown fog of winter. He no longer enjoyed the distance between his house on Joy and the shop, between one refuge and the other. He stopped looking at the faces of passersby; instead, he lowered his eyes, respecting the privacy that desperate people demand. Cleveland became for Eddie an unreal city, grayer and colder, covered by a pall that made it difficult to breathe. As time passed Eddie saw more businesses boarded up and more homes abandoned, markers in a graveyard of lost dreams.

"It's payday," said Harvey, handing Eddie a thin envelope.

Eddie liked being paid in cash. It was the only good thing about a world without banks. Eddie opened the envelope and counted the money; then he took half and gave it back to Harvey.

"I don't need half," said Harvey.

"Yes, you do. I saw the bills on your bench today. The shop can't stay open without heat and lights."

"Even so." Harvey tried to stuff a five-dollar bill into Eddie's shirt pocket.

"Look. It's the only way," said Eddie. "The business needs money to make money. Your father said so."

"I know, Doc. But you need to live."

"What good'll it do me if the shop closes?"

Harvey put the money in his pocket. "They say this mess'll clear up by the middle of next year."

Eddie shrugged. "I keep telling Jessie that there's still plenty of rich people. People who never trusted banks. People who hid their money. More than enough to buy a new radio."

"That's right," said Harvey.

"Enough to fix old ones on the blink," said Eddie.

"It's undeniable," said Harvey.

"I'm glad your father's not here to see this." Eddie looked at his empty workbench. "He got out just in time."

"I guess he did," said Harvey.

LETHEA STRONG went to Fred's Radio & Repair only once. Her employer, Dr. Madison, owned a temperamental Philco, a table-top model that patients pointed to with affection as the sickest thing in the Doctor's waiting room. The radio went silent on a regular basis, but when it disappeared for more than a week, Dr. Madison's patients began to fret; they missed the object of their derision; a few even canceled appointments. Lethea took it upon herself to visit Fred's shop, hoping she could get Eddie to speed up the repairs. She found out that the radio needed a diode from New York, that Eddie could finish the job in five minutes once he had the missing part. Lethea told Eddie that Dr. Madison's practice depended on the radio. "That's funny," said Fred. "Our practice depends on it too." Lethea laughed and extended her hand to Eddie. "I delivered all four of your children on time! See what you can do about that radio, okay?"

Lethea shook Eddie's hand. "This boy's finally a man," Lethea said, winking at Fred. "I knew Eddie when he needed Jessie all the time, leanin' on her for this and that. Now, here he is with a firm handshake. Let me see your other hand." Lethea looked at Eddie's hands, a deep habit from her childhood. Eddie had long, feminine fingers. "These hands are made for careful work. You see, he's turnin' red like he never thought of it. Well, let me tell you somethin' else you boys never thought of. Hands tell stories. I learned that from my mother."

LETHEA STRONG was born somewhere outside Columbus. Forced to make herself an orphan, she ran away at eighteen. She couldn't recall her mother's face, but she remembered the hands that washed and brushed her hair, that lifted her out of the snow when she was a little girl. Lethea remembered her mother's black skin and the contrast of her father's white fingers resting on her mother's arm. "My little girl is milk chocolate," her father said. Lethea looked at her light brown skin and smiled.

Lethea was fourteen when her mother died of typhoid fever. Ben Strong blamed himself, having dug the well that provided the contaminated water. There was no bottom to his grief. He refused to go to work or to church; he sat in the same dirty clothes day after day. Lethea cooked as best she could. She listened to him weeping; she listened to his footfalls as he moved from room to room. "Thea," he said. "You gotta help me forget. I can't do it myself."

Lethea didn't know if she could help him forget. She missed the bright flowers that once filled her mother's garden. She missed how her mother and father laughed when they were together. She yearned for the softness of her mother's hands, for the games she played with her mother, tracing letters on each other's palms and then trying to guess the words, passing a walnut from fist to fist and then trying to guess which hand. Seeing the sadness in her father's eyes made Lethea wish that she could take her mother's place. She watched the way older women walked and talked; she tried to keep the house just like her mother had left it.

Ben Strong finally returned to the world. He found work. He talked to people again, but he never resigned himself to the loss of his wife. He began to drink, and as the years passed he gradually grew numb, a disease that began imperceptibly with a tingling in his toes and fingertips. His hands, once so gentle and compassionate, began to tremble, began to fumble and break the objects of his life. He craved the comfort of anything beautiful and familiar. He wanted nothing more or less than the touch of his wife; he wanted his wife to reach out and steady his hand.

Lethea grew. Ben discouraged the first boys who came courting, keeping Lethea in the house like a married woman. He bought her fancy dresses for church, compared her hair to the softness of rose petals, praised her for the sureness of her hands. The more Ben fawned over his daughter the more she appeared to be his wife. He coveted the inflections, the supple movements, the ample breasts and hips that belonged to Lethea's mother. His fascination became obsession. He wrestled with the grotesque weight of his desire, tried to beat it down by drinking all night at the local saloon. But liquor didn't blind him to the woman in his house.

It began when Ben went to Lethea's room to say goodnight. He told her he wanted to rest his head for a short while, but he fell asleep and woke hung over and embarrassed just before dawn. He went to her room the next night, asking if she'd mind a little company. He didn't touch Lethea. Sometimes he came late, other times early in the morning. He began to tell Lethea lies, saying that Daddies will sleep with their daughters when the woman of the house is away.

So it went. Lying. Lying to her. Lying next to her.

Ben didn't say his daughter's name. He rolled over on top of her and forced himself into the body that was so like the body of his wife. "You gotta help me forget," he groaned. Lethea made a sucking sound like a throat being strangled; clumsy fingers tried to wipe away her tears. "You're all I got." Then the voice sounded cruel. "You gotta make me forget."

Ben forced the lock until Lethea stopped locking the door. Lethea lay beneath him and made no sound or movement. No tears. In the morning, Ben said that he would never touch her again, that it was the bottle possessing him, that he hated himself for doing such things to his only child. The voice that spoke to Lethea was filled with contempt and self-loathing. It wasn't a voice that Ben recognized.

The nightmare leached into daylight when Ben gave Lethea a gun for her eighteenth birthday. "Thea, I want you to use this to protect yourself. When I come to you, I'm not in my right mind. If I ever open your door again, I want you to shoot me. Promise me that. Promise you'll shoot me if I come to you again."

Lethea put the gun beneath her pillow because her father ordered her to do so. She slept alone for three nights. She prayed for escape, for purity, for absolution. But on the fourth night she heard him come stumbling into the house; a glass broke on the kitchen floor, and then her bedroom door opened and a heavy weight of whiskey and sweat fell on her like death. Lethea pulled the gun out from beneath her pillow, but she failed to shoot; she held the gun, her arm outstretched, waiting for him to finish. Ben pulled himself from between her legs but stayed on top of her. He ran his hand down the length of her arm until he felt the gun in her hand. He pressed her finger on the trigger, making her bring the gun to his head. "I gotta forget," he whispered. Lethea couldn't pull the trigger. Her body convulsed with terror. With a steady grip, Ben Strong held the hand of his daughter, squeezed the hand of his daughter, until the bullet released them both.

Lethea fled the night her father died and eventually found herself in Cleveland. She invented a new past for herself, for Dr. Madison, who took her in and trained her as a nurse and midwife. She told no one her story until she was ready, until she was very old and surrendering herself to sickness. "I am harder than amber," she said then. "I used my hands and built a livin' house. I drew strength from the misery of my teenage years. And I thank God my body has no memory for pain. I survived because I was never with my father. My body was beneath him in that bed, but I wasn't. My soul was absent. He couldn't touch it. My soul went off to a safe place, somewhere filled with soft birds. With the smell of damp earth after a light rain. My soul stayed in hidin' there. That's what saved me in the end."

Lethea never married. She had no sons or daughters of her own. But everyone agreed that the children on the west side were all Lethea's children. She delivered more babies than she could remember, and the families she served became her extended family. Everyone owed her a life, perhaps more than one, and some people believed that a birth without Lethea meant bad luck for the child.

Lethea watched her children as they grew; she held their hands, letting them feel something powerful and familiar, the first hands that touched them when they came into the world.

"WELL, LOOK at you. You're still the prettiest woman in Cleveland."

"I doubt that. And you've not seen the women in Mayfield. Oh Lethea, it's good to see you. But you shouldn't have come all this way. It's cold."

"I enjoy the walk. And I like trains. Sometimes I think about gettin' on one just to see where it'll take me. But you look settled in. Train must a been early."

"Only ten or fifteen minutes."

"And how was the ride?"

"Peaceful. Mayfield's not so far by train."

"It's a far piece by wagon. Much further on foot. I forget sometimes you live out there. I start walkin' over to Joy and then I remember. How are the children?"

"As good as can be expected. They have a fine teacher. Philip hates the tent."

"And Myron?"

"Better. At least I think he's better. His brothers and sister have been watching over him at school. But he's scared most of the time now."

"Just a baby," said Lethea. "And already he knows too much."

"He keeps looking over his shoulder."

"He'll be all right in time."

"I know. I have to be patient."

"I worry about you in that tent."

"I feel like I've lived there for a hundred years."

"Well, we don't have to make this station your new camp. I have lunch waitin' for us."

"I hope you didn't fuss."

"Of course I did. How often do I get a visitor from Mayfield? This is a special occasion. Maybe I'll just keep you here for a couple-a-days. Eddie'll think you left him."

"Eddie came in with me. We left the children with the Johnsons."

"You mean that man ran off without even sayin' hello?"

"He came in to see Harvey. Some new scheme about Fred's

Radio & Repair. Harvey had something to do this afternoon, so Eddie felt like he couldn't wait."

"I'll forgive him. He's the one missin' my lunch. Let's go."

Lethea took Jessica's arm and the two women walked out of the station. They passed familiar houses on comfortable streets, nodded to drivers who stopped at crosswalks. They passed old trees, leafless in winter, standing like sentinels on front lawns, promising a new family of leaves in the summer ahead. They looked down Joy.

"I can't see the house," said Jessica.

"Can you hear the children?" asked Lethea.

"I can hear them, but I can't see them."

"They're playin' in front of your old place."

"I hear them."

They passed through Lethea's tiny gate and into the house that was Jessica's second home. Lethea watched Jessica hang her things on the coat rack.

Jessica smiled. "Split-pea soup?"

"Just the way you like it."

"And to be in a house again! With windows, and carpeting, and shelves for all your keepsakes."

Lethea poured two cups of tea. "How's Eddie managin' these days?"

"I thought he'd waste away after Fred's closed. It was worse when we arrived in Mayfield. Eddie never drinks, but he lived in a stupor at first."

"He has a tired heart."

"Sometimes too tired."

"Workin' at Fred's pumped up his handshake. Made 'im a foot taller."

"He loves radios."

"Does he love you?"

"Yes, he loves me. And the children, too."

"I don't know why you married that boy. You have more fire in you than he can handle."

"I didn't know what I wanted."

"But you were smart. A young girl, yes. But always smart."

"Not always."

"You knew what you wanted."

"You're never satisfied, are you?"

"Bein' satisfied is like bein' dead."

"I don't know what I thought. What I was feeling."

Lethea looked at the clock. "I've got all afternoon."

"You're stubborn as stone."

Lethea waited, stirring the soup.

"I wanted some sort of direction. The future seemed strange—hard to imagine. I wanted someone to give it shape."

"And you thought Eddie would do that?"

"He was handsome—not overbearing, like my father. He wanted me."

"Of course he wanted you!"

"He was gentle. I saw his tenderness, his decency. I thought he would rise above selfish and cruel men like my father."

"He never lied to you?"

"No. He courted me just as he is. 'My humble champion.' That's what I called him. I refused to see him as anything less."

"And what do you see these days?"

"It doesn't make any difference now."

"That's not what I mean. I saw you squintin' down Joy like a helpless old woman. My Lord, Jessie, I thought you'd get lost between my front door and the kitchen. Why do you think I met you at the station?"

"My eyes aren't that bad."

"I said you were a smart girl. Well, I'm old and much smarter than you. Don't tell me your eyes are just fine."

"I have enough to worry about. The children—"

"I worry about the children too. I told you I'd take Margie and Myron if you wanted me to."

"I couldn't ask you—"

"You didn't ask. I offered. I understand about your family, but bein' blind won't do them any good."

"We don't have enough money. The little bit we saved is all we have to live on."

"Oh, I hate money. I don't have the money either. I'd give it to you if I did."

"The doctor said I'd have to stay in the hospital for a week after the operation. It's all too expensive."

"You have to tell Eddie."

"For what? So he can feel worse? He can't find work. He was a ghost for two months when the shop closed."

"Tell him you need an operation. He'll figure it out sooner or later. He probably knows already. He just can't admit it."

"It's not the right time."

"You have to."

"But there's nothing he can do."

"Now don't get me riled. Eat your soup."

EDDIE WALKED down Lorain Avenue with his cap pulled low over his eyes. The street looked the same, but the windows saved no image, no ghost of what he was once in this place. The sounds and smells had changed, even in the short time he'd been gone, and the soap-swirled door of Fred's Radio & Repair stood out like a white hole, a whitewashed dream in a block of dirty brick buildings.

Crime in Cleveland was on the rise; so too were temporary shelters and suicide. Men and women spent part of each day in bread lines. These were the observable effects of the Depression. In the next year, unemployment would claim twenty-five percent of the national work force. The newspapers would count 85,000 bankrupt businesses and 5,000 failed banks, a quarter of a million people evicted from their homes. Eddie didn't anticipate these facts. He, like many people, tried to ignore the magnitude of the situation.

Eddie would have liked to ignore Harvey as well. The boy never valued his father's legacy. How could he? He could barely manage a screwdriver. How could he appreciate the intricacies of electronic repair? Eddie held Harvey responsible for the store's demise. There was no one else to blame. And there was no one else to talk to about putting the business back in operation.

When Eddie opened the door of DeCarlo's Café, he saw Harvey sitting near the window reading his paper.

"Doc Tollman," said Harvey, rising from the table and smiling. Harvey put out his hand and Eddie shook it.

"Hello Harvey."

"Have a seat. Can I buy you lunch?"

"Yes."

"So how's life out in Mayfield?"

"I'd rather be in Cleveland."

"That bad, eh."

"Not as bad as it could be."

"Things aren't good here either."

"So I hear."

"Arnal's Cleaners closed. And Talking Leaves Books went out of business about a week after we did."

"I heard."

"Is the family okay?"

"The children are in school. Sometimes I think they like living out in the country. But it's hard on the younger ones. Jessie needs glasses. I guess we're all okay."

"You want a hamburger? I'm havin' a hamburger. Hey, Tony. Me and my friend here want burgers with fried potatoes. And we need coffee." Harvey pointed to the newspaper on the table. "I can't believe what's happening. Every day the unemployment lines get longer. People are living on the streets in cardboard boxes. Those guys on Wall Street back in '29—they should've all jumped. The ones who didn't jump should-a-been pushed."

The coffee came. "Thanks," said Eddie. "So you wanted to see me about opening the shop."

"That's right."

"What makes you think we can do it?"

"The fact that I have brains and a certain undeniable charm. And the fact that you want it even more than I do?"

"Big talk. Big talk won't keep it open."

"I'm not so sure. I have the money. You have the dedication." Harvey put three teaspoons of sugar into his coffee. "I need your expertise. Hell, I can replace a burnt-out tube, but anything more complicated than that and I begin to sweat."

Eddie smiled. "Okay, you've made your point. You said something about money."

"I don't have all of it. But I have more than anyone else you know. If we pool our resources—"

"So we open the shop. Where do we find enough customers?"

"I've been cultivating a couple of commercial accounts. A good friend of mine is the night manager at the Chancellor Hotel. The owners want to put new boxes in every room."

"Never heard of it."

"It's a new place. It used to be the old Wellington. My friend tells me it's Hearst money behind the takeover."

"Have you forgotten that I live in Mayfield?"

"Stay in town during the week. You can sleep in the shop."

"I can't leave my family out there alone."

"It'll only be for a few weeks. After that you can get a place and bring them back to Cleveland. You said you'd rather be here."

"Let's say all this is possible. Where do you plan on getting the rest of the money?"

"Well, that's where you come in. You must have a little nest egg set aside."

Eddie stood up and began buttoning his coat.

"Where are you going? You haven't had your lunch!"

"What makes you think I'm fool enough to give you any more money?"

"I know. I didn't do right by you in those last days. But I learn from my mistakes. You always had the right idea. You said we have to put money into the business if we expect to make money in the end."

"Your father said that."

"And he was right. You're right."

"No. It's not possible. My family needs that money. We're hangin' on out there with cat claws. You still have a furnace. You still have indoor plumbing. From where you sit, it may not seem like a big risk. For me, it's everything."

"I don't need that much. You wouldn't have to give me all of it. I know it's a gamble, but it's your only ticket back to Cleveland."

Eddie's stomach rumbled when the hamburgers arrived. He took two large bites.

"Listen Doc, you have a gift. You know that. But you'll lose it if you live out in the country too long. Do you think RCA feels the bite? I doubt it. And you can bet they're designing new models all the time. I've seen some of the new console jobs. They're like the White Star line of radios. You'll get out of touch if you don't get back on a workbench."

Eddie chewed.

"I don't want to lose money any more than you do. I wouldn't be here talking to you if I thought we'd end up in the hole."

Eddie wiped his mouth. "I can't do it."

"Won't you just think about it?"

"I can think about it. But it won't do much good."

"Just think about it, Doc."

"I have a question."

"What's that?"

"I don't see what's in it for you. You never liked the shop. What's the problem? Not enough money for hamburgers?"

"I have enough. But nobody knows how long this thing is going to last. I might run out."

"You'll run out sooner if we go bust."

"I know. But I can't just stand around waiting for the end. I need something to do."

"That's the first thing you've said that makes any sense."

"So you'll think about it."

"I might. I'll let you know."

"You've just made Dad a happy man."

"I didn't peg you for the sentimental type."

"My father was sentimental. Not me. I'll bet he's smilin' right now."

chapter three

WINTER IN Mayfield demanded heavy clothes, layer upon layer of cotton and wool, galoshes and leggings, and a big tin of bear grease for my father's leather boots. We stoked our wood stove every hour and kept it going all night, using up dry cords of maple and hickory that we cut and stacked long before the first snow. For more warmth, we piled tarps and heavy rugs on the floor, hung a maze of blankets against insidious drafts. We ate summer vegetables and fruit that Mother canned in the fall, and we froze fish and venison, gifts from the Johnson farm, in a metal can outside the tent. Snow in a bucket kept milk and cheese cold. Sometimes, when the temperature rose just above freezing, the tent was almost cozy, except that my hands were never warm. My fingers, despite the constant rubbing, always felt stiff and brittle, ready to snap like icicles.

Margie ignored the cold, or so it seemed, and she always managed to make us forget the misery of going out to get wood or water from the well. She rarely talked about the weather. She refused to count the days until spring. Walking to school on the coldest mornings, she made us play word games, forcing us to make the trip without dwelling on the distance or our frozen feet.

"Goddamn, son-of-a-bitchin' tundra," said Phil.

I laughed. Cursing the elements was my brother's new habit.

"I thought you liked snow," said Margie. "You always built snow forts and igloos and snowmen—"

"He loved the snow," I said. "When we lived in Cleveland."

"I don't l-l-love it anymore."

"How can you say that Myron?" asked Margie. "You loved it before. You loved it when we were back home. When Phil took you to the park and you went down the hill on your sled."

"I know."

"And didn't you love it last week when we made angels next to the tent?"

"I don—I don—I don't know."

"You're just saying that to be like your big brother. You like it when he swears."

"Hell yes," I said. "It's as much fun as anything else."

"What about you, Stephen?" asked Margie. "Do you still like the snow?"

"Sure. It's okay with me. I don't take it personal."

"Phil, do you really hate the snow?"

"Margie," I said. "Give it up."

"It's the same snow as in Cleveland," said Margie.

"It's not the same," said Phil.

Margie made no reply. None of us did. We walked the rest of the way in silence, running and stumbling in fresh powder when we heard Miss Dossin ring the bell.

School days went on forever when winter had its way. Temperatures below freezing meant no recess or lunch outside, no retreat from the day's failures or embarrassments, no escape from the pecking order or the snobbery of Felda Lane. Phil and I developed the habit of ignoring most of what went on, except when it concerned Myron, but Margie involved herself in all disputes, major or minor, that erupted within the walls of Mayfield School.

Margie was tough and unfailingly honest, and so it seemed natural that the girls, and even some of the boys, looked to her for guidance. Her penchant for truth earned her a grudging respect, and she became the arbiter of petty squabbles, an advisor to the lovelorn, and the savior of any girl rejected by Felda Lane and her sidekick, Sarah Shaw.

Margie, without realizing it, became exempt from the general habit of Tollman disdain. On most occasions, the kids relegated Myron and me to the lowest rungs of the social ladder. They feared Phil and left him alone, knowing that he was capable of inflicting pain. Margie was the only Tollman for whom they expressed genuine affection. They gradually included her in their games, asked her for help with their arithmetic; they even depended on Margie—when delicate matters required diplomatic art—to take up their arguments with an angry Miss Dossin. Margie earned her place despite the shortcomings of her brothers. I was happy for her. More than that, I was proud.

The latest controversy at school revolved around Felda Lane and Sarah Shaw, a disagreement over the possession of treasure— a gold medallion found at Carson's Bend. It began when Felda bragged about walking on the old, rotting planks that covered the mouth of the well. She dared her good friend Sarah to do the same. Sarah wanted to wait for spring, but when a week of southern air melted what little snow was on the ground, Felda made a case for doing the dare right away. "By springtime," said Felda, "the boards might be rotten. Then you won't be able to do it like me. My daddy says the sheriff's gonna cap the well. If they do that anytime soon, then you might as well forget it. It doesn't mean anything unless you walk on those old boards."

The two girls hiked to Carson's Bend. Felda went first, proving that she'd done it before and could do it again, the damp wood creaking and groaning beneath her weight. Sarah started out after

Felda reached the other side, walking slowly as the wet planks bowed, feeling the spring beneath her feet. When Sarah got to the middle, she started bouncing.

Felda let out a squeaky, high-pitched laugh. "Sarah," she almost sang, "you're crazy as a loon."

"I dare you to come up here and bounce with me," said Sarah.

"It won't hold both of us."

"How do you know?"

"I can hear it cracking."

"Will you come up and bounce by yourself then?"

"This is my dare. I don't have to do it your way."

"It's my dare now. I'll tell everyone you wouldn't do it."

"I'll tell everyone you're a crazy loon," said Felda.

"Are you scared?" screeched Sarah, bouncing harder.

"Yes," Felda screamed.

"Will you tell everyone I scared you?"

"Yes, I'll tell."

"Do you promise?"

"Yes," said Felda. "Just stop!"

Sarah ran to the other side. Climbing down, she put her foot on a mound of wet leaves and pine needles at the base of the well, and when she slipped, her heel turned the mound over. It was then that Felda saw something sparkle. "It's a gold coin," she said.

"Let me see," said Sarah.

Felda brushed away the dirt.

"That's not a coin," said Sarah. "It's jewelry. It has somebody's initials on it."

No less excited about her find, Felda wiped the yellow wafer with her scarf and put it carefully into her pocket.

"What are you doing?" asked Sarah.

"I'm keeping it," said Felda.

In the days that followed, Sarah insisted that her foot and her fall uncovered the medallion; it was hers because she kicked it free. Felda argued that she saw it first, that Sarah, falling on her face, would never have noticed it. The disagreement festered. When Felda wore the medallion on a gold chain, showing it off to Miss Dossin before school, the argument escalated into an all-out battle.

As often as circumstances allowed, Sarah sat on Felda's lunch.

Felda waited for Sarah to leave her desk, whether for board work or the outhouse, and then tipped Sarah's inkwell.

Sarah passed notes that confessed undying love for Myron and signed Felda's name.

Felda called Sarah "a clumsy wart."

Sarah called Felda "a selfish cow."

All this might have gone on for the rest of the school year, but then Sarah found out that the medallion belonged to somebody— somebody dead—and that made the situation serious. Engraved on solid gold were the initials W.R. Sarah's mother said that Welby Rose was the name of the boy who fell into the well, when the well still had water, at Carson's Bend.

We all wanted to see the medallion up close when this fact became common knowledge. It suddenly inspired awe, floating on Felda's freckled skin like a golden moon. It shadowed us with death, bore witness to the end of breathing for one like ourselves. The medallion was grotesque and beautiful. It became a sacred charm, recalling a name, Welby Rose, which rolled off our tongues like poetry.

This new attention surrounding Felda only increased Sarah's frustration, and the two girls went at each other until their friends asked Margie to somehow settle the argument.

Most of the kids assembled on the steps after school. Felda kept fingering the medallion while Sarah spoke her mind.

"Felda should at least let me wear it some of the time."

"I will not," said Felda. "And if you try to take it, I'll kick your shins black and blue. Don't you know about finders-keepers?"

"But you didn't find it by yourself."

"I know. You think I owe you something just because you're clumsy."

"You see, Margie. Felda won't listen to me."

Margie bit her lower lip and nodded.

"Does that mean you agree with her?" asked Felda.

"Not exactly," said Margie.

"Well, who exactly do you agree with?" asked Sarah.

Margie looked at Sarah. "I don't agree with you." Then she turned toward Felda, who began to smile. "And I don't agree with you."

"I'm going home," said Felda. "This is a waste of time. I found the medallion. It belongs to me."

"It belongs to me, too," said Sarah.

"I thought it belonged to Welby Rose," said Margie.

"Everybody knows that," said Sarah. "My mother knew the family."

"So what," said Felda. "So it belongs to a ghost."

"So it belongs to his family," said Margie, standing between the girls like an ambassador offering a peace treaty. "It belongs to his mother. She's the one who should have it."

"Oh, you think you're so smart" was all that Felda could think to say. I heard the confusion in her voice. She hadn't anticipated Margie's point.

Sarah turned red, searching the faces around her for support. But the kids had adopted Margie's opinion as their own, and their expressions condemned the two girls as greedy and thoughtless.

"Just give the medallion to Miss Dossin," said Margie. "She can get it to Welby's mom."

It took a little more than a week, but Felda handed over the medallion and eventually forgot her enmity against Sarah. But I had little interest in whether or not Felda and Sarah would renew their friendship. For me, the whole episode culminated on the school steps, sharing the simplicity and the beauty of Margie's best moment. In all the weeks of bickering between the two girls, in all the jokes and conversations about who would possess the medallion, no one suggested, or even considered, the idea of returning it to its rightful owner. Only Margie saw what needed to be done.

Later, when Miss Dossin unraveled the whole story, discovering my sister's suggestion, she wrote a note and complimented Margie for her "moral sense." Margie asked me what Miss Dossin meant by "moral sense."

"She means you're a good person," I said.

"Am I?" asked Margie.

"When you're not a brat."

"Do Myron and Phil think so too?"

"Ask them."

"Stephen, are you a good person?"

"No. I don't think so."

"And Phil?"

"I don't know. He never got a note from Miss Dossin."

MARGIE'S growing popularity became, for Phil and me, a measure of our family's worth. We admired Margie's natural talent for politics, recognizing her as a serious player in the game of schoolhouse status, bragging to anyone who would listen, especially Mother and Father, that Margie would someday be a teacher—or even a judge. We watched her meteoric rise from the sidelines, keeping our distance; we didn't want to remind the others that she was the sister of misfits, of dead wood.

As much as Margie captured our attention at school so did Wormwood's black shack fire our imaginations, our need for adventure, on cold days that kept us near the tent. It all began as a game. "Watchin' for the worm," we'd say. But under the endless gray of winter, it became our obsession.

Each day, as Phil and I walked to and from school, looking across the Chagrin River through leafless trees, we had a clear view of Wormwood's shanty. We never saw Wormwood, only the squat hovel where he lived, and the more he stayed out of sight the more ghostly he became. Sooty smoke rising from the chimney pipe told us when Wormwood was home. When we saw no smoke, we supposed that Wormwood was out foraging for food or gathering firewood. We said that Wormwood spent most of his time peeking through farmhouse windows at families reading the newspaper or listening to the radio, at mothers and fathers arguing over unpaid bills, at brothers and sisters weeping over a dead puppy. A good day for Wormwood, we laughed, might be finding a woman's old stockings in the trash.

But Wormwood's tiny house, more than the life we invented for him, remained the object of our fascination. In summer and fall, Wormwood stayed out of mind, masked by leaf-filled trees. But seeing his shack every day in winter—a black smudge on a field of white—being aware of it, like a sliver beneath the skin, spurred our interest, our flowering contempt.

"I wanna see the inside," said Phil.

"The inside of what?" I asked.

"Wormwood's shack."

"Are you nuts? Should I look for a straitjacket?"

"C'mon. Tell me you're not dying to see it."

"That's right. I'm not dying. We'll end up in Wormwood's trophy case."

"You don't have to come."

"I didn't say that. Are you looking for something particular?"

"No."

"Just for the hell of it then."

"Don't you wanna see how the ol' Worm lives?"

"You're serious." I looked at Wormwood's shack. "What are you gonna do?"

"I've been watching that chimney now for two or three weeks. He's never home on Thursday afternoons. Gets back some time after dark. It'll be easy to take a look when he's not there."

"I suppose you'll just walk right in."

"I don't know." Phil cracked his knuckles. "Bet he doesn't lock the door. Or maybe one of the windows."

"You won't break in—"

"Not so he'd notice."

"I bet," I heard myself say, "we'd be the only two people on earth, besides Wormwood, to see what's in there."

"Wanna go or not?"

"Thursday?"

"Like I said."

I thought of nothing else for the next three days. Phil convinced me not to talk about it for fear that someone would overhear and ruin the plan. We saw smoke on Tuesday, the small chimney pipe puffing against snow, and then thicker smoke, probably damp wood, on Wednesday. On Thursday, nothing rose from Wormwood's flue.

We waited until just after sunset and then asked Mother if we could go over to Johnson's well for water. She said we had enough for the wash tub and tomorrow's breakfast. But we insisted, saying that we wanted to go, it being a clear evening and no wind.

We took the path that led to the Johnson farm, but after we crossed the river, walking on a bridge of downed trees to avoid the thin ice, we turned upstream toward Wormwood's place. In only a few minutes we reached the last line of trees that bordered the clearing where Wormwood built or found his black shack. Phil hid the bucket under a pile of bramble and dead twigs.

"Looks like he left the lights on," said Phil.

"What d'ya mean?"

"Look at the window."

Against the gathering twilight, I saw a faint, almost imperceptible glow. "He must be in there," I whispered.

"How could he be without a fire?"

"I don't know. Maybe he's cold blooded."

"Let's just wait. Until it gets a little darker."

"I'm cold."

"So am I," said Phil.

The wait was short. Night fell like black fog, obscuring the outline of Wormwood's shack. But the window grew brighter, and we watched the wall inside for shadows, for any sign of life.

"He's not there," said Phil.

"How can you be sure?"

"I'll make sure."

Phil ran from the cover of the trees and reached the side of the shack, crouching below the lighted window. He listened and then stood up slowly, peeking over the sill. He looked inside, in both directions, then signaled me to come over.

We walked around to the front door, looking through the thick dark for movement, listening for the rustle of Wormwood's coat. We tried the door, testing Phil's theory. He was right. The door was unlocked.

"Jesus, Phil. What is all this?"

Burning candles on plates and saucers ringed the room, the light from all sides confusing my brother's shadow with my own.

"You're right about Jesus," said Phil. He pointed to a large crucifix, with a muscular body of Christ, tortured and bloody, that dominated the shack. Surrounding the crucifix, on rough-hewn branches nailed to the wall, were votive candles, undulating in the draft, and small statues of Jesus and Mary, even some of the apostles.

"Shut the door," said Phil.

"Let's get outta here."

Phil sucked in his breath. "Strange shit."

"Let's go."

"In a minute."

The only furniture, in addition to the wood-burning stove, was a table and chair, a bed, and a small chest of drawers with an open Bible on top. Puddles of hard wax cracked beneath our feet, and a pot full of candle stubs sat on the stove.

"He's gonna burn this place down," I said. "You can't leave candles like this."

"This place'll never burn," said Phil.

"What's that supposed to mean?"

"Wormwood's got God on his side."

Phil opened the first two drawers of the chest in rapid succession. He found shirts and socks, sheets of paper filled with handsome writing, and tobacco.

"Look at this shit," said Phil, opening the third drawer. He pulled out something white.

"What is it?"

"I think it's a wedding veil. It's a lot like Mom's. You know. She keeps it in the cedar chest."

"Do you think Wormwood was married?"

"Hell no. He probably stole it." Underneath the veil was another piece of white cloth.

"It feels like satin," said Phil.

"Is that the wedding dress?" I asked.

"No. I don't think so." Phil held it up by thin straps. "I think it's underwear. It's for under a dress."

We both heard a snap. Phil stuffed everything back into the drawer and closed it. He stopped, listening for Wormwood.

"It was a deer," said Phil.

"Please," I said. "Let's get the hell outta here."

"Out the window then. You first."

I didn't breathe again until we were back in the trees and Phil uncovered our bucket.

"Let's run to Johnson's," said Phil. "Mom will ask too many questions if we don't hurry."

When we got back, Margie and Myron were in trouble, making Mother and Father angry enough to take turns yelling, so no one asked why it took such a long time to get a bucket of water. The tent looked good to me; it felt safe. I was glad to be there.

Nothing that Phil or I had imagined compared to what we found in Wormwood's shack. We wanted his place to be a dungeon, rank with the air of catacombs; instead, we found a chapel, a bizarre, forbidden grotto. Still, something about it was ghoulish, and I couldn't shake off the shadows—our looming silhouettes—that seemed to follow us when we ran.

IN FEBRUARY, on a sunny, unseasonably mild afternoon, Lethea Strong came to Mayfield, walking up from the village, following the road that went past the schoolhouse, then along the Chagrin River, until she finally set foot on Tollman property.

"Lethea," I announced, as she emerged from the woods like

Mother Nature's right-hand woman; her green bonnet bounced with each vigorous step. Phil heard me and came running.

Lethea opened her arms and I almost knocked her over. She laughed and Phil hugged her from behind. "Well, aren't you two just the best lookin' boys I've ever seen."

"You say that every time," said Phil.

"That means it must be true," said Lethea.

"I didn't think it was you," I said. "I thought I was seeing things."

"Why? What do I look like? A ghost? You'll have to wait a few years for that. Not that I'd mind one bit."

"What are you doing here?" asked Phil.

"Is that your idea of a welcome? What do you think I'm doin' here? I'm visitin' you."

"But we didn't know you were coming," I said.

"Your mother knew. She didn't want to tell you, though, in case I couldn't make the trip. She thought you'd be disappointed if I didn't show up."

"Margie and Myron are gonna be mad," said Phil.

"They're not here?"

"No."

"Where'd they get off to?"

Phil shrugged. "It's Saturday. They're off somewhere playing." Phil caught my smirk. We both knew that Margie and Myron were at the construction site hoping to see a family or two of ducks.

"Then I'll just have to wait until they get back. I have to give them their surprise."

"What surprise?"

Lethea reached into her shoulder bag and pulled out something wrapped in wax paper. "Hard to come by these days," she said.

"You should visit every weekend," said Phil.

"Mind your teeth, now," said Lethea.

"Candy-store apples!" I said, tearing the wax paper and drooling.

On the end of my stick was a beautiful ball of caramel and nuts. The fruit was firm and fresh, and the mixture of apple juice, golden caramel, and salt exploded in my mouth like God's own fireworks.

Phil licked his brown fingers. "Just leave Margie's and Myron's with us. We'll make sure they get 'em."

Lethea laughed. "I wasn't born yesterday, ya know. I'll just keep the other two here in my bag."

We walked Lethea to the tent. Mother and Father heard us coming and came out into the sunshine, open arms reaching for Lethea.

Mother squinted at our dirty faces. "Boys, did you say thank you?"

"We forgot," said Phil. Then we both thanked Lethea, kissing her on the cheek.

"You're welcome. But your Mama shouldn't have to remind you."

"We'll remember," I said. "If you come visit us again next week."

"Finish those apples outside," said Mother.

Phil and I, slurping and chewing, nodded agreement. Father raised the tent flap, following Lethea and Mother inside.

"Should we go find Margie and Myron?" I asked, still preoccupied with the apple.

"They're not gonna stay out all afternoon. They'll be back soon enough."

"What do you wanna do?"

"Nothin'."

"That's what we've been doing all day."

"Lethea's here. I'm goin' in when we're done." Phil took a bite of his apple and chewed. "I gotta ask her something."

"What?"

"I wanna see if she needs any help around the house. Over the summer. I was thinking I could work at her place."

"You just want to go back to Cleveland."

"So what?"

"So it's not fair."

"What's not fair?"

"Why should you be able to go and live in Lethea's house while I have to stay here with Margie and Myron?"

"Why not? You'd be the oldest then."

"I won't let you. I'll jump out of a tree and break my leg. Then you'll have to stay. You'll have to stay and help take care of me."

"That's stupid and you know it."

"I'll do it. I'll break both my legs."

"Stop talking like an idiot."

My apple was gone and the stick tasted bitter. "Well, Mom won't let you go."

"How do you know?"

"She'll say she needs you here. She always says that." I ripped up a handful of grass. "I get sick of it sometimes. I get sick-a-you sometimes."

"Of course, no one gets sick of you," said Phil. "You're such a goddamn prince."

"I'm not special like you. Everyone treats you like you're something special."

"You know, Steve, the only thing that runs more than your mouth is a duck's ass."

"Say what you want. But you know I'm right. The kids at school get out of your way. Miss Dossin treats you like royalty. And Mom can barely stand to have you out of her sight."

Phil took a step toward the tent.

"And now you're going back to Cleveland for the summer."

"It was just an idea."

"You'll go. You always get what you want. You—"

Phil raised his hand, motioning for silence. We heard voices rising, first Lethea's and then Father's.

"C'mon," said Phil. "Let's see what's going on."

Father's words trailed off when Phil raised the flap and we walked into the semi-twilight of the tent. "Can't you boys find something to do?" His voice sounded hoarse.

"They can stay right here," said Lethea.

"It's not your place to say so," said Mother. "Eddie's their father."

"And, after you, I'm their mother. I'm too old and ornery to be told what I have a right to do or not to do. The boys need to know what you've been goin' through. They need to hear it just as much as your husband needs to hear it."

My father looked destitute, somehow incomplete, sitting at the table with Lethea and my mother. He rubbed the stubble on his cheek. "Why do you keep saying that? You make it sound like I don't care."

"I know you do. But you don't care enough to see things for what they are. You like to keep things comfortable. You drop things off in the back of your mind where they won't bother you too much."

My father tried to speak but Lethea cut him off. "How often do you ask about her eyes?"

"That doesn't—"

"I want to know." Lethea turned to my mother. "When was the last time he asked you?"

"I don't remember," said Mother. "But asking is beside the point."

"It's the whole point," said Lethea, shaking her head. "Hopin' the problem will just go away and heal itself is a child's game. It's neglect."

My father searched Lethea's face for mercy. "Is this what you want the boys to hear?"

"They'll hear it soon enough," said Lethea.

"Hear what?" asked Phil.

"Go find Margie and Myron," said Mother.

"Your mother's goin' blind," said Lethea.

The words broke over me like a heavy wave. Father began to say something but Lethea's glare silenced him. He bowed his head as if he were in mourning, as if he were a penitent waiting for redemption.

"How do you know?" Phil's question jabbed like a punch. "How can you say that? Who told you?"

Phil's voice was grim and desperate. I looked at my mother, realizing that she had lied, knowing that I had allowed myself to ignore the truth. Phil had tried to tell me—pointing at her when she threaded a needle, nudging me when she helped us press flowers—but he hadn't believed it himself, not entirely.

"Lethea, that's enough," said Mother. "We've been friends for a long time. I want you to leave here as my friend."

"That's right, Jessie. I'm your friend. And I love you too much to let you sit here and lose your eyes without sayin' my piece. I suppose you think you're some kind of saint, keepin' all the worry and pain to yourself. Well I don't think you're a saint. Your family will suffer. They'll live with nothin' but guilt."

"But the doctor's wrong," said Mother. "My eyes are bad, it's true. But I can still see. He said I'd be blind by now, but I'm not."

"Jessie talked about getting glasses. Maybe that's all it is."

"And what do you know about it? Just because you can fix fancy radios doesn't mean you know about her eyes."

"Mom," said Phil, the word sharp with outrage. "What are you talking about?"

My mother looked at Phil. "The doctor said I need an operation."

"That's not what you told us."

"That's right, Philip. Your Mama lied to you. She lied to save you the worry. Now don't be frettin' and gettin' all hurt. Sometimes people lie to protect you. You have to be grown up enough to understand that."

"Then we'll go to Cleveland," said Phil.

"It's too expensive," said Mother. "We don't have the money."

I could see the shame rising in Phil's face. "Why didn't you tell us? Me and Steve can work. Dad could've told us if you didn't want to."

"I didn't know," said Father.

"That's no excuse," said Lethea. "Anyone with eyes—"

Mother cut her off. "There's no work for men like your father. What would boys do to earn enough? We just don't have the money."

"That's what I've come to talk about," said Lethea.

Father looked up. Mother discounted the remark, turning again to Phil and me.

"How much money is it?" asked Phil.

"Much more than we have," said Mother.

"Are you gonna listen to me?" asked Lethea.

"You've already said enough," said Mother, more fatigued than angry.

"I've saved a little," said Lethea. "And I've talked to Dr.

Madison. He says he can put up half the money as a loan. Now I know you have a little bit set by. I figure you wouldn't have to use all of it. With Dr. Madison and me puttin' in with you, maybe we could do it."

No one spoke. It took time for Lethea's words to register, to reveal their meaning completely. My mother rubbed her forehead and her eyes. She reached across the table and squeezed Lethea's hands.

"Then you can have the operation," said Phil.

"I don't know," said Mother. "Eddie, what do you say now? If Dr. Madison put up half?"

"Maybe," he said.

"What do you mean maybe?" boomed Lethea. "This ain't somethin' you think about."

Mother reached out for Phil and me. "The operation may not work."

"It'll work," said Phil. "Why would Dr. Madison give us the money if he thought it wouldn't work?"

"You have to do it," said Lethea. "At least then you have the satisfaction."

"Phil. Go in the bottom drawer of the armoire. You'll see a cookie tin with stars on it. Bring it here."

Father went over to the stove and poured himself some coffee. Phil brought the tin to the table and Mother opened it. Inside was money. Mother started counting while Lethea looked on, smiling, and asked my father to warm up her cup. Then Mother drew her eyebrows together, wrinkling the skin above her nose.

"This is less than half of what we had."

Father put down his cup.

"What happened to the rest of the money?"

At that moment my father wore a face I'd seen before, a face of complete helplessness, an expression that relinquished all responsibility, and this time I saw something worse, an absence of feeling, a blank paralysis, like the face of a statue.

"I gave the money to Harvey," he said.

My mother's hands made the only sound, gathering the bills with trembling fingers and returning the thin roll to the cookie tin. She moved her hand in circles over the lid, pressing firmly until it closed. "Philip, put this back where you found it."

"What's wrong?" asked Phil.

My mother shook her head.

"Don't we have enough?"

Father looked at the floor.

"How much?"

Silence.

"Is it gone?"

More silence.

Phil let out something like a growl and brought his fist down on the table directly in front of Father. Then Mother's arm snapped in a short, deft movement, her hand slapping the side of Phil's head. She hit him so hard that he crumpled on the floor and wept.

Lethea stood up like a pillar of stone rising. She fixed her eyes on my father—her whole body ready to wreak violence. Then it passed.

"I understand," she said.

She pulled the caramel apples out of her bag and put them on the table. That was all. She gathered herself and walked out of the tent.

I tied back the flap and watched her go. And by the time I turned around, Mother held Phil in her arms, rocking him and holding his head to her breast. He never looked so small.

————

My FATHER made a trip to Cleveland, not long after Lethea's visit, hoping to reclaim his stake in the restoration of Fred's Radio & Repair. The train moved through a freezing rain that increased his apprehension. He told himself that he wouldn't beg. He would simply explain the situation and demand the money. No man whose wife was going blind could be called a welcher. My father told himself not to worry. But the first inklings of disaster came to him on Lorain Avenue, some three or four blocks beyond Joy Street, when he noticed the shop's green awning gone and a sign proclaiming Kovac's Delicatessen over the window. Then he walked to Fred's house and found a statement from the bank taped to the front door. Harvey was nowhere to be found. My father went to the bank begging for a forwarding address, for any trace of Fred's son, who, my father bitterly complained, stole more than money or a man's dream of radios.

After that we made ourselves believe that mother's eyes would hold out until summer. Spring mending-time on the farms promised work, maybe enough, we all said, for Phil and me. We talked about saving our share of the money, knowing that Lethea and Dr. Madison would still make good on their promises. My mother reported every day that she could see as well as the day before. She stacked firewood, brushed Margie's hair, told us stories, and checked our faces after washing, and the harder she worked to make our lives seem normal, the more Phil's hatred for my father grew.

We passed the balance of February in a state of profound anxiety, wary of quick and awkward movements, as if winter had wrapped each of us in a fragile skin of ice. We lived in our cocoons, protecting ourselves from one another, hating ourselves for being poor. At the same time, February kept flirting with spring. We hoped for an early thaw and release from the creeping stiffness of the cold. When temperatures plunged, we retreated into our shells, growing more and more accustomed to the necessary hardness.

Then, like a punishment for milder days, the heaviest snow of winter came, with an accumulation of two or three feet in a week. We couldn't go to school or spend much time outside. We went in pairs to the outhouse and took shifts digging out the woodpile. We kept the roof clear, letting the snow build up around the tent for better insulation. Two or three times a day the entrance needed shoveling. We all took turns; not because we were dutiful children, but because we wanted to escape the closeness of the tent.

I remember the silence of snow, the deep privacy of it, walking to Mayfield village to mail a letter, feeling the cold brass of the post office door. One afternoon, on a trip to Johnson's farm for supplies, Phil and I sank to our thighs in powder, and for a long time we made no sound, and I felt the absolute hush of winter as a pressure in my ears, as if everything in the world had been wrapped in cotton. I tried to pull up one leg, but then the other would sink deeper.

"We need goddamn snowshoes," said Phil.

I started laughing. "Can you get out?"

"Yeah. If I roll out."

I rocked backward into the snow and my legs broke free. When I stood up, I sank again, but this time only to my shins. We started to walk and I thought I heard twigs snapping, but then I realized that Phil was cracking his knuckles.

"It's gonna take years to get to Johnson's place," I said.

"Yeah," said Phil. "With any luck, this shit'll melt by the time we get back."

IT WAS A dazzling, sun-flooded morning after two days of snow when Margie wanted oatmeal for breakfast. Mother stoked the fire and poured some water in a good-size kettle. She measured the oats by the handful, two handfuls to one portion, and then Myron filled her palm with salt and she sprinkled it into the water on top of the oats.

"Philip." said Mother. "Bring me the milk and put out the cream."

We sat at the table, wrapped in coats and blankets, waiting for the water to boil.

"Make it thick, Mom," I said.

"I'll do what I can."

"Is there brown sugar?" asked Margie.

"There should be plenty. Somebody find it. I bought a pound the last time we went to the village."

"I'm going to make golden porridge," said Margie. "My stomach's been dreaming of brown sugar and cream."

"I had a dr-dr-dream last night."

"Not another one," I said.

Myron nodded. "Ma-Ma-Margie got m-married."

We all laughed.

"How do you know she was getting married?" I asked.

"She was w-wearing wa-wa-white."

"What did my boyfriend look like?"

"Ugly."

"You're mean," said Margie, over more laughter.

"Was the guy wearing a black suit?" I asked.

Myron nodded.

"An ugly man in a black suit. Too bad, Margie. Sounds like an undertaker."

"That's enough, Stephen," said Mother.

I smiled at Phil but he wasn't listening.

"That oatmeal will be ready soon," said Father. "Stephen, you can set the table."

Margie snickered at me as I stood up to get the breakfast bowls and spoons from the sideboard.

"You two better stop it," said Mother. "Margie, the oatmeal's ready. You can serve."

As soon as all the bowls were filled and Mother sat down, Margie cornered the tin of brown sugar. We passed the cream and waited, and then Myron reached across the table and tried to take the tin from Margie. My father stared into oblivion stirring his oatmeal. My mother said nothing.

I sweetened my voice. "Margie, if there's any left when you're finished, we'd like some on this side of the table."

Margie kept digging into the brown sugar and Myron tried grabbing it again. My mother, unusually intent on her oatmeal, still said nothing. I gestured to Phil that he should take the tin from Margie, but he kept staring at Mother and then at Myron.

"C'mon, Margie," I said. "My gruel is getting cold."

Myron, tired of reaching across the table, rose out of his chair and lunged for the brown sugar. This time Phil dropped his spoon.

"Mom," he shouted.

Mother's face went white. "Philip, you frightened me."

"Not now," he groaned, passing his hand in front of her face. Her eyes saw nothing. She sat absolutely still and waited for the next word. She forced a smile, a final effort to protect her secret.

Margie jumped to her feet. Myron grabbed my jacket and pulled so hard that the sleeve began to tear. Phil stood up and swore at my father, but then he couldn't catch his breath.

He backed away from the table and wiped his cheeks. He

opened the china cabinet, taking down the book of pressed flowers. He put the book under his arm and zipped up his jacket. Then he ran out of the tent.

Before anyone could say anything or ask any questions, I followed him, the shock of sunlight on snow stinging my eyes. His tracks were easy to see, but he moved faster than I could match, traversing deep drifts and blankets of fresh powder. I walked for a while without catching sight of him, and then I knew where he was going and I started to run.

Phil was already standing at the well when I reached Carson's Bend. I saw him struggle to raise one of the old heavy planks and push it aside; then he leaned over the short stone wall and looked down. I called my brother's name, running and sinking in snow. He didn't turn or wait for me.

He held my mother's book. It was filled with girlhood flowers, with flowers my father had given her long ago, with flowers from the garden in Cleveland. It was the book we filled with wildflowers from the woods and with leaves we collected in the fall. Between some of the pages lay pieces of lace, thin and yellow, unfolding in delicate turns, and locks of hair curling beneath yellowed tape, and old letters speaking of love and once important dreams. It was a book of photographs, colors, and shapes, images of my mother's life bound between cardboard covers. Phil hugged the book to his chest and then, in the next moment, let it go.

I got to the well and shoved Phil aside, thinking that somehow I could snatch the book into daylight. But the well offered no sight or sound, no hope.

I started back, shielding my eyes against the brilliant, glaring snow. I stayed ahead. I wanted him nowhere near me.

chapter four

MOTHER MANAGED well enough inside the tent where the arrangement was her own and familiar, but the woods outside harbored new and unexpected obstacles. She said that roots, rocks, and tree stumps seemed larger in the dark, that the Chagrin River, running high with the first melt-off, sounded like a waterfall. Slush and mud scared her now, and so did the creaking of dead trees. Her head tilted toward every snap and rustle, saying that a sound so big must be a bear. "That's not raccoon or deer. Don't tell me it's just wind."

Hours of near silence came with my mother's blindness. She told us to keep quiet all the time, made us listen with her, while she trained her ears to do the work of her eyes. Myron wanted her the way she was before, so he acted out, trying to monopolize her attention. On bad days, Margie stepped in, reprimanding her charge and then mothering him, and when Myron calmed down beneath her touch, beneath fingers that caressed and soothed him, her hands as skillful as my mother's, I knew that Margie possessed a power I lacked. I began to think of my hands as clumsy and feeble, and I shoved them deep into my pockets.

Phil and my father refused to speak. They refused to look at each other or exchange the necessary pleasantries that living in one room demands. If Father stood where Phil needed to go, Phil waited. There was no tap on the shoulder or simple request to get by. Just reticence. When Phil sat at the table with Mother, Father kept to his cot. They tolerated each other at meals. Without pause, Phil devoted himself to walling out my father. So did I. It was a wall built with methodical precision, with a steady but cruel patience.

Margie took Myron on long walks in the warmer weather, and when they returned one afternoon, just before dusk, they came into the tent, all smirks and knowing glances, trying to hide their bubbling and giddy exuberance. Between them was a secret, the closest thing we had to a sacred bond.

"Hey, Myron," I said. "You and Margie find trouble?"

"N-No trouble," he said, smiling. I could almost hear him giggle.

"You can tell me what happened. I won't tell."

Myron looked at Margie and she shook her head.

"Margie," I pleaded. "I'm your best brother and you won't tell me."

"Since when are you my best brother?"

"I heard you say so. You told Mom I was your favorite just the other day."

Myron narrowed his eyes and shook his head.

"Don't listen to him, Myron. I never said any such thing."

"Maybe it wasn't Mom. Maybe you said it to Miss Dossin."

"You're just trying to start something so that one of us'll give in."

Myron sat on his cot like a sphinx perfecting a smug and superior attitude. Margie danced around my questions and managed to withhold the details of their adventure. She thought, at the time, that there was nothing I needed to know.

Margie and Myron were in ecstatic cahoots over a stone they'd found in the woods. Myron saw it first and thought it was a chunk of black glass, its curved, shiny surfaces in sharp contrast to the snow. He picked it up, impressed by its cold weight, and polished it with his sleeve.

"It's as big as your hand," said Margie.

"Wa-Wa-What's this?" Myron pointed to a bright streak of red that ran down the center of the stone.

"I don't know," said Margie. "I've never seen a rock so shiny. It's beautiful. You have to keep it."

Myron ran his finger down the red line. "Ma-ma-maybe it has a heart."

"Let's take it back," said Margie. "So everyone can see."

Myron tried to see his face in one of the stone's many mirrors, a smooth facet that looked like the work of a sculptor's chisel. Then he thought of something. "Margie, I c-c-can't take it back."

"You have to. What do you mean you can't? If you don't want to, I will."

Myron turned away, shaking his head and brooding.

"I don't understand you. Everyone should—" Margie's throat tightened like a fist. She turned Myron around and pushed the hair out of his face. "Then we'll keep it," she said. "Just you and me. As our magic stone."

Myron smiled. "We can w-wish on it."

"We'll bury it. And we'll make the spot where we bury it our secret place."

They found a dead tree and broke off a branch that was thick enough to use as a shovel. Not far away was Margie's favorite maple, a hard-barked giant that made the reddest leaves she'd ever seen. They started digging and found the ground still frozen, but they managed a shallow hole, and they gently laid their shiny black stone in the earth.

"Before we cover it up," said Margie, "we have to do something special." She looked at Myron, searching for an idea. She poked her toe at the small pile of overturned dirt, and then she looked up through the bare branches of the tree. "I know." Margie took out her pocketknife and carved two stars and a crescent moon low on the maple's trunk. "This way you'll be able to find it without me. And the stardust and moondust falling on the stone will keep it safe."

When Margie finished, Myron traced the stars and moon with his finger.

"Let's make a pledge," said Margie. "Put your hand on the red line." Margie put her hand over Myron's. "I swear I'll never tell another living soul about this magic stone or this secret place. Say, I swear."

"I swear."

"I swear that I'll never tell another living soul about the wishes I make on this stone." Myron was silent, so Margie kicked him.

"I swear."

"I make these promises on the heart of this stone, and if I ever break them, then my own heart will break."

"I p-p-promise."

Then Margie giggled, cracking the solemnity of the moment, and Myron giggled too. They covered the stone and tried to make the spot look pristine, untouched by human hands.

"We better get back. The sun's going down."

Her words were swallowed by a stiff wind rising out of the west; it rushed through stark limbs and made a hollow sound like voices chanting in a church.

"Sounds like go-go-ghosts."

Margie squeezed Myron's hand. "I'm here. We're together. There's no reason to be scared."

They started walking, but before they'd gone very far, they looked back, proud of their mysterious secret. When they looked again, Wormwood stood between themselves and the tree. His face, a white board squeezed between his black collar and his black hat, conveyed no sign of ill will. He didn't move. He just stood there, watching them go.

Myron whooped. Margie slipped and fell and started laughing. Myron helped her up and they ran as fast as they could. When they reached the clearing and saw our tent, they fell on the ground gulping cold air.

"YOU HAVE more money than you need," said Mother. "Don't buy anything that's not on the list."

Phil checked his pocket. "Do Margie and Myron have to go? They slow me down."

"You'll walk slower," said Margie, "if you have to carry everything yourself."

"She's right," said Mother. "Besides, what's your hurry?"

"I thought you wanted me to clean the stove. Who'll dump the ashes?"

Mother smiled. "It'll keep until you get back. Stephen's here. I'll be fine."

"When will Daddy be back?" asked Margie.

"You'll probably beat him home. Mayfield's not an easy place to look for a job. The farms are far apart."

Myron kissed my mother's cheek and so did Margie. "Stay warm, you two," said Mother. "We don't need any more colds around here." Phil hugged her with all the strength he could muster. Then Phil turned to me and saluted. "Send the cavalry if we're not back by sundown."

"Yes, Sir," I said. Myron turned on the way out and shot a spitball at my head. He was lucky that Mother couldn't see.

"It's your turn next time," she said.

"It's okay. I didn't wanna go anyway."

"That's hard to believe."

"I'm not lying. I really wanted to stay."

"You're sweet to say so."

"It's because," I began, and then I let it go.

"Stephen. What is it?"

"Remember when we lived in Cleveland," I said. "Sometimes when I was the first one home from school we'd walk over to Chatterton's Department Store and look at all the fancy clothes and things in the windows. Then you'd take me to Sander's."

"Where you would always order a chocolate soda or a chocolate milkshake."

"And you always ordered soup. And I would take your saltines and dip 'em in the chocolate foam. I liked the sugar and the salt on my tongue together."

"You are a strange boy."

"We never do anything like that anymore."

Mother laughed. "Well, I still eat soup. As for windows—"

"That's not what I mean," I snapped, angry with myself for calling attention to her eyes. "I liked that it was just you and me. Even when we didn't talk about anything."

Mother reached over and touched my face; she ran her fingers across my forehead and down my cheeks.

"You're tickling my nose."

"Keep still. I'm trying to see if you've changed at all."

"I look exactly the same."

"You're handsome."

"But not as handsome as Phil."

"I wonder—"

"What?"

"If you're going to spend the rest of your life comparing yourself to your brother."

"Everyone else does."

"You really don't know. Do you?"

"Know what?"

"You have something your brother doesn't have."

"Bigger feet?"

Mother laughed. "Well, yes." Then she squeezed my shoulders. "You look like me. Sometimes you look more like me than Margie."

"So I look like a girl. Thanks a lot."

"No. That's not what I'm saying . . ." Her voice trailed off.

"What's wrong, Mom? Did you hear something?" I listened and then looked out of the tent, but I saw nothing.

"I worry about Phil," she said. "Anymore, I hardly know who he is." Then she smiled. "I never worry about you."

Now's a good time, I thought. Ask her now or forget it. "Why didn't you punish Phil for taking your book?"

Mother tilted her head to one side. "It wasn't mine anymore. I gave it to him. Remember?"

"But it had all your stuff in it."

"I know. It's hard to understand."

"Weren't you mad?"

"A little at first. But not really."

"I was mad."

"There's no reason for that." Mother tapped her temple. "Everything that was in that book is right here."

"But I liked it. I miss —"

"It doesn't matter anymore. Memory is the only thing that matters." She pulled her jacket tight around her shoulders.

"You cold?"

"Let's have some tea. Put a pot of water on the stove."

I took two cups out of the china cabinet. "Where's the strainer?"

"It should be in the top drawer of the sideboard."

"Mom. Why did you say that about Phil?"

"Say what?"

"That you don't know who he is anymore."

Mother smelled the tea. "He's changed. The longer we live here the more he changes."

"I don't think he's changed so much."

"Maybe not. I don't see as well as I used to."

"Will you promise not to be mad if I ask you a question?"

"I promise."

"Naw. Forget it."

"That's not fair. You can't ask permission and then not ask the question."

"It's about your eyes."

She sat up straight. "Ask me anything."

"What's it like?"

She stayed quiet for a long time, and I shifted in my chair, regretting that I brought it up. I could hear the water boiling.

"At first it was like being locked in a cellar. But then I realized that I could still see light and sometimes shadows."

I put three tablespoons of tea into the pot.

"Now I want to ask you a question."

"As long as it's not about girls."

"No. It's not about girls. I was wondering. When Phil and your father are together, do you ever see them talk?"

"No. Never."

"And now you're following your brother's example. You keep pretty much to yourself when your father's around."

"It's his fault that you can't see."

"All right. Blame him if you have to. Be angry. But don't let it live in you like slow poison."

"Is that why you're worried about Phil?"

She gave no answer. "The tea must be ready."

I poured, the fine leaves collecting in the strainer, and then added extra sugar to my cup and a teaspoon to my mother's.

"You're a smart boy, Stephen. You think like I do. But you'll have to be careful. Your brother may want something from you."

"Phil's never asked me for anything."

"Not yet. But someday he will. He'll need what you have. He'll ask for it."

"There's nothing I have—"

"Suppose you couldn't give him what he wants."

"I don't follow."

"Suppose he wanted an arm or a leg."

"That's weird."

"No. Think of it like a game. Say he came and asked you for your hands. What would you do?"

"Can we talk about something else?"

"Use your imagination."

"Okay. I'd tell him he could have my hands when I'm not using 'em."

"Suppose he asked for your heart."

I took a tiny sip of tea but it burnt my tongue. "I guess I'd say no. It'd kill me."

"That's right. See what a smart boy you are. That's why I never worry about you."

THE SPRING thaw was harsh. Alternating between days of sunshine and leaden skies, soggy earth and ice, it swelled and squeezed the ground so that anything left living seemed to rise and fall in spasms of pain. Parts of the riverbank crumbled, exposing gnarled fists of rock, red clay, and roots. The heavy snow left blank spaces in meadows and along the road, and in the line of reddish, forked bushes that against all odds would strain to bear fruit by summer.

Only dying trees remained the same. Each one stood through winter without feeling or desire, without passion for the soil, having no need to grip down like the burly oaks or hickories, and winter, as if rewarding the patience of the numb, smoothed and polished the trunks of dying trees until the wood glowed an ethereal white. The creaking and groaning was louder in the spring, and as I listened to these sounds, I admitted to myself, tentatively at first, that winter in Mayfield had changed me.

I began to understand spring as only a promise of life, a life that demanded commitment but offered no guarantees. I whispered to the trees that I wanted to live, that I would make the necessary promises, that my brothers and sister would make the necessary promises, to the world and to our family, but I didn't understand about living then or the strange twilight of betrayal, the likelihood of failure—not because we give up or grow old, but because we are bound to promises that living will not let us keep.

I filled my nostrils with the sweet, earthy smell of damp ground, watching the snow disappear a little each day. The people in Mayfield called it spring mending-time, and with a little help from Mr. Johnson, my father got a job on a nearby farm. He stayed there three nights a week, a relief for Phil and for me too, and we said to each other, more than once, "The old man's gone and the gloom's gone with 'im."

Phil and I made money delivering bags of fruit and vegetables for the greengrocer in town. We'd report after school and find four or five bags ready for delivery to some of the bigger houses off the square. We made two bits per bag plus tips. Then Miss Dossin hired us to do some work at her place, washing windows and carrying furniture up to the attic. Cleaning out and whitewashing her basement was a big job; it took us two Saturdays.

"We have to be careful," said Phil. "It's easy to paint yourself into a corner."

"Where do you wanna start?" I asked.

"Let's do the walls first. Then the floor, starting at the back and working toward the stairs."

Phil was better than me with a brush, so he did all the cutting in. I followed with a roller.

"How much will we have after today?" I asked.

"Sixteen bucks."

I scratched my nose, careful not to get paint on my face. "Never thought we'd make money again."

"We're lucky."

"You call it luck. I call it work."

"We'll be lucky to get out of that tent."

"I'm staying," I said, puffing up my chest. "That sissy shit in the city's not for me."

"Don't swear. She's right upstairs."

"No slick shithouse for me," I whispered. "I'll take a tree anytime."

"That's not funny."

"Okay, okay. If we throw in with whatever the old man's making, it might be enough to get us back to Cleveland."

"How do you know?"

"I heard the old man say so."

"That doesn't mean shit."

"Who's swearing now?"

"You know he's full-a-crap."

"I heard Mom say it, too."

"That's different."

Miss Dossin left two glasses of lemonade at the bottom of the stairs. Phil stood his brush next to his pail, and I ran my roller dry and then propped it on the edge of my paint pan. We sat down on the steps and sipped the sweet and sour juice, trying to make it last as long as we could.

"Are you still in love with Miss Dossin?" I blurted out. "Don't hit me . . . don't hit me . . . don't hit me," I pleaded, bracing for the blow.

"Keep your voice down, you jerk. I won't hit you."

"Then are you?"

"I was never in love with Miss Dossin."

"Margie said you were."

"Margie's not right about everything, you know."

"Well, then, do you still like her?"

"You like her, too. So let's drop it."

"Not like that."

"Like what?"

"You know."

"No. I don't know." He looked up the steps and then lowered his voice to an absolute whisper. "Do you think Miss Dossin is pretty?"

"I think she's beautiful."

"Have you noticed her teeth?"

"What about 'em?"

"Perfectly straight and white."

I nodded.

"What color are her eyes?"

"Green," I said. "Sometimes."

Phil looked up the steps again. "And when she wears her yellow blouse, the one with the loose buttons, have you noticed the shadow right here?" He pointed to the center of his chest.

I felt butterflies in my stomach. "And you can see her shoulders and arms are perfect when she wears the sleeveless one."

"Then you love her, too."

"I do not."

"Then what was all that about her shoulders and arms?"

I took a big gulp of lemonade. "Is that love?" I asked.

"Maybe it is. I don't know."

"Did you ever tell her that she's beautiful?"

"Of course not."

"But she knows how you feel."

"What d'ya mean?"

"The way she looks at you. It's different. She doesn't look at me like that."

"You're just saying that."

"No I'm not. Whenever she looks at you, she looks like she's ready to cry."

"And you think that's a good thing."

"Not the kind of crying Myron does. It's a different kind."

"You don't know what you're talking about."

"I see it. I see a lot of things now. Just like you taught me. That's why she picked us to come here. She didn't pick Todd Lincoln."

"She picked us because we need the money. She's paying us. Remember? We better get back to work."

"Just admit it. Admit that you love her."

Phil picked up his brush, already stiff and dry, and dipped it in the whitewash to loosen it up. Then he began and I loaded my roller, the paint splattering in a fine mist as I started. We finished the walls and then slowly rolled our way to the stairs, careful not to track wet paint up the steps. When we came up, Miss Dossin was sitting at the kitchen table correcting papers.

"Can you boys come again next Saturday? I'd like to clean out the shed so it's ready for summer."

"We'll be here," said Phil.

I moved toward the door, and then, feeling the butterflies back in my stomach, I said, "Miss Dossin, we may not be in school next year."

Phil squeezed the back of my arm.

"Stephen, you have to go to school."

"That's not what I mean. We may move back to Cleveland."

"Oh," said Miss Dossin. "How wonderful."

"We don't know for sure," said Phil.

She smiled. "I'll keep my fingers crossed."

"You should move to Cleveland, Miss Dossin. And teach wherever we go to school."

"Thank you, Stephen. But I could hardly do that." Then she tried to fix Phil's unruly hair. "You have paint on your face."

"I'll take credit for that," I said.

"Wait a minute," she said. She took a small towel out of the kitchen drawer, wet one end, and began wiping Phil's cheek. "I'll really miss you boys if you go."

Phil said nothing. I did the same.

"That should do it," said Miss Dossin. "See you Monday."

We stumbled out of the house like two boys drunk on ambrosia.

I pushed Phil. "Why didn't you say you'd miss her too?"

He pushed me back. "Why didn't you?"

"She wasn't talking to me."

When we got back to the tent, Mother had dinner waiting. We told her how much money we made and then Phil put it in the cookie tin that Mother still kept in the armoire. She shared our excitement and wanted to hear all about our day; she even forgot to tell us to wash, so Phil ate supper with paint in his hair.

"It sounds like Miss Dossin has a lovely house."

"And big," said Phil. "For one person."

"And you're going back next Saturday?"

"She has tons of work," I said.

"Miss Dossin is a wonderful teacher," said Mother. Then she tipped her head as if listening. "Do you boys think she's pretty?"

Phil almost choked.

As IT HAPPENED, we didn't clean out Miss Dossin's shed the following Saturday, nor did we have a full day of school on Friday. Miss Dossin came down with the flu. Everyone said it was the change of season.

I was disappointed. Phil was too, though he denied it. He only talked about the money. I told him we'd make it up later. "It's Miss Dossin that I miss."

We'd made no other plans, so Saturday rolled out before us like a clear road. Margie and Myron went out early, but we hung around the tent, ignoring the rustlings of my father, and played game after game of checkers. Phil always took black and he always won, capturing two and three of my red pieces at a time and forcing me to crown his kings. My mother, entertained by my groans of defeat, sat at the other end of the table with her pincushion and thimble, sewing with no less precision than when she could see. Of course, she no longer threaded needles by herself, and sometimes she needed help finding the split seams or tears. These were the only concessions my mother made, and her finished work was smooth and strong, better mending than any of us with eyes could manage.

Just before noon, Myron came back, and he was crying.

"Is Margie with you?" asked Mother.

"She'll come b-b-back in a little w-w-while."

"Where is she?"

"Don't n-n-know."

I knew Myron was lying.

Mother hugged him. "Did something bad make you cry?"

Myron kept silent and rested his cheek on my mother's shoulder. When he went around to his cot, I followed him. I cupped my hands around his ear. "Is Margie in trouble?"

He shrugged his shoulders.

"Can you tell me what happened?"

He shook his head. "I p-promised."

"That's what I thought."

When I got back to the table, Phil was folding up the checkerboard. "Let's go out and do something," he said.

"Like what?"

"You should go," said Mother. "The sun's out. It felt so good on my face this morning."

"C'mon," said Phil, cracking his knuckles. "We'll think of something."

Once we were outside Phil told me that he wanted to do some tree climbing. With plenty of snow still on the ground and the temperature only a little above freezing, I thought the idea was premature. "It's too cold," I said. "The trees are still bare and slippery."

"I don't wanna wait," said Phil.

"Shouldn't we look for Margie?"

"She's okay. Maybe we'll see her once we're up."

"Let's wait awhile. Until it's warmer."

Phil shook his head. "We might be gone by then."

I appreciated the irony of his impatience later, because the climb we made that day turned out to be our last. I should've made a speech to mark the occasion, to acknowledge the passing of a simple pleasure. But it never occurred to me that Phil and I would stop climbing trees.

We found a giant elm with stretches of smooth bark turning white. I told Phil what he already knew, that he shouldn't be fooling with a dead tree. "More of a challenge," he said.

This time I decided to try, shimmying up the slippery trunk until, reaching and pulling, I bellied over onto a broad, sturdy limb. We were already a good ten or twelve feet above the snow, and I looked up through the maze of bare branches, becoming shorter and thinner toward the sky, and I knew it would be a race to the top.

Phil began, taking the sparser side of the tree. I could hear switches snapping and twigs cracking as he rose. I tried to stay close to the main trunk and use the bigger forks for footholds. Sometimes I slipped on crumbling bark and saw the slick, bone white skin underneath that would someday claim the entire tree and make it treacherous to climb.

Halfway up I started to get scared. I slowed, perching on each new limb to study my next move. Whenever I stood, stretching for a firm grip, my legs started shaking. I found myself in a clutch of thin branches, and then I stopped.

Phil kept going, competing with gravity and brittle wood. I could feel vibrations, the slight movements of the tree under his weight. It wasn't a windy day, but, as high as we were, even a breath of air moved the elm. Sometimes it made a mournful sound like the keening of old women.

My neck hurt from looking up. "How high are you going?"

"All the way," said Phil.

"Will it hold?"

"Has so far."

Phil swung his leg out over empty space and stretched, rising higher and higher. I heard something snap, and a small twig fell through the branches until it stopped a few feet above me.

"You okay?" I called.

"Yeah."

"Looks like you made it. Are you starting down?"

"I got another fifteen, maybe twenty feet."

"I can't see any branches from here."

"There's one good one. If I can stand on it, I can clear the top of the tree."

It looked short, the offshoot of a bough that forked out of the main trunk below. Phil raised himself and got a foothold, his arms wrapped around the bough, and as he pulled up his other leg, I heard a loud crack.

"You fuckin' son-of-a-bitch," yelled Phil. I thought I saw him fall, but only the broken branch tumbled through the tree. I felt the elm sway and saw Phil clinging to crumbling bark, shouting at the sky, "You bastard. You can kiss the ass'a the devil. Eat his shit. I'll show ya how."

Then Phil started down and I waited for him, holding my breath when branches bowed beneath his weight. When we reached the safety of the thick, lower limbs, I asked him what the world looked like from up there.

"Don't know," said Phil.

"Did you see Margie—or the tent?"

"I had to watch what I was doing. I never looked out. I didn't see anything."

We finally landed on soft snow, and my legs stopped shaking as we walked, glad to be back on solid ground.

"I won't climb bare trees anymore," I said.

"We won't," said Phil.

When we got back to the tent it was too quiet. We found Myron standing just outside the entrance; from a distance, he looked like a nervous old man, twisting his hat and looking around.

"M-Margie n-n-never came b-back," he said.

Phil stopped and squinted at the trees that formed the perimeter of our clearing. Then he pulled back the tent flap and the three of us went inside.

"Where's Dad?" I asked.

"Mr. Johnson came by. Said he needed some help over at his place. Your father went with him." The lines around my mother's mouth showed worry. "And Margie's still out. Myron says she went to look for something. She might be lost."

"Margie's too smart to get lost," said Phil.

"You're probably right," said Mother. "Remember when we first got here? She found a bird that couldn't fly. She didn't come home all day."

"That's right," said Phil.

Myron looked at me, his face stricken with uncertainty and fear. I sat him down and put his hat on the table. "Myron, where's Margie?"

"He says he doesn't know," said Mother.

"He knows something," I said.

Phil stood behind Myron's chair and nodded for me to go ahead.

"Myron, I know you promised, but Margie could be in trouble. She wouldn't want you to keep a promise if she needs help."

"She m-m-made me swear."

"That doesn't matter," said Mother. "You have to tell us what happened."

Myron struggled. Between tears and fits of guilt, the words and phrases came out. We learned about the black stone with the red streak, and the secret place at the foot of a maple tree where

Margie and Myron made their pledge. "We went there t-t-today b-but the stone was g-g-gone. He-he has it."

"Who has it?" asked Phil.

Myron squirmed in his chair. "W-Wormwood."

"What's Wormwood?" My mother pursed her lips, as if the word tasted sour.

"You won't like it," I said.

"Just tell me."

Phil cut in. "It's a name. It's what we call the old guy in the black shack."

Mother made no lecture. "Myron, why would this Wormwood want your stone?"

"He wa-was there."

Phil pulled on the back of Myron's chair. "What do you mean he was there?"

"After we b-b-buried the-the stone, he came out. He was wa-wa-watching."

"Mom, we gotta go," said Phil. "We'll find Margie. I promise."

We ran, following the trail through a stand of ancient trees, then across the meadow and down to the river. We crossed and scrambled up the bank, running again through thick woods until we reached the clearing and Wormwood's shack.

Phil pounded on the door. We backed away and saw a thin line of smoke rising from the chimney. Phil pounded again. This time we heard something inside, and then the door opened, only a crack at first, and we saw Wormwood's eye.

"Come to pray?" The words came fast from a throat filled with sand.

His owl-like eye paralyzed me, but Phil swaggered a bit, trying to see inside, and managed to speak. "Where's my sister?"

"I show it," he said. "Body of Christ. Breathing."

"Is she in there?"

He rubbed the stubble on his face. "Is is was."

"Margie," shouted Phil. "Margie. Can you hear me?"

Wormwood cracked the door a little more, shielding his eyes from the late afternoon sun, and then the door swung open until we could see all of him.

At first I couldn't believe that the little man standing in front of me was our nemesis. Up close, without his hat and coat, Wormwood was a short, frail old man with toothpicks for arms and legs, a pitiful scarecrow. It looked to me as if a sneeze or a coughing fit would break two or three of his ribs.

Wormwood took a step forward. I looked again at his pinched face and drooping shoulders and it dawned on me that he was harmless. I felt unkind and foolish. I could see the crucifix and the vigil lights. Margie was nowhere in sight.

Phil lowered his voice. "Did my sister come here today?"

Wormwood nodded.

"And you talked to her?"

"Body of—"

Phil cut him off. "I know. The body of Christ."

"—of sin," said Wormwood.

"What sin?"

Wormwood was silent. He looked at his hands that were palsied and wrinkled.

"So my sister came here," said Phil. "And she asked for the rock."

"I give it. Black bread. Devil's stone. I give it." Wormwood looked again at his hands. "A soft thing. I give it. For the body of sin."

"What do you mean, soft?"

"To match evil."

"C'mon," I said. "Margie's not here."

Phil looked at Wormwood. "Do you know where she is?"

"Is is was."

We started walking away and Wormwood stepped outside. "Black bread. Devil's stone. River rock," he called. "A soft thing. For the body of sin." We didn't speak until we lost sight of Wormwood's shack.

"She's probably hiding it right now," I said.

"Why would it take her all day?"

"I don't know. Margie can be pretty particular when it comes to secret places."

Phil let out a sigh of relief. "At least the Worm never touched her."

"I know."

"He's a lunatic," said Phil, almost laughing. "And puny. He's nothing more than a bundle of sticks. Margie could snap him in two."

"D'ya think Margie's on his mind? Ya know—in the way we thought?"

"She's on his mind, all right. But all Wormwood wants is somebody to pray over."

The image of Wormwood kneeling in benediction over Margie was strange, but it wasn't as fearful or grotesque as some of the other postures I'd imagined.

We fanned out and Phil saw footprints near the road that looked like Margie's, and Phil said, "I know where she is." Then we ran, the running more difficult on the road without trees or branches to grab, and several times we slipped when the crusty snow was slick or the slush turned to mud. We finally saw the row of evergreens, and I felt the sting of wet needles on my face as we pushed through the trees calling Margie's name.

The basements looked like open wounds between aisles of white, melting snow. I heard the trickle of water against concrete, the splash of feathers being washed.

Phil saw it first, the black stone marking the basement that was furthest from where we stood. Again we called Margie's name, waiting for her to dart out from behind a tree, knowing that she was probably watching and laughing somewhere nearby. When we got a little closer, I could see the vein of red rock in the stone, and then what I thought was a shadow became clear, and I saw that the smooth, troweled cement that formed the top of the basement wall was no longer smooth, a large chunk had fallen away. And then Phil let out a scream, and I saw a flash of white, and he ran down the rotting wooden steps, splashing and stumbling in knee-deep water, until he reached Margie, who floated face down, her clothes bloated and heavy, wearing a white veil.

Phil turned her over and blood ran from the black welt on her forehead. I heard him say she's not breathing, and then I heard a trickle of water and my head began to spin . . . began roiling like the swollen river, and I thought I heard waves, swells of white silk filling the air around me, and I thought I saw ghosts, old boatmen, rowers of tree-bark, carrying cold voyagers to Lake Erie, and I held my own body, rocking and praying like a child in need of motherly hands, waiting to be cradled . . . as my brother cradled the drowned body of our sister, the wet whiteness of Margie, in his arms, rocking, kneeling on the cold concrete floor of the basement, and the spring runoff lapping the walls, and my brother, cradling and rocking and weeping for the last time.

BOOK TWO

Katherine

chapter five

THE THING to remember is that I met Stephen first. I noticed his hands, as he wrapped my book in brown paper, a strange beginning for me. Usually it's the eyes. Neither of us spoke, of course— but that night at the meeting I told Laura I'd met a boy. She asked me what kind of boy, and I told her, forgetting my own predilections, that he was a poet. Poets bore you, she said. That's right, I said. I don't really know what he is. He must be a lover of books. Laura gave me a sultry look. And did he open you and crack your spine? We haven't talked, I said. I liked his hands.

On any other day, a detail such as hands would've escaped me. Something startling would've demanded my attention, like a newspaper headline, especially in those last years before the war, before the saboteur, the kamikaze man, the homunculus with a black stain beneath his nose made me abandon all newsstands, made me hate smug journalists and slick politicians who refused to condemn him, who looked the other way while he made the world his butcher block. But hands obsessed me on this particular day because I had tried a small piece, a not altogether ambitious piece, by Rachmaninoff, and my reach failed. So I stood waiting for my book, comparing my hands to Stephen's hands, jealous of his long, male fingers that could stretch, I supposed, an octave and a half.

I went back to the store the next day and asked for a biography of Beethoven that was long out of print. Stephen verified what I already knew, and then he searched for a remaindered copy with more enthusiasm than seemed natural. I was, after all, a not so regular customer. He asked me if a book on Bach would do. I pointed out that Bach is hardly Beethoven, but I thanked him anyway for his consideration. Do you like music? I held my breath after asking the question, knowing that if he shrugged his shoulders or grunted, I would choose not to see him again. I like Chicago jazz, he said. Divine, I said, closing my eyes. Those were the first real words between us.

I milled around the store for another half-hour, pretending to look for something that would replace the fugitive Beethoven, as if anything possibly could, and then the old woman who worked in the store told Stephen it was time to take his break. He started for the door, but I stepped out from between the stacks and cut him off. He almost fell over me, as good an icebreaker as anything, and when he regained his composure, I asked him if he wanted to go for coffee. He stuttered something and said Myron must be rubbing off. Who's Myron? My little brother. Oh.

The café was dark, it being a rainy afternoon, and we took a table in the back and ordered coffee. I offered Stephen a cigarette. He declined, sitting there like a man without a single vice, and then I waited for him to light mine. I leaned toward Stephen. I held the cigarette close to my face and brushed it with my lips, but I had to make a show of looking for the ashtray before he finally realized what I wanted. He checked his pockets, fumbling keys and change in a fluster, and then apologized for having no matches. I took out my lighter and lit my cigarette. You'd have thought from the look on Stephen's face that he'd never seen a woman smoke before.

I gave him a chance to start the conversation, a social function

I always claim for myself, and for an agonizing period of silence, I oozed patience. My mother implores me to slow down; she says good things come to those who wait. But patience is a virtue I find incompatible with my nature, and, anyway, Stephen was busy with the cream and sugar. I asked him if he liked the shop.

He looked around. It's all right, he said.

I mean the bookstore.

Oh. He nodded. Better than a factory.

Quieter, too.

Very quiet, he said.

What else do you do? I asked.

How do you mean?

Boating, tennis, polo . . . political subversive?

I take care of my family.

You're married?

No. It's my mother and me. And two brothers.

Myron, right?

Yeah. Phil's my older brother. He works too. Between the two of us, we make enough money for rent and groceries. Myron's still in school.

And your father?

Stephen stirred his coffee. What about you? What do you do?

I play piano.

Really? And you make a living at it?

I took a long pull on my cigarette. I'm saving money. My plan is New York.

Where do you play?

Massimino's Music. I'm the sheet music sampler. Lambert calls me his player piano.

I've only seen the place.

There's a little glass booth in the back with an upright piano in it. I sit there and practice and wait. Then a customer brings me a sheet from the rack and I play him or her a few bars. Some can barely read music, so they want to hear how it's done. Some want to make sure they're buying the right song. There's always a few who just want to hear me play.

Good pay?

Lousy. But plenty of time to practice.

That's like the bookstore. I spend most of my time reading.

Any favorites?

He didn't have to think. Hemingway, he said.

Of course.

I suppose he's not much for a girl.

That's not true. There's something egalitarian about Hemingway. Men and women are the same for him. They're all shits.

Stephen laughed. Who do you read?

Marx, Dreiser, Dos Passos, Lewis.

Then you're a reformer.

I'm a communist. Most everyone I know is a communist. I waited for Stephen to make the next move. He sipped his coffee and said nothing. Capitalism collapsed of its own weight, I went on. It was inevitable.

I'm not much for economics, said Stephen.

I jabbed the ashtray with my cigarette. Were you born here?

He nodded. I've lived here all my life, except for a year in Mayfield.

Where's that?

East of the city. We lost our house and my father moved us out there.

Relatives?

No. A tent.

I didn't know whether he was kidding, and I didn't know

whether I should ask. Stephen saved me the trouble. It's a long story, he said.

So your father passed away?

No. He left. He knocked around Cleveland when we came back. He found work and then quit two or three times.

I'm sorry.

No reason to be sorry. Stephen finished his coffee. I need to get back. He dug in his pocket for money.

It's on me.

No. I can't—

If you want to see me again, you'll let me.

Stephen smiled. Can I call you? I wrote my number on a clean napkin and handed it to him. He stood and turned toward the door. Then he hesitated. What's your favorite song? he asked.

I don't have a favorite song.

Well, whose music do you like the best?

You know that already. Stephen looked puzzled. Beethoven, I said.

And do you have a favorite symphony by Beethoven?

Not a symphony. *Sonata Number Fourteen, in C-sharp Minor.* Do you know it?

Stephen shook his head.

MY INTEREST in Stephen made no sense from the beginning. I wore my black hair rather long in those days, and I rarely looked at a man, according to Laura, unless he also had dark hair and dark features. Laura took the point further, saying that I pursued only those men whose eyes were the same shade as mine. She called me narcissistic. Maybe so, but for a girl I spent precious little time in front of a mirror.

Stephen's hair was the color of sand, shiny and coarse, and he combed it straight back like Clark Gable. His eyes, of course, were another thing. Beautiful and blue, with that soulful touch of sadness that I find irresistible. His face, too, was beautiful, almost pretty. No stubble or shadow, no razor nicks, very clean cut altogether. I might have said boring had there not been kindness in his every move, a tenderness that seemed impossible.

And what to do about politics? Stephen—and I knew this after our first conversation—was the first apolitical person I ever met. His family absorbed him. So did survival. But watching a man move through life with so little interest in the machinery of the world was a new and perplexing reality for me. How could I introduce him to my friends? What would they talk about? My trepidations were considerable.

Half my friends thought that I was Jewish. I let them believe what they wanted, though my initial ignorance of high holy days gave me away to some and remained a mystery to others. My parents were intellectuals and liberal, that much was true, but they were also Protestant, with fair hair and skin. My father accused my mother, after I was born, of sleeping with Al Ventimiglia, a smoldering Italian who lived next door and who always kissed my mother's hand over the fence.

My father worked like an uncompromising zealot, giving time to committees and practicing law for poor people. Everyone in the neighborhood knew that he hated Henry Ford and loved Paul Robeson because he talked incessantly, history and current events swirling in a whirlwind of words, holding forth on the Trotskyites, the Wobblies, Sacco and Vanzetti, the Spanish Loyalists, Hitler, and the inevitable war in Europe. He insisted I play the piano, and he paid for the best teacher in Cleveland until I finished high school. His biggest disappointment was my refusal to go to college, which should've come as no surprise since he described institutions of higher learning as male-dominated bureaucracies doing their best to turn young Americans into mindless consumers or, he said, something worse.

My mother worked for the Party. I guess you could say that she handled public relations, though she disliked titles as a rule. She befriended powerful reactionaries — people who used words like Bolshevik strikers, Red terrorists, Black anarchists — and tried to win them over, serving them tea and homemade cakes, disagreeing with them in a very agreeable tone of voice, proving to them that communists are civilized after all. She lived for social justice, which, I decided much later, was a way of living without desire. The women who almost choked on my mother's cookies and crumpets lived in large houses; some of them were chauffeured in expensive cars. But my mother wanted none of it. She made no comparisons. She at no time asked my father to abandon clients who were unable to pay. And when the houses outside our picture window began to fall apart, began to peel and sag from neglect, she would sit in her green armchair, smoothing the folds of her dress, and ask me to play her something lovely, something that would make the world seem alive again, and fresh.

My parents cared about music almost as much as they cared about politics, but for me it was the other way around. It happened that way because the piano made me the center of attention; it drowned out the radio and cut through conversations, forcing whoever was in the room to notice me. I decided at an early age that I liked an audience. I liked people's eyes on me. I felt the piano imbuing me with powers to mesmerize and seduce; I made arpeggios and chords and glissandos that listeners took as the intimate expressions of their own passions and regrets.

Music, said Beethoven, allows the mute man to speak; a melody, like a flash of insight, is the profound equivalent of his innermost thought. When I was young, I wrote a letter to Beethoven on the back of a recital program, and I made him this promise: If music lives in the gut, if it lays bare the heart, if it fills whatever emptiness we carry, then I will live like music.

I WAS A sexually precocious teenager, much to the dismay of my mother and father, who were progressive in all things except sex, and usually over dinner or just before the arrival of relatives, I would report the latest development in my carnal explorations, like the day I let Jimmy Kobus take a good look at my breasts, or the night just after my fifteenth birthday when, like a molting bird, I decided to cast off my virginity as a belated present to myself. This event, unlike the others, I announced over breakfast—in a flush of morning-after ebullience. My father nearly expired of scrambled egg inhalation.

The man I let between my legs was a boy of eighteen who, with his stepfather, organized labor unions. He talked with passion about Tom Mooney and William *Big Bill* Haywood. He sang Joe Hill's song about *pie in the sky.* He told me, through fits of pacing and arm waving, about Joe Hill's execution in Utah, by firing squad, after management framed him for murder.

And let's remember, he said, that the Industrial Workers of the World backed Joe. The moneymen wanted Joe out and the Wobblies knew it.

My labor organizer seemed to me a boy my parents could embrace, except that he talked about fucking as frequently and with as much fervor as he talked about the history of the labor movement. Fucking, for him, was a political act, though he had no interest, I realized later, in a balance of power. He said that the proof of a man's convictions could be seen in the woman he fucks.

I believed him and, for a time, became the standard-bearer of his cause.

My next affair was less successful and not the least bit intellectual. I met him at Tringali's. He worked the counter, a brooding Italian who scooped ice cream, ladled hot fudge, and sprinkled peanuts. He flirted with me and always remembered that my favorite treat was the fresh strawberry sundae. After a while, he made it with two extra scoops and then finished with a flourish of whipped cream. I started meeting him when he got off work, and we took long walks, sometimes along Lake Erie, and on a bench in a public park I let him raise my skirt and run his hand over my thighs, and I pressed myself against his warm palm until he made me gasp.

He asked me, the next time I saw him, if I could go away with him for a weekend. To Detroit, he said, to visit family. We'll take the train. He seemed so romantic and sophisticated, so European, and he wanted me to meet his relatives. My parents, quite naturally, would say no, so I made up an elaborate lie, convincing them that every girl in my class was going to a weekend slumber party at Laura's house. They trusted me. I knew they'd make no attempt to verify my story.

I started packing my overnight bag, stuffing it with more clothes than necessary for a trip across town, and somewhere between my pajamas and my lace brassiere, I began to have second thoughts. What did I know about this older boy with black, curly hair? What if he had no relatives in Detroit? What if he was violent, forcing me to perform unnatural acts before he threw me off the train? More than once I heard my father say, when he thought I wasn't listening, that Italians—like the one living next door—have animal desires.

I almost broke down and told my mother, but my pride and resourcefulness won out. I resolved that I could handle the situation as long as I could defend myself. I ran around the house looking for small weapons that would not be missed. I loaded my purse with a screwdriver, a heavy wrench, a scissors, and an ice pick; I even took a short, sharp file out of my father's grooming kit. I showed up at the train with a bloated suitcase and a rattling purse.

We were only two stops outside Cleveland when my escort opened the berth and pressed his bulge against my hip. In other circumstances, I would've welcomed his advances, but both the train and Detroit seemed foreboding and uncontrollable. I clutched my purse and rang for the conductor, a broad shouldered man with a dour face who checked our tickets and, unwittingly, shrank my erstwhile lover's ardent desire.

After that, my confidence gave way to embarrassment, my sexual allure to awkwardness, and I became sullen and withdrawn. At the next station, my sexy, Italian sundae-maker put me on a train back to Cleveland. He, of course, went on to Detroit and a weekend filled with steamy pasta and red wine. My sudden appearance at home posed no difficulty. It's my period, I said. It was good you came home, said my mother. My father looked at the ceiling. I don't want to hear about it, he said.

So by the time I met Stephen, I was an experienced, almost jaded, woman. I thought I knew what men wanted. For entertainment, I plotted the course of my relationships and found my calculations all too accurate and inevitable. But Stephen was different. After that first coffee and conversation, we saw each other almost every day for a month. We went to the movies, cheap restaurants, a cooperative gallery run by artists I knew, and all the proper museums; we went book-browsing and people-watching, and Stephen came to my house and ate dinner with my parents. Stephen had no close friends, at least no one I ever met, so I, ignoring the potential risks, took him to meet my cronies. It wasn't long before Stephen put up with whole evenings of Marxist theory and endured, with charming patience, suspicious inquiries into his own political disposition. We did everything that courting couples do, but there was nothing physical between us. Of course, my mother and most of her friends would've thought me outrageous for sleeping with anyone before marriage, but sleeping together wasn't so much the point. Stephen and I rarely held hands and, despite my willingness, we never kissed. He usually said good night to me with a friendly, familial hug. I thought for a while that he found me unappealing. Then something more interesting occurred to me; perhaps Stephen was homosexual. It was a deliciously exotic idea—one that I soon abandoned. And then it came to me; Stephen was a virgin.

Imagine. I could do little more than wait. I decided that Stephen was a test, an ironic payback for all my years of impatience. I went over my mother's words again, extolling the virtues of delayed gratification, but this time I heard more clearly a tone of complacent and self-righteous superiority, and in the end I decided that affection should always be expressed, and I still believe, even after the way things turned out, that there's nothing noble about abstinence.

I want to ask you something, said Stephen. I thought, given the look on his face, that he was going to propose. Instead, he wanted to know if I would come to his house and meet his family, which was another thing I'd been waiting for, and then he told me why he hadn't invited me sooner. My mother's blind, he said. This revelation caught me off guard. Just when I thought I understood the shape of his life, he said or did something that changed everything. Will I meet Phil and Myron, too?

Just Myron.

I've wanted to meet your mother, I said.

I CONFESSED to Laura that I was nervous about going to Stephen's house. Meeting his family is all so serious, I said. Laura pointed out that any hesitation on my part contradicted my impatience with Stephen. She was right, of course. Stephen assured me that his mother was more open-minded than most, that she was generous in her acceptance of others. I thought of her blindness and worried that I might find it somehow distracting. Then the day arrived and I accepted, quite happily, the silliness of my apprehension.

Jessica Tollman made me feel at ease from the start. She was beautiful, just as Stephen had said, but her beauty was pure, completely unadorned and unpretentious, with a face that belonged more to the prairie than to a gray and rusting city like Cleveland. Her movements, despite her blindness — or perhaps because of it — were economical and graceful. Mother, said Stephen, I'd like you to meet Katherine Lennox. And Mrs. Tollman turned from the fireplace, extended one hand, swept her hair back with the other and smiled. Is it Katherine, then? She asked. Or do you go by Kathy? Mostly Katherine, I said. Though some of my close friends call me Katie. Then I hope someday, said Mrs. Tollman, to call you Katie. She squeezed my hand, a firm grip. She asked me how I liked the house and wanted me to describe the things I saw. I get a better picture, she said, if more than one person tells me what they see.

Having a roof means a lot to Mom, said Stephen.

And I suppose it means nothing to you, said Mrs. Tollman.

Stephen gestured that I should sit down. I was trying to explain, he said.

You've told her about Mayfield, haven't you?

Yes, I said. I know all about it.

Then there's no need for explanations. Mrs. Tollman moved to her chair without difficulty. I've been very jealous of my son. He tells me that he visits you at the music store and that you play for him.

Stephen is my best customer, I said. But Lambert Massimino— he's the owner of the store—is always asking me why the boy with the baby face never buys any music.

Mrs. Tollman laughed. You mean he hasn't caught on.

Not yet, said Stephen.

Are you good? asked Mrs. Tollman. Or very good?

I looked to Stephen for help.

She's excellent, said Stephen.

I didn't ask you. I already know what you think. Mrs. Tollman sat there like she could see me. Are you excellent?

My teachers—

I don't know your teachers. I want to hear it from you. Are you good, very good, or excellent?

I'm embarrassed, I said.

Don't be, said Mrs. Tollman. I want to know what you believe. Life is too short for polite humility.

I took a deep breath. I'm excellent, I said, feeling the tension in my stomach dissolve. Then I started to laugh.

Mrs. Tollman smiled. Now, doesn't it feel marvelous to say so?

Yes, I said.

You're a lucky young woman. Some people have talent, or a gift, but they find it too late.

I think my father found it for me.

Don't give him too much credit. You had to find it for yourself.

I wish someone would help me find dinner, said Stephen. Where's Myron? My stomach's about ready to cave in.

Myron's visiting Lethea. Like he does every Saturday. He'll be home soon. You know, Stephen, Lethea asks about you constantly. You should make the effort and go see her.

I will. Stephen gave me a conspiratorial look. It's just that I've been busy.

Then take Katherine with you. Lethea loves company.

I'd like to meet her, I said. Stephen's told me a lot about her.

Has he told you, said Mrs. Tollman, that she's threatening to go to Washington. She wants to talk to Eleanor Roosevelt face to face.

I wanted to hear more about Lethea, but Myron burst through the front door and came to a sudden standstill, shifting his weight from one foot to the other while Stephen began to introduce me. Myron's hair was curly and some of it spilled over onto his forehead. His thick eyebrows and square jaw made him look tough, older than a high school senior. I'd barely said hello, and then, stuttering and walking backwards, he apologized for being rude, said he hoped that I would understand and bolted for the bathroom.

That's Myron, said Stephen.

Glad to meet him, I said.

Stephen and I set the table. Mrs. Tollman asked Stephen to fill the green water glasses while I, equipped with a scissors and specific directions, went out into the yard and cut five or six tulips. By the time I had the flowers in a vase, Myron reappeared and we all sat down. I kept looking at Stephen and wondering what else we should do, but I gradually realized that Mrs. Tollman ruled the kitchen and wanted no more help than was necessary to serve the meal.

The chicken was golden and juicy, falling off its bones in tender segments, and the mashed potatoes went down like warm, creamy custard. Stephen smiled and told his mother when I tried to sneak a second helping of green beans, which were long and tender and laced with sautéed onions. Strangely enough, I do not remember dessert. I say strange because dessert, for me, is the memorable moment, the grand crescendo of any meal. But I do remember that Stephen kept filling my cup with fresh coffee, and we all talked more than I thought possible about food and flowers and music. And somewhere amidst all the talk was a moment of great sadness and beauty when Mrs. Tollman, her hands feeling their way to the vase of tulips, drew out one of the flowers and caressed the stem with her fingers and touched the petals to her lips.

At one point, Stephen and Myron were in the kitchen rinsing dishes, and Mrs. Tollman lowered her voice and confided to me that she liked having another woman in the house. I love my boys, she said. But with Margie gone, I sometimes feel outnumbered.

I'll side with you in any argument, I said. Just give me the word.

Mrs. Tollman looked straight at me. And how is it in your family? Who outnumbers whom?

My father tries to hold his ground against my mother and me. I'm the only child. My parents are very modern.

So is my oldest. He says he won't have any children at all.

You mean Philip.

Yes. Has Stephen told you? He works—

For the railroad.

Exactly. He's a gandy dancer.

I kept turning the lid on the sugar bowl. I always thought those words sounded sweet.

It's a fanciful name, said Mrs. Tollman.

My grandfather loved locomotives, I said. He loved to tell stories.

Mrs. Tollman tilted her head. When I was a girl—and I won't mention the years I'm speaking of—trains seemed mysterious and grand. Everyone rode. Suddenly it's 1939 and whole railroads are shutting down.

The money's gone elsewhere, I said. Politicians are paid to lay roads and not track.

You make it sound like a crime.

It is.

And do you believe what they say? That trains will soon be obsolete?

Absolutely. And your son may be out of a job.

A thought lit up Mrs. Tollman's face. Maybe he's not so modern after all, she said.

Do you want him to change his mind? About having kids, I mean.

I don't know. I don't know if he wants to be a father.

Does he look like Stephen?

You can tell they're brothers. But Phil always looked older than Stephen. It's the black hair. I think he started shaving when he was sixteen.

I hope I get to meet him.

You will, said Mrs. Tollman. He'll be home for a week or so in June.

Is that for sure? asked Stephen, drying his hands and then throwing the dishtowel at Myron.

According to his last letter.

Good, said Myron. That m-m-means free t-tickets.

Planning a long vacation? asked Stephen.

Myron smiled. J-J-Just a long ride.

IN THE DARK fields of my imagination I nurture a dream of loco-motives. My grandfather—I sometimes called him Casey Jones—worked for the great Pennsylvania Railroad, and when I was a little girl, before piano or politics, my only desire in life was to be an engineer. My girlfriends at school thought it queer, and the boys, without exception, laughed at the idea of a girl piloting a train. I could say, with the cool confidence of hindsight, that I was unconventional. But there was nothing unusual about a young girl riding the rails with her grandfather, plunging through moon-filled nights, swaying gently across open fields, the window open and my hair streaming in the wind.

My grandfather, after he retired, used to walk around the house reciting poetry, usually Whitman, and the poem he favored was *To a Locomotive in Winter. Thee for my recitative,* he would bellow. And then a long pause before—*Thee in thy panoply, thy measured dual throbbing and thy beat convulsive.* He would forget words or lines, even long passages, but he always roared, without variation, *Thy black cylindric body, golden brass and silvery steel, Thy great protruding head-light fix'd in front.* And then . . . *Fierce throated beauty! Roll through my chant with all thy lawless music.* . . . The neighbors thought he was insane, and I thought he was a beauti-ful old man, and I know now that he understood things about America that I will never understand. Something about the prom-ise of a Baldwin K4, 4-6-2, hand-stoked until 1930, pulling a Pennsylvania Railroad freight. Or go back, way back, to the begin-ning of the Baltimore and Ohio, a thirteen-mile line to nowhere in 1830, but then the Mohawk and Hudson Railroad laid more track, and soon, as my grandfather said, steel begat steel, until it was everywhere that trains arrived. After fits of poetry, my grandfather poured forth the history of the Union Pacific, the Central Pacific, and the Southern Pacific, and he explained, often with tears, how the Baltimore and the Ohio became the Pennsylvania Railroad, how all the independents were gobbled up by giants.

Born in New Hope, Pennsylvania, my grandfather landed his first job with the Baldwin Locomotive Works, a company that built more steam engines than anyone else in the business. And it was through Bucks County that my grandfather rolled for the first time in his Baldwin-built 4-6-0, a locomotive they called the New Hope & Ivyland, as if it were made especially for my grandfather and me. And in the last weeks before he died, he took me twice to the Cleveland switching yard to gaze at a moth-balled engine we'd visited several times before, the Pine Creek Railroad's little balloon-stacked number 6, still wearing its bright red badge from the Lima Locomotive Works. This is the one, Katie, he'd say. This is the one that built America.

My grandfather missed the beginning of the end; death spared him the torment and the disappointment. He went to his grave believing that trains would carry us into the next century. He had no idea that people would slowly abandon the railroads for sleek, new automobiles, which were, to his mind, lousy tin lizzies. Making a midnight run, he'd say, is like absolution. The crisp night air washes your face with the hopes and dreams of every man who ever laid track or rode the rails. And you can feel the constancy of the engine, marking time, moving through the rise and fall of towns and cities like a rushing, silver river. *Type of the modern,* I still hear him proclaim, *emblem of motion and power— pulse of the continent.*

I remember my grandfather well, and for him I nurture a dream of locomotives, a dream of railroads as they were before the crash, before Henry Ford and Harvey Firestone, before bankrupt lines, forced to sell their trains, gave up mile after mile of hard-won distance and, like migrating birds, arrived where they began.

As I grew older, the music of trains filled my head, the rhythmic clicking of the wheels like a rolling bass for my left hand, and the sharp bells and whistles, the expurgations of steam, like a staccato melody for my right. I played Gershwin and knew that he too heard the trains, and sometimes my fingers ached from hammering his locomotive sounds, my piano ready to burst like an over-stoked engine.

And while I played furious odes to long forgotten railroads, while the years went by and the world changed, I began to see trains as wild contradictions, inexplicable oppositions. Things that were ponderous but graceful, inelegant but beautiful, cold but erotic. And when I stand in a museum now, surrounded by dark, unmoving steel, my stomach flutters and my heart beats double-time. The fear and the fascination come back.

By June, Stephen, under my restless direction, began kissing me goodnight, and although our kisses were tightlipped, quick and dry, I took these awkward clutches as a sign of passion still to come. Stephen's lack of experience, I told Laura, and his maddening determination to be a perfect gentleman conspire quite naturally to slow us down; his charm and his virtues keep the fire from sparking.

Despite my self-satisfying explanations, I craved intimacy, and so, after a long night of deliberation, I decided to take Stephen trestling. I call it trestling because it was beneath a trestle, with a train roaring overhead, that I first had the idea, but trestles really have nothing to do with trestling.

The idea is to get as close to a fast moving train as humanly possible without losing your nerve. It's an experience that overwhelms your body with sound, with unstoppable fury, with skin jangling tremors and up the spine shivers, and when the train is gone and you rest in the settling air and silence, the heightened sensitivity to everything that surrounds you borders, for me, on ecstasy.

My first time happened by accident, standing beneath the trestles of the Rainbow Bridge when a locomotive pulling freight came up and over; suddenly, my adolescent legs felt warm and jittery, as if a swarm of bumblebees were buzzing beneath my skin. After that, I began to wonder what it would feel like to sit on the gravel railroad bed as near the track as I could. I began to experiment, always by myself, getting closer each time. It became my private game, my secret obsession, so taking Stephen with me wasn't a casual matter.

I explained to Stephen that trestling only works at night. Engineers, I said, keep watch as they go, and in the daytime a good engineer can see anything that's near the track. In broad daylight, we'd be blasted with a screaming whistle and screeching brakes. It has to be dark. And we have to do it in the country where the trains run at full throttle. I know a place.

How do we get there?

We can borrow my dad's car. You have to believe me. Trestling is no good in Cleveland. The trains slow down as soon as they reach the city limits.

I proposed the idea on a Sunday, sitting on Stephen's front porch watching a storm roll through, and so it must have been a Monday evening when we drove west along Lake Erie and then southwest on Detroit Road.

Is it much further? asked Stephen.

Not far, I said. Doesn't the air smell delicious?

I love driving on warm summer nights, said Stephen. I love the road and the open windows.

Sometimes I could just keep going, I said.

Where would you go?

It's not where that's important. It's just the going.

Stephen leaned out the window. Is that a full moon? he asked. I can't tell for sure.

I looked up through the windshield. I don't think so, I said. But it's bright. If we sit in the moonlight they'll see us for sure.

Maybe we should wait for clouds.

No. Tonight's perfect. All we have to do is find a spot with trees. If you sit in the shadows, then you're almost invisible.

How do you know there'll be a train tonight?

I know the schedule.

You know everything about trains, don't you?

Almost.

What if they changed the schedule without telling you?

It's possible. I've been stood up once or twice before. But not very often.

I parked the car on the dirt shoulder of the road, and we walked out through tall grass toward a line of silhouetted trees that formed a hedgerow along the railroad track.

How long before the train? asked Stephen.

We're early. Probably twenty or twenty-five minutes.

This reminds me of my brother.

Which one?

Phil. We'd do stuff like this all the time. Crazy things. Especially when we lived in Mayfield.

We passed through the row of trees. Do you think this is crazy? I asked.

It's crazy and beautiful, said Stephen. Like you.

The rails looked like liquid silver in the moonlight, and we took two steps up to the gravel bed and saw, not far from where we stood, the shadow of a tall tree falling across the track. We walked into the shadow. This is it, I said. And I sat down slowly, pulling my knees against my chest, smelling the creosote of the crossties.

You can't sit that close, said Stephen.

Of course I can.

But how can you stand it?

I've done it before. It takes practice. At first, I thought the train would throw me over, leave me face down in the gravel. But you learn how to hold your own. You don't have to sit this close.

The track's on fire, said Stephen. Then he sat down and faced me.

You're sitting the wrong way, I said. The train'll come from the west.

I know, he said. I want to see you right now. We still have time.

Let's whisper, I said.

Did you ever do this with your grandfather?

I let out an embarrassed giggle. I haven't done this with anyone, until tonight.

And what if I can't do it? What if I pull away as the train passes?

Then we can try it again. If you want to.

You won't think less of me.

No. You're willing to try. That's enough.

Is it?

Relax. Let yourself go.

You say the same thing when I listen to you play.

Exactly.

Have you always lived like this?

Like what?

I don't know. Stephen shook his head. What's that?

I felt a vague pounding and told Stephen to lower his ear to the rail. I can almost hear it, he said. It's like an echo running through the steel.

You feel it, I said, before you actually hear it.

Stephen turned around and sat next to me. Are you sure you're not too close?

I'm sure.

We waited. I was aware of our nearness, our breathing, as the ground began to pulse, a faint vibration at first, but then more and more until it started to tremble. I heard the steady beat of the wheels and a long, howling whistle, and then, as if a demon had suddenly spit fire, a yellow shaft of light erupted from the darkness. Behind the glaring beacon was a rushing sound like white water and I saw the outline of the locomotive plunging toward us and I felt the engine throbbing, its pressure ballooning in my ears, and the warm night wind pushing against my face like a fast-running current. My skin tingled as the roadbed shuddered and shook. And then it was upon us like an avalanche — the swelling pant and roar, the convulsive onrush, a gale pulling my clothes and hair. I let myself ride on the fury, on the raging cacophony of steel on steel, and the bones of my body bounced until, in a final, relentless surge, the last car flew by, leaving a wisp of startled air.

I knew that Stephen sat beside me, but for a long time we said nothing, and I felt open then like a palm held out, open as a sunflower, without shelter, hideless and unhidden. Every inch of me seemed electric, attuned to every creature that lived in the summer night.

And then Stephen kissed me, a deep and soulful kiss, and I waited for something to move through me, to forcefully take me over. There was nothing.

I looked up at an unfamiliar sky and shivered as I found what a fragile thing a dream of passion can be; where I expected to feel excitement and elation, I felt a sudden emptiness instead, and I knew, as the shock of it stunned me, that somehow Stephen and I had missed each other, perhaps from the start.

After all my vulnerability and joy, I felt myself running down like an overwound clock. I thought I should report myself missing, as if I'd slipped, quite accidentally, into someone else's body. I needed to be alone. And when Stephen reached for me to steady himself, as we walked back together to the car, I wanted to close myself up, crawl inside a shell where Stephen could not find me, where he could not love me after all.

NOT LONG before puberty, in my last year of dolls and maternal dreams, I begged my parents for a little brother or sister. They explained—in a roundabout way—that capitalism depended on and therefore encouraged middle class breeding to provide a surplus population of consumers. They were not going to place their love or their lust in the service of an immoral, economic system. I made serious faces while they repeated their well-rehearsed lecture, and just at the moment when they thought I understood, or so the story goes, I would stick out my lower lip and talk about Laura and her two sisters and whether or not I would suffer, as my mother once said, from the 'only child syndrome. I rode on my father's back and whispered in his ear that our family needed a baby, and I promised to take care of it when it came. And when I sat on my mother's lap, I spoke incantations over her tummy, coaxing it to get big, wanting, I thought, someone to share my games. I whined and badgered and insisted until my father asked his nephew, who was younger than me, to come and stay with us for a month. Think of him as your baby brother, said my father. At least for a little while.

For the first few days I took up the role of big sister with a fervent passion. I played with the dull boy, told him scary stories before bedtime, and showed him how to hide my mother's disgusting green peas in his napkin. But after a week as a dutiful sibling, the charm of having a brother began to wear off. I resented the fact that I was no longer the principal contender in mealtime conversation. By the third week, I hated my cousin and learned my first hard lesson about asking for something that, in the end, I didn't want. After that, my desire for a sibling waned, but the cycle of wanting something and then rejecting it—sometimes with great embarrassment or sadness—persisted. And so it was with Stephen.

Sometimes I recognized the cycle as it began, but still I did nothing about it, as if I craved disappointment or, even worse, some sort of existential ennui. But my lack of feeling for Stephen came as a grave surprise. I pushed my past experiences aside, told myself that what I saw on that first day in the bookstore must still be there, buried, perhaps, and almost forgotten, but still there. Patience, I said. Stephen will reveal himself. My feelings will change.

Oddly enough, Massimino's Music became the place where I talked about Stephen the most. Lambert liked to tease me by inquiring about the intentions of his best, non-paying customer; he worried that I would run off and get married and leave him alone in the store.

You must warn me, he said, so I have days enough to order a new sign.

In the window was a placard that provided the following information: *Lambert Massimino, Proprietor; Katherine Lennox, Pianist.*

My heart breaks when you go, he said. But even if you marry and stay, I will need a new sign.

No you won't.

But you will be Lennox no longer.

If I ever get married, which at this point is absurd even to consider, I'll keep my own name.

Lambert smiled. Perhaps the boy will change his?

Maybe he should, I said.

You will have to pardon me. I am an old man.

Lambert took out his feather duster and began fussing over the oil paintings that decorated the walls of the shop. With the exception of three or four landscapes, each canvas offered the face and the figure of a woman, some old and some young, some with children in busy domestic scenes and some quite alone in bistros or sidewalk cafés. The collection showed Lambert's impeccable taste; whether sumptuous or muted, impressionistic or realistic, each painting offered a vision of extraordinary beauty.

Lambert hummed to himself while he dusted. Is the boy not in love with you?

He is.

Then your face should be the face of the girl who has just discovered a magnificent bouquet. You should be this girl.

I have wanted to be, I said.

Lambert put down his feather duster. Is he a good boy? A caring boy?

Yes.

But there is nothing else?

I wanted to say that I wasn't sure, that it would be prudent to wait a little longer and see, and then Stephen walked through the door arm in arm with Philip Tollman, the gandy dancer, his dark and brooding brother.

They came in with a gust of bravado — Stephen bursting with pride, ready to show off his hero. There was something magnetic between them, a sympathy or understanding, a charisma that, I later realized, diminished when one was without the other.

Lambert shook Phil's hand and said, Perhaps you will listen to music and buy it too. Then he went back to his paintings.

Katherine, said Stephen. This is the guy I've been telling you about.

I feel I know you already.

Phil took my hand. Wish I could say the same. Stephen's been trying to fill me in since we left the station. What he didn't tell me is that you're the most beautiful girl in Cleveland.

Phil doesn't waste a minute, said Stephen.

Thank you, I said. But now that you're back, I think you should take a good look around.

I haven't been gone that long.

At least not long enough to pick up any new lines, said Stephen.

I mean what I say.

You better, said Stephen.

Stop this right now or you'll make me a vain woman.

Vanity, said Phil, is the honest face of beauty.

There's a new line, said Stephen.

With his brother, Stephen seemed more relaxed, his wit sharper, and for a moment I thought I saw the thing I liked. C'mon you two, I said. Take me away from here. I need coffee.

Then you're here for the whole week? I asked.

Probably two.

Since when? asked Stephen.

It's a slowdown. The union's putting pressure on the home office.

Stephen shook his head. What union?

The Brotherhood of Railway Clerks, I said.

Phil's eyes shot across the table. That's right.

Ask her anything about railroads, said Stephen. She knows it all.

I'm impressed, said Phil. You a Vanderbilt?

Right passion, I said. Wrong politics.

Why the slowdown? asked Stephen. What do they want?

Better wages and hours, I said, pulling out a cigarette. Better working conditions.

Phil struck a match and leaned across the table. The union's been bleeding, he said. That's what the old-timers say. They say membership is running low.

Doesn't sound like the right time for a strike, said Stephen.

It's not a strike, said Phil. Just a slowdown. I don't know whether it's the right time or not.

The owners know what's going on, I said. They think low enrollment means apathy. They're counting on it.

Where did you find this woman? asked Phil.

She found me, said Stephen, raising his cup. Damnit, he sprayed. You gotta be careful with this stuff. It's hotter than blazes.

You're lucky to be in a union, I said.

I'm not a member—not yet, anyway. I can't afford it.

You could afford it if the union got you a better wage.

What do I do in the meantime?

That's a point, I said. Do you like it? Being a gandy dancer, I mean.

I like the free passes. I go up to Buffalo almost every weekend with some of the guys. The dance halls there are always crowded. Last month I went up to Niagara Falls.

Sounds fun, I said. What about the job?

It's just that—a job. I get tired of it.

I thought gandy dancers were the 'lifeblood of the road.'

Phil smiled. Who've you been talking to?

My grandfather. He was a dancer for a few years.

What did he tell you?

Not much. He said gandy dancers move up and down the line looking for bad stretches of track. They take out old crossties, then wrestle new ones up to the roadbed and tamp them down. If the rails are shot, they have to splice in new steel. The gandy dancers keep the whole thing going.

That's about it. But you make it sound like a glamour job.

I laughed. Don't you like the image?

It'll take some getting used to.

You'll join the union as soon as you get back, said Stephen. Talk to Katherine long enough and you'll be packing Marx in your suitcase.

I'm surprised, little brother. I didn't think you'd fall in with radicals while I was gone.

If you think Katherine's dangerous, wait till you meet her parents.

I don't think I'm dangerous. At least not to the New York Central Railroad.

Phil laughed. No. But what about the poor saps working the line? You know—the lifeblood between Cleveland and Buffalo? Most of 'em would be afraid of someone like you.

But you're not, said Stephen.

I'm not a sap, said Phil, cracking his knuckles.

Can the railroads survive? I asked.

Survive what?

Highways. Automobiles. No passengers.

They may be short on travelers, but they're never short on freight.

I've heard that, I said. I'm not sure I believe it.

And I'm not sure the situation is as bad as they say. New York Central wants us to think our jobs will disappear tomorrow. If they keep us scared and grateful, then they figure we won't strike.

Now you sound like Katherine, said Stephen.

Phil smiled. No reason to insult your girlfriend. I'm just a gandy dancer. And gandy dancers are simple and crude.

It's true, said Stephen. You haven't heard him cuss.

I bet I could keep up, I said.

I don't doubt it, said Phil.

So what do you wanna do while you're home? asked Stephen.

Sleep. Take it easy. Phil finished his coffee. I plan on going to Mayfield.

It's been a while, said Stephen.

Phil nodded.

Stephen looked at me. Will you come with us?

She has to, said Phil.

I smiled and accepted the invitation. Phil insisted on paying the check, ignoring loud protests from his brother, and we walked out and turned down Lorain Avenue, toward the storefront where one afternoon I'd stood with Stephen and a handful of strangers watching a baker turn dough, where Stephen had whispered to me about his father and Fred's Radio & Repair. Now as I approached the place with Phil and Stephen, I expected one of them to say or do something, make a solemn speech or gesture, as if we were visiting a grave. But there were no words, not even a pause. The silence went on for several blocks, the street almost empty, until we passed a pawnshop with an accordion in the window.

How long have you played piano? asked Phil.

As long as I can remember.

On one side of the accordion was a trumpet and trombone. On the other side was a black clarinet. It looked to me like all the musicians in Cleveland had given up their instruments. No one ever pawns a piano, I thought.

THAT NIGHT I went to the movies with Laura and talked only about Phil. I called him cocky, argued that meeting him put my feelings for Stephen into perspective. Laura said that I was lying. She told me my voice sounded higher, like the day I met Stephen at the bookstore. Laura cautioned me, pointing out, in a flourish of motherly concern, that I really knew nothing about Phil. But that's where Laura was wrong.

Phil stood an inch or two taller than his brother, with a shock of black hair that sometimes fell across his forehead. His thick eyebrows and thin mustache were black, and his eyes were dark as coal, black pearls brimming with sadness, the same sadness that first drew me to Stephen. But Phil's eyes, so different from his brother's, jumped with fury, with pain. I had never seen eyes so indignant.

Phil almost strutted when he walked, as if he dared anyone to question his ownership of any place he happened to be. His humor, at least what I saw of it, displayed all the qualities of a cactus, and while he exercised restraint with me, he liked to dominate conversations, sometimes with a maddening, unearned confidence, a boldness of manner that, like my own, masked a deep well of insecurity and apprehension. His self-assuredness was hypnotic, but his attitude was less than outgoing. I saw him— even on that first day—as overbearing, enigmatic, and aloof. All around him was an aura of gloomy magnetism, a dark shadow that jolted my stomach like whiskey.

THREE DAYS later we made our pilgrimage to Mayfield. The gray struck me at first, as if the sky, trees, and meadows composed a palette of neutral tones. The month may have been June, but the leaden clouds colored the day like winter. I felt anxious on the train, studying the faces of strangers, checking my watch more than was necessary. When we arrived, I saw a woman waiting for her husband, and the smile on her mouth was the deadest thing I'd ever seen, alive enough to have strength to die. We followed the road away from Mayfield Village, hearing a tractor's steady drone beyond a line of poplars, and I couldn't shake the woman's face or the conviction that the days and hours of this place were somehow running down.

A light rain, almost a mist, made grass and flowers heavy, whole fields of wild carrot leaning and bowing, and all around us the leaves, like the few that had fallen from ash trees and elms, no longer seemed green. The leaves curled at the edges, dripping silver beads, clinging to black branches like tired children.

I walked behind Phil, and Stephen walked behind me, and we said very little, lulled into silence by the growing stillness. After some distance we left the road, taking a trail that cut through shrubbery and woods and a line of dead trees, and then I heard something that sounded like wind, though the day was breathless, and the trail dropped off a bit until it leveled out beside the Chagrin River.

The rain made rings inside rings and rivulets trickled into the slow-moving stream. Without the sun, the water looked stolid, a channel of ashes, flowing, I imagined, into the opaque depths of a dark harbor.

Coming back here, said Phil, makes me feel old.

His voice floated out over the river and became part of its silence. I saw far ahead of us, at the edge of the heavy woods in the distance, a field of white flowers. It looks like a bed of feathers, said Stephen.

Then someone take me there, I said, and cover me with soft petals.

We stood on the bank near a long, flat stone, and I wondered about the end of my life. What will I sing when my hands freeze with arthritis and fail? What will I hope for when the moon leaves me in an ocean of darkness, when the weight of the past leans against nothing? Perhaps the clouds and the rain, or maybe the river, made me sad. I wanted to hold that sadness for a while. It felt like the company of a good friend. It felt peaceful.

I tried not to move, telling myself to be still like an old tree, but then Stephen broke the spell. If the river had a voice, he whispered, what would it say?

I've seen shit, said Phil.

I don't think so, I said. Something mournful, maybe, or wise. That's it — something wise.

We began walking again and I heard the river making words; it sounded like an old woman speaking of what it is like to wait without hope, to watch the daylight inch across the ground. The voice made a poem out of cankered fish and rotting logs, and then it said something I could barely understand. I listened hard, trying to get it all, trying to get it right, but in the end all I could hear was a whisper. I thought it said this: *everything is unbearably over with*.

Stephen stopped us. Do you hear that?

What? asked Phil.

That sound. It's like wind in bare branches.

We listened.

Everything is unbearably over with, I said.

Stephen looked over his shoulder. What?

The river. That's what it said.

I didn't hear it, said Phil.

You weren't listening, I said.

Phil suddenly smiled. You'll have to teach me, he said.

We continued on and walked past the meadow of Queen

Anne's lace. Not far from there the river curved, forming a high shoulder on our side of the bank. After the bend was a wooden footbridge.

That's new, said Stephen.

Would've made life a hell-of-a-lot easier, said Phil.

How'd you get across? I asked.

Fallen trees, said Stephen. Shallow spots.

Sometimes we swam, said Phil.

We crossed on the bridge and turned upstream until the trail disappeared. Then we bushwhacked our way through thick woods until we came to a clearing and a black shack with broken windows and a sagging roof.

What's this place? I asked.

Our neighbor lived here, said Phil.

Stephen said that your closest friends lived on a farm.

This guy wasn't our friend, said Phil.

We walked up the creaking steps to the door. It was rotting from the bottom up, turning green with moss, and it hung from one hinge. The little house was empty except for half-burned candles scattered across the floor and puddles of hardened wax everywhere.

All these candles, I said. I looked at Stephen for confirmation.

Stephen nodded. I wonder who got the crucifix?

Wormwood took it with him, said Phil.

A board cracked beneath my foot and Stephen said, Nobody's been here for ages.

Just as well, said Phil.

We stayed inside for a few minutes and Phil crouched against the wall looking at the floor. He picked up a candle stub and scratched the wax with his fingernails. He tossed it aside and picked up another one, and then Stephen walked over and put his hand on his brother's shoulder. Phil stood up and we walked out into the rain; it felt like a blessing after the brittle decay of Wormwood's shack.

We went back across the footbridge and walked downstream until we came to a field of tall grass. Phil stopped once or twice and pointed to what he called markers on the tree line. Then he and Stephen decided that the path they were looking for was overgrown, so we were forced to make our way up from the river through a wash of dripping grass. We pressed through a stubborn line of blackberry bushes and then into dark woods once again. This time we came out into a small clearing. Phil and Stephen argued over the exact position of the tent, but after a fit of pacing and head shaking, they finally reached an agreement.

This was the place, said Phil. Sometimes it's hard to remember what it was like.

I remember all of it, said Stephen.

The day we tore it down, said Phil. That's what I remember best—watching the shithole collapse like a punctured balloon.

Myron cut his hand, said Stephen.

And Mom sat on the wagon we brought over from Johnson's farm, said Phil.

I had questions I wanted to ask them, but somehow it felt wrong for me to intrude. Instead, I listened to them talk and curse, and I watched Phil's face grow darker and darker as Stephen went on with his memories. I sunk deeper into my own melancholy, feeling the weight of the overcast sky and the steady drizzle that seemed to make everything around us hang its head. I knew, of course, where our next stop would be, and I wasn't at all sure that I wanted to go.

I followed Phil and Stephen, trying not to think, wanting to see again the open space near the Chagrin River. But we continued away from the water and into the woods and through a grove of dead trees, silver smooth ghosts that once were giant elms, ashes, and maples. The rain made the skin of the trees glisten, and I caressed the cold wetness and said the trunks felt like silk.

More woods passed in a blur until we were on a dirt road that gradually curved back toward the river. We walked in silence for more than a mile, and then on the right was a row of evergreen trees. We turned off the road and Phil held back an armful of soft, pine-scented branches, and then I saw three depressions in a clearing of scrub grass, and I knew that this was the place where Margie had died.

They filled 'em, said Stephen. And then he described, as he had done once before, the open basements and the ducks and the late afternoon in spring when they found Margie face down in the cold and muddy melt-off. Phil was silent. He walked the high ground around the sagging earth, and I drifted after him, caught unexpectedly in the wake of his sadness.

It's no good, said Phil.

I came up close to him after he said that and let myself lean against him. Phil looked at me and put his arm around my shoulders. He rested on me for a moment, but then he moved a short way off.

I hate this place, said Stephen.

So do I, said Phil.

Then why do we come?

I have to.

It doesn't change.

I know.

It doesn't change anything, said Stephen.

WHEN WE got back to the city that evening, Phil insisted that I play for him. We left our sopping shoes at the door and dried off as best we could before shooing my parents out of the living room and opening the piano. I was in no mood for a sentimental ballad, and an upbeat number I couldn't possibly bear. Only Beethoven suited me, and the only piece I yearned to play was my favorite, though Stephen had listened to it more than once, sometimes the whole thing, other times in bits and pieces.

I had no choice. My fingers found the notes without my thinking, but Phil sat in the chair like a statue, still preoccupied, I knew, with the day's journey. I watched him through the first movement, and then, as I approached the *Allegretto,* I saw him give in to the music. He hunkered down in his chair and seemed to me like a wolf in darkness perking up his ears. I played Beethoven then like I have never played him since. And when I was finished, my fingers trembled.

What is it? asked Phil.

Sonata Number Fourteen, said Stephen, in something or other minor.

In C-sharp Minor, I said.

Lousy title, said Phil.

It's the *Moonlight Sonata,* I said.

You never told me that, said Stephen.

You never asked.

Once more, said Phil.

I can't. I'm too tired.

Just a little, said Phil.

I started again and was only a minute or two into the first movement when Phil abruptly stood up and said he needed to go. I'm sorry, he said. I didn't realize the time. In an instant, he was gone.

Stephen looked at me and shrugged his shoulders.

Maybe he doesn't like Beethoven, I said.

He liked it, said Stephen.

How do you know?

I'm his brother.

THE NEXT night was up to me, my turn to take Phil and Stephen on a guided tour. We had dinner at The Third Coast, apéritifs at The Sign of the Steer, jazz and more drinks at Fat Face Fenner's, and then we stopped for a nightcap at the Silverbird Saloon. At each bar we ran into friends of mine, most of them members of the Party, an outspoken group of misfits who all conspired to recruit Stephen. He put up an admirable resistance. Phil ignored most of what was going on, said it was too late to make him a convert.

You certainly know your way around, said Phil.

It's 1939, I said. A woman can't afford not to.

Is this a standard routine for you two?

Stephen laughed. Hardly, he said. We've been to the Coast before. But the rest is news to me. Stephen put his hand over mine. Why haven't we done this until now?

Because I haven't been here to do it with, said Phil.

Is that right? asked Stephen.

Both of you needed some cheering up, I said. But I'm afraid my friends have ruined that.

Not at all, said Phil.

Would you like to go to New York? asked Stephen.

I always go to New York, said Phil.

I mean New York City.

No.

Why not?

Too expensive.

Katherine's going. She's going to make a great career in New York City.

Phil raised his drink and so did Stephen. To Katherine in New York, said Phil.

Listen, Phil, said Stephen. If I handled both our expenses, would you go with me?

You're supposed to go with Katherine.

I want you to see it too.

He'll probably get there before us, I said.

No point in that, said Phil.

All my life I've wanted to go to New York City, said Stephen.

All your life? asked Phil.

Stephen nodded. It was a quiet dream. I never told you.

Then go. You can go anywhere you want.

I'll be too old before I can do it. I can't get started.

Don't be a fool, said Phil.

Stephen looked at me like a lost child. I felt sorry for him. The idea had taken hold of him and now he had it badly.

I can't stand it, Stephen said. Sometimes I feel like my life is already used up.

You're drunk, said Phil.

I mean it, said Stephen. I feel like my life is going . . . just going.

Life can go wherever it pleases — with or without me, said Phil.

You can say that now, said Stephen. But what happens in ten years?

I say fuck it, said Phil.

I wanna go to New York City. Maybe there I can get caught up.

Going to another city — even another country — makes no difference, I said. You end up living in a straight line. You keep moving until you lose your friends — your family too.

Then I'm fucked, said Stephen.

No. You're drunk, I said.

How do you know? asked Phil.

His eyes are flying at half-mast.

I can see that, said Phil. I mean that other stuff. How do you know about living in straight lines?

I lit a cigarette. My grandfather, I suppose. My mother too. Some people need straight lines. Some prefer circles.

But then you end up where you began, said Phil.

That's inevitable, I said. It's what you collect along the way.

You mean your phony friends?

What did you say? asked Stephen.

Your brother said that my friends are phony. And he's right about some of them. I poured part of Phil's drink into my empty glass. I'm sure you're very careful when it comes to choosing your friends.

I don't have any friends, said Phil.

So it runs in the family.

I'm likable, said Phil. It's just hard to keep in touch.

Stephen's chin had sunk into his chest. But he wasn't a sloppy drunk. He stayed in his chair and dozed like a gentleman.

The waiter stopped at our table, stooping beneath an enormous tray of empty glasses.

Do you want another drink? asked Phil.

Do you?

Another whiskey for me, said Phil. And a vodka gimlet for the lady. Bring some coffee for Sleeping Beauty.

We sat there without speaking, both of us keeping an eye on Stephen. I listened to the steady murmur of voices. The sound made me feel warm, quite cozy altogether.

Poor Stephen, I said. It seems we've run him down.

Don't be angry, said Phil. But you're not the right woman for my brother.

What's this? Disapproval?

Not exactly.

Okay. Then . . . you feel a sudden urge to protect him.

I always have.

And I suppose you know the right woman.

Not for him.

Are you flirting with me?

Not so anyone would catch me.

And are you afraid of getting caught?

The drinks came. I let Phil pay the waiter.

Do you know how they trap a lion or a tiger? asked Phil.

No. But I imagine it's cruel.

Lions and tigers return to a place of remembered beauty. That's where they set the trap.

And you, no doubt, are a lion. Or are you a tiger?

Nothing so noble.

Then why worry?

It's just my habit. I return to places of remembered beauty.

You are flirting.

It's a game. I can't think of it as anything more than a game.

Why's that?

I believe you're spoken for.

You should know by now that no one speaks for me.

Is that true?

I'm not good at games. I forget the rules.

I'd be better if my brother wasn't sitting at the table.

Do you want to kiss me? I whispered.

Let's not talk about it now.

I knew it in Mayfield. And then later, while I played for you.

You don't forget the rules. You make up new ones as you go.

But it's true.

I think I should take Stephen home while he can still walk.

I ran my fingers through Stephen's hair. His head tilted toward me. I care for him, you know.

He loves you, said Phil.

Yes, I know. That's my fault.

Stephen slept on my shoulder in the cab. Phil and I said nothing more. We stopped at the Tollman house first, and I watched Phil and Stephen stumble up the front walk, waiting until they were inside. I asked the driver to take me for a ride, and we drove the deserted downtown streets and out along Lake Erie until I could no longer think about it all. The cabby was at the end of his shift, so he finally took me home.

PHIL AVOIDED me for two days, even to the point of changing his plans. Earlier that week, Stephen had arranged a visit with Lethea. He got very excited. But when the evening came, Phil begged off at the last minute.

That son-of-a-bitch really pisses me off, said Stephen.

Don't be angry, I said. It'll spoil our visit.

I'll be what I damn well please. That's your philosophy, isn't it?

What do you mean?

Nothing. I never mean anything. That's the beauty of talking to someone like me. You never have to take me seriously.

Maybe we shouldn't see Lethea tonight.

You backing out too?

No. I want to go.

Good. That makes one of us.

We can do it some other evening. Use me as an excuse if you need one.

C'mon, we'll miss the bus. Lethea's waiting.

You sure you want to go through with this?

I'm sure.

The bus driver looked like an ex-boxer, a no-neck bulldog with a crooked nose and a cauliflower ear. His hands were huge on the steering wheel, and he kept looking at us in the rearview mirror. The bus was like a church, more than half full and no one making a sound. I asked Stephen if he wanted to talk before we got to Lethea's. He looked at the bus driver and shook his head. I'm not taking any chances, he said.

The little woman who answered the door was Lethea's neighbor; she told us in a thick, Italian accent that Lethea had been chattering all day about our visit, and then she took us into the living room. Lethea sat in an opulent wing chair, a throne of plush cushions and emerald green fabric, and she smiled and set aside her needlepoint as Stephen introduced me.

I leave now, said the neighbor, kissing Lethea on the cheek.

Thanks for lookin' in, said Lethea. Then she turned to Stephen and me. I'm lucky to have such friends.

The little woman nodded to us and went out the way we came.

So you're the young lady I've heard so much about. Lethea held out her hand.

What's Mom been saying? asked Stephen.

Only good things, said Lethea. She shook my hand and took a close look at it, and then she asked to see the other one.

It's you everybody talks about, I said. I've heard enough stories to fill a book.

Lethea laughed and motioned for us to sit down. Where's that rapscallion you call a brother?

I don't know, said Stephen. He was supposed to be here.

Too busy, said Lethea. All you young people are too busy.

He'll see you before he leaves town, said Stephen. He told me to tell you.

I couldn't guess Lethea's age, but she looked very old, very tired and venerable, as if she'd lived each day of her life to a point of profound exhaustion. Deep lines scored her face, and sometimes her laughter ended in a fit of coughing and gasping.

Heard from your daddy? asked Lethea.

Stephen shook his head. You ask me every time I visit. You ask the same question, and I give you the same answer.

Lethea ignored Stephen's exasperation. On the coffee table was a plate of cookies. Lethea pushed the plate toward me and told me to help myself. You've probably noticed, she said. The Tollman boys get worked up about their daddy.

Let's not talk about it, said Stephen.

Stephen and his brother figure their daddy is a good for nothin' who doesn't give a good goddamn—

Stephen started to say something but Lethea kept going.

—Well, maybe he is worthless or maybe he ain't. Maybe he thought he was doin' you all a favor.

I wanted to change the subject for Stephen's sake, but everything I thought to say seemed obvious or absurd. It must have been difficult for Mrs. Tollman, I said.

Jessica just keeps goin'. I thought she'd break when her little girl died. She couldn't get over it for a while—that's where the older boy gets his stubbornness. But then one day she just picked up and went on with her life. It's all anybody can do.

How've you been feeling? asked Stephen.

Damned awful, said Lethea. It's too late in the day to make small talk. If we can't talk about what's important, then I'd prefer we not talk at all.

Stephen had been perched on the edge of the couch, but now he sat back and sulked, an obvious attempt to make me the center of conversation. I rifled the drawers of my brain looking for a question, for anything to say, but I kept coming up short. Lethea knew what was happening, and she saved me. Tell me somethin' about yourself, she said.

I blurted out the first thing that came into my head. I'm a communist.

Is that a fact? Lethea said. Where'd you pick it up?

My parents.

Somethin' like religion. Is that it?

You could say that. But I don't think the founders of the faith would appreciate the comparison.

We know it by its disciples, said Lethea. Not by its disclaimers. Is communism your work?

I play the piano, I said.

That's right. Jessie talked about that. I should've remembered after lookin' at your hands.

My hands are too small.

Too small for what?

Rachmaninoff.

To hell with him. You got strong hands.

Thank you, I said.

I'm only tellin' you what I see. Lethea took a handkerchief out of her sleeve and wiped the corners of her mouth. Damn medicine, she said.

Can I get you something? I asked.

Just relax yourself. I got all I need right here. Lethea waved her hand toward the end table next to her chair. It was loaded with pills and bottles of milky liquid and a pitcher of water. You're a strange girl, said Lethea.

Why do you say that?

In my day girls played piano in the parlor—not in concert halls.

I'll settle for a publishing house in New York, I said.

Lethea laughed and coughed. I hear New York City is a lively place. You ever make up your own songs?

Sometimes. But I throw them away.

You shouldn't do that.

This time I laughed.

Lethea went on about music. How her mother sang to her before putting her to bed and how she felt pride, years later, when the first Negro musicians started playing in the clubs around Cleveland. I never went to such places, she said. But I saw the posters at the streetcar stops.

Lethea poured herself a glass of water and took a long gulp. Then she changed the subject abruptly: So what are you doin' with Mr. Sour Grapes over there?

Now don't start on me, Lethea, said Stephen.

I been on you ever since you started to shave. You should be grateful. Not everybody gets my undivided attention.

Stephen managed a smile.

Lethea waved her hand in my direction. You've hooked a live one here.

Any advice? asked Stephen.

Stop messin' in deep water.

I suddenly felt exposed. I wanted to crawl under the couch.

This girl's too much, said Lethea. I've seen it before.

Lethea, said Stephen. You're a hard woman to love.

I'm only tellin' you what I see.

I looked down at the floor and saw Stephen's shoes. I wanted it to be Phil sitting next to me. I wanted to say it out loud.

You still at the bookstore? asked Lethea.

Almost every day, said Stephen.

You thinkin' about stayin' there?

I doubt it.

What then?

I'm still looking, said Stephen. I'd like to write for a newspaper. What I'd really like to do is write a book.

A book you say. What kind?

Short stories.

Then go to it.

It's not that easy, said Stephen. You don't just sit down and start writing a book.

Why not?

Well, for one thing it takes practice.

Then start practicin'.

But you have to have something to say.

Let me understand this. You're thinkin' you'd like to write a book, a book filled with stories, but you've got nothin' to say.

That's not what I mean.

That's more or less what you said.

I mean . . . you have to be ready to write.

How do you know when you're ready?

I don't know.

Then it seems to me you could spend a considerable time waitin'.

Katherine, said Stephen, can you save me from this?

You're on your own, I said.

I'll tell you what, said Lethea. Why don't you write a story about me? Katherine says she's heard enough to fill a book. I'm not shy, and I'm certainly not humble. I've got more than you'd ever want—she tapped her forehead—right here.

That's a wonderful idea, I said.

You can interview me, said Lethea. I know things you'd never imagine.

Stephen reluctantly gave in and promised to bring his notebook on his next visit. Then Lethea, after a spell of coughing, apologized for cutting our visit short. I'm not the social lion I once was, she said.

Lethea stayed in her chair and we said good-bye.

Come back again, said Lethea.

I'll come.

Do somethin' for me?

What's that?

Play your music loud. Play it so an old, deaf woman like me can hear it.

I smiled. I'll do my best, I said, and I bent down and kissed her cheek.

Lethea held my face between her hands. Go on now, she said.

We showed ourselves out and walked back to the bus stop in a light rain.

I think we should talk, I said.

Not tonight, said Stephen.

Why not?

I'm talked out.

That's funny. You didn't say much all evening.

I don't feel like talking. Is that all right?

The bus came and I stepped up, giving my ticket to the driver. I heard the door close, but when I turned around, Stephen was not behind me. The bus pulled away and I saw him walking slowly down the street, his hands thrust deep into his pockets.

I WALKED the long way home from the bus stop, oblivious to the rain and the lateness of the hour. I looked into the well-lit rooms of houses, into the private spaces of strangers, and occasionally, when my timing was good, I saw shadows or a flicker of motion, a few fleeting signs of life. The dark windows on my block glowed with the spectral light of street lamps. I stopped for a moment and heard the night noise of the city, and then fancying myself a composer of nocturnes, decided to stay outside for a while and listen. I had almost reached the front walk of my house when I heard my name and Phil stepped from between two bushes onto the pavement.

His sudden appearance startled me and I felt short of breath. I thought you were busy, I said.

I am, said Phil. I've been waiting.

Water dripped down his face and the shoulders of his jacket were soaked through. He'd been standing in the rain for a long time.

You could've come with us tonight and saved yourself the trouble, I said.

I wanted to see you alone, said Phil.

All right, I said. I'm alone.

Have you told him yet?

Told him what?

That you don't love him.

I tried to walk past him but he grabbed my arm and turned me around. You're talking about your brother, I said.

Do you think I feel good about it? It's just as bad for me.

It's worse for Stephen.

Then you didn't tell him.

I've wanted to. I've tried before. I even tried tonight but he wouldn't talk to me.

He knows.

What does he know?

Phil loosened his grip on my arm. I'm in love with you.

You'll have to tell him that yourself, I said.

I'll do it, said Phil. I'll tell him.

Why should I believe you?

I see no reason not to.

I moved a little closer and tried to see his eyes, but the shadow on his face was too dark. You say you love me?

Yes.

You did say you love me, didn't you?

I love you, goddamnit.

Then tell him.

I'll tell him that . . . and more.

Is there more?

Phil looked toward the house, saw there was no one, then pulled me close and kissed me. I slid my arms under his jacket and felt his heart racing.

chapter seven

WE RAN ACROSS the baseball diamond behind Pleasantview School, the full moon icing the field down after a humid day, the grass feeling cool and fresh. We were looking for a private place, a shadowy recess, moving through the night like leopards, eyes wide and searching as we made our way to the darkest corner, just inside the fence, where the silhouette of a tall tree clutched the sky with its giant arms.

Phil took off his shirt and spread it out on the ground like a blanket. I did the same with my skirt. I ran my hands over his chest, his skin moist and electric, and I kissed him and bit his lip and broke away and began to unbutton my blouse. I did it slowly, wanting him to watch me, wanting his eyes to take me in like moonlight. I lifted one strap and then the other, my shoulders awash with silver, and then the clasp gave way and my breasts stiffened, aching for the pull of his mouth.

Phil laid me down on our bed of clothing and I felt the long strength of his legs, his tongue traveling my hips and thighs, his hands touching my face. I kept my eyes open like a wanderer, an explorer, trying to absorb all the sudden beauty of the visible world, and before long I floated beneath his weight, rocking in the full embrace of his body.

I shivered. I sensed the ground sliding out of reach below. I rose toward the sky like an open hand waiting for rain, and we clung to each other, arching and sinking with the ebb and flow of our blood. I saw everything imitate our movements, our turnings, the stars, clouds and leaves shifting and spinning, slowly at first, whirling into a heavenly mess, into a fierce, indecipherable language.

It all went too fast, always too fast, and I wanted the whirling never to stop. I wanted the world in motion for as long as I could stand it, so before either of us could catch our breath, I stood up naked like a child and did a cartwheel out from the shadows.

Phil looked around like a just-discovered thief. Katie, come back, he said, before someone sees you.

I cartwheeled again and felt the night air between my legs like water. I laughed then, feeling the total exhilaration of freedom, and I returned to where Phil sat watching me and began to dress. Put on your clothes, I said. I have an idea.

That's a funny smile, said Phil. What are you thinking?

When I went to this school, I said, I'd climb up the downspout and hide on the roof.

We're going up there? asked Phil, pointing at the gymnasium.

Of course not, I said. I'm talking about that little building in front. The one with the flat roof.

Phil was visibly relieved. What's up there anyway?

Me, I said. And I started to run.

I remembered my old footholds as if I'd done it the day before, and then I swung one leg over the gutter and pulled myself up. Phil followed me.

Lamps burned on all sides of the school, but the roof was deliciously dark, still warm from the day's sun. We sat for a minute and gazed at the neighborhood lights, and then Phil leaned over and opened my shirt. He took a handful of my hair and pulled it until my eyes looked up at the moon. He kissed me. Then he rolled back on his shoulders and raised his hips, pushing down his pants. I want you on top, he said.

I stood with his body between my legs. I raised my skirt and dropped to my knees, using my hand to guide him, trying to hold off at first to make it better, like the first bite of chocolate, then filling myself and feeling his pulse inside me.

When it was over, when my body finally said stop, I felt like a swimmer being pushed by the tide toward shore. How absurd my life seemed then, knowing that I would soon tiptoe up to my room, my bed—both owned by my parents—and sleep a cold and lonely sleep without my lover. To be cast up after an interlude was the condition I came to dread—to return to the same routine when certainly something in me and around me had changed.

We climbed down.

My skin feels prickly, said Phil.

I rubbed my arms and felt it too. It feels like someone's sticking me with tiny pins, I said.

It's from the roof, said Phil. The tar—there's glass in it.

We both started to scratch and complain and walk faster until we reached my house. Phil turned on the garden hose and sprayed me. I washed my arms and legs and then I held the hose on Phil. He opened his shirt and cleaned his chest and shoulders, but then he had to let the water run inside his pants. I tried not to laugh, but I couldn't help it. My wet hair felt cool against my neck and shoulders, a welcome relief from the late July heat.

More than a month now, I thought, since the first time Phil had talked about leaving, of going back to work, and I had asked him, capriciously, not to leave. I never imagined for a moment that he would give up his job. I knew what the money meant to his family. I had asked him to stay knowing that it was impossible.

When you go, I said, I want a clear sign, a door shut by accident on my hand, a sliver pressing its point beneath my skin.

We had said good-bye on a Sunday, just a few days after our first kiss, but on the following Monday I found Phil waiting for me in front of Massimino's Music.

I'm not going back, he said. Piss on the railroad. I'm staying for the summer. I'll look for a job in town. The money I've got should last till September.

I don't remember what I said. I don't remember thinking. I felt myself letting go, giving myself over to an impulsive rush of days, plunging ahead through whatever time we had, wild to be falling forever.

In my excitement, I began talking to flowers and trees, sometimes tables and chairs, even the vegetables that I cleaned and chopped for dinner. I ate artichokes. I took one for lunch each day and met Phil in Penny Park for picnics. Phil was intimidated the first time. He hadn't approached an artichoke before.

Is it edible? he asked.

It's delicious, I said.

Is it cooked?

Steamed.

What do I do?

You peel it. Like this. Then you pull the meaty part between your teeth. Like this. I closed my eyes. There is no greater joy, I said, except for the dipping in salted oils.

Phil took a green leaf and raised it to his mouth. He seemed to like it. We ate until most of the thick, outer leaves were gone. I put the artichoke in his hand.

You keep peeling, I said, until you come to the heart—and its still slickery thistle.

Its what?

Its slickery thistle.

I can't even say that.

Watch closely, I said. With this part you have to be careful. Sharp edges protect the more vulnerable flesh. But soon, you see, the small blades fall away . . . and it gives up its heart. I wanted Phil to eat from my fingers. Take a bite, I said.

I don't want anymore, he said.

It's part of the ritual, I said.

I'm too full.

I ate the rest of it myself, ate it reluctantly, with less pleasure than I expected, and then I lit a cigarette and we walked back to Massimino's.

I've never been happier, I said. I said it two or three times more, trying to fend off my apprehension, a pool of doubt that had lately begun to gather, as it often happened in those days, without warning.

I felt something after the first time Phil and I made love, something that gave me pause. I tried not to think about it, wrote it off as awkwardness, a passing mood. It was something rooted in Phil, a hardness, a core that would not give in, and as the nights began passing in a blur, I felt it again. It haunted me, though I had no intention of stopping. On bad days, I took comfort in my music, fueling it with our passion, playing myself out, hoping my fears would soon fall away.

I spent all my time with Phil. Laura told me later that she hated me, abandoning her without so much as a word. My parents had rarely seen me so obsessed. I think it scared them, and they left me alone, believing, I think, that the whole affair would soon burn up of its own heat. The only time my father said anything was when I asked repeatedly, with very little compunction or consideration, to borrow the car. Take it, he'd say. The older generation likes to walk.

I started stealing my mother's underwear. Borrowing says it better, but it felt like stealing, standing over my mother's open drawer looking for something different, something sexy that an older woman keeps as her secret. Phil thought it was strange until I found a black negligee that pushed up my breasts into perfect orbs—sister moons, I called them.

Pretending we were fugitives, racing against dawn, Phil and I drove out along Lake Erie, and when he saw what I was wearing beneath my raincoat, his eyes widened with desire, a craving that excited me. I would not let him touch me. He had to watch while I knelt on the seat and leaned forward, and then, lawless as I was, I opened the car door and stepped out into the night. Phil kept calling me back but the place where we had parked was dark and secluded and I wanted to feel the breeze off the water on my skin. I could hear Phil's breathing as I moved a little further from the car. My heart pounded; it demanded audacity; it made me eager for danger, for the risk of being discovered. Phil moved to the passenger window, and I could see his breath mixing with the air. The fury of my heart pounding and the excitement between my legs made me want more, and I turned around so that Phil could see me, and I pushed the thin straps of the negligee off my shoulders and felt diaphanous folds of silk fall around my waist and then my ankles, and I stood there letting the darkness wash over me, and I saw an aching in Phil's eyes as I walked back to the car and covered him with my body like a siren just risen from the lake.

JULY DISAPPEARED like a fast-moving train, and so it was a brutal, tar-melting afternoon in August when a sad ghost of Stephen, a

shade with black circles under his eyes, caught me leaving
Massimino's after a profitless day. I saw him far down the street
coming toward me.

He's waited long enough, I thought; now he wants to have it
out. I was distracted, my fingers shaking and my head swimming
after hours at the piano. I could've ducked into a store and tried to
avoid him. I made up my mind not to.

You look lovely, said Stephen.

I'm sorry, I said. We should've talked before this.

Too late for that, he said.

Do you want to do this right here? I asked.

Let's walk, he said.

An old woman in filthy clothes sat on the curb holding a coffee
tin. Stephen stopped and gave her a quarter; the coin clanged and
rattled in the bottom of the can.

I hate my brother, he said.

It should be me, I said.

Then I'd hate myself, said Stephen.

The words struck me, even at that moment, as something
Stephen had rehearsed. He used the same line in the letters he
wrote, long missives that came through the summer and fall until
the weather turned cold. He wrote to me like a poet haunted by
loss, by the memory of a ghostly moon, barely visible with light
from the sunken day.

I have your book on Beethoven, said Stephen.

What book?

The biography you wanted. The one you were looking for the
first time you came into the shop.

He must make me suffer, I thought. I've tortured him so infer-
nally that he must go back like this into the past. He must make
me think of it again.

Do you still want it? asked Stephen.

You're very kind, I said.

That's too formal, said Stephen. I don't need much, you know. Just a word or two, that's all.

Is Jessica angry? I asked.

My mother doesn't talk about you anymore. You're not a safe subject in the house.

Is she well?

She misses you. She won't say it, but I know she does.

I miss her too.

Once she confused your name with Margie's.

That's sweet. But it feels strange.

Get used to it.

That's not a pretty thing to say.

We sat down on a bench in Penny Park, a different bench from the one Phil and I used. Mothers sat everywhere rocking their baby carriages and fanning themselves. I rummaged my bag for a cigarette.

You don't know my brother, said Stephen.

Give me time, I said.

He's like a jigsaw puzzle losing its pieces, said Stephen. When he cares about something and it fails him, he loses another piece.

If you're trying to talk me out of loving him, it's too late.

You don't see him like I do. He walks around the house like a frightened man.

I said to myself that Stephen's words were false. This is all too clever, I thought. He's the scared one—not his brother. But a stricken image of Phil stuck in my mind; it fed my burgeoning doubt.

I'm the kind of woman he needs, I said. And you know it.

I need you too, said Stephen.

I'm sorry, I said. I'll say it as many times as it takes.

I'll do anything, said Stephen. I know what I'm up against.

No you don't, I said. I made you love me. I did it. And that's the whole point. It shouldn't have happened that way.

Why not? Because you changed your mind?

I lit my cigarette and said nothing.

Explain it to me, said Stephen.

Don't make me say it, I said.

All right, I won't.

Stephen, it won't do any good. But if I try just once, will you give it up?

I won't promise you that.

I worked too hard with you. Do you understand? Everything with you was too deliberate, too careful. With Phil there was no second-guessing, no waiting. It just happened.

Stephen's eyes wandered sadly across the park, and then without the slightest warning, suddenly thrown by uncontrollable forces in the air, he burst into tears, wept without the least shame, sitting on the bench, streams of water running down his cheeks.

Did you ever love me? asked Stephen.

I thought I did.

And now you love Phil.

I go too fast, I said. I wait for no one. It's not something I'm proud of. I ran my fingers through Stephen's hair and he managed something like a smile, wiping his face with the back of his hand.

I'd like to hate you, said Stephen.

The whole mess is my fault, I said.

I can't hate you, he said. It's me. I'm to blame.

No you're not, I said.

You were impossible, said Stephen. Then he shook his head. I don't mean that, really. It's just—I felt small whenever I was with you. You're smarter than me. You care about everything. I remember the time a bee got stuck in the window wiper of the car. You stopped and set it free. A yellow jacket, for God's sake—but you took care of it.

But not you, I said. I never took care of you.

I didn't let you, said Stephen.

I could've done more, I said.

You have talent, said Stephen. Everybody loves you. I think I was jealous for a long time. Stephen touched my leg and made me look at him. I thought you could change me, he said.

That's too much, I said. More than I can do.

I know, said Stephen.

You always held back, I said. What were you waiting for?

Forgiveness, he said.

This wasn't a word I expected. What do you mean? Like a priest?

For everything, he began, then he stopped and looked around at the women with their children in the park.

I refused to hear it. I made explanations, told him he needed to look at me with clear eyes. I'm stubborn, I said. Selfish, too. I take what I want and I'm not polite about it. Why should I forgive you? How could I forgive anyone? It would be a considerable presumption.

I've been on a speeding train, said Stephen. And I've looked out at boulders in open fields. And the train sways and pitches and I think, we can't bear disaster, like the rocks. One slight bruise and we die.

You'll be all right, I said.

I don't know anyone on the train, said Stephen. And then a man comes walking down the aisle. I want to tell him that I forgive him, that I want him to forgive me.

I can't give you what you want, I said.

Stephen squeezed my hand. I know, he said. That makes us even.

We walked a little by the lake and then Stephen said he had to go home. I didn't see him again until September.

As it turned out, most of what I did with Phil stood in sharp contrast to the things I did with Stephen. Phil, unlike his brother, despised bookstores and museums, so we spent the bulk of our time taking long drives, usually in the opposite direction from Mayfield, or walking down to the marina on muggy nights and arguing for hours over which sailboat we would steal. Phil knew a guy named Nick who worked on a rich man's yacht. One Saturday, with the owner out of town, Phil convinced Nick to give us the keys to the ship. We strolled the railed decks and commandeered the master stateroom, and all the while I struggled to leave my capitalist disdain on land, though, truth be told, I betrayed my beliefs with less guilt and consternation than I expected.

So you feel like a traitor, said Phil.

I'm trying not to, I said. It'd be worse if we were going for a cruise . . . or if we'd been invited.

We brought food and a bottle of champagne on board. Phil wore a nautical hat for the occasion and insisted that I call him captain. I refused. We sat on an overstuffed couch and ate cheese and bread and drank the sparkling wine out of fine crystal flutes that we found in the galley.

Phil finished his champagne and upended the bottle. It's all gone, he said.

Would you like more? I asked.

I'm fine, he said.

I drained my glass and held the champagne on my tongue. I got up on my knees and made Phil rest his head on a pillow; I kissed him and the bubbling liquid flowed into his mouth. I started loosening his belt and he caught my wrist, squeezing it hard.

What's wrong? I asked.

Nothing, he said.

You're lying. You never stopped me before.

I don't feel like it right now.

You're still lying.

I'm not.

Then explain this, I said, rubbing his groin.

He pushed my hand away. Just once, he said, I'd like to be the one to start things.

I don't like to wait, I said.

Everyone knows that, said Phil.

His words took me aback. Are you being old-fashioned? I asked.

I didn't mean it like that, he said.

Good, I said. I haven't much interest in virtue.

Or chastity, said Phil, smiling at first and then laughing.

Or hypocrisy, I said.

You always have the last word, said Phil.

Let's get some air, I said, and I started to get up.

Phil took hold of me and pushed me against the back of the couch. It's my turn, he said.

I suppose it's only fair, I said.

We kissed.

That's right, he said. It's social justice.

You are a communist, I said.

No, he said. An opportunist.

Now I feel used, I said.

I'm sorry, he said, kissing me again.

I'd like to feel well used, I said.

Katie, this is my turn, he insisted.

Sorry.

Take off your clothes, he said.

I struggled out of what I was wearing while we kissed, and then in one movement he was inside me with only his pants open and the rest of his clothes still on.

I hate it, he said. I hate that you ever loved anyone but me.

Say it again, I said. Say it louder.

Phil thrust himself deep into my body, chanting the words over and over, sometimes shouting and sometimes whispering.

I tore open his shirt, wanting to bite his skin, needing to inscribe his body in some permanent way, a sign that marked him as my lover. I sunk my teeth into his shoulder.

Make me feel it, he said.

But before I could do anything more he arched his back and shuddered; then he slowly eased down until his head rested on my breasts.

LYING ON the couch, wrapped around each other like vines, no sound other than our breathing, I wanted something different. I wanted Phil to tell me a story. I craved the intimacy of words. I wanted to crawl inside his hard shell, his protection, and dig down until I found whatever it was at bottom that ruled his soul.

As a matter of principle, Phil loathed talking—the only thing he liked less were people who talked too much—so picking the right moment was essential. We were entirely alone; only one person knew of our whereabouts. The yacht swayed gently, nudging the dock like an old friend. The solemn hush of the marina enfolded us. Despite such delicious privacy, Phil put up a strong wall of resistance.

I can't think of any stories, said Phil. Especially about him.

You just don't want to, I said.

There's nothing to tell.

There must be, I said. You and Stephen hardly mention him.

You go first, said Phil. Tell me a story instead.

I've told you everything, I said. I talk all the time. I'm surprised you still love me.

I like the sound of your voice.

Flattery won't help.

You're always pushing me, said Phil.

Oh really, I said. You don't need much coaxing when it comes to some things.

Have you always been this way?

What way?

So greedy.

You're greedy too. You just won't admit it.

What's in it for me if I tell you a story?

See what I mean?

What do I get? asked Phil, cracking one or two of his knuckles.

If you let me pick the story, you can have whatever you want.

Phil took a deep breath. All right, Katie. Have it your way.

I want to know why he left, I said.

Phil tried to get out of it. He swore at the ceiling and made a show of being angry, but I held my ground. Finally, little by little, through fits and starts, he began the tale, telling me first about radios and his father's great talent, about the grateful customers who spoke of Eddie as a wizard, a man that could conjure up voices and music from a cheap box of wire and thin air. All that was before the crash, and when the Tollmans came back from Mayfield, there was very little repair work to be had, so Eddie took a job as a short-order cook.

Bacon 'n eggs, burgers and steaks sputtered and splattered grease until Eddie's white apron turned brown. He cleaned the griddle every few minutes with a steel spatula, watching the drip pans fill with white ooze. He rarely ate at the diner himself; the constant odor of fried food nauseated him.

Eddie hated the lunch hour rush, an exhausting marathon run by people who barked orders and gulped food and made life miserable for the waitress and the busboy. The busboy was actually a man, a retarded, middle-aged man, and every so often a few customers poked fun at him, or they bet good money on the time it would take him to clean up their mess. On what would turn out to be Eddie's last day, the busboy tripped over a truck driver's foot. A tray of plates and glasses went flying and the whole place broke into laughter. There ain't no radio in here, said the trucker. A man needs entertainment with his food. Eddie burned the truck driver's sirloin to a cinder and told the waitress, who thought it was a mistake, to serve it just as it was. Then Eddie took off his apron and quit, walked out through a horde of booing patrons, leaving the griddle cold and the customers hungry.

After that, Eddie worked part-time repairing sewer lines for the city. The money was good but the job almost destroyed his hands. All the digging and dirty water in cold weather cracked his skin until he had to pack his gloves with Vaseline. Phil heard him weeping one night while Jessica wrapped his hands with a warm compress of oil and herbs. He stayed with the job for more than a year, and just when he thought something full-time was in the offing, Eddie got a paycheck and a pink slip, and a slap on his back from the foreman.

Phil was eighteen years old then, ready to receive his high school diploma, and nothing could change his mind about his father; he still hated him for the stupidity that had made Jessica blind, for the indecision that Eddie's face advertised like a bill-board. Phil said it was guilt, not character, that gave Eddie his strength; it was Jessica's misery that made him work hard.

After losing his job with the city, Eddie bounced around town for a while, coming home some days with wild promises of a new career, coming home other days with a hangdog look and a mug of cold coffee.

It was a celebration, the Fourth of July, when Myron ran up to his mother and asked for more fireworks. All day long, Stephen and Myron had been exploding paper cups with the neighborhood kids, but now with dusk falling, everyone's eyes anticipated Roman candles and bottle rockets, bright trails of light to etch the night sky.

Jessica asked Eddie to run and get some sparklers for the boys. Eddie wanted Phil to go, but Jessica said it was a father's job, like getting the tree at Christmas. Eddie turned off the radio and put on his shoes and sport coat. Phil watched his father walk down the porch steps and away from the house. And when Myron and Stephen were asleep and the clock chimed twelve, the Fourth of July disappearing without fireworks, Phil told his mother to stop waiting, to lock the front door. Sudden and swift and clean as that the ties gave. The finality of it was like death, said Phil. I only think of him as dead.

My FATHER, being very much alive, called the summer of 1939 portentous, a time filled with harbingers of war and, as it concerned me, wars of love. It was true, of course, but I didn't know how true until the first weekend of September when my parents were called away to Akron.

A colleague of my father's, an old friend from his law school days, had died unexpectedly of a heart attack, and my father had been asked by the family to speak at the memorial. My mother felt the loss as well, and her mood was somber as she arranged the details of the trip. I helped her pack, trying to respect her sadness, but I kept making suggestions and talking too fast. Slow down, I thought. She'll see your excitement. All I could think about was the empty house, having it all to myself for two nights.

They left early on Saturday morning, and I spent the rest of the day making my own preparations. I set out my clothes for the evening and then took a long bath in sudsy water scented with lavender salts. I softened my hair with vinegar and brushed it when it was dry, counting one hundred strokes or more. I shaved my legs and rubbed my skin with sesame oil.

I took Phil out to one of my favorite, very cheap restaurants. We ate spaghetti and drank red wine, and we finished with heaping forkfuls of ricotta cheesecake. After that, we went to the Silverbird Saloon, where I filled the time, leaden time, with vodka gimlets and cigarettes. I wanted the evening to go faster, anxious as I was to tell Phil about my house without parents, to ask him if he'd stay the night.

It was just before twelve when we left the bar. The streets outside sparkled in a misty rain and we walked for a while without talking. Phil seemed far away; he kept looking at our reflections in shop windows, kept turning around as if he expected a thief to approach us from behind.

I want to tell you something, I said.

I'm listening, he said.

It's a surprise.

Phil looked at me and smiled. What?

My house is empty for the weekend.

Where'd they go?

Akron.

For what?

None of that's important, I said. Will you come over?

Of course.

And spend the night?

Phil sighed. Do you think that's a good idea?

Why not?

Living at home complicates things.

I thought of that too, I said. But we can't keep sneaking around.

We've hardly done that, said Phil.

Then don't decide now. You can stay if you like . . . or go.

Phil was uncomfortable in the house. He made a small fire and then leaned against the mantelpiece in a strained counterfeit of perfect ease. When he finally took a seat, he kept some part of himself always in motion, a foot tapping or fingers drumming, a leg moving up and down as if he were pumping a faulty brake. He cracked his knuckles and jumped up at odd moments to poke and prod the burning logs.

We kissed and I slid over to the end of the sofa so that Phil could put his head in my lap. I closed his eyelids gently and pushed the hair off his forehead, and after a while he began to relax. I watched the fire dance, its yellow light flickering on the walls, the ceiling busy with shadows. We should go upstairs, I whispered. Phil nodded and I led him up the steps. We lit candles in my room and turned down the bed. By then the nervous boy of the living room had disappeared, and we made love quietly, touching each other with deferential confidence, with the firm, satisfying comfort of old lovers.

Katie, sweet Katie, he chanted. I love your name.

You say it like music, I said.

You're beautiful.

Not beautiful enough, I said. Then I ran my hand down the

length of Phil's body. I am your own lean animal, I thought, the cat at your belly, the fox at your hip.

I wanted sleep, wanted to luxuriate in the warm sheets of my bed, but my mind refused to cooperate. My thoughts kept racing, thinking about the future. My fingers fiddled with the blanket. I sat up and looked for a cigarette.

Don't do that now, said Phil.

All right, I said. Can we talk?

If you like.

Do you ever think about how much we look the same?

That's crazy.

No it's not.

Yes, but you're beautiful. I'm something else altogether.

I kneeled up on the bed so I could see myself in the mirror. I pulled my hair into a tight ponytail. Now, if I practiced your scowl, I'd look just like you.

You better not.

I pinned my hair into a tight bun on the back of my head. Why don't you let your hair grow?

For what?

For me. Let it grow a little longer.

It's too long as it is.

No, let it grow a little longer and I could cut mine and we'd be just alike.

Don't ever cut yours.

I should. It's always in your face when I kiss you.

I like it.

Do you like it that we look the same?

We don't.

Not now, maybe. But if your hair was longer and I cut mine, we'd both be alike.

I don't think so.

I can show you.

Show me what?

How much we look the same.

Stop saying that.

You said we could talk.

But it's crazy. I'll never look like you.

I can prove it.

How?

Promise you'll go along?

Where?

Not where, silly. Go along with what I do to you.

Sounds dangerous.

Just promise.

Tell me what it is.

If I do, you won't let me.

Then why should I promise?

Am I asking too much?

No.

Well, then?

All right. I promise.

I slid off the bed and opened the top drawer of my dresser. Close your eyes, I said. I took out a brush, an eye pencil, and a compact. I sat down next to Phil. Sit up, I said, but keep your eyes closed.

First I brushed his hair, pressing it tight against his head like mine. Then I opened the compact, filled the tiny brush with rouge and began to brush his cheeks.

Phil jerked away and opened his eyes. What the hell is that?

You promised.

For Christ's sake, Katie. How much can a man take?

A lot more than this. C'mon, don't be scared.

I'm not scared.

Yes you are.

Phil snorted and shook his head like an ornery bull. Then he closed his eyes and sat still. I heightened the color of his skin, and then I deepened his eyes with the black pencil.

Don't move, I said. I have to do me. I went over to the mirror and highlighted my face the same way. Do you want to see? I asked.

I'm not sure.

Phil came over and we looked at ourselves and each other in the mirror.

I look strange, said Phil.

That's not a nice thing to say, I said. You look like me.

Only a little.

You do. You shine even brighter.

You can't say that.

Look at my face, I said. My skin looks muddy.

I don't see any difference.

Good. I want us to be all mixed up. That way we never have to worry.

About what?

The nights.

What if one of us had to leave?

Then the nights would be long, I said.

We got back into bed and held each other and listened to the house creaking and the trees rustling just outside in the shadows.

We'll have a wonderful life, I said. You'll love New York.

And what will I do in New York? asked Phil.

It doesn't matter. I'll make enough for both of us.

Let's go to sleep, said Phil. I'm tired.

And someday, if I'm really good, I'll do concert tours in Europe.

I know you will.

And we'll learn everything there is to know about foreign lands.

Katie, you should sleep, said Phil.

But there was no sleeping for me. Moonlight came in through the open window and I watched it move slowly across the bed.

I WOKE UP scared, my body feeling half its weight. Phil was gone. The twilight just before dawn made my room and the street look unfamiliar. I pictured him dressing in the dark and slipping out. I searched for a sign, something left behind like a button or comb, but I found nothing.

Phil failed to call on Sunday and I went without sleep, rattling around in empty rooms like an insomniac. When no message arrived on Monday, I assumed the worst, an accident or illness, an emergency at home. The waiting was intolerable, but I had agreed to stay away from the Tollmans' house, never to visit or telephone for Stephen's sake.

I went to work and sat with my closed piano until customers forced me to play. I smoked an endless string of cigarettes and refused to stop in Penny Park for lunch. Lambert tried to console me. He bought me Italian ices and talked about business and the weather, how he wanted to sell the store and move to Florida before another winter killed him.

By the middle of the week, I was desperate, no longer willing to wait or keep my distance. I wondered if Stephen would be there or what I would say to Jessica if she answered the door. The house had never seemed so small to me as it did that day when I stopped on the front walk and peered through the picture window in the hope of glimpsing Phil.

I knocked and Myron opened the door. He invited me in but I assured him that I was fine on the porch. I said I wanted to see Phil, and Myron managed to say that Phil wasn't home. Do you know where he is? I asked. Myron shook his head and told me to wait.

Through the sooty screen I smelled the sweetness of Jessica's baking. I heard no voices or footfalls, and Myron was gone for a long time. Then Stephen came out and we exchanged a polite hello and I asked him about Phil. Stephen thought I was kidding, and then his face went white. I thought you knew, he said.

I braced myself for the thing he would say next. All my nerves stood at attention and waited, but Stephen's lips were frozen. He stood there holding the door open as if he were suddenly struck dumb.

Tell me, I said.

Phil's gone, said Stephen. He shipped out yesterday.

My first impulse was to accuse Stephen of lying, but he went on about going to the recruitment office with Phil in August, about Phil's physical and his subsequent orders, about Phil's dream of joining the Army Air Force and becoming a navigator, maybe a pilot.

I said something absurd—like 'thank you' or 'I appreciate it'—before I turned and walked down the steps. Stephen said he was sorry.

Remember this, I thought. Always remember. Never, never forget. This is what it feels like when half the world falls away. I heard birds in the trees singing, and people went about their business as if the earth and the sun still mattered, as if the moon would always rise happily and whole.

I told myself to cry. You cannot grieve properly, I thought, until something inside you breaks. But after I had walked for a while and looked in shop windows and smoked a cigarette it wasn't any good. It was like mourning the death of a stranger.

chapter eight

WHAT IS THERE to say about a person who leaves? Concerning the hands or face, hardly a thing. Even less about the voice or certain words repeated in the dark. Much can be said about the gap, the lack, the empty space that now becomes you like a glass slipper.

I have been grieving since you've gone, I said. I talked to no one who could hear me. I have this grief because you are a ghost and a thief. Your absence steals my presence. Soon, I thought, I'll lose my dignity.

In the days that followed I came to treasure anything discarded, all the lonely artifacts of life that people cast off as obsolete and worthless. I fancied myself a connoisseur of the pawnshop window, recognizing the cherished ring, the engraved retirement watch, the trumpet abandoned by a hungry musician.

I walked the crowded streets at rush hour waiting for Phil suddenly to appear, and I sat in Penny Park, a feeder of pigeons, unearthing strange words amidst the din of traffic. There is a sickness in me, I thought. Something vague that waxes or wanes. It floats in me like a dead child.

I talked to myself about lies, the different ways that people lie, with or without words, in laughter or in silence, revealing very little of their hidden selves. I'd once read a story by Chekhov in which the main character, an unfaithful husband, comes to the realization that *everything important, interesting, essential, everything about which he was sincere and never deceived himself, everything that composed the kernel of his life, went on in secret.* At the time I thought the idea was deliciously romantic, a spark of mystery, a darkness in the human heart which makes love risky and, above all, exciting. Now the notion struck me as specious, an ambitious rationalization for cowardice, for the inability to confront and pursue the things we want or need without fear, and I felt silly thinking of it as I once did, as profound insight, as wisdom, when the real lesson of the story, its universal tragedy, is the knowledge that two people can live inside each other's skins and remain strangers.

After a few weeks of wandering I found myself on Laura's doorstep, and she took me back and cared for me even though I had neglected her over the summer. I expected her to be angry, to make a few smug declarations about the kind of men I pursue, but her eyes were gentle and forgiving, and I was thankful for such generous company. She listened to me like a big sister and held off the impulse, which I'm sure she felt, to shake her head and recount her warnings about love and obsession, about going too deep too fast.

Sitting in Laura's kitchen, I told her the story of my parents' courtship, a circuitous affair with so many starts and stops that no one, not even my grandparents, held out any hope for marriage. The first wedding day was canceled despite the fact that the chapel had been reserved and the invitations sent. They set another date only to reschedule it twice. Equivocation is normal, I said. Except for me.

That's your gift, said Laura.

I laughed. Now you're making fun of me, I said.

You know I'm not, said Laura. You throw yourself into everything—politics, music, men. You always leap without looking. It's your way.

It's dangerous, I said. It's a fool's way.

Maybe so, said Laura. But it's why people adore you. They admire what's reckless. They want to know how you manage.

Not very well I'd say.

That's not true. Things fall apart . . . and then you regroup and start over again.

I'm tired.

You should be.

I pulled out a cigarette but didn't want it by the time it reached my lips. Lately, the rotten things taste bitter, I said.

You should come to a meeting, said Laura. Everyone's been asking about you.

I don't want to right now.

It might do you some good.

I can't focus. I'd have to pretend I'm interested.

You could just drop by and say hello.

I shook my head, remembering my father's remark that wars of the heart must be settled before engaging in political battles. I'd be obliged to make small talk about the state of my life, I said. I'd have to lie.

Laura rolled her eyes. Worse things have happened.

I tried the cigarette again, but it was no good. Do you think we depend on lies?

I don't think about it, said Laura.

I know we do. I hear myself lying about something or other all the time and I don't question it.

It's the same for everyone.

Of course it is. We learn how to lie when we're very young, and then we practice and perfect our technique until the world is filled with expert liars. Life depends on our collective skill. In the end, if we're very good, we can convince ourselves that we're not lying at all, that everything we say is true.

Bleak but accurate, said Laura. Did you ever lie to Phil?

I don't think so.

To yourself?

All the time.

About what?

I chose not to say it. I needed something not quite true to soften the blow. My doubts, I said.

That tells me nothing.

I sidestepped again and then I stopped. It's always the same, I said. I can feel a person turning, stepping back almost from the start, but I ignore it.

Do you want more coffee? asked Laura.

I'm swimming in it now, I said.

He'll wind up overseas, said Laura.

Or worse, I said. When I told my father what happened, it almost took the wind out of him. I'd never seen his face so sad. We'll soon be at war, he said. It's coming and no one can stop it.

I can't picture that boy in uniform, said Laura.

Phil's not much of a boy, I said.

I suppose not, said Laura.

I discovered, thanks mostly to conversations with Stephen, that Phil had been thinking about enlistment for quite some time, mentioning it in letters to Jessica even before he came home for the summer. At first, no one believed he was serious, nor did anyone realize how much Phil wanted to leave Cleveland and his father's ghost behind. Working for the New York Central Railroad was his first step, but in the end he needed more distance.

Eventually, it all became too clear. Phil quit his job knowing that the military was his ticket out. More than once I'd thought it strange that Phil's attempts to find work in town were sporadic and haphazard. He'd said he had enough money to last the summer, but he didn't seem overly concerned about going broke in the fall. Of course, my ballooning ego, my not altogether realistic ego, kept me from seeing his true ambition.

Stephen had gone with Phil to the recruitment center. The first time was early in August, and the officer there asked Stephen if he wanted to join, but Phil shook his head. My brother has to stay home, he said.

Stephen waited while Phil had his physical and took the intelligence test. Afterward, they stopped for a beer, and that's when Stephen asked Phil what he intended to do about me. Phil, quite naturally, told lies. Katie's okay with this, he said. We've talked it out. She's going to New York anyway. You knew that from the beginning.

So that's it, said Stephen. It's that simple.

It's not simple at all—but what can I say? I didn't think you'd want the details.

Is she going to wait? asked Stephen.

We haven't talked about that. If Uncle Sam enters the war, there's no use making plans.

Stephen confessed that at that moment he could've cold-cocked his brother, but he backed off. How did things get so fucked up?

I came home for the summer, said Phil.

For a while, Phil didn't exist for me in any imaginable location, then later I attached him to military names and numbers: Fort Hayes in Columbus; the Selfridge Air Base outside Detroit; the 554th AAF Unit; Airplane Inspector, class 750. I knew none of these designations at first, but in the end I referred to Phil only in these terms. I liked the impersonal integrity of place names and titles, the substance, the physical certainty.

As AUTUMN wore on and the days turned cold, I made preparations to move to New York. Aunt Lorraine, my mother's sister, wrote to say that she had taken some time over the summer to spruce up the guestroom in anticipation of my arrival. She said Uncle Larry, a columnist with the *Times*, was ready to take me around town and introduce me to people who, according to him, had influence.

Somewhere between the phone calls, the train ticket, the failed attempts to clean out my room, I put in my last day at Massimino's. Lambert gave me a dozen red roses and said—with lovely, exaggerated gestures—Now I go under. You will come back for spring visit and the windows will be boarded up and the door will be locked.

You'll do better without me, I said.

No one comes to buy the music. They come to hear you play. And because they are grateful, and because they feel sorry for me, they will sometimes purchase a song or two.

You've been very good to me, I said. Maybe your next pianist will not only play music but sell it too.

There is no one, said Lambert. I have the sign in the window for two weeks. I put an ad in the paper. No one comes. No one wishes to play.

Somebody'll show up, I said.

Yes, but this some-*body* will be just that. Not an artist.

You should move to New York and open a store.

I am too old. Cleveland is already enough to kill me. If I go to New York I will not live long.

Winters in New York are mild compared to Cleveland.

So I have heard. But there are other kinds of cold that a man fears.

Don't say that. It makes me want to stay.

No. You must go. You must take a chance and prove what you can do. There is nothing here for one like you.

You are my Italian papa, I said. I will miss you.

Come visit me before I die.

You're too stubborn to die.

Lambert started laughing. My wife, when she was alive, she say the same thing.

If it's true that people hardly see a place until they leave it, then I hardly saw Massimino's, that notable relic, that cozy museum of music, until my last day, and as for its curator and woeful sage, I never met another man who was so in love with beauty. Even the rusty streets of Cleveland and the walk to Penny Park looked different, more vivid, suddenly fresh. Like a lesson in tone and movement, the weeks before I left were filled with unexpected revelations, and because the world seemed deeper, more complex, my feelings went back and forth between surprise and introspection.

My father talked more to me than was his habit, postponing appointments or letting the phone ring, and I heard beneath his words a tone of regret. He wasn't sure he liked me living with Lorraine and Larry. Too conservative, he said. And then he went on telling me how he'd always wanted to live in New York himself, how he'd had a chance a long time ago but stayed in Cleveland for my mother. At least, he said, you're finished with that Tollman boy—it makes things easier. He always called Phil 'the Tollman boy'; he called Stephen the same thing. And as he sat on the edge of my bed, I tried to imagine how my life would've been different if my father had done things that left me no choice but to hate him. I knew I'd be someone else entirely if my father had been a weak man, or a selfish man, or a man who could calmly and quietly walk off into the city night. But now there was nothing for me to say. I hardly knew how to thank him, as he sat slumped over on the edge of my bed looking tired to me for the first time.

Will you write? I asked.

It'll be hard work you know, trying to decipher my scrawl.

I'll have Mom give me some lessons before I go.

Good idea. Look at this hand, Katie. Used to be like granite.

I couldn't see any movement, but he insisted that his 'shakes' were getting worse. I'm losing control, he said. And he told me about the old days when he could write an entire letter without one slip of the pen. No ink blots, he said. And nothing crossed out. I argued that I had never in my entire life written a perfect letter. He smiled then and said my fingers weren't made for writing.

Hands have a mind of their own, he said. And I thought of a story that my father always told young lawyers, the story of Adolph Myers, a schoolteacher from Pennsylvania, whose expressive and caring hands were said to want unspeakable things, who was slandered, beaten, and run out of town by a mob of blood-hungry hands, who lost his home and his closest friends, though the lying child recanted his story, and who, my father said, never taught again but kept his hands forever hidden from view.

Hands, I decided, betray us without warning. Just at the moment when someone says hold on, hold on tight, the fingers will refuse to curl, there will be no grip. Someday my reach will fail—the idea frightened me—and pressing a key will cause pain and perhaps then I will understand what it is to be abandoned.

My mother, not unlike my father, sighed with what I thought was relief when I told her Phil had gone. We talked in the kitchen while she was making bread. I'm sorry, Katie, she said, sprinkling flour and rolling dough. I waited for her next words, something reassuring but pragmatic, an insight, perhaps, that would mildly suggest that she'd known what was going to happen all along. Instead, she surprised me with silence and, even more peculiar, there was a delicate expression on her face, something weary and wistful, and it made me wonder what it was about my situation that touched her so deeply.

I'll be fine, I said.

Of course, she said. You're an independent woman.

It's very difficult, I said.

She put down the rolling pin. I know.

I cannot resign myself, I said.

It will take a long time, she said.

Her words gave her away. Was there someone for you? I asked.

I was very young.

I'm very young, I said.

It was before I met your father. So long ago I hardly remember anything about it.

I don't believe you.

She shook the flour off her sleeve. No, Katie. Not now.

You have no choice, I said.

You're just like your father, she said. You always get your way.

Not always.

She looked at me and I thought she was going to apologize. Then she took up the rolling pin and started talking.

His name was Martin Fury. He was a coal miner from Kentucky who came north to Cleveland to work in the steel mills. I met him on the streetcar. My father, after learning that I was in love, called him a vulgar boy, an indecent boy. He swore and turned red. I'll not have him handling my daughter with black coal under his fingernails, he shouted.

My mother stopped and began kneading the dough.

There must be more, I said.

There is.

So your father kept you from seeing him?

That's right.

And what about Martin Fury?

He hadn't come around for a week or so when he showed up in the middle of the night, dead drunk, pounding on the front door and waking up the whole house and half the neighborhood.

I laughed. So he was a man with backbone.

I don't know, said my mother. He demanded to see me, and when I came out of my room—against my father's wishes—he asked me to elope with him. He wanted me to walk out right beneath my father's nose dressed only in my nightgown and leave everything behind.

Did you think about it?

Maybe. It's hard to remember. I do remember that he was beautiful in the doorway, drunk but beautiful, telling my father that dividing two people who were in love was a sin against creation. You know, Katie, I was afraid for a while that you and Phil might elope.

We had nothing to run away from, I said.

My mother nodded. I suppose not.

So what happened to Martin Fury? Did you ever see him again?

No, said my mother, in a very matter-of-fact tone. He died that same night.

My mouth fell open in amazement. I thought for a moment that I should comfort her, take her in my arms and hold her, but then I realized that the whole affair had played itself out long before I was born. I was thirty years too late.

I asked her how he died and my mother explained that she

knew nothing more than what had been reported in the newspaper. 'Martin Fury was last seen in a local tavern just before closing time and was found at daybreak on a waterfront dock beaten to death. The nature of the injuries suggests a blunt instrument was used.'

I had no idea, I said.

Of course not, silly. How could you?

Did you hate your father after that?

At first I was angry, particularly when he used the murder as a vindication of his judgment. But, like most parents, my father only did what he thought was best. I loved Martin because he seemed dangerous, but I know now it wouldn't have lasted very long.

No doubt my mother was right, but then I realized that something ineffable lived within her. I could hear it in the lilt of her careful words. And I began to understand what it is that exists in memory, the images that return to us again and again as if in dream, piling up like water behind a dam, forming a pool of doubt that swells over time and weighs heavily on what we think and feel.

I saw with clarity the weariness of my mother's face; she carried the ghost of Martin Fury like a second self. And the sigh I heard when I told her Phil was gone wasn't a show of relief; it was an acknowledgment, a sad declaration that only the very strong or the very brave or the very lucky leave themselves or the people they find in one piece.

My mother returned to her baking. You'll find another young man in New York.

But he won't be the same, I said.

No, said my mother. Probably not.

MAYBE IT was seeing my parents in a new light, or maybe it was needing to make peace where I had left animosity—I can't say for sure—but I made up my mind to visit Jessica Tollman before I left town. I stopped by the bookstore and asked Stephen if he would arrange it; he resisted at first, but then he gave in, doing it as much for his mother, he said, as for me.

The evening when I went to see Jessica was crisp and cool with a hint of wood smoke in the air. I passed homes already fitted with storm doors and storm windows to fend off the autumn chill, and as street lamps sputtered to life, I saw my shadow gliding across empty lawns and porches.

I walked up to the Tollman house and, like the last time, Myron was the first to answer. I stepped inside and Jessica called from the kitchen that she'd be right out. When I looked past Myron, I saw Lethea Strong sitting in the living room.

You didn't come to see me, said Lethea. So I came to see you.

I meant to, I said.

Now don't go apologizin' and fallin' all over yourself. I know what's been goin' on. I hardly expected you.

I smiled and sat down, but stood up again as Jessica swept into the room. Hello, Katie, she said. I'm glad you're here.

She seemed truly magnanimous, offering me the same smile and handshake that she'd offered me before. After Phil and I got started, I'd always imagined her angry, annoyed at the very least, but when she pulled me close and embraced me, some of my fears began to dissipate.

So it's New York at last, said Jessica. Stephen says you're almost ready to go.

I thought I'd be gone by now, I said. I've changed my ticket twice.

There's no hurry, said Lethea. Go when your feet say so and not before. Lethea wiped the corners of her mouth with a handkerchief. Why don't the two of you sit before your dogs give out.

We sat down and Jessica said that she'd put a pot of cider with mulling spices on the stove, and Lethea asked if she could have hers with a cinnamon stick, and then there was an uncomfortable moment of silence and Lethea said, Somebody say somethin' before I fall asleep.

I came to say good-bye, I said.

Is that all, said Lethea.

I looked at Jessica. Do you mind if I smoke?

I do, said Lethea. Can't breathe anymore when someone stinks up the room.

I put down my bag. I'm sorry, I said. Sorry for making problems between Phil and Stephen.

You didn't do it by yourself, said Jessica.

I'll say she didn't. But she's hankerin' to take the blame.

I never intended—

I know, said Jessica. But blaming you or Phil . . . or Stephen for that matter, won't change what's happened.

You're very kind, I said.

Kindness has nothin' to do with it, said Lethea. It's the way things are.

It's not fair, I thought, that both of them should be so comfortable. I felt ridiculed by their ease, their confidence. At the same time, nothing in their words or manner was intended to hurt me; they were direct and honest, and so, of course, they said things that cut close to the bone. There was very little, I realized later, that could make them angry or vengeful.

Have you heard from Phil? I asked.

I've had a few letters, said Jessica. He's stationed outside Detroit. A place called the Selfridge Air Base.

Lethea laughed. Phil's learnin' about airplanes with another boy named Crash.

Jessica ignored Lethea's remark. Stephen said that you didn't know anything about it. Phil's enlistment, I mean.

No, I said.

That makes two of us, said Jessica. Stephen promised not to say a word, believing, I suppose, that Phil would tell me in his own time—which he did. He said good-bye on the same day he left. I could still feel the kiss on my cheek when I heard the screen door slam. He was gone that fast.

There's been plenty a leavin' in this family, said Lethea. You'd think a bright boy like Phil could figure out the proper way to do it.

Is there a proper way? asked Jessica.

There is, said Lethea. You don't keep walkin' when someone's expectin' you to come back. And you don't run out the door as if bloodhounds are snappin' at your heels.

There may be a proper way, said Jessica. But there's no easy way.

I don't understand it, I said.

Phil's been the most difficult, said Jessica. The most unpredictable. More and more it's like he's walking on a tightrope.

And he's not much good at it, said Lethea. The boy's had no balance since the day he was born.

Jessica nodded. That's true. Losing his sister was a poor start.

He told me about Margie, I said.

We're not speakin' a Margie, said Lethea. Phil lost two sisters. The first was his twin. She followed him outta the womb stillborn.

He didn't tell me, I said.

No surprise there, said Lethea.

Then Margie died, said Jessica. And Phil was impossible. He blamed his father, of course . . . but secretly he blamed himself. Jessica smoothed the folds of her dress. His grief was strange.

Weren't nothin' strange about it, said Lethea.

There's so much I don't know, I said.

Lethea remembered that I'd been to Mayfield, and she asked me to tell her what I'd seen, so I described the grayness of that day and the silence of the Chagrin River, and when I mentioned the place where Margie had died, both Jessica and Lethea, assuming I hadn't been told, recounted the story of the black stone with the red streak and the strange gift from Wormwood and the edge of the concrete wall that somehow gave way.

Phil found her, said Lethea. Stephen was there, but Phil got to her first. And by the time Stephen made his way down, Phil was already in a state, ragin' with tears and profanity against God, as if all the hope in heaven had been used up. He wouldn't let Stephen touch her. And when twilight fell, Phil raised her out of the water and carried her up the steps and down that long, icy road and through the woods. Carried her all the way by himself and laid her down inside the tent and wrapped her in blankets and held her, tryin' to warm her body with his own, not wantin' to let her go because when he did he'd have to say to himself, now my sister is dead, and he refused to say it, he refused to say it or think it, tryin' not to give in, wrappin' himself around her, holdin' tight, tighter than his own life, until Jessica and Stephen had to pull him away.

When Lethea finished, I looked at Jessica, who was sitting with her eyes closed. I expected some kind of response, but Jessica said nothing. Her body was completely still.

My nose tells me the cider's ready, said Lethea. I'll get it.

Absolutely not, said Jessica, opening her eyes. You're a guest in my house. I'll tend to the cider.

After Jessica was gone, Lethea asked me if I was all right. Looks to me like you could use a little brandy in your cup.

I feel stupid, I said.

Happens to me all the time, said Lethea. I've loved these Tollman kids like they were my own. I get to thinkin' sometimes that it hasn't been easy, and then I think of her. Lethea motioned toward the kitchen.

Katie, said Jessica, coming back into the living room, I'd appreciate it if you'd pour the drinks.

I was happy to have something to do with my hands, and I poured cups for each of us and placed a cinnamon stick on Lethea's saucer and offered her the shortbread that Jessica had arranged perfectly on a small plate.

Just what a fat woman needs, said Lethea.

What about New York? asked Jessica.

I'll be staying with relatives, I said.

That's a new arrangement, isn't it? You weren't planning to go by yourself.

That's right, I said, wondering what Jessica really thought of me. I planned on Phil going too.

So I would've lost him either way, said Jessica.

Maybe so.

After that, no one made a sound, even the house refused to creak. The utter stillness bore down on me like death, and I stopped chewing, afraid that both of them would hear the shortbread crunching between my teeth.

He should've gone with you, said Jessica.

A-men to that, said Lethea.

Thank you, I said, almost spilling my cider.

You'll be fine in New York, said Jessica. You have music. It'll be your best company.

I stayed for a long time but remembered no other words, only gestures and expressions, the lovely and hypnotic grace of Jessica's hands, the boldness of Lethea's smile. I walked home along deserted streets trying to imagine Phil in uniform, wondering what he was doing at that precise moment. The smell of wood smoke was heavier now and the clouds had disappeared with nightfall, making the sky look like an endless sheet of black slate.

I TOLD MYSELF to go, chided myself for thinking that a message would come, a simple word of reconciliation, an apology. Finish packing your bags, I thought, and call a cab.

I went through the same ritual almost every day, but my suitcases remained unlocked and my music stayed open on the piano, and when I did go to the train station it was only to check and double check the timetables or exchange my ticket. Aunt Lorraine, who had expected me before Halloween, now began to call once a week inquiring about the date of my arrival. At first her calls were pleasant, her voice filled with the solicitude of a concerned parent, but her tone changed after a while, evolving into something more querulous, more impatient, and she suggested, as my explanations piled up, that I stay in Cleveland for Thanksgiving and catch the first express to New York after the holiday.

I admitted to no one that I was waiting for a letter from Phil, and when the mailman showed up empty-handed day after day, I made excuses to soften my disappointment. I defied logic, convincing myself that Phil had no time to write and that he would phone instead.

I hung around the house like a morose child. My parents, I'm quite sure, had more of me than they bargained for, putting up with my studied indifference, my efforts to appear composed. Laura, of course, was the only person who called, and knowing me better than most, she forced me to admit that I was waiting for something else.

Jessica had mentioned more than once—and with a great deal of motherly enthusiasm—that Phil had put in for a holiday pass, so I knew that in all likelihood Phil would be coming home for Thanksgiving dinner. I also knew that only one train arrived from Detroit each day.

I couldn't take the chance of missing him, so I started my vigil on Monday night, sitting in dark mahogany pews, the station like a solemn, futuristic cathedral. I smoked and tried to read magazines but found myself glancing up at the clock every few minutes, and then at precisely 11:49, I made my way out to Platform 3 and stood in the near dark listening for the sounds of an approaching locomotive. Everything around me was still, except for a few scattered housewives who had come to meet the train and collect their commuter husbands.

And when I saw the black engine from Detroit blustering into the station, shouldering its way up to the platform, my stomach felt strange and my heart quickened. I couldn't stop what I was doing, nor could I stop the train, and I had no idea what I would say once Phil stepped onto the platform, his jaw set firm above a military collar. He'll walk right by me, I thought. I'll be an invisible face in the crowd. But the crowd was small because of the hour, and I waited near the porter's booth and watched businessmen and a few old women struggle off with their luggage. Phil was nowhere to be seen. When I was certain that the train was empty, I left the station and went home.

Tuesday was much the same, except the engine seemed sluggish, worn out, followed by a long procession of dark compartments. A few more holiday travelers and some soldiers got off, but soon there was no one, and the porters counted up their meager tips.

On Wednesday night the time went faster and the feeling in

the station was less lonely. A crowd of people waited for their loved ones, and as the train glided toward the platform, I noticed that the passenger cars were lit and nearly full. Then came the slow click of the wheels and the engine easing off—such sad and beautiful music, I thought. A little boy waiting with his mother kept smiling at me and then hiding his face; the two of them looked otherworldly, stripped of color by moonlight that shone through the towering clerestory. In that instant the station seemed heavenly, metallic but magical, like a giant grandfather's clock.

I played peekaboo a little longer and then lost the boy in the sudden rush of people. The first uniform I saw frightened me and I felt a catch in my throat. I watched families and couples and lone travelers walk by, but Phil was not among them. The stragglers came next, fretting about whether it was too late to get a cab. Finally, a grandmother suffering from gout came down the steps with the help of two conductors.

No holiday passes for new recruits, I thought. But I stayed until the platform was almost empty. I looked down the length of the cars and then began walking toward the gate; I'd gone about half the distance when I turned and looked again and saw Phil stepping off the train.

He stretched and buttoned his jacket and fiddled with his duffel bag. I walked over and heard myself say, You certainly take your time.

He paused to catch his breath. I was asleep, he said. He picked up his duffel bag and then he put it down again. What are you doing here? Who told you—?

I was hoping for a tearful reunion, I said. I imagined a scene with moonlight and fog and swelling violins.

Hello, Katie.

Hello.

It's good to see you.

Is it?

Yes. It is.

You look lovely in your uniform.

He looked down at his sharp creases and smiled with a hint of pride.

Have you learned to fly an airplane?

No. I check the mechanical systems. But I'm learning navigation.

That should be useful.

I thought you'd be in New York by now.

Me too.

You're going, aren't you?

Yes.

You're still in Cleveland, for Christ's sake. Just pick up your bags and go.

Maybe you can give me a few pointers.

I deserve that.

Yes. You do.

I didn't think I could leave if I had to say good-bye.

That's pretty—but it's bullshit.

Phil pinched the bridge of his nose as if he were suffering from a headache. I don't know what to tell you.

Tell me something true. If you can't do that, then don't say anything at all.

Stephen still loves you.

That's a cowardly way to say it.

Call me a coward then.

Don't tell me you left for Stephen's sake.

No. But it's easier this way.

So you made the decision for both of us.

I made it for me.

That's better.

Katie, why did you come here?

I'm not sure. I pulled out a cigarette and Phil struck a match and cupped his hands close to my face.

Are you pregnant?

I jerked away. You bastard. Is that what you think? You think I've been waiting around this station to tell you that? I don't know you at all. You're a lousy bastard.

I'm sorry, Katie. You caught me off guard. When I saw you again I didn't know what to think.

You're just a scared, selfish bastard.

Phil looked around but there was no one in sight. Can we go somewhere?

We can say whatever we have to say right here. There's no better place.

Phil leveled me with his black eyes. There was nothing for me in New York.

How do you know?

I'm not as clever as you, Katie. I knew I couldn't live up to it. I knew you'd get bored.

Go on. If you keep going maybe you'll get to the truth.

That's all there is.

C'mon. You can do better than that.

I don't know what you're talking about.

No. Maybe you don't.

Phil reached for his duffel bag. Let's get a cab. I could use a drink.

I'll get my own cab and my own drink. I flicked the ash off my cigarette. I came here to see if you looked the same. I wanted to know if you'd recognize me.

You're very beautiful. We're both still the same.

I don't think so.

Phil wrinkled his forehead in disbelief. Let's go. We'll take a ride through town.

I've done that already. More than once.

I'm sorry, he said.

His apology was no help. It's strange, I said. Standing next to an empty train late at night makes everything so civilized.

I tried writing, he said. But I gave up.

If I ask you a question, will you tell me the truth?

Yes.

It was all good, wasn't it?

Phil lowered his eyes. Too good.

One of the porters walked by and tipped his hat. I smiled and the tension in me gave way. Will you ever come to New York?

I can't.

Don't be sentimental.

I can't.

I cajoled him again and then stopped. There's something else, I thought—something mercenary. Then I felt it like a fist in my stomach. I dropped my cigarette on the platform and ground it out with my toe. Is she from Detroit?

Phil winced and looked away. Grosse Pointe, he said.

You are learning to fly. And you're flying fast.

You asked for the truth.

Take it from me, I said. Steer clear of the sun.

I'm sorry, he said. I didn't expect it. She came out of nowhere.

No, I said. She came from a dignified house with a lovely manicured lawn. Does she know you'll soon be shipping out?

Phil opened his duffel bag and took out his gloves. There's not much anyone can do about that, he said.

You'll be worse off without me, I said.

He tried to pull on one of the gloves but it was too small. Army issue, he complained. He turned up the collar of his jacket and waited for me to say something.

Keep your head down, I said. Don't forget.

Katie, he said, and then he paused, his hand almost touching me. I won't.

ON THE FOLLOWING Monday I went to the station alone. I walked through the turnstile and out onto the platform and gave the porter my bags and boarded the train for New York. I listened to the train's powerful and dissonant music — the incessant banging and clanging and rumbling — as the conductors made everything ready for departure. Then the heaviness of cold steel began to grind and I felt the first lurch forward.

BOOK THREE

James

MY FATHER was a son-of-a-bitch. So said the milkman, the mail-man, and the paperboy. So said the neighbors who walked by our house on their way to church.

Old Knute next door made son-of-a-bitch a regular part of his greeting. He'd say, Hey Tollman, ya son-of-a-bitch, stop trying to poison my dog.

Zip it, said my father. I won't take no smear. Then he told Knute to keep the damn dog in his own yard. I don't call my dog damn, said Knute. His name is Ralph—and my gate's always latched. Then explain to me, said my father, why each morning I find a steaming pile of crap on my lawn. We reap what we sow, said Knute, biting his sodden cigar and smiling.

Let 'im stew, said my father, turning aside, talking more to him-self than to me. He liked a stiff drink after going up against Knute, griping and making threats, but he never went after Knute's shaggy cocker spaniel, not in any deliberate way, even when it did piss him off.

Knute had every reason to suspect foul play. That summer my father peppered the yard with a special kind of bait, a mixture of tuna and rat poison, a lethal treat for the neighborhood alley cat. Knute's dog tunneled under the fence. Ate the stuff just once. Then he staggered home and sprayed liquid shit all over Knute's welcome mat and porch steps. Knute got ugly after that and took to fertilizing our lilies of the valley with Drano.

My father steeled himself against friendly conversation, particularly with Knute. Friendship wasn't something he cared about. He had no lifelong buddies, only acquaintances at work. His habit of solitude, his indifference, felt like an insult to most. Perhaps it was.

You could say he earned the right to be ornery. He hated his job. Sometimes he hated my mother. He seemed to hate the things young people were doing. This is one god-forsaken year, he'd say, looking at the paper, looking out at the street in front of our house. It was 1968. I knew almost nothing about him. I wasn't in the habit of listening or knowing.

MY FATHER drank. He enjoyed whiskey and beer and thought himself a rather stylish boozer. He went through three stages whenever he got liquored up. First he was silly, a harmless, short-lived stage. After a few more drinks, he sank into a sullen and sarcastic melancholy. In this stage it was necessary for those around him to become invisible. No one wanted to fall under his gaze and risk a turn as the topic of conversation. Finally, after Sunday dinner and a full weekend of drinking, he turned angry and abusive. A cruel drunk.

His disposition spilled out of the house. Most of my pals, some of them awestruck, clammed up around my father. It wasn't so much anything he said or did. It was the possibility of violence, something just behind his eyes or under his voice. Whatever it was, it made people edgy and tight.

Not everyone on our street reacted the same way. Knute's daughter, for one, said exactly what was on her mind. She told stories about my father to her wide-eyed girlfriends. Mr. Tollman wears darkness like a ghoulish cape, she once said. He casts a pall over our block. After checking the dictionary, I had to admit she was right. Another time she pointed at my house and giggled. It looks unfriendly, she said, even in the best weather. That made me laugh. Tell me about it, I said. It ain't on the list of preferred hangouts.

Only the bravest came over, even when the house was empty. Sometimes we stomped around and barked orders. We called each other rum-dumb, dumbass, and good for nothin' bum. These were my father's favorite expressions. Welcome to the School of Hard Knocks was another. My father considered himself a surviving graduate and commissioned instructor of the school. I was one of his favorite pupils. Manhood, for him, meant living without sympathy, compassion, or forbearance. It demanded a bitter kind of silence, the strength to show no weakness, to suffer alone and to leave alone those who suffer.

MY FIRST lesson came early.

It started like this: The bell rang. I twisted around in my desk to ask the girl sitting behind me for a paperclip. I felt a stitch in my side.

When the pain grew worse, I complained. Ignore it, my father said. It'll get better. I waited and the cramp became debilitating. My mother took me to a pediatrician who diagnosed the problem as walking pneumonia.

My father was put out by the news. I could see it in his face, a mild expression wavering between impatience and disgust. I tried to walk without holding my side or doubling over, but on Thanksgiving I broke down. One of my Grosse Pointe aunts said I was sick. She said somebody better do something about it.

The doctor in the emergency room gave me a rectal exam. I felt his finger touch something tender. He ordered a nurse with long, red hair to shave my lower belly. They put me to sleep after that. I slept while the doctor opened my side and removed my ruptured appendix.

I woke up with a tube running out of my nose. I could feel the tube in the back of my throat. It sucked poison out of my stomach. It dripped green and black fluid into a glass bottle. I ran a high fever for three weeks. My black-and-blue ass got three shots a day. Two were antibiotics, one was morphine.

The doctor, I learned much later, told my parents I was going to die. My parents kept this information to themselves. I didn't know what to think. Their worried faces struck me as strange, out of character at the very least.

I considered myself an embarrassment. I knew I was weak for allowing myself to get sick. So why was I getting more attention than I ever thought existed in the world? My mother bought me presents and smuggled pizza and hamburgers into the hospital. But her efforts to feed me were misguided. Anything more than a bland diet made me wretch. The redheaded nurse frowned at me. She rolled up my bedding in a huff and gave my mother a dirty look.

My father fed me ice chips from a paper cup. I remember something gentle about his movements, his hands. I remember the tiny plastic spoon looking silly between his giant fingers.

At the hospital, in the presence of doctors and nurses, my father was a changed man. His round shoulders seemed to speak of uncertainty, humility, even defeat. At that moment I felt calm, as if I were floating in the eye of a storm. But the stillness did not last.

MY APPENDECTOMY became a short scar. My father, like a man coming to his senses, shook off his brief spell of tenderness. Life returned to business as usual.

I soon became the proud owner of a Columbia Gold Flyer. I

learned to lubricate the sprocket and chain. I polished the chrome wheels. My lock went with me wherever I went, and I allowed no one to borrow the bike unless it was for the sole purpose of carrying a girl on the handlebars.

I raced around on that sleek two-wheeler until the day I entrusted it to God. Leaving it unlocked at the front doors of St. Veronica's Church seemed all right at the time. I needed to find my music teacher, the parish organist, to change the day of my lesson. It'll only take a minute, I told myself. And besides, no one will take a bike parked at the church steps. It's too serious a sin.

I walked home and didn't stop crying until I stood in the doorway to the family room. Somebody swiped my bike, I said. My mother looked up from her sewing. You did lock it, didn't you? She said this in a pleasant, if disinterested, voice. No. I stopped at church, I said. I only left it for thirty seconds. My father lowered a corner of his newspaper. You should've hung a sign on it, he said. A big sign saying STEAL ME. He glowered at me for a moment and then his face disappeared behind the paper.

SPRING WAS my father's favorite season. After the long winter, he looked forward to getting outside with his boys. Equipped with heavy rakes, my brother and I yanked dead grass out of the lawn. We dug out weeds. We mowed, trimmed, edged, swept, and fertilized. We dragged soggy leaves and debris out of flowerbeds. We made way for crocuses, for tulips. We weeded and weeded again. We labored slowly because we found, early on, that efficiency made time for more and more chores.

Strange to say it now, but there were no lilacs in the spring of 1968, no sprigs of purple or white. We thought, given our inexperience, that the ice storms of March had killed the first buds. We were not far wrong.

April arrived like a car on fire. Television and magazines showed pictures of the dead: soldiers and civilians in Vietnam; Martin Luther King in Memphis. Not even the gardens along Lake Shore Drive had lilacs that year.

The Detroit Free Press reported King's murder in a voice of flat apprehension. Riots broke out in Washington, D.C., Baltimore, Chicago, and Boston. Fires burned in Detroit. This time, though, the violence died quickly. James Brown pleaded for peace and brotherhood. Outrage subsided to grief.

Despite the calm, my father made himself ready for reprisals. Half the city went up last year, he said. I remembered the summer before and the smoke rising over the tallest trees and the ash settling in our back yard. He said, All niggers need is a reason. They can still torch the other half.

Uncle Stephen was up from Cleveland and spoiling for a fight. Keep calling 'em niggers, he said. That way I won't feel bad when they burn you out. My father grunted and turned away. Uncle Stephen chased after him. At least be consistent, he said. Lethea was a nigger. Mom's a nigger—My father stopped and let out a sigh of disdain. She must be a nigger, said Uncle Stephen, spitting the words at my father's back. She lived in the projects too.

Uncle Stephen was different. He had a desk job at a GM assembly plant. He skipped college, but he always wanted to talk about something he'd just read. When he was young, he wrote a book of short stories. It was rejected by editors and never published.

I always thought of Uncle Stephen as a writer, even before I read his book. He spoke well, like a writer should talk. My mother said I was a lot like him, but I was never sure about that. He read poetry in his spare time. His politics leaned to the left. He said Bobby Kennedy was the only hope for the Democratic Party. My father grunted again. You better vote for Kennedy, said Uncle Stephen. He's the only one who can save you. My father narrowed his eyes. You wouldn't be so slick if you lived here, he said.

This place *should* be burned down, said Uncle Stephen. Cleveland too, for that matter. We live on desecrated ground. Fire is as good a way as any to make it pure. Probably the best. You talk like a dumbass, said my father. Uncle Stephen smiled and said, Don't call me a dumbass in front of Jim. He won't respect me. He respects you too much already, said my father.

IT SEEMED like Uncle Stephen spent more days in Detroit than he did in Cleveland. Whenever he could, he showed up for a visit. Sometimes Uncle Myron came with him, but Uncle Stephen, a confirmed bachelor, usually made the drive by himself. He never missed Thanksgiving, Christmas, or a holiday weekend. Once in a great while he stayed with us, but most of the time he took a room at the Parkcrest Motel on Harper Avenue. His life struck me then as cosmopolitan and free.

It was exhausting, arguing with my father at every turn, but Uncle Stephen was fearless, tenacious—a little too honest at times. Rarely did he let things pass. He went after my father, pushing and prodding, always trying to bend him. I listened to it all.

For a while I kept score. I assigned points as new disputes developed or dissipated. It was often difficult to declare a winner. My father's weapon was condescension. This and his flinty silence defeated almost everyone.

Most arguments centered on politics, family, or the auto industry—UAW infighting, the plant in Cleveland versus the Tech Center in Detroit. The bouts over Grandmother were the worst, short rounds with unexpected jabs.

GRANDMA TOLLMAN lived in a retirement home in North Olmstead, a suburb of Cleveland. She was stubborn and capable, but age and blindness had made it dangerous for her to live alone. Uncle Stephen hated putting her in the home, but my father insisted and Grandma Tollman, after a bad fall in her old apartment, finally gave in.

Uncle Stephen was of the opinion that we didn't visit Cleveland enough. If Mother could see, he said, she'd forget what you all look like. My father shrugged it off. We visit plenty when the weather's clear, he said. Uncle Stephen shook his head. Since when does winter last seven or eight months?

They poked each other about Grandmother all the time, but any talk concerning Grandfather was strictly off limits. He died before I was born—or so I was told. But then Uncle Stephen rocked the boat, saying, rather offhandedly, that that may or may not be true. No one knows for sure, he said. The bastard's dead, said my father. He would've shown up again if he were alive—just like a bad penny. We should try to find him, Uncle Stephen said. My father ended the argument before it could get started. Go ahead, he said. But don't forget. If you do find him, he lives out of your pocket—not mine.

WHEN UNCLE MYRON came for a visit, everything changed. Talk that bordered on altercation upset him, so my father and Uncle Stephen gave each other a wide berth.

Uncle Myron believed that a family should stay together—whatever family there was—and so he never went anywhere without his dog, a Doberman pinscher named Max. The animal looked vicious enough, but he never growled or barked. What a pathetic, sorry-ass dog, said my father. It never makes a sound.

Max stayed in the yard while my uncles were in town. My brother and I played with the dog and tried to make it speak. It just can't bark, I said. Maybe it's mute. My brother lobbed a tennis ball toward the cherry tree and Max went after it without much enthusiasm. He's a tired dog, said my brother. He got old before his time.

I remembered wisecracks about Myron's bald spot and shuffling gait. Most of these came from my father. He introduced Myron as his older brother. He called Myron and Max the geriatric twins.

UNCLE MYRON rented a house in North Olmstead that everyone else in the family referred to as a one-bedroom box. The housewife next door cut his postage stamp lawn, and a maid showed up once every two weeks. A delivery boy from the corner market left groceries on the front porch. Uncle Myron refused to drive. He shied away from public transportation. Except for the daily exercise of his dog, he rarely went out. The only redeeming feature of the little house was a large, fenced-in yard. This was Max's exclusive domain. Uncle Myron could sometimes be seen opening the back door for Max or closing it behind him.

Uncle Myron started out young like everyone else. Then somewhere around his twenty-eighth birthday the glassworks in Cleveland hired him as a maintenance man. Every morning he filled a tank in the yard with gasoline. The tank fed blow-fires that heated up powerful ovens in the plant. Uncle Myron had to climb a rickety ladder to do the job. He spilled gasoline on the way up. One day the tank exploded and down came Uncle Myron with three ruptured vertebrae. He suffered no paralysis, but his hands and feet trembled and eventually grew numb. He couldn't walk for almost a year. When his spine finally healed, he found that he could walk again, but the feeling in his hands and feet never came back. This forced him to apply for permanent disability. The glass-works operated as a non-union organization and the owners told Uncle Myron that the accident had been his own fault. He worked as an unarmed security guard after that. By the time I got to know him he was living alone in his tiny house, collecting state money and taking care of Max.

THESE WERE the men I watched: Uncle Myron, Uncle Stephen, and my father. I observed the way they moved, the way they acted around each other. I looked to them for approval, even accept-ance. So did my brother. We imitated their mannerisms and their no-nonsense dispositions. When we saw a characteristic we liked, we easily found it in ourselves. When we saw a characteristic we didn't like, we wrote it off. It never occurred to us that something might be missing.

MY MOTHER, Carrie Ann, was one of thirteen children. As a middle child, she felt deprived. It's not easy, she said. You live with eight sisters and four brothers—see how you like it.

The sire of this brood was James P. Carnelli, my grandfather and namesake, who came to America from Milan. He built a small construction company and left it to his sons. Everyone in the fam-ily said he passed away too soon. They were right.

The brothers took over and lived well, but the company died a slow and shameful death. My Italian uncles, passionate men with a taste for the good life, lacked my grandfather's vision, not to mention his business sense. They should've listened to one or two of their nine sisters, a formidable group of natural-born supervi-sors, managers, and bookkeepers. They chose, instead, to shield the girls from worldly considerations. We did the accounting, said my mother. Our fingers bled with paper cuts. But they made the decisions without us.

Excluding the girls wasn't difficult. The customs of my grandfather's Italian-Catholic lineage made no provision for bright and capable young women. The sons inherited the business and its proceeds; the daughters were left to marry as best they could.

Marriage prospects were excellent. The family's big house stood on Three Mile Drive in Grosse Pointe. The sisters had the pick of the lakeshore crop. They married promising young men: lawyers and small businessmen and mechanical engineers. My mother married a man decorated in the War, an Army Air Force machinist who looked like a movie star in uniform. Over time the glamour of the uniform wore off. A few of my mother's sisters wondered out loud as to how Carrie Ann ended up with a man like Phil. They compared my father to their husbands and decided my mother deserved better.

Your father was something to see, she said. I liked the attention, the kind of attention that surrounds a man in uniform. She capitalized on his flying jacket and silk scarf. She relished the shock value of his checkered past. She felt reborn when her closest sister declared him bold, dark, and dangerous, forbidden fruit for a Catholic girl, a wrong turn on the long Carnelli road. Stepping out, she had discovered something perilous, a poor man who possessed the physical charm of Errol Flynn. She accepted his proposal as her first and last act of rebellion.

For my father, Carrie Ann was a lovely, Italian aristocrat or, to be more precise, a meal ticket. She represented access to a world that had long been hostile to the Tollmans. She came with the mansion on Three Mile Drive and the expensive cars my grandfather drove. She came with the cottage on Lake Saint Clair and the mahogany Chris Craft runabout. She came with the just-scrubbed smell of success.

It was understood that my grandfather would pay for a large wedding. It was also understood that he would buy each of his nine daughters a first home. But his plans for his sons and his business were not understood — at least not by my father.

Carrie Ann delivered the first house. It stood as the last benefit of her family's wealth. She then delivered my brother and me and the two bedroom ranch was suddenly too small. My father sold it. He got a good price. Even so, the only house he could afford was a squat bungalow on the east side of Detroit.

My mother followed the example of her sisters and compared my father to all the professional men who married into the family. We should live in Grosse Pointe, she said. We're the only ones who don't. She treated our Detroit neighbors with disdain and made disparaging remarks about our white trash relations in Ohio. She let it be known that visiting Grandma Tollman in the housing project made her physically ill.

The unbelievable thing was this: my mother's revulsion wasn't enough to thwart her duty. She made all the trips to Cleveland. She arrived with a smile on her face and participated in family small talk while my father drank beers with his brothers. I suppose she made these visits out of a rigid sense of Catholic obligation. Maybe she thought of it as penance. She even pushed my father to go when the weather was bad.

I went with them until I began high school, but we never made the journey with any sense of joy. Grandma Tollman felt this. She always gathered her shawl around her shoulders, even in the middle of summer, as if a cold draft had come in with us.

My father preferred to stand or pace and my mother sat in a Windsor chair to the side of Grandma Tollman's recliner. My mother tapped her foot and rattled off a long list of inquiries. Grandma Tollman made quick answers. Then she asked me how I was doing in school and if I was still playing the clarinet. She got excited when I changed to flute. You get your talent from my mother, she said. She played the flute. She always played *Green Sleeves* when I was a little girl.

Like most children, I asked an endless string of rude questions. Why does Grandma Tollman smell funny? Why is her skin so wrinkled? Who poured the milk in her eyes? I asked such things until I got old enough to understand. Her skin was once like yours, said Uncle Stephen. Smooth as a baby's behind. But you'll have to imagine her eyes. Make 'em emerald . . . or the deepest shade of jade you've got.

I'd stare at Grandma Tollman, at the white film covering her eyes. Her long, lean fingers trembled as she pulled back her hair or smoothed her skirt. I've got the shakes, she'd always say, and then she'd give me a wry smile, as if she'd known all along that I was the only person in the room looking at her.

At no time was I ever alone with Grandma Tollman. My parents never brought her up to Detroit, and I never thought about going down to Cleveland on my own, even after I could drive. I picked up my father's habit of making excuses, so I had plenty of reasons not to go.

To escape the guilt, to make restitution, I spent more time with Grandma Carnelli. It really came down to this: I could see her without making a long trip. I could visit her without smelling urine and disinfectant. I could look into her eyes.

Grandma Carnelli was a frequent guest. She invited herself for lunch or dinner. She helped my mother bake Italian coffeecake and holiday cookies. She even lived with us—much to my father's consternation—for one month out of every year. She bustled around the house like a little general. She bragged about the peasant strength in her arms and legs. She talked to the air. She whispered her dead husband's name when she thought no one could hear. She spoke with him every night.

A GREAT MANY girls lived in the neighborhood and most, like my mother and grandmothers, were confusing, especially the confident and mischievous ones who knocked on Knute's front door. Twice or three times a week they called for Knute's daughter, Selena. They talked and giggled until Selena came out. The girls seemed certain of their beauty, and Selena was the most beautiful among them. Her hair was luxuriously thick and straight. Her hands were graceful and mysterious.

Selena was named after Knute's mother, who came from Greece to Detroit by way of Ellis Island. Selena inherited her father's black hair and dark eyes and her mother's olive skin. She played the piano. She turned eleven that spring but insisted her age was thirteen. There was a seriousness about her face, a calm sophistication that seemed not the least bit unnatural. At eleven years old she was more of a woman than most of the older girls I knew. I adore the sound of flute and piano, she said. Come over any time.

I should've taken her up on her invitation. I should've tried. I don't know classical, I thought. I'll make a fool of myself. In the end, though, it was Selena's playing that intimidated me. Her depth of feeling, even in the simplest compositions, unnerved me.

She chose pieces with exotic titles: *Gymnopedie, Gnossienne, Sarabande,* and *Nocturne.* I repeated the words after her but never pronounced them correctly. We talked about famous composers when she wanted to. There is, she said, a strange beauty that comes from sadness. I wanted to know if she'd read that or made it up herself. I didn't ask. I didn't want an eleven-year-old, even if she was a prodigy, explaining things to me.

Sometimes we played Monopoly or Clue. Sometimes we took Ralph out for a walk. But most of the time I listened to her music, whether sitting in her living room or standing outside her house or lying beneath the cherry tree in my yard. Her delicate phrases floated on the air. They haunted windows and doors. All the events of that summer were inextricably bound to the melodies Selena played.

My brother, Paul, aspired to be a professional musician in those days. He began his career playing accordion and guitar in a wedding band, letting me sit in now and then, teaching me the basics. I tried clarinet on our first gig, but my performance drove Paul crazy. You make every song sound like a polka, he said.

We were very mediocre in the beginning. Somehow, though, we stayed with it, serving as audience to each other when no one else would.

Paul's gifts included a good sense of pitch and time and a fine ear for harmony. He moved from accordion to piano and eventually played lead guitar. I gave up the clarinet for a jazzier flute and learned how to play electric bass. Both of us could sing better than most musicians we knew. After a while we were almost good. Then the war came.

Paul's draft number was low. Vietnam felt remote but inevitable, like a bully waiting at the edge of a sandlot. I'm tired of fighting, said Paul. He was speaking of my father, not the war. I can pay for my own place, he said. I can get a job. I wanna go — but not to

Vietnam. He didn't look at me when he said it. You're fucked, I said. It's out of the frying pan and into the fuckin' inferno.

MY FATHER disliked the fact that his sons were musicians. He believed that rock 'n' roll led to muscle cars, loud stereo systems, strange politics, and general irresponsibility. My brother added fuel to these fears by producing a long string of poor report cards.

The argument usually started at the dinner table with the same gestures and the same words. First my father would salt his salad. Then he'd bang the table with the salt shaker like a judge pounding his gavel. My mother usually chose this moment to speak up. Now Phil, she'd say, don't get on your high horse. Following the established pattern, my father would wave off her words. Look at these god-forsaken grades, he'd say. Paul would sit with his elbows on the table and his hands clasped over his plate. Sometimes he cracked his knuckles. What a rumdumb, my father would intone. What a good for nothin' bum. On weekends the words were slurred with booze and the quarrel often escalated into a beating.

My brother's senior year offered more of the same. In February, as a calculated perversion of Valentine's Day, the assistant principal of East Detroit High School sent my parents a warning letter. It said this: If Paul's grades do not improve, he will not graduate in June.

After that, each test and progress report became a possible occasion for violence. My mother called the school once a week. Paul's grades kept straddling the borderline between success and failure. His diploma remained in question.

So it was—in that strange and brutal spring without lilacs—that Paul and I found ourselves forever at the dinner table, stupefied and hungry, subject to my father's shopworn routine. One evening his monologue involved me. This new twist caught me off guard. I could see Paul moving in his chair, growing restless.

My father said, You're starting out behind the eight ball—and that's where you'll stay. You've even got Jim believing that things'll be great behind the eight ball as long as he's with you. He wants to be a musician. He wants to be like you. My father focused on me. Go ahead. Be like your brother. Be a good for nothin' bum. Leave him out of this, said Paul. Jim's good in school. My father's glare called for silence. He's good now, he said. But if he follows your example, his grades'll wind up like yours—in the toilet. My father kept talking. Paul pushed himself away from the table and walked out of the kitchen. My father gave him a minute or two to come back, and then he wiped his mouth and got up. I followed.

My father walked slowly, his right hand balled into a fist. We passed through the living room. Then we entered the hallway leading to the bathroom. I heard water running in the sink. It stopped. The door opened and my brother turned and stepped out. That's when my father nailed him, doubling him over with a forearm to the stomach. Paul fell against the wall and the force broke the wainscot molding. He rushed my father with his shoulder down. My father sidestepped, catching my brother's feet, and Paul hit the floor on his hands and knees. All this happened with deadly precision.

My father picked up the broken molding and stormed off. I asked Paul if he was all right. Fuck off, he said.

ONE SATURDAY afternoon, after the eaves were scraped and painted, my brother took the keys to the Oldsmobile without asking my father and we drove down to Cobo Hall for the annual Auto Show. Cruising down I-94, loud music pouring through open windows, I suddenly felt the urge to sing, to drive all the way to Chicago just for the hell of it.

Paul was confident behind the wheel of a car. He talked about music and waved his hands like a child. He cracked his knuckles on the dashboard. He said he wanted to get a present for Char. We sang *Incense and Peppermints* and *Apples, Peaches, Pumpkin Pie.* My brother turned up *Mrs. Robinson,* and long before the DiMaggio verse, he started yelling, Where's Joe? C'mon Joe baby. Where's Joltin' Joe?

Cobo Hall overflowed with women, chrome-heavy cars, and homegrown rock 'n' roll. Mitch Ryder and the Detroit Wheels played one end of the auditorium and the Bob Seger System played the other end. We sat in futuristic concept cars. We ate hot dogs and drank root beer.

We found a booth with a pinstripe artist who also did customized T-shirts: peace signs, caricatures, cartoons. Paul thought the blue hippopotamus was cool and that Char would like it. It was the cutest of the lot, but we called it boss or bad—never cute. Paul bought one for Char and one for himself. Then he bought one for me.

We stayed late and listened to Seger's last set. Driving home, we didn't speak. The chilly night air washed over us while the radio played Janis Joplin, The Four Tops, Johnny Rivers, and Eric Burden and the Animals. When we pulled into the driveway on Lincoln Street, my father sat waiting for us on the porch. I reached over and dug my fingers into Paul's arm. Got a story? I asked. Hang loose, said Paul. He set the parking brake and turned off the engine. I'll say we went shopping. I rolled my eyes. That's right. Show him Char's T-shirt. You're dipped in shit if you say shopping. Shopping for what? My brother smiled. A Mother's Day present.

PAUL HAD brought Char around for the first time less than a year before, a picnic at the Paint Creek Cider Mill. Her eyes were blue, flecked with yellow and green. Her face gave away everything she thought or felt. I thought at the time that I'd never seen a face so honest.

Char met Maria that day and together they made the picnic something of a miracle. They unpacked a plate of barbecued chicken and small containers of pickles, vegetables, and potato salad. I tried to help. I stole a taste of this or that before they were ready. I managed to spill a glass of iced tea.

The day grew clear and bright. Red, orange, and yellow leaves fluttered in a steady breeze. We ate near the stream, away from noisy children and their beleaguered parents. Paul and I were unusually quiet. Maria said so. I caught myself watching her hands. I wanted my own to be less greedy, less awkward. I looked at her shoulders and breasts. I stayed close to her all day, leaning against her arm or resting my hand on her thigh.

Char and Maria liked each other immediately. They established a routine of unspoken communication. I'd say or do something uncouth, or Paul would, and then Char would frown or roll her eyes and Maria would commiserate with a sympathetic nod.

Paint Creek was a place of light. Even at dusk the brilliant leaves surrounding us seemed to rise up and color the sky. We lingered until most of the people had gone, until the waterwheel made the only sound we could hear. Night came quietly then, falling around us like black rain, soothing us with its calm and private darkness.

In the gathering moonlight, we listened to Char talk about the future. I'd like to teach, she said. Or start a school, maybe. Imagine—to build a school. My brother smiled. He bucked the constraints of any plan. He dreamed big dreams and lived from day to day.

Maria, of course, believed in planning ahead. We took each other's virginity in tenth grade, and in that same year Maria asked me about marriage and whether or not I wanted children. But I couldn't see myself in a distant place or time. The next day or the next week was the best I could do.

THE MONDAY after the Auto Show I ran into Paul and Char leaving school. I noticed the T-shirt right away. It makes your eyes look bluer, I said. They talked about eloping, getting away before the draft notice showed up. Is that your new plan? I asked. It sounded like one of Paul's halfcocked ideas. Where will you go? What will you do for work? Paul waved his arms like a drowning man. You ask too many questions, he said.

WHEN THE GUYS at school asked me why I was going steady, I explained it this way: I'm in love with an older woman.

Maria and I were the same age, true enough, but at seventeen she eclipsed me. We both went to East Detroit High, but I didn't meet her in the cafeteria or at a school dance or even at a party. Instead we met at Carlucci's Café on a Friday evening when everyone else in the world seemed to be fucking.

The corner booth where Maria sat was dark. At first I thought I saw her laughing, a strange thing to be doing by herself, and then I realized that she was weeping. Look at those tits, said the guy in front of me. He was waiting for a meatball sandwich. I took a long look but it was no good; her crying got to me. I stared at her while I ordered my pizza. I dropped my change.

Everything on the table in front of her had its place: glass, candle, ashtray, purse. Her long hair slid across her shoulders like silk. Her skin was dark, darker in the half-light. I wanted very much to touch her. I walked over with a slice of pizza in one hand and a stack of napkins in the other. I offered her a napkin.

She told me she didn't want to talk about it. The last guy just split, she said. He hit the street right before you walked over. I told her that my life was an exercise in bad timing. She laughed for a second and then resumed her crying. I sat across from her and ate my pizza and waited for her to stop. I asked her if she'd ever been to a Tigers game. She said yes. I said that another Tigers game would do her good. What kind of good? she asked. Good for the soul, I said. The ballpark is like church—only better. She said that going to the game with me meant nothing—even less than nothing. She supposed that we could be friends and not much else. I agreed.

By the time junior year was over we understood more about sex than the coach who taught Health Class. We did it in cars, tents, and swimming pools, in bathrooms and on balconies, in her basement with her parents upstairs. We did it behind a convent and in the bell tower of a church. I remember places that were safe, even beautiful, and some that were far outside the city.

I remember Maria running ahead of me through the woods. This night wears like a loose dress, she said. Sharp branches scratched our arms and thighs. We found a clearing and a stark, silhouetted cabin and a door already open. Lying beneath her, I could almost feel her bleed.

BY THE END of May we knew that my brother would graduate. In an impressive come-from-behind effort, he managed to pass all his final exams with scores high enough to offset his previous grades. My father observed the occasion with three words: I'll be damned.

With my father's permission, Paul bought his first car. He used the money he made from odd jobs and wedding gigs. He bought an old Mercury Comet, black with a red leather interior. It ran rough when it was cold and the window wipers worked intermittently, but it was a car and it belonged to Paul.

On commencement day my father got drunk. So did many of the graduates. Paul stayed sober and walked through the ceremony and tossed his cap at the end. Then he went cruising with several of his buddies.

My father parked himself on the porch that evening. He's stewing, said my mother, shrugging her shoulders. About what I don't know. My father kept drinking. At midnight my mother asked him what he was doing. He said he was waiting for Paul.

Paul pulled up not long before daybreak. He ignored my father and went around to the side door. A few minutes later I woke to the sound of Paul's voice. You son-of-a-bitch, he yelled. Don't do it you son-of-a-bitch. But my father was deaf to the words.

He raised the tire iron over his head repeatedly, bringing it down on the hood and the windshield of my brother's Mercury Comet.

The neighborhood came to life. Voices from dark houses cheered or booed. Some wanted more. More, it seemed, than my father was willing to give. After a minute or two of silence I heard someone say, Show's over.

Light from the corner lamp made my father a silhouette. His black figure leaned against the car. Broken glass glittered on the street.

c h a p t e r   t e n

UNCLE STEPHEN had driven up from Cleveland to see Paul get his diploma. He'd come in late on Friday. Nothing on the radio, he said, except the shooting. I wanted to shut if off, but I couldn't do it. They say a doctor in the crowd found Bobby holding his beads and crucifix. They say he was telling Ethel, It's all right. It's okay.

Saturday had begun with the telephone ringing, rumors about graduation being postponed, as if the day could easily fall apart. Anything unbroken seemed suddenly out of place: my brother in his cap and gown, the procession, the clear sky. Both the salutatorian and the valedictorian quoted Kennedy in their speeches. Uncle Stephen closed his eyes while the students spoke. I saw tears on Maria's face. She squeezed my hand until it started to sweat.

When Uncle Stephen stopped to say good-bye on Sunday morning, he saw the battered Mercury Comet. I described the front porch vigil and Paul coming home late and my father wielding the tire iron. Uncle Stephen surveyed the damage and asked if Paul was okay. I guess so, I said. He took off this morning. I haven't seen him since. Uncle Stephen looked up and down the block. Took off on foot? On foot, I said. We took a few steps toward the house. If you're looking for Mom and Dad, I said, they're at church. That stopped Uncle Stephen. First he smiled and then he began to chuckle. I gotta go, he said. Tell your old man I'll be back in town for his birthday. What about this shit? I asked, pointing at Paul's car. Uncle Stephen shrugged and got into his blue Corvette and started the engine and swung out of the driveway. He'd gone halfway up the street when he put on the brakes, dropped the Corvette into reverse and rolled back. He waved me down to the curb and leaned across the transmission console toward the passenger window. Listen, he said. Have a beer with your old man. Get him talking about his Air Force stint. Ask to see pictures.

I watched the car stop at the corner and then turn. My father spoke to me when I was in trouble, I thought. Or when I had chores to do. Otherwise our conversations revolved around the Detroit Tigers, the Cleveland Indians, and the weather. You can ask a man like my father for permission to use the car. You can ask him about which tool to use for a particular job around the house. You can even ask him for a buck or two, when he's in a good mood. But you don't ask him about his life. Maybe I was wrong. Maybe he would've spilled his guts had I asked him about the War. I doubt it.

PAUL STAYED away for four days. I knew I could find him at Char's house, but I didn't mention this to my parents. My mother spent the time wringing her hands and blaming my father for chasing her son out into the streets.

Because my mother couldn't imagine her boys having sex, she never thought to call Char's parents. She couldn't picture my brother crawling up an ancient oak tree or climbing through an open window. She never considered the possibility of Char's bed and my brother in it. My father knew better, of course, but he said it'd be a cold year in hell before he'd spend his time tracking down a good for nothin' bum.

On the fifth day Paul showed up and claimed his car. He drove it over to Char's place and parked it in the driveway where he could begin repairs. After a week or two Paul started coming home to sleep, but he always left the Mercury Comet somewhere out of sight.

WHILE ALL this went on I kept thinking about my father's time in the army and the last words Uncle Stephen had said. I decided to forgo a face to face with the old man, but I did open the big cedar chest that held my mother's wedding dress and my father's Army Air Force uniform. In it I found photographs and letters and my father's military decorations, his ribbons and his Bronze Battle Stars. I also found a ragged copy of a poem. Scribbled in the margin was a note from Uncle Stephen to my father. It said, *Thought you should have this.*

I read several of the letters. About half were written in India and North Africa. The rest were written in England. Most of the letters were short and filled with descriptions of cities and villages. Once or twice my father described the different airplanes that he inspected and repaired. He used the salutation My Dearest, rather than my mother's name.

Nowhere in the writing did I hear my father's voice. The tone was unfamiliar. In several letters he spoke about coming home, seeing the States again and visiting the house on Three Mile Drive. One letter ended with a strange postscript: "The work is bad. We feel more like grave robbers each day." This one was the last, dated a year before the armistice. I searched the cedar chest, looking under old clothes and photo albums, but I found no others. Lost by the army, I thought. Or locked up with thousands more in a dead letter room.

I wanted a reason for the missing letters, something to do with security or procedure, but there was no official explanation. The simple truth was this: my father stopped writing. He just stopped. Uncle Stephen said later that Carrie Ann, fearing the worst, sent inquiries addressed to General Eisenhower. Her efforts earned a document from the Secretary of Defense, an active duty list that included my father's name. She received no other word.

THE NEXT TIME I saw Uncle Stephen I told him about the letters I'd read. I showed him the poem. He had to sit down when he saw it. I remember this, he said. I came across it not long after the war. He tried to smooth out the paper. What does it mean? I asked. He handed it back to me: It means exactly what it says.

I read the poem again.

EARLY IN 1943 Philip Tollman left North Africa. His new orders took him to England, an airfield sixteen miles east of Northampton in a place called Chelveston. He was a master sergeant by then and a veteran of almost four years.

Starting in 1942, flying from Chelveston and other fields like it, the Royal Air Force had dropped incendiary bombs on German cities. This established a vicious pattern of attack and retaliation. Then, in preparation for the allied invasion of France, the United States joined the Royal Air Force, reinforcing the British squadrons with fighter units and heavy bombers, including the B-17 Flying Fortress.

Philip Tollman understood the guts of a B-17 better than his own. He wrote while he was in training that the B-17 fuselage was more home than a man could ever want. He knew how the plane worked and how it was supposed to feel. He flew several missions as a flight engineer, but his specialty was inspection and repair, so he spent most of his time on the ground.

By the summer of 1943 the combined British and American

forces flew round-the-clock raids over Germany, using as many as seven hundred planes, targeting Essen, Cologne, Dortmund, Nuremberg, Stuttgart, and Hamburg.

The Royal Air Force specialized in night flying, having perfected a system of nighttime attack after the Battle of Britain. The system, it was said, yielded a margin of acceptable loss. The crews went out in healthy planes and delivered their midnight payloads. With luck, they made their way back at dawn, often in wounded machinery. It was the same for the squadrons of the Army Air Force, except that they specialized in sunshine raids and the precision bombing that daylight made possible. The aircraft of choice for these missions was the B-17. The bombers left in the morning flanked by fighters, then limped back at dusk, sometimes without escorts.

Philip Tollman and his crew of machinists were responsible for keeping the B-17s at Chelveston in the air. He'd arrived at the airfield feeling that this assignment was the reason he'd enlisted. Now he could put his brain and his hands to good use. He'd been repairing one plane or another since his enlistment, but the B-17 was larger than life. These bombers, adopted by their crews and named after buxom pin-up girls, were ferocious machines bristling with American power and sex.

Philip Tollman surveyed the base at Chelveston and felt the dreamlike impatience of India and North Africa slipping away. Assigned to remote airfields, repairing cargo and surveillance planes, he'd felt absurdly absent from the war. Now he knew he was in it.

THE FIRST forty-eight hours were quiet. Rain and fog grounded the planes; on the third day the weather cleared. The mission for the American squadron involved industrial targets in the Ruhr valley. The *Go* order came early. Ground crews prepped the planes. They flagged the fighters and B-17s into a cloudless sky.

The machinists felt the full weight of time when the planes were gone. They moved as if they were living underwater. No one spoke about the mission. No one spoke about individual crewmates. They spoke only about the B-17s. They repeated the names as if conjuring up a spell of good luck: Big Betty, Naughty Nancy, Raging Rita. If they finished work on an ailing plane, they paced the airfield and glanced now and then at the horizon. Over hands of gin rummy they waited for sunset and looked up at the encroaching darkness. Then they heard the engines.

All but two of the bombers returned, and two others touched down as best they could without landing gear. The planes came in quickly. They seemed to fall out of the black sky like avenging birds.

The belly landings were the first priority for Tollman and his crew. They drove out in jeeps alongside the fire trucks. No one was allowed to enter the planes until all fuel leaks had been neutralized and all electrical fires snuffed out. The procedures went smoothly. Doors were pried open, pieces of torn fuselage were cut away.

It was on this first night of service that the commanding officer conferred on Philip Tollman an unexpected measure of authority. Tollman, he said, give the clear for boarding order when you're ready. And it was on this night after securing and entering a damaged aircraft, after evacuating the injured, that Philip Tollman found the severed hand of a ball turret gunner still gripping the gun.

Finding body parts in a flak- and bullet-riddled plane was neither common nor uncommon. It happened. Some of the oldtimers thought it auspicious that the new master sergeant had made his find on his first night out. Now, they said, he could relax for a while before the next one. When it occurred, though, no one was thinking about relaxation. Jesus fucking Christ, everyone heard, squinting into darkness. Who's that? It's Tollman, someone said. Wha' de say? He said, Jesus fucking Christ. The new master sergeant had moved forward in the plane and found the topside turret splattered with blood and crazed with web-like cracks. His light ran over the gun and finally came to rest on the hand. A fusillade had sliced through the gunner's wrist while he was firing. The hand itself was not mutilated. It was as if the hand had been separated from the arm with surgical precision.

No one had told Philip Tollman about the washing out that was necessary before repairs could begin. He had received no training in the use of a hose and sponge, no debriefing on the smell of burnt flesh. Before Chelveston, he'd thought gut-bucket was a colorful figure of speech and nothing more.

In his time working on the B-17s, Philip Tollman or the men of his company found bone fragments, fingers, ears, forearms, lumps of melted skin and hair, and blood—black blood sprayed like paint on every possible surface. The master sergeant himself found an eyeball cradled in a nest of exposed wires.

He'd been there only three months when he started praying for moonlight. The moon's silver, he wrote, makes everything black and white. He soon referred to the planes as dark caves, as stinking mausoleums. He'd wanted to be a career man before the United States entered the war. The B-17s at Chelveston changed his mind.

One of the men in Tollman's crew talked about everything he saw. He ran off at the mouth, retelling the horror to himself, to whoever would listen. He fidgeted on his chair a great deal. He slapped his forehead and cheeks like a man killing mosquitoes.

His fellow men, unable to ignore him or convince him to stop, called him a chattering idiot. He's got the talking disease, they said. They ordered him to shut his mouth. After a long day, they threatened to break his jaw.

None of this changed the man's behavior. He listened to no one but himself. Wherever he went, he made things messy. He declared himself out of it, detached from the regular chain of command. No one could gag him or make him sit still. Several crewmen complained and Tollman passed the complaint up the line.

The man was given new paperwork. He ignored these orders and the next day was dragged off the wing of a damaged B-17. After that, he spent his time sweeping barracks and cleaning latrines. No one cared if he spoke endlessly to a tired broom. It wasn't long before he refused to sleep, filling the night and neighboring dreams with nonstop talk.

Philip Tollman, keeping his distance, observed the swift progression of the talking disease. He listened to the man at mess speaking to his plate of food, heard him mumbling through evening inspection and common prayer. He watched as two crewmen rose in the dark each night and strapped the man to his bunk and taped his mouth. The disease, after all, couldn't go unchecked. The machinists needed their sleep.

The situation ran on for weeks and then the man disappeared. Everyone noticed, but no one said a word. Those who remained kept their hands out of sight. They concerned themselves with work and weather reports. They talked only about difficult repairs.

In September of 1945 Philip Tollman separated from service at Fort Sheridan in Illinois. He was given an honorable discharge and mustering out pay of three hundred dollars. It was also in 1945 that a man named Randall Jarrell wrote a poem that would later make him famous. Philip Tollman cared very little about poetry or the careers of poets. His brother knew this but sent him the poem anyway.

> *From my mother's sleep I fell into the State,*
> *And I hunched in its belly till my wet fur froze.*
> *Six miles from earth, loosed from its dream of life,*
> *I woke to black flak and the nightmare fighters.*
> *When I died they washed me out of the turret with a hose.*

I REMEMBER reading the poem several times and looking at a photograph of my father in full uniform. He wore his hat with a rakish tilt and sported a pencil-line mustache, much thinner than the thick, dark eyebrows that called attention to his darker eyes. I noted the firm jaw, the high cheekbones, and the perfectly proportioned nose. He was a handsome man. No doubt about that. It would've been good to know him on the day this picture was taken, I thought. Something in his eyes and in the set of his mouth seemed inviting. Nothing about the face in the photograph intimidated me. Nothing at all.

I kept the poem with me for several days and then copied the lines into one of my school notebooks. I returned to the attic, and putting the poem back where I'd found it, I looked again at my father's photograph. Seeing it the second time was different. It made me think of things: my father raking leaves and then watching me jump into the bright pile; my inability to throw a knuckler no matter how many times he showed me; the heaviness in my gut when his car pulled into the driveway after work.

And then I remembered my mother talking to her sister, the one she was closest to, describing a time I'd never seen, the years after the war, before Paul was born and then me. There'd been almost five years without children, a circumstance unheard of in my mother's family. There were nightmares, she said. And waking up with the room in total darkness and the bed soaking. He'd complain the bed was no good. Like everything else. Not nearly so friendly as it looks. Sometimes he'd mention a name. One of his men. But he never kept in touch. Never wrote a letter or visited anyone. Then my brother gave him a job, she said. He was better after that. He learned to drive the big trucks. Brought home cigars that my brothers gave him. But then there was trouble. Some of the hired men started saying things. I never knew what. He quit. Or maybe my brother fired him. Who knows? He said he hated Detroit. I didn't understand because he'd always loved the city. Going to ball games and out for music and dancing. Maybe Detroit was ugly after Delhi and London. I'm not sure what he thought of me. He could be well-liked, you know. That builder out near the golf course liked him. That summer was good. He came home with sawdust in his hair. He brought me flowers. He seemed better. But then the winter came and less work. I tried to get him out. I said we didn't have to dance. We could just listen. But he refused. By the next summer I was pregnant. He decided there wasn't enough money so he looked for another job. The job he has now. My father gave us his blessing. We had our own money. Enough even to travel. But there was no time and nowhere to go.

I put the photograph on top of the uniform. I took in the sweetness of cedar. I moved carefully, trying to leave the thick dust in its place. I closed the chest and turned the key in the lock. I started down the attic steps and heard music from Selena's piano rising up the stairwell.

I paused for a moment and concentrated on the rolling figure that I knew was the work of her left hand. It anchored the melody, which was light but touched with melancholy. It reminded me of summer rain. I strained to hear it after I made my way down, but the notes got lost. My ears filled up with the drone of an electric fan and with a sound that had become overly familiar, the trembling of my mother's voice.

You're nothing but a louse, said my mother. It's not like I stay home when it's time to visit Cleveland. My father pointed out that a weekend visit wasn't the same as having his mother-in-law move in for the entire month of July. I know. I know, said my mother. You'd put her in a home. That's your solution. My mother's blind, said my father. She belongs in a home. He started toward the kitchen door. My mother glared at his back. You're lucky she's blind, she said. My father turned on her then, his eyes black with contempt. I married the queen of bitchdom. My mother's face filled with blood. My father pointed his index finger and said, Take it somewhere else. Find another man who likes cozying up to an iceberg. Then he waved his hand as if to wipe my mother off the planet. She ignored it. She took a step toward him and thrust out her chin. You're a lousy bastard. You've got nothing to offer but a drink. Call me whatever you like. That won't change the fact that I'm right. I'll say it again. You're lucky she's blind. You're lucky because it gives you an excuse. Shut up, Carrie Ann. You don't know what the hell you're talking about. I know, said my mother. I know better than you. You think she did it for you. You think she let herself go blind. Well she didn't. People don't let themselves go blind. She chose it. She chose it—just like I chose to marry you.

My father walked out and slammed the door. My mother glanced at me and then collapsed into a chair and started weeping. I wanted to say something that would make her stop. I wanted to tell her that things would be better for all of us if she left him. But I said nothing.

I needed some air. I got outside and saw my father crouched

beneath the cherry tree. He was listening to Selena play. I wanted to hang around and hear the music too, but seeing him there spoiled it for me.

WHEN GRANDMA Carnelli moved in she brought with her six pounds of butter. My father suffered a mild heart attack at forty and my mother, on the advice of my father's physician, started cooking and baking with margarine. Vegetable fat made no sense to Grandma Carnelli. She said that nothing edible could be made with margarine. Her cookies, coffeecakes, and pastries were tributes to unsalted butter. She made no apologies. She buttered her breads and muffins and finished the ritual with a sprinkle of powdered sugar.

Grandma Carnelli loved Whitman Samplers and hot fudge. Cannolis and chocolate chip cookies were her favorite snacks. In the summer she drank orange sodas made with creamy vanilla ice cream; she made orange sodas almost every night about an hour or so before she went to bed. She spared herself and her family no indulgence when it came to sweets and desserts. This was one good reason for her undying popularity with the grandchildren; it was also the reason why the dentist shook his head each time I went for my regular check-up. I remember her always asking about the dentist. Giacomo, how many cavities this time? Usually I told her the truth. And usually she'd smile and say it was okay and drop a Hershey's Kiss in my hand.

WE REARRANGED the house when Grandma Carnelli moved in. She slept upstairs and Paul and I moved into the basement, which suited us fine, given the fact that Paul's stereo was downstairs along with a second phone. As subterraneans we saw my father less. We felt comfortable in the basement, especially in summer.

Char and Maria visited often but didn't share our enthusiasm for underground living. They complained about the absence of light.

With Grandma Carnelli in the house, my father spent most of his time behind the newspaper. He didn't engage her in conversation. Most of the time he ignored her when she spoke to him. When her idiosyncrasies or incipient deafness aggravated him, he usually stomped out of the room. Sometimes he lost his temper and shouted at her. My mother lost her patience too, and then my father would join her in a show of solidarity. In this mood, they talked about Grandma Carnelli behind her back.

One evening my father asked a simple question. Why doesn't the old bat get a hearing aid? Because she's a stubborn cuss, my mother replied. Just like somebody else I know. My father rustled his newspaper. Tell me again why I put up with all this shit. My mother turned her head like a stage actress in her best moment. Do I have to? My father grunted. We won't get more than a dollar when the old bat croaks. Maybe not, said my mother. But that's more than you'll ever inherit. My father went back to his paper and my mother went back to her mending.

We lived with an obvious double standard. I never once heard my father call his mother an old bat. It was true, of course, that she never moved in with us, but even if she had, he would have treated her differently. I knew this after my last trip to Cleveland. The three of us had already said our good-byes to Grandma Tollman, but as we left the room my father paused and said he'd catch up in a minute or two. My mother and I were almost to the elevator when I realized I'd left my jacket behind. When I walked back into the room, my father was handing his mother a yellow rose. He seemed to have conjured it up out of thin air. He turned and looked at me while Grandma Tollman touched the flower to her lips and smiled. I could tell by the look on my father's face that he hadn't wanted me to see this gift. He hadn't wanted my mother to see it. I picked up my jacket and left. We never said a word about the rose.

BY JULY Tiger Stadium was my second home. Maria and I spent most of our afternoons and evenings there. I like to think that we made this choice because we wanted to observe the sacred rituals surrounding baseball, because we wanted to participate in sports history as it unfolded. We probably went because it was cheap. Even so, the spectacle of a winning team kept us going back.

The Tigers had been in first place since early May. Now it looked to many fans, even the most jaded, that the Tigers would hold that lead and take the American League pennant for the first time in twenty-three years. Every game that summer seemed to be a sellout. Every billboard and bumper sticker advertised the slogans of the faithful: *Detroit Tigers: On the Ball; Hear the Roar; Sock it to 'em Tigers.*

Sports writers for *The Detroit News* and the *Free Press* called the team *The Comeback Crew.* It was true. They ran off with games that seemed impossible to win. Down three or four runs in the ninth inning, the team would rally. Bill Freehan or Dick McAuliffe got the ball going. Then Mickey Stanley and Jim Northrup hit for extra bases. Bringing home the runs fell to Al Kaline, Norm Cash, or Willie Horton.

Kaline had been a Tiger for sixteen years. He'd hit his 307th home run in May, breaking a long-standing record for the most home runs hit by a Tiger. He'd been an all-star thirteen times. He'd won the Golden Glove ten times. His interviews and public appearances revealed intelligence and charm. If the Pope had been a baseball fan, he would've made Al Kaline the patron saint of Detroit. The press called him the old pro, the ballplayer's ballplayer. For us he was an anchor, a member of the family, living proof of integrity and stability.

Kaline broke the Tiger's home run record in May, and then he broke his arm. Despite the benching of our hero, Maria and I kept going to the games. There was more to it now than a winning team. We wanted to be there when Kaline came back, when he took his place again in right field. We ate bag after bag of roasted peanuts and let the shells pile up at our feet. We washed down the salt with Vernors.

I loved the smell of the ballpark, a sweet mix of dirt and grass and steamed hot dogs and beer. I loved the grit beneath my feet and the stickiness of the chairs. I loved the short left-field wall and the impossible depth of center field. I loved that Maria had fallen in love with me here and that I'd fallen in love with her. I loved the scent of her skin, the way she whistled, the way she walked and talked and watched. I loved the excitement of our bodies melding with the excitement of the game. I loved the way she kissed me when our team took the lead.

There were times at Tiger Stadium when we felt safe, when we felt a certain kind of hope for Detroit and for ourselves. Baseball, we knew, followed its own tragic cycles. Great players faded into bitter legends of injury and dissipation. Others betrayed the game itself or were betrayed by it. But in those days we ignored the changing seasons. Always we returned to the ballpark, the satisfying geometry of field, fence, and foul line. It stood as a bulwark against losses we could not imagine. Losses we could not understand. Somehow we felt that the world would make sense only as long as we stayed in our seats.

THE FIREWORKS that July were higher and brighter than any I'd ever seen. Streamers of green, gold, and silver illuminated the sky and the Detroit River and the downtown office buildings. Ravaged streets were awash with color. Belle Isle glowed beneath the sparkling rain. The light warmed every upturned face, and everyone — grandparents, parents, and children — struggled to fix in memory one shade or shape, one flash of beauty that for a moment transformed the darkness.

I watched Maria watching the fireworks, and I looked over at Char sitting close to my brother, her eyes fixed on the heavens, and I felt the urge to speak, to say something so unexpected and so hard that it would stop time, something that would keep us in this moment for as long as we wanted to stay. I thought I felt a word or phrase take shape in my mouth, as if a lost or ancient sound were welling up in me, but then it was gone.

The grand finale startled me. Maria smiled and told me to look at the sky. I did. When it was over we drained the cooler and followed the crowd up Grand Circus Park Boulevard to where we'd left Paul's car. Let's not go home, said Maria. I wanna see more. The smell of gunpowder lingered in the air. I can't take anymore explosions, said Char. My ears are ringing. So are mine, I said. Paul smiled and turned on the radio.

THE WEEKEND after the fireworks we all went to Belle Isle again, this time for the unlimited hydroplane races. Powered by airplane engines, these boats flew above the water at tremendous speeds, so fast that an accident often meant the disintegration of the craft and the death of the driver. Fans liked to say thunderboats, rather than hydroplanes, and for good reason. When the Roostertail or the Electric Eagle or Atlas Van Lines came out of the south turn toward Belle Isle, opening its throttle for the straight-away, the vibration and the sound took hold of a body like an earthquake.

Everyone near those boats felt the rapture of speed on water. We thought of the drivers as living each moment to the limit, as men hoping to claim the intangible — not money or a gold cup — a state of grace, maybe, or freedom. I imagined myself the driver of a great machine. I didn't like the heaviness of my legs. I wanted, instead, a sleek bullet of steel and wood to take me away from earth, to carry my body to a place it could not otherwise reach. We cheered the drivers as they ran nose to nose for the finish line, and if a boat disappeared in a wall of white spray, we understood the sacrifice.

Between heats we swam in the Detroit River, then stretched out in the sun. We ate our picnic lunch and drank iced tea. Paul wanted someday to own a powerboat. He argued with Maria about the type and size of boat he planned to buy. Fiberglass is cool, said Maria. Paul shook his head. Fiberglass boats are faster, said Maria. That means better skiing. My neighbor has a wooden boat and he spends more time with it out of the water than in. All he does is sand and paint and varnish. And he does it under my bedroom window. You should help him, said Paul, cracking his knuckles. Maria laughed. No way, she said. Why are wooden boats such a big deal? They look good in the water, said Paul. Oh, I know, said Maria. It's what boats are supposed to be made of.

We stayed for the last heat and then swam again while the crowd thinned. Normally we'd have waited until dusk, leaving only when the police closed the park, but there'd been a stiff breeze out of the northwest all day and storm clouds were gathering upriver. Paul and I knew that Mom and Dad were out for the evening, so we suggested going back to our place. Char thought Paul was crazy until he explained that we'd have the house to ourselves — except, of course, for Grandma Carnelli.

PAUL PARKED the car around the corner just to be safe. Char and Maria walked ahead of us. Paul and I were still talking about the thunderboats as we approached the house and heard the television blaring. Grandma Carnelli, taking advantage of her time alone, was watching her favorite show, *Truth or Consequences*. The rest of the neighborhood was listening to it with her. We went in to say hello and Maria turned down the volume. I asked Grandma Carnelli if she remembered Char and Maria. You insult me, she said. How could I forget? And are my grandsons treating you like they should? Char and Maria took this opportunity to air their grievances. They said that Paul and I were incapable of remembering special occasions, like birthdays, anniversaries, and Valentine's Day. They said they enjoyed music but didn't like competing with it all the time. They said they loved to go dancing, but they only danced with each other. I thought dating a musician would be great, said Maria. You know, a guy with rhythm. A man who can dance. Musicians don't dance, said Char. Grandma Carnelli laughed and said, Sounds like you're all very happy.

We asked Grandma Carnelli a few questions and got her talking about Grandpa and the old days, and she told us the story of my uncle Jim, her first born, a hockey player who died of internal bleeding after a stick jabbed him in the stomach. He'd been scouted the day before by the Detroit Red Wings. She changed the subject after that, saying that my mother was a precocious beauty when she was a little girl. She said that Carrie Ann read important books like *Jane Eyre* and *Wuthering Heights* while she was still in elementary school. Then Grandma Carnelli talked about Italy and how poor her family had been and how my grandfather had promised her a better life.

It had begun to rain while she was talking, and now a flash of lightning broke her train of thought. Enough stories, she said. She asked Char and Maria if Paul and I could play a few songs for her. Char and Maria said yes. Paul and I jumped at the opportunity.

No one else in our family ever asked us to play, except Uncle Stephen.

We all went downstairs where Paul and I had set up a makeshift studio. Paul found a couple of song bibles and we played the standards that Grandma Carnelli said were her favorites. Paul alternated between electric piano and guitar, and I went back and forth between bass and flute. We played *Moonglow, Fools Rush In, My Funny Valentine, As Time Goes By,* and *My Foolish Heart.* We played *Blue Moon, Sentimental Journey, I'm Thru With Love,* and *Moonlight Serenade.* Then we played songs for Char and Maria, songs by the Beatles and Buffalo Springfield and Van Morrison. We did some Motown. We did Elvis and Del Shannon and Sam Cooke. We played every song we knew and many we didn't know. In between songs we listened to the rain. Grandma Carnelli stayed for all of it. Selena wandered in after we'd been at it for a while. We had a grand chorus for *Brown Eyed Girl.* We played until Mom and Dad came home.

On the last Sunday of July a policeman showed up at our front door. He asked my father if he'd heard a shotgun blast. My father shook his head. The officer checked his notes. The call came in around noon. Anyone else in the house hear anything? You can ask my mother-in-law, said my father. But she's deaf. I laughed and decided to head back to the kitchen. What about your boy there? The question made me feel like a man in a lineup. If I didn't hear anything, said my father, then what makes you think he heard anything? The policeman tipped his hat. Sorry to bother you, he said.

My father closed the door. Nothin' but dead wood, he said. That's what my tax money pays for — a cop with more belly than brains. I guess he's bored stiff.

'Dead wood' was another of my father's favorite expressions. He used it to describe welfare recipients, politicians, and priests. He used it to describe most of the men he worked with at the Tech Center. He had no regard for middle management, college graduates who sat behind desks and collected big paychecks without breaking a sweat. He had no regard for the janitorial staff. Broom pushers and toilet swabbies are overpaid, he said. Only the model makers in my father's shop were spoken of with respect, and some of them were written off as bachelors or rummies.

I thought of General Motors as loaded with dead wood. I imagined employees piled high in offices. They looked to me like stacks of lumber, not unlike the stacks of mahogany and pine that my father smuggled out of the Tech Center and stored in our basement. GM was bloated with people and raw materials. The Tech Center had too much of everything. My father judged and apportioned this excess.

After living in Detroit for twenty-three years, my father felt surrounded—both figuratively and literally—by dead wood. Trees in the neighborhood, even trees we planted, were beginning to die. A case in point was the small black maple in our back yard.

On the Friday before the policeman showed up we cut it down and pulled up the stump. We were forced to do this work without Paul. My brother had received a graduation card from Aunt Elvira inviting him up north for a few days in July. Up north meant Aunt Elvira's cottage on Lake Huron. Paul loved the place, especially the boathouse and the boat. My father knew, of course, that weekend chores would take longer without Paul, so he came home early on Friday and dragged me out to examine the black maple for the last time. Half its branches were bare. We could point to the scars and cracks made by the winter ice, but we did not see the tree's misery until we started cutting. A cross section of the larger limbs revealed disease and rot. Something had wormed its way into the tree; it was eating the tree from the inside out. A similar thing had happened to the mountain ash in the front yard. I remember my mother's grim face when the branches began to fall. My father kept saying, It has to come down. The words sounded like a prayer. He repeated the words while he sawed and chopped. It has to come down, he whispered, speaking to no one, not even himself. He said the same thing now.

We were still sizing up the job when I asked my father if he'd seen the nest of cardinals in the young pine tree near the fence. He nodded. It's lucky the mother put her nest over there, he said. It's a good choice. Evergreens are scrappers. Winter knocks 'em for a loop but they never stay down. I heard chirping and looked in the direction of the sound. I caught a glimpse of the mother's red crest as she disappeared behind a screen of branches.

The black maple went quickly. We stacked the logs and then started on the roots, trying to loosen the stump. We could burn it out, said my father. The idea of a bonfire appealed to me. Want me to get the gasoline? My father shook his head. We'd have to dig a trench first. It'd have to be wide and deep or we might set the whole place on fire. On the shelf in the garage is that long chain — the heavy one. Get that instead.

We looped the stump and some of the fatter roots and then brought the car around the side of the house and attached the chain to the trailer hitch. We were almost ready to start when the neighborhood alley cat came out from behind a honeysuckle bush. It was a ragged animal, much larger than a regular house-cat, bearing scrapes, hot spots, and a chopped ear. It was white and orange with large, green eyes. Its shoulders moved up and down like the leopards I'd seen at the zoo.

My father seemed unaware of the cat as we made our way back to the stump to check and tighten the chain. I was about to ask him if I could start the car when his level hand told me that I shouldn't move or make a sound. The cat stared at us, standing amidst my father's roses like a statue.

For a second the whole world became stone. I didn't breathe. I heard blood rushing in my ears. Then my father's arm whipped into motion and the hatchet that had been on the ground between us sailed straight for the cat's green eyes. The animal bolted and was gone. The hatchet kicked up dirt and slammed into the fence. Goddamn alley cat, said my father. He'll think twice before he comes back.

I WOKE UP early on Saturday. Long shadows crowded the back yard. I poured myself a glass of orange juice and put the cereal boxes on the kitchen table. Soon the floor creaked and the china cabinet in the dining room rattled. I heard these sounds every time my father walked through the house. He came into the kitchen and walked over to the sink and looked out the window. Won't rain today, he said. His face hardened after that. Christ almighty, he growled. Then he rushed outside and ran toward the pine tree.

When he got there he had a heavy rake in his hands, but he was too late. I walked up behind him and saw the mangled nest on the grass and two or three feathers marking the mother's struggle. My father held the rake with two hands across his body. She didn't build it high enough, he said.

My father backed the Oldsmobile out of the garage and drove away. He left without giving me instructions. He left without saying where he was going. I toyed with the idea of taking off, but I didn't have the guts. I went to check the list of chores but it wasn't there. I wandered around outside and then stretched out under the cherry tree. I heard Selena playing scales. I decided to wait.

My mother came out and swept the back porch. Where's your father? She asked me this without any agitation in her voice. I got up slowly. I don't know, I said. Maybe he's gone for good. My mother stopped sweeping and walked over to where I was standing. Watch your mouth, she said. Some people get what they wish for. I almost smiled. Fine by me, I said. She turned and headed back toward the house. She sharpened the edge in her voice. You should show more respect than that, she said. I followed her. Why should I show respect? He doesn't respect me. My mother kept walking. We went through the back door and into the dining room. She turned and faced me. You and your brother are both ungrateful. You're both selfish—just like your father. The comparison infuriated me. What do you expect? I said. We've had a good teacher. My mother nodded. So you've picked up his sarcasm, too. You say awful things about your father, but you live under his roof. You eat the food he buys you. She sounded more like Grandma Carnelli than herself. We don't live with him, I said. We live around him. You know it better than anyone. For God's sake, we have to walk on tiptoe any time he's in the house. My mother raised her hand. That's enough, she said. You don't have it so bad. I should've allowed her the last word. I should've given her that. I said, You're right. I'll eventually get out. You can't.

In that instant she shrank. Her housedress suddenly sagged, hanging on her bones like old skin. She lowered her head and moved toward the kitchen. Grandma Carnelli stood in the doorway. She tightened her lips. She looked at me as if I were a stranger.

When my father came back he had four cans of cat food and a tube of rat poison. He rummaged through the kitchen cupboards looking for clean margarine tubs. Above the fridge, said my mother. My father grabbed a stack and went out into the garage.

Seeing the old skull and crossbones surprised me. I don't get it, I said. I thought the stuff didn't work. You said the cat ate it up — even liked it. My father put portions of cat food in each tub and then stirred in large dollops of rat poison. This brand is stronger, he said. You see. It even smokes a little. The other kind never smoked.

That afternoon we trimmed the bushes along the back fence and sprayed the roses. When we were finished we placed the cat food around the yard. I went over and checked the latch on Knute's gate.

My parents attended eight o'clock mass every Sunday. So did Grandma Carnelli, no matter where she was living. I came upstairs at nine and the house was still empty. Probably Father Hastings or Father McGovern, I thought. Neither could resist a captive audience. I forgot about breakfast and immediately checked the tubs. Three of the four were licked clean and surrounded by the cat's unmistakable paw prints.

My father was not in a peaceful state of mind when he came home from church. He said, Hastings loves himself. You'd think he invented the English language the way he talks. Offer it up, said my mother. If boredom is the only cross God gives you, you're lucky. My father changed into his work clothes. Well? Did the cat take the bait? Three times, I said.

We set to work scraping and priming the window frames on the back of the house. It wasn't bad working in the shade, and Grandma Carnelli brought us cold glasses of iced tea. We finished four windows before noon.

I've got fresh salami, my mother said. She opened the butcher paper and the sweet smell made me hungry. I followed my father downstairs and we washed in the set tub. I came up first and took the chair closest to Grandma Carnelli. My mother asked if I wanted mayonnaise or butter on my sandwich. A good grandson would take butter, I thought. I almost chose it. Then I changed my mind.

I'd taken a huge bite of my sandwich by the time my father sat down. I looked out the window and watched the roses bending in the breeze. The blooms were pink, yellow, white, and orange — and then some of the orange spilled out of the flowerbed. I stopped chewing. Dad, I said, cramming the salami and bread into my cheek. It's the cat.

He ran through the house without making a sound, and by the time I was up from the kitchen table and in the dining room, he was heading for the back door and loading his shotgun. He shoved in the second shell and locked the breech. In one movement he kicked the screen door open and raised the gun. The cat turned and panicked. It froze in the very second that my father squeezed off both barrels.

The etched glass of the china cabinet shuddered. Antique plates slipped and shattered. My mother screamed. Grandma Carnelli clapped her hands in delight. Loud enough to raise the dead, she shouted.

My father let out his breath. The recoil should've dislocated his shoulder, but he was rooted to the floor like an old stump. The blast had taken out two or three roses. Now there was bright red splattered on the rest. I smelled the powder and heard the breech break open. My father pulled the spent shells. The salami and bread were still wadded in my cheek.

I watched my father stand the shotgun in the corner behind the china cabinet. I watched him go back to the kitchen table and pour his beer. Then he walked over to the counter and spread a thin layer of mayonnaise on two slices of Italian loaf. Next came a careful stack of salami, lettuce and tomato. He made it himself because my mother had gone outside in a flurry of concern about the neighbors.

We ate in silence. I washed down what was left of my sandwich with the beer my father didn't finish. It was then the policeman showed up, the cat still in pieces in the back yard.

chapter eleven

LETHEA STRONG said, You get ninety-nine years of bad luck for killin' a cat. Lethea didn't say this to me. I never heard her speak. She died in Cleveland on the first day of September in 1945. She died while looking at postcards that she kept in a shoebox.

Lethea's name would mean nothing to me if not for Uncle Stephen. The short stories he wrote and never published were about her. One of the stories included a list of her favorite sayings. Uncle Stephen always talked about Lethea. He made her a legend in our family. He said he owed her that much.

A priest visited Lethea on the last day of her life. He wasn't there to hear her confession or perform the last rites. The call was social. The priest and Lethea talked about the end of the war. Lethea said, At least now I know it's done. The priest had come to tell her about the Tollman boy. The one, he said, with the stutter.

Is he runnin' with those hoodlums again? He's not to blame, said Lethea. The child's been left out too many times. The priest shook his head. No, it's not that. Myron tells me he'd like to be a priest.

Lethea did something then that made the priest uncomfortable. She laughed. She laughed and coughed for a long time. So Myron's lookin' to sign up, she said. He's finally found a club that'll have 'im as a member. Did you know the military passed him by? They said his stutter made him unfit for service.

The priest adjusted his collar. Well, he could present a certain kind of risk in dire situations. Lethea laughed and coughed again.

What do you know about it? You've never been in the line of fire. Not in your uniform. The priest sized up Lethea. It depends which fire you're speaking of.

Lethea laughed for the third time. She did not cough. Fair enough, she said. But Uncle Sam should've taken him. His oldest brother went in before the whole thing got started. Long before Pearl Harbor. Oh, it's easy enough to understand. Myron wanted to take care of his mother. But Jessie had Stephen for that. So Myron felt odd about stayin' home. Then when the military brass said no, he started runnin' with gangs. He's not a bad boy. He just wants to belong.

You know all the children on the west side, said the priest. You brought most of them into the world. I thought you'd like to know that one of them has been chosen by God.

Then I hope God unchooses him, said Lethea. He's been alone most of his life. The kind of alone that's difficult to understand. And now he wants to join God's fraternity and live without a woman and die without children.

The priest had never known Lethea to be so forthright. You've lived without a husband, he said. He waited for an explanation. He waited for a second cup of tea. He said later that Lethea's last words followed him out the door. Tell God to leave him alone, she said. Tell him to choose somebody else.

Lethea must have struck a bargain with God. Maybe she offered her own life for Myron's freedom. Maybe she bartered her soul. Whatever the price, God sacrificed his potential shepherd.

THE SEMINARY turned out to be an unfriendly place. It became, for Myron, an impossible regimen of intellectual and moral discipline. Six months put him back on the streets of Cleveland looking for work.

Myron found a job and his first and only love at a service station. For the first few weeks he pumped gasoline and checked dipsticks and washed windshields. He exchanged pleasantries with the young wife of the grizzled and gap-toothed proprietor. The wife and Myron's boss lived in a small apartment above the garage. Sometimes the wife totaled the receipts and locked the cash register before closing. She flirted with Myron whenever possible. She said she liked the way he handled fan belts and spark plugs. She asked if she was the reason for his stutter.

On Tuesdays and Thursdays the boss played bingo at the neighborhood church. So on those evenings Myron washed his hands and visited the wife upstairs. He left the smell of gasoline on her body and on the bed. It was a Thursday before payday when the boss came home early from bingo and found the boy he'd trusted sweating on top of his wife. Myron lost love and two weeks' pay that night. He nearly lost his balls.

He drifted from job to job after that. He never found the woman that Lethea wanted him to find. Eventually he stumbled into the glassworks and a monastic life with Max. Lethea looking down must have felt betrayed. She must have questioned God's goodness, His sense of fairness and proportion.

OF COURSE the seminary and the young wife were still ahead of Myron on the day of Lethea's funeral. He listened to the priest speak mystical words over the coffin. He and his brother Stephen and six other young men had been asked to carry the casket to the hearse. Incense filled Myron's nostrils and organ music filled his ears. He thought he felt the grace of God giving him strength.

Lethea's funeral was the largest that anyone could remember. All the west side families filled the church and the overflow of mourners filled the steps and the street around the waiting cars.

And as the coffin moved through the crowd, some of the people thought they felt the pressure of a hand, or two hands, upon their arms or faces.

Jessica Tollman was the first person to speak of it. She sat in a pew reserved for herself and her two sons Stephen and Myron. Stephen had brought two photographs. One was a faded picture of Margie standing on the porch of the Mayfield schoolhouse. The other was a picture of his older brother in uniform. The pall-bearers were called. At that moment Jessica felt familiar hands cradling her face. She even tried to touch the person that seemed to be in front of her. She found nothing but air.

Stephen felt a weight on his shoulder in the minute before he raised the coffin. Myron thought he felt fingers on his lips. Other friends came forward with similar stories in the days after the funeral. In time people believed that the touch they felt was Lethea's. Her way was unmistakable, they said.

Jessica's eldest son was crossing the Atlantic on the day Lethea was buried. He read Jessica's telegram when he arrived at Fort Sheridan. The excitement of being back in the States and the antic-ipation of his discharge made the news of Lethea's death almost irrelevant. He traveled to Cleveland. He listened to his mother and brothers describe their experiences at the funeral. He said he hoped such things were impossible. The next day he left for Detroit.

ONLY UNCLE Stephen and Grandma Tollman knew about Myron's time in the seminary and his ill-fated love affair. My father was out of the loop. He barely spoke to his family in the months just after the war. His days were filled with my mother and the big house on Three Mile Drive and plans for the wedding.

Myron was smart to keep his life under wraps. He probably knew that my father would ridicule his bid for the priesthood. I realized this when my mother, against my father's wishes, took a job in the St. Veronica rectory doing secretarial work for the parish priests. She came home each day with anecdotes about her bosses. She talked about their patience and understanding and good humor.

If I never worked, said my father, I'd be patient and understanding too. My mother scrunched up her face. I recognized the expression. Her mouth and nose did the same thing when she discovered spoiled food in the refrigerator. Father Helner cares about people, she said. My father looked at my mother as if she were a child. And who pays him to care? he asked. I do. I put five bucks in the basket every week. I carry him on my back like dead wood. My mother would not give it up. Your five dollars, she said. All you can think about is your five dollars.

Paul walked in and saw me listening. Rarely did I interrupt. This time, though, I couldn't help myself. Seeing Paul pumped up my nerve. Why do you go to church? I asked. Why do you give the church your money if you don't believe in it? My father turned his eyes toward me. He seemed surprised that I could speak. Because I promised your mother I'd go with her as long as we were married.

You need a lot more than church, she said. Paul passed through the kitchen and tossed an unopened letter on the table. Then let's trade jobs, said my father. You go to the Tech Center and I'll go to the rectory and have lunch with the priests. I wouldn't mind eating stuffed olives and finger sandwiches for a change. My parents paid no attention to the envelope. It'd be good for you, said my mother. Maybe they can save you. My father steadied himself for the kill. A leech can't save the body it clings to, he said.

My father left the kitchen by the side door. My mother went out into the dining room. I walked over to the table and saw a government seal on the envelope. I knew what it was.

Paul came in and saw the letter opener in my hand. Don't bother, he said. I already know what it says. I knew that to believe it I had to see it in print. The language was terse. The military wasted no words.

ON THE FIRST day of August Grandma Carnelli moved out. On the second day Paul burned his draft notice. The rooms in the house already felt empty. I imagined them emptier still. Paul and I kept our beds in the basement, complaining about the heat upstairs. We talked about Canada. We listened to presidential candidates promise peace with honor in Vietnam. We knew about napalm and fragmentation bombs. We knew what Warren Christopher and Robert McNamara looked like.

We were learning fast that summer. Names and events washed over us in waves. Every television screen and newsstand shouted the names James Earl Ray and Sirhan Bishara Sirhan. The constant repetition threatened to drown out everything else. Conspiracy theories were discredited. Ray and Sirhan joined Oswald in a trinity of lone assassins. In the background, Benjamin Spock pleaded for gentler parenting. Abbie Hoffman and Jerry Rubin worked to foment bloody revolution. Black Panthers shot it out on the streets of Oakland. The Fugs played the Avalon Ballroom in a mythical city called San Francisco, and Phil Ochs sang in support of the *Resistance*. All this took its time getting to us in Detroit. Paul and I were still trying to figure out Hendrix and Haight-Ashbury and *Sgt. Pepper's Lonely Hearts Club Band*. I remember going back to Elvis, to Gene Pitney, and the Righteous Brothers. I had to. Their music made sense.

I think now that my brother and I were blessed by an inescapable Midwestern dullness. Rust Belt pragmatism blinded us to the real news. Paranoia and political double-talk convinced us that the world's business went on in secret. For all this we should've been grateful. We were never forced to confront the world as it was.

It would've been impossible for us to conceive of Agent Orange or McNamara having doubts about Vietnam. We read about LSD and Timothy Leary, but somehow we missed the bus and the Merry Pranksters, missed the bus driver, Neal Cassady, who walked off one morning into oblivion. We missed Allen Ginsberg mourning his muse. We went to the movies and watched *The Graduate*, *Bonnie and Clyde*, *Guess Who's Coming to Dinner*, *Cool Hand Luke*, and *In the Heat of the Night*. The stories raised questions without offering solutions. They presented more possibilities than we could use. In our neighborhood we saw families on welfare; on television we saw Jean-Claude Killy and Peggy Fleming winning gold medals. We knew Ed Sanders as a member of The Fugs, but we didn't know his poetry or his mentors, Kerouac and Olson, or that in the company of Ginsberg and others he attempted to exorcise the grave of Senator Joseph McCarthy. We didn't take seriously the Governor of California. We didn't think about Richard Daley's announcement that *from now on police will shoot to kill arsonists and shoot to maim looters*. We couldn't possibly imagine Charles Manson hanging out with Brian Wilson at the old Will Rogers estate on Sunset Boulevard. We didn't know that Manson played guitar or that the bloated Beach Boy called him the Wizard.

Most of that summer got away from us in the end. We were certain of our confusion. That much I remember. We were certain that the war in Vietnam would not end, that Paul would go first and I would follow. We were certain that King and Kennedy were dead.

———

AUGUST WAS hot. Asphalt turned spongy and steamed in the rain. It radiated heat all night. Flowers wilted and trees collapsed. Street people hunted for shade and water. No corner of Detroit escaped the light.

Paul lived for the heat. He moved through high humidity like a tropical cat. He barely broke a sweat. I hid from the sun. Sticky air hung on me like sandbags. I knew that standing in an open field at midday required strength. Full exposure demanded a specific kind of honesty. I felt better in the shade, even more comfortable under a roof. I felt freer at night.

August delivered twelve consecutive days without rain or clouds. A dozen days of unbroken sunlight. Such clarity was unusual for Detroit. God must be looking for something, my mother said. That's crazy, I said. How can God lose anything if he sees all things? My mother smiled. Don't be so smart, she said.

I woke up each morning and looked for clouds. I did dances for rain. I wanted to hear thunder rumbling in the distance. When I was very young and my mother put me to bed, she told me stories. And when we heard a storm approaching, she'd say the elves were bowling. I pictured gnomes with long beards and stocking caps playing ninepins on a cloud. And I remember my surprise when I found the same image in *Rip Van Winkle*. Later I found notebooks in my mother's hand filled with words. For many years she wrote down almost everything. I never asked her why she stopped.

Somewhere in that time of unbroken light Maria announced that she was five days late. My stomach rose into my chest. Her body usually ran with the precision of a clock. But she told me not to worry. She said we'd be okay. I told her to let me know the minute anything changed. I said I could handle it.

I cursed the humidity and the sun. I told Paul and he told Char and they sat with me some of the time and admitted that they'd been through it before. Did you use anything? asked Paul. It was the right time of month, I said. Paul looked at Char. He cracked his knuckles. There's never a right time of month, he said.

Through the long afternoons I sweated and prayed oh Jesus Christ don't let her be pregnant. Dear Jesus please don't let her be pregnant. Please please please sweet Jesus. If you'll only keep her from getting pregnant I'll do anything you say. I won't complain about anything ever again. There's not a single kind of problem that I will call a problem if you get me out of this problem. I believe in you. I'll tell everyone in the world to believe in you.

On the third day of waiting Maria called very early in the morning to say that she'd started. The next night Maria and I slept together. I had some difficulty at first. When we finished, we talked about being pregnant—how it's not such a scary thing. I never told Maria about Jesus. I never told anybody.

DINNER DURING the August heat wave was a quick and mostly silent affair. My mother cooked meals on top of the stove in an attempt to keep the kitchen cool. My father didn't appreciate her efforts. I feel like I'm sitting in the oven, he said.

No one offered a word about Paul's draft notice. Each sweltering day gave way to the next without hope of conversation. I kept waiting for someone to say something. I blamed the heat. Too much daylight makes people tired.

My mother served chopped meat on potato with green beans every second or third evening. Paul smothered the steaming blandness with ketchup. My father didn't complain about the repetition. Chopped meat on potato was one of his favorite meals. But one night near the end of the heat wave, near the end of my mother's dependence on chopped meat, my father put down his fork and looked across the table at Paul. What do you plan to do?

he asked. Paul milked the moment for what it was worth. About what? he shrugged. My father kept looking at him. About Vietnam? My brother dragged his fork through the thin grease on his plate. I've been talking to an advisor at Macomb, he said. My mother brightened when she heard this. That's why school's important, she said. Now you can get a college deferment. My father shook his head. They're going to do away with just about all deferments, he said. I read it in the paper. Paul looked again at his plate. He said, The guy at school doesn't think so.

I don't give a rat's ass about some college advisor. You're not going. You can take a walk across the Ambassador Bridge instead.

I heard the familiar voice, the harsh cadence of the words, but I thought for a moment that this wasn't my father. I wondered if he'd been drinking. I wondered if Uncle Stephen had planted the idea.

If he goes to Canada, said my mother, he'll be a criminal. They won't let him come back. My father answered her without hardness or condescension. Leaving home is one thing, he said. Dying is another.

I stared at my father. I wanted to remember what he looked like just after he said those words. I tried to memorize his face but there wasn't enough time. He leaned back in his chair. How long before you have to report to Fort Wayne? October tenth, said Paul.

School will have started by then, said my mother. Then you can get your deferment. My father lost his patience. Maybe if he was a senator's son he'd get one. But I'm telling you, Carrie Ann, school won't keep him out. Not anymore. My mother began stacking the dinner plates. You think you know it all, she said. The Pastorelli boy is a draft dodger—and now no one at church talks to the family. My father said something about churchgoers and my mother called him a louse, and then Paul wedged himself into the argument. I've asked Charlene to marry me, he said. For a moment there was unspoiled silence—but only for a moment.

My mother said she wouldn't allow it. My father agreed. They left Char out of it at first and talked about her parents. Mr. Kingsly was the owner and operator of Brighten Buffing. He was in the business of finishing steel and chrome for the auto industry. His wife watched over the books and their six children.

I've known people who operate shops, and I've known the people who work for them, said my father, and most of 'em wind up bankrupt or worse. Paul decided to throw fuel on the fire. Mr. Kingsly offered me a job, he said. My mother dropped a handful of silverware. Do you hear that, Carrie Ann? Your darling boy plans to work in a sweatshop. It should be quite a homecoming after Vietnam.

And I suppose Mrs. Kingsly loves the idea, said my mother. She knows a good thing when she sees it. My parents had met Mrs. Kingsly and most of her daughters at a school event the year before. The encounter fluttered with friendly smiles and gracious handshakes, but after a while I sensed my mother's snobbery. Several of the girls embraced my parents, talking effusively about Paul and Char as the perfect couple. When we returned home, my mother rattled around the house in a nervous state. Char's sisters are wonderful, I said. My mother nodded. They're very open, she said. After that she said she needed a bath. Now she insisted that Paul was being manipulated. That's a family of opportunists, she said.

Paul was pummeled with questions. Who's paying? Is she pregnant? What about the future? How will you support a wife? Why now? Why not wait? Paul answered none of these. He said he couldn't go to Vietnam without marrying Char. Then it's simple, said my father.

My mother asked Paul if he'd thought about a reception. My father pointed out that there was no reason to think about a reception because no one was getting married. Paul said that Mr. and Mrs. Kingsly had offered to host a small party in their basement. My mother's voice became shrill. Your aunts and uncles have never set foot in Roseville. My father almost smiled. Not a basement in Roseville, he said. That's for sure. My mother picked up our greasy plates. This is what happens when you run around with tramps, she said.

My brother flinched. I could see no other register of his animosity. He headed for the door and I followed him. My mother told us to sit down. We ignored her. My father did not move.

Once we were outside, Paul said, The two of 'em can go to hell for all I care. I don't want 'em at the wedding. I'll have a better time if they're not there.

What will you do? I asked. Paul stopped and leaned against the fender of the Oldsmobile. I'll do what I want, he said. I'll get married without 'em. I knew that Paul was resting on the car because he'd been told not to. I don't mean that, I said. I'm talking about going over. You know, splitting on a permanent basis.

Paul didn't say anything at first. He turned his head in the direction of Selena's house. Coming from the windows was a drifting, plaintive song. The melody kept wandering, somehow circling but never quite returning to its central theme. Sounds like she's making it up as she goes along, I said. We listened for a long time. If it was just me, said Paul, I'd go and try my luck. This surprised me. I knew that if I were drafted I'd make a lot of noise about going to Canada. I also knew that when the time came I would never go. You've got more guts than me, I said. Paul ignored my admission. But I can't ask Char to do it. She loves her family. I think it'd kill her if she was that close but could never see them.

There was nothing to say after that. Selena's song kept going, rising up into the twilight like a prayer.

IN THE LAST weeks of August, Paul and I played six or seven gigs. We did a wedding, an anniversary party, and a bar mitzvah. We played a coffeehouse and a church picnic, reconfiguring the wedding band as a folk-rock quartet. We even played the Roostertail when two members of Fingal's Cave were hospitalized with food poisoning and Paul and I were asked to sit in.

Char and Maria came to the most of the jobs. They moved around the rooms and halls listening for problems with feedback and overall balance. They always commandeered a table for the band. Paul and I checked in with them between sets. Char sometimes made a list of the songs that she thought sounded the best. Maria enjoyed eavesdropping on the dance floor. She usually gave us a rundown on what the audience liked or didn't like.

During some of the breaks Char and Paul made plans for their wedding. They wanted a small ceremony in a chapel followed by a gathering at the Kingsly house. Char insisted on inviting the Tollman side of the family. Paul was against it. Never leave anyone out, said Char. Let them decide for themselves. Maria agreed. The two women also agreed that chocolate cake with chocolate frosting was more daring and certainly more appealing than traditional white cake with vanilla frosting.

Whenever a lull in the conversation occurred, Maria brought up Chicago. She wanted the four of us to go. She wanted to hang out during the Democratic National Convention. I kept telling her that Paul and I had booked too many gigs, but she ignored me. She said we could go early in the week and stay for just a day or two. We could take the train. She said that a lot of kids were planning to camp out in a place called Lincoln Park. Then they'll sleep with the cops and the National Guard, I said. We knew that Mayor Daley in preparation for a flood of demonstrators had shored up his police force with over six thousand soldiers. Maria said the Yippies were providing free concerts in the park: The Fugs and Country Joe and the Fish, and the MC5. There might be free LSD, she said. We could swim naked in Lake Michigan.

I slept well into the afternoon on the day before the convention opened. Maria woke me up by throwing a copy of *The Detroit News* on my bed. She said we were missing all the fun. On the front page was a picture of a pig. Maria didn't wait for me to read the article. That cute little guy is Pigasus, she said. The Youth International Party says he's their candidate for president. I don't want to go, I said. Neither does Paul.

Where don't I want to go? Paul asked, coming down the steps. Chicago, I said. My brother kissed Maria on the cheek. I try to avoid tear gas, he said. Maria believed that the kids would out-number the cops. Once the crowd gets big enough, she insisted, there's nothing they can do.

Maria was correct in theory, but the theory did not prove itself in Chicago. Far fewer demonstrators showed up than the Yippies or anyone had hoped for. As the week wore on, Daley and his cen-turions played it their way. In an effort to survive, some of the smarter kids living in Lincoln Park went to Marshall Field's and bought football helmets.

Rather than Chicago, Maria and I drove up to Ann Arbor for a day. We smoked marijuana in the park and bought a handmade candle from an ancient black man who lived in his car. We found stairwells and back alleys and subterranean doorways, and we unzipped our jeans and laughed and looked over our shoulders, struggling to prolong our unbearable excitement.

In those last days of August I tried to think about everything other than Vietnam. I made myself worry about school. I made Maria rearrange her schedule so that she could help me with chemistry. It seemed impossible to me that by next spring we'd be graduating. I thought about buying my first car, about going to college and getting out of my father's house. I thought about the wedding. I pictured Paul and Char living in a quiet place outside Detroit. After a while, nothing worked.

Paul accepted no bookings for September. He told the guys in the band to start looking for someone else. He gave me some of his electronic gear and sold a guitar that he no longer played. We began breaking up our basement studio. I hate it when summer ends, I said. We unplugged microphones and rolled up cables. I hate packing, said Paul.

I SAW A LOT less of Paul after Labor Day. He started classes at the community college and he stopped eating dinner at home. He'd show up after dark to take a shower and change his clothes. He'd leave again just before midnight, when Mother and Father were asleep, to spend the night with Char.

Senior year started for Maria and me, and with it came more homework than I could manage. My important class was Satirical Literature. I signed up for the elective because it was taught by Wayne Bogich, the best teacher in the school.

Not everyone shared my affection for Bogich. Some students called him intimidating. Some went further, calling him egotistical and condescending. He was, I suppose, an acquired taste. I tolerate nothing less than perfection, he said. I pursue nothing less than the sublime.

In opposition to common belief, Bogich insisted that stupid

questions exist. He said that needless repetition was the hobgoblin of little minds. He confessed that he hated students who complained about his favorite books. Your lack of compassion, he said, pierces my armor. He often told the story of a lion pursued by inexperienced hunters. There is nothing more tragic than incompetence, he said. It delivers death painfully and without respect.

He taught us logic through debate, maintaining absurd positions for the sake of argument. One student argued that the earth was round. The student lost. Anyone with courage enough to voice an opinion was fair game. Using sarcasm upped the ante. You can't have a battle of wits with me, said Bogich. You're totally unarmed. At all times there was a kind of electricity around the man. He shook his mane of dark hair. He flashed his black eyes. He dared us to follow the fury of his mind. For me Bogich was more than an English teacher. He was a way of life.

As a sophomore I had Bogich for Composition. That year he drove a yellow Cadillac to school and wore expensive suits and kept a huge roll of money in a gold clip. He made bets with students, flashing fifty and hundred dollar bills with the flamboyance of a lottery winner. The teachers at East Detroit High made him the president of their union. I'm the Hoffa of higher education, he said.

In class he taught the mechanics of writing with clarity and precision. He made the mastery of language a necessity. Those not up to the task were thrown out. Some were thrown over while sitting in their desks. Billy Kosmos, whose mouth ran like a leaky pipe, spent most of his time staring at the ceiling in his upturned chair. In such moments, Bogich appeared to be a spontaneous imp, a very smart boy in a man's body, but to underestimate his purpose was deadly. Today's lesson, he said, is everything that happens in this classroom. If you haven't the time or patience to study everything, then leave.

Unlike other teachers, he admitted to playing favorites. Teachers are lying, he said, if they deny having favorites. All human beings fall victim to favoritism and most teachers are human beings. He often identified his preferred students by asking them to sit in the first desk of each row. Students at the front of the class will receive higher grades, he said. He explained the school's grading system as a calculated extension of the capitalist economy. I'm the boss, he said. You guys are the laborers. The people I've put up front do the best work so they receive a higher rate of pay. Of course, some of the people up front do mediocre work, but they look good—and somehow their mediocre work looks good. These people get the highest grades because in the real world they'll get the highest pay.

Occasionally a school administrator showed up to observe Bogich in action. Most came and went in silence, though this wasn't always true of the sallow assistant principal. He asked, Do you think your theology is sound? This question came in the middle of a Bogich reverie about the sex life of Jesus Christ. I have my own trinity, said Bogich. The Father is drama, the Son is surprise, and the Holy Ghost is fun.

As a junior I took a class from Bogich that most of my peers advised against: Research Paper. The requirements for the final project included note cards, a detailed outline, twenty pages of text, formal footnotes, and a comprehensive bibliography. Points were assigned for each stage of the writing. Bogich insisted on depth and style. He demanded that we follow the rules. The final step was an oral defense. A committee consisting of two students and Bogich examined each writer. Don't worry, he said. If you've done the work, then the oral defense'll be fun. If you're a plagiarist, whether full-blown or marginal, there'll be nowhere to hide.

In the middle of that year Bogich abandoned his Cadillac and started driving a Harley Davidson to school. He carried his helmet in one hand and his briefcase in the other. Sometimes he wore leather pants that matched his leather jacket. In the spring he started skydiving. Billy Kosmos asked him why he wanted to jump out of planes. Well, said Bogich. My doctor says I have a heart condition. He says I should avoid excitement. No one at the time took him seriously. We all laughed at the joke. It turned out that congenital heart disease had killed most of the men in the Bogich family before they were fifty.

On the first day of Satirical Literature, Bogich complained about his knees. He said they were useless. Where most people have kneecaps, he said, I have water balloons. He made a remark about oversleeping, about heaving his alarm clock at the wall. He said that satire was the only consolation in a fallen world. A rumor was circulating that his wife and kids had left. I didn't believe it.

Wayne Bogich died the night before our third class. He was forty-four. He was cleaning his collection of guns when one of the rifles discharged into his stomach. His wife and kids had been gone for several months. There was no one there to find him.

The school community displayed equal amounts of grief and outrage. School officials described his death as senseless. Some students wept. Others felt nothing. There was a short eulogy in the school newspaper.

I thought about his death for a long time. I tried to imagine his hidden life. I wanted to find a recognizable pattern, something familiar and less threatening. But the logic escaped me until I was older. Only then could I assemble the order of events—the motorcycle given to a friend, the trusts arranged for the children, the guns in a careful row waiting to be cleaned.

When it happened I shared my sadness with no one. Then, as the months passed, I found myself telling anecdotes about Bogich to anyone who would listen. I repeated his words. I tried to remember everything. Most people were polite. Some were pleasantly entertained. I made up nothing. I retold the stories he told and tried to explain their meanings. But his one essential lesson eluded me until I was far away from East Detroit High School, far away from the house on Lincoln Street. It was the story he told most often, the tragedy of a belly-shot lion, enraged with pain, waiting in the brush, waiting in absolute silence, to spring the last time into darkness.

CONSIDER this: Roger Bacon, a thirteenth-century monk, dipped a candlewick into a mixture of potassium nitrate, charcoal, and sulfur. He hoped the black powder would make the flame larger and brighter. It worked, but only for an instant. The candle flared and popped. The eruption snuffed out the flame. When he increased the powder the reaction became more and more violent. No amount of powder could keep the light burning.

A fourteenth-century German monk named Berthold Schwarz used the black powder to propel a small ball of lead. This was the first cannon. Refinements in design meant the cannon could be reduced in size. Soon it was small enough to fit comfortably in the hand. The portable cannon was convenient. It could be concealed beneath a loose fitting shirt or a military waistcoat. Someone called the diminutive cannon a gun. The fuel for the gun was Bacon's black powder. Everyone called it gunpowder by then.

Cloistered monks, men of education and spiritual beauty, gave gunpowder and the gun to civilization. Bogich must have known this, I thought. Irony is the only faith in a fallen world.

Addressing the Democratic National Convention, Senator Eugene McCarthy said, America is made of guns. Yes, I thought. And the Midwest is made of guns. And Michigan and Detroit and

East Detroit High School and Lincoln Street and my back yard are made of guns. I made a list of guns that I knew intimately or had observed in passing: an unloaded, antique derringer that Grandma Carnelli carried in her purse; the BB gun that my father gave me when I was ten; assorted hunting rifles in the trunks of cars; my father's shotgun; a Saturday night special beneath a cab driver's seat; another in a paper boy's bag; Bogich's collection of firearms; and a plethora of pistols that were fired into the sky on a cool September night when the Tigers became the undisputed champions of the American League. Even Knute next door asked me with a wink if a shotgun had prompted Paul's sudden wedding plans.

I began to realize that many of the people around me kept guns at the ready. I knew a guy who lived above Baldo's candy store. He could lay his hands on just about anything for the right price and at least three day's notice. His own collection included a grenade launcher. I also knew that most of the men in my neighborhood paid dues to the NRA. They called it a club for sportsmen. They spoke passionately about the Constitution and a citizen's right to bear arms.

Like all men of deep conviction, the neighborhood members of the NRA were tested. They were faced with a picture of Huey Newton sitting on a makeshift throne with a shotgun as his scepter. They were incensed and frightened. They should have been flattered. The Black Panthers had chosen the gun as their chief arbiter. They obviously understood the advantage of firearms when negotiating demands. They were observing the law of the land. They wanted to protect their bodies and their property. They wanted their own club.

Huey Newton and Bobby Seale were nothing more or less than students of culture. They knew that a white man with a gun commanded a certain kind of attention. They assumed that a black man with a gun would not be ignored. They were correct.

In September, leaders of the Black Panther Party announced that they would be sending representatives to Detroit. The *Free Press* speculated that the Panthers were looking to induct new members. Their stated purpose was to *shore up the besieged black community after the assassination of Martin Luther King and during a time of ongoing racial strife.* My father didn't believe a word of it. They're coming to burn down the rest of it, he said. The FBI says they've got an army of five thousand.

No one knew when the Panthers would arrive. No one knew where you could go to find one. None of this mattered to my father. He started drinking on Friday night. By Saturday evening he believed that the Panthers were in town and stirring up trouble. He sat on the front porch and watched cars as they drove by the house. He leaned forward in his chair whenever the faces going by were black.

Maria was away with her family for the weekend. Paul was with Char taking care of last minute details for the wedding. My friends were out on gigs. I could've gone for a walk. I could've spent some time at Carlucci's Café. Instead I stayed home.

My mother started to worry when the old man refused to go to bed. He would not give up the porch. Lots of niggers out drivin' tonight, he said. They're having a fine party. You can hear bottles rollin' around.

My father's favorite combination was a shot an' a beer. On the weekends he drank shots and beers all day. He said the whiskey warmed his stomach before the coldness of the beer. By the time my mother went out to talk to him he was drinking double shots. She picked up his empties and said she was going to bed. You can do that, he said. You can sleep through anything. My mother glanced at the empty street. She came into the house and asked me to sit with him for a while. Throw a blanket over him when he passes out, she said.

I sat down on the porch steps. My father didn't acknowledge my presence. The only sound was Selena's piano. He was listening, moving his head as the melody rose and fell. No one was out walking. Most of the houses were dark.

I saw one, said my father. He didn't look at me when he said it. You saw one what? I asked. He took a long time to answer. A bottle, with a piece of rag stuck in the top, he said.

I didn't believe him. You can't see a thing like that from here, I said. I wanted him to pass out. I wanted to go to bed.

I saw it, he said. Then he got up and went into the house.

I had enough time to gulp down a fresh can of beer he'd left behind. I crushed the can and stepped inside. I was turning the deadbolt on the front door when he walked out of the living room darkness with his shotgun. You're with me, he said.

He led me into the garage and we took down the heavy extension ladder. We stumbled and scratched the Oldsmobile. I didn't ask what we were doing or why we were doing it. We carried the ladder around the back of the house and leaned it on the gutter where the roof was low. Let's go, said my father.

I thought about deserting him. I thought about taking his keys and the car and getting away as fast as I could. Then I thought about him drunk and by himself on the roof. I followed him up.

Jesus fucking Christ, he said, slipping on the dewy shingles. Somehow he managed not to slide or drop the gun. We made it to the peak and crawled over to the chimney. The night was moonless. It was perfectly still except for our breathing. Selena had stopped playing.

I heard cars in the distance. I saw headlights through the

branches of big trees. My father sat at the top of a valley with his shoulder against the chimney. I sat next to him. He pulled two shotgun shells out of his back pocket and opened the breech. I could see his fingers shaking when he loaded the gun. He took a deep breath and steadied himself.

He's getting ready to kill someone, I thought. He's getting ready to shoot. For a moment I floated outside myself, looking down on the absurdity of the situation. Then a car suddenly appeared and nearly stopped in front of the house. My father took aim. The driver seemed to be looking for a particular address. The car moved off slowly and my father lowered the gun.

We sat watching for a long time. I regretted drinking the beer. My mouth was dry and I had to piss. I asked him if we could go down. He did not answer. He kept his eyes on the street, turning his head toward any sound that seemed out of place. At one point a helicopter flew overhead. A long time after that we heard the squeal of tires and a car raced down Lincoln. It stopped at the cross street and burned rubber as it turned the corner and sped off.

The hours paralyzed me. I spent most of the time massaging the cramps in my legs. I rolled over on my side when my ass fell asleep. My father stayed awake all night.

From my perch on the roof I saw very little that was human. I did see two stray dogs and a fat raccoon. Something that looked like an enormous rat darted through the light from the street lamp. What I did not see were demonstrators, agitators, rioters, Black Panthers, or Molotov cocktails.

My father and I climbed down just before daylight.

IT'S NOT RIGHT, said my father. It's just not right. He muttered these words to himself or to my mother like a man in a trance. He seemed to say nothing else in the days just prior to the wedding. On the morning of the ceremony he had a shot an' a beer for breakfast. He stood in the kitchen and bent back the fingers of his left hand. I waited for the sound but his knuckles would not pop. He pushed and pulled until a sudden pain made him gasp. He spoke again, repeating himself like a scratched record. He had another shot an' a beer while my mother took a bath. The booze amplified his refrain.

Uncle Stephen came by early and asked me if I wanted to ride with him. His blue Corvette sparkled in the sun. My father had gone back to bed. My mother was still in her robe, moping around the house like a deserted woman. She didn't acknowledge Uncle Stephen. She told me to straighten my tie. If you and Dad decide to come, I said, don't let him drive.

I should say good morning, said Uncle Stephen. He looked in the living room and then disappeared down the hallway that led to the bedroom. I waited in the kitchen. I caught my reflection in the toaster and fussed with my collar. Uncle Stephen was back in no time at all. He kissed my mother on the cheek and dropped his keys into my hand. You drive, he said. Uncle Stephen smiled when he saw the astonishment on my face. You're wearing a classy suit, he said. You get to drive a classy car.

ONLY A FEW people were waiting at the chapel when I arrived. The bride was nowhere to be seen, but two of her sisters, radiant in their formal gowns, were decorating the altar with flowers. Paul and Mr. Kingsly stood in the door of the sacristy. Paul kept checking his cufflinks. Mr. Kingsly kept adjusting his vest. Paul let out a deep breath when he saw me. You're early, he said. How'd you get here? I answered him quickly and casually. I drove the 'Vette, I said. Paul looked around, fingering the buttons on his coat. So where's Uncle Stephen? I brushed some lint off my brother's lapel. He had to run an errand, I said. He says it's a surprise.

Little by little the chapel filled up with friends and family. The entire Kingsly clan was there. So were most of the musicians from the east side. Most of my mother's sisters and brothers came from Grosse Pointe. Grandma Carnelli came too, and I escorted her to a front pew reserved for special guests. Then Uncle Stephen walked in with Uncle Myron and between them was Grandma Tollman. It was the first and only time I'd seen her outside the nursing home. She wore a deep green dress. Her long, silver hair fell in waves across her shoulders.

My two grandmothers sat together, one short and the other tall, one with peasant hands and the other with long, graceful fingers. Uncle Stephen and Uncle Myron sat behind the two women, leaving space in the first pew for my parents. They showed up at the last minute. They came in after Char and the rest of her sisters and Maria had arrived. My mother wore her well-rehearsed smile. My father wore a concrete face, like a patient late for a dental appointment.

The music started after my parents sat down. A young priest came out of the sacristy and stood on the lowest step in front of the altar. He gestured that we should stand. Then the organist began a joyous march and Char walked down the aisle with her father. The wedding dress and beaded veil made her seem untouchable and luminous. This is my sister, I thought. This is my brother's wife. Mr. Kingsly said later that he took hold of Char's arm like a man on roller skates. Good thing she was there to hold me up, he said.

I missed most of the ceremony because my father kept talking under his breath. Grandma Tollman shushed him several times. So did Uncle Stephen. Even my mother glared at him once or twice. He ignored all of it. Something amused him during the exchange of vows. I heard the beginnings of a chuckle, but no one else seemed to notice.

Maria nudged me when the priest told Paul that he could kiss the bride. There was an awkward silence after the kiss, and then the organist began the recessional. After that, Paul and Char greeted everyone in the vestibule of the tiny church. Uncle Stephen told Paul that Grandma Tollman was his wedding gift. Then he smiled and slipped an envelope into Paul's hand.

Mr. Kingsly was last in line, and I remember how Char embraced him, kissing him on the mouth and touching the deep lines on his neck. And in return Mr. Kingsly hugged his daughter as if he were seeing her for the last time. I watched him kissing her cheek and holding her dark hair between his fingers. The moment was beautiful and strange, so deeply personal that I wanted to look away. I tried to catch Paul's attention, but he was surrounded by friends. I asked Maria if she liked my suit. I asked her what she thought of the ceremony. I decided that making small talk was hopeless. My eyes kept going back to Char and her father. Stop staring, said Maria. I pulled her close to me and said I was sorry. No reason to be sorry, she said.

I asked Grandma Carnelli if she was going to the party at the

Kingsly house. She said she would if she could get a ride. Maria has a car, I said. Come with us. Maria liked the idea and wouldn't take no for an answer.

Most of my mother's family passed up the reception. But all the Tollmans came, including Max. Even my mother and father came, countering Paul's prediction that they'd cut out after the ceremony. My father set up shop near the bar, drinking highballs for a while and then whiskey on the rocks. He kept to himself most of the afternoon and evening while my mother did her best to socialize.

Some of the band members had brought instruments and equipment, and soon everyone wanted Paul to play a few songs. I joined him and so did the other guys and we played straight through to dinner. Maria handed me a beer somewhere in the middle of it all, and I heard myself making the same sad apology that I always made when I left her alone at a party. Play as long as you want, she said. You'll have to make this one last. But I didn't play very well after she said that. I started to think. I couldn't stop myself. I kept losing my place and forgetting the words.

Grandma Carnelli began dozing after dinner, so I told her I'd take her home. She promised Paul and Char that she would pray for a long and fruitful marriage. She hugged Maria and my mother.

GRANDMA was snoring by the time I got to Gratiot Avenue. I passed East Detroit High School. I passed a few of the bars where Paul and I had played. When I slipped over the city limit and into Grosse Pointe, I felt like a cat burglar. It must have been the silence in the car and my expensive suit.

I helped my groggy grandmother into the carriage house at the rear of my uncle's estate. I saw a light on in one of the bedrooms and wondered whether cash or jewels or both were locked in the safe. I imagined myself wearing white gloves and pausing on the staircase when it creaked beneath my feet.

Pulling away, I rolled down all the windows. The night air was cool and clean, but it didn't make me feel any better. I kept spinning the radio dial looking for a sad song. Nothing seemed to fit. I ran one yellow and two reds going back.

WHEN I GOT there, Maria was sitting near the bar with my father. I could see what she was doing. She was trying to draw him out. Trying to take his mind off the liquor. She'd done it before, though once it ended badly when my father stumbled and tore the sleeve of Maria's blouse.

The Kingsly basement looked well-used, filled with disheveled tables and dangling streamers. The party had begun the inevitable process of winding down. Paul ate the last piece of cake. Char ran upstairs to get out of her wedding dress. Mr. Kingsly poured himself a serious drink and sat down for a quiet moment with his wife. My mother sipped tea and continued a conversation with the young priest who performed the ceremony. She also kept an eye on my father, hoping that he'd go to the bathroom or wander outside for a breath of fresh air, waiting, I suppose, for the right moment to take him away. And Uncle Myron, ensconced at the Tollman table, puffed on a fat cigar and blew smoke rings at Max.

I sat down next to Max, interrupting Grandma Tollman in midsentence. Everyone at the table had been listening to her and now they looked at me. Is this a private conversation? I asked. Uncle Stephen reached over and laid his hand on my arm. Good work, he said. Ma's been talking about the old days. Maybe now she'll change the subject. Grandma Tollman sipped her water. Don't count on it, she said. John Kingsly, Char's only brother, sat across from me. He wanted to hear more. You can't stop now, he said,

You're just getting to the good part. A few of Paul's friends had also joined the table. They agreed with John. Over Uncle Stephen's shoulder I saw Maria with my father. She kept moving his drink, hoping he wouldn't find it.

James, you're just in time, said Grandma Tollman. I was telling everyone about a certain Miss Dossin, a schoolteacher, who caught the fancy of your father and your uncle Stephen. Myron too, but he wasn't old enough to fall in love. Uncle Myron rolled his cigar on the edge of the ashtray. I n-n-never loved anyone but . . . but you, M-Mom. Everyone at the table laughed. Phil was the man in love, said Uncle Stephen. Miss Dossin hardly knew I was alive. Grandma Tollman flattened her hands on the table and leaned forward. You're only telling half the truth, she said. Phil was smitten—there's no doubt about that—but so were you. Uncle Stephen twirled his finger next to his head. My mother can be a little crazy, he said. Someone chuckled, and then Grandma Tollman said, Well, if I'm crazy, then what does that make you? I'm not the one who came home with frostbite. Uncle Myron laughed. I *almost* got frostbite, said Uncle Stephen, because the ice broke and my feet got wet. Grandma Tollman nodded. That's the truth, she said. But he's not telling you all of it. Grandma Tollman lowered her voice like a woman revealing an important secret. It was a Sunday afternoon. It was bitter cold . . . *and* it was Miss Dossin's birthday. The faces at the table looked expectantly at Uncle Stephen. My son wanted Miss Dossin to have her gift on the actual day. He couldn't wait until Monday like everyone else. He wanted to be first. And he didn't want his big brother to see it.

Uncle Stephen was chagrined. He made a few mock protestations and then he smiled. All right, Mom, he said. Get on with it. You obviously know more about it than I do.

She told us about the frozen river that Uncle Stephen had to cross to get to Miss Dossin's house. She described the cracking ice and the water coming up over his ankles and the scramble to the bank. Anyone with winter experience would have turned around right then, she said. But not my son. On he went, walking all the way into town. His boots were frozen stiff by the time he got back. I unlaced them and pulled them off. His toes were purple. Needless to say, he wouldn't tell me where he'd been or why he'd stayed out so long. I'd almost forgotten about it, but then Miss Dossin sent a note saying how sweet it was that Stephen had left a gift on her doorstep. It was a simple thing. He'd carved the words Happy Birthday into a bar of perfumed soap. Miss Dossin said it was lovely.

Uncle Myron slapped Uncle Stephen on the back. Where'd you g-get the soap? Grandma Tollman seconded the question. I stole it, said Uncle Stephen.

Grandma Tollman made apologies for her son, the thief. She said that it's sometimes hard to know what your children are up to. My kids were always wandering off, she said. Margie was the worst. But Stephen was almost as bad.

I glanced again in the direction of Uncle Stephen and saw my father using Maria to prop himself up. I considered whether or not my father still had it in him to wander off, to turn the corner and disappear for a while. But then I remembered him going on about Cleveland, about the locations of buildings and streets, especially with Uncle Stephen. Listen little brother, he'd say, you were always roaming around and getting lost. But you have to look where you're going if you wanna get back.

I'd never taken much of it seriously until my father said, You were looking for him. Like you expected him to be standing on a street corner waiting just for you.

I looked at Uncle Stephen and pictured a young man searching the streets of Cleveland for his father, walking with the same determination that took him through the snow to deliver a bar of perfumed soap. I imagined him going out every night, wondering why it was that his father had slowly and steadily given up.

Char came down the steps. She wore jeans and tennis shoes. She looked like herself again. She said something to my father and then she hugged Maria. She came over to the table with Paul to say good-bye. I listened to the chorus of farewells. I watched the hand shaking and the kisses.

I thought about life without my brother. I tried to imagine how the days would be different. He hadn't lived at home in any conventional sense for a long time, but now his leaving felt official and permanent. His old accordion and his clothes and his stereo were gone. All his things were now in the Kingsly house. The newlyweds would have the comfort of an attic apartment until Paul reported for duty. They would honeymoon at the St. Clair Inn for two nights.

I followed Paul and Char up the steps and out onto the driveway. I shook my brother's hand. Char's sisters had tied a *Just Married* sign to the Mercury Comet, and now they threw handfuls of rice. The grains scattered across the black roof and hood like tiny hail. The car started rolling away from me, backing down the driveway. Paul looked over his shoulder and Char waved.

I waited for them to pull away. I tried to look happy. I tried not to feel sorry for myself. They'd been together almost two years. I'd known from the start that someday they would marry. I'd simply overlooked the fact that it would happen so soon. Marriage was for men and women, for people much older than we were. Marriage was the end of something.

Just then my mother came out of the house with my father in tow. You can come home with us, my mother said, dangling the keys. No thanks, I said. I'll catch a ride with Maria. My father was loaded and talking to himself again. It ain't right, I heard him say. Ain't right. He leaned on my mother like a punch-drunk fighter.

I was ready to go inside and find Maria when the Mercury Comet pulled into the drive and stopped. Char got out and ran around the front of the car. She touched my face. She said she was sorry but with all the confusion she'd forgotten to say good-bye properly. She kissed me on the mouth. She hugged me. In the next instant she was back beside my brother and the two of them stole away, speeding down the street toward an orange moon.

UNCLE STEPHEN surprised everyone by staying in Detroit for a week. I met him for lunch the day after the wedding. We talked about my father's drinking and Paul going to Vietnam. I told him that Maria and I had decided to date other people. He said he was sorry. It's okay, I said. We're cool. We just thought we should. We need to make sure.

Uncle Stephen nearly choked on his ham sandwich. I think you're a damn fool, he said. Then he drilled me with his eyes. You keep saying we, he said. Does Maria feel the same way? I swallowed a mouthful of potato chips. I think so, I said. Uncle Stephen hung his head over his plate. Now I know you're a fool. It's your idea and you talked her into it. Well, go ahead and test the waters. Dip your stick as often as you please. But don't expect Maria to be there when the tide goes out.

I tried to backpedal after that, but nothing I said seemed to work. After a while we dropped the subject. We talked about music for a time, but Uncle Stephen kept looking around the restaurant and checking his watch.

He paid the bill and then he pulled a newspaper clipping out of his wallet. This is the reason I'm staying in town, he said. The clipping advertised a show at Baker's Keyboard Lounge. I didn't know you were into jazz, I said. He smoothed out the small square of newspaper and pointed to a name. Never heard of her, I said. My ignorance came as no surprise. Uncle Stephen explained that Katherine Lennox was a hot ticket on the club circuit, a musician's musician. He said he had a reservation for three for the Sunday night show. Katherine Lennox is an old friend, he said. She knew your father too. He said nothing else about her.

I fired off a salvo of questions. Uncle Stephen answered only one or two. Katherine is a woman that both your father and I knew before the war, he said. He refused to elaborate. Have you talked to her lately? I asked. Have you heard her play? Uncle Stephen counted his change. I've seen her a few times, he said. Your father's not seen her at all. That's why we're going.

I shook my head like a wet dog. I was flabbergasted. You mean Dad's going too? Uncle Stephen laughed. I talked him into it yesterday, he said. With a little help from Maria. Now it's my turn to laugh, I thought. The old man was three sheets to the wind yesterday, I said. He won't remember a thing about it today. Then I reconsidered the reservation for three. It suddenly made sense. Mom turned you down, I said. Uncle Stephen nodded. She doesn't like nightclubs, he said. She hates jazz.

I FOUND my father bent over his workbench when I got back from lunch. His hands were steady. He remembered his conversation with Uncle Stephen. He said he was going. He said it was okay with him if I came along.

We worked in the yard that afternoon, edging flowerbeds and pruning bushes. I stuffed the cuttings into plastic bags. One of the overfilled bags split and spilled on the side drive. My father didn't seem to notice. He made no observation or suggestion. I proceeded to clean up the mess.

My mother interrogated my father over Sunday breakfast. Who is this Katherine Lennox anyway? she asked. If she was such a good friend, then why haven't I heard about her before this? And why are you going on a work night? It's a school night for Jim.

My father explained that his friendship with Katherine Lennox went back more years than he cared to remember. He pointed out that he knew none of my mother's girlhood friends and that he certainly didn't recall any names. He supposed that Katherine's name had come up once or twice, but who could possibly remember a passing conversation from twenty years ago. Jim's going, he said, because Stephen didn't want to waste the ticket.

My father said all this in a subdued, almost amiable voice. He seemed willing to explain things further. His benevolence was disconcerting. He stayed in for the remainder of the morning. He stayed in all afternoon, catching up, he said, on domestic chores. He sharpened my mother's knives, replaced the belt in the vacuum cleaner, changed the air filter in the furnace, and patched a crack in the dining room ceiling. He seemed lighter on his feet, moving quietly through the house, moving efficiently from one job to the next. He drank water when he was thirsty.

UNCLE STEPHEN picked us up after dinner. By then my father's mood had changed. He complained that his sport coat needed pressing. He argued with Uncle Stephen about the best way to go. This car rides like a brick, he said. These bucket seats are made for midgets. I sat sideways in the back and watched the neighborhoods change. It was a long trip.

The valet took the car and left the three of us standing at the curb. Let's get a drink before we go in, said my father. Wharton's Bar is just down the street. Uncle Stephen stopped to tie his shoe. They serve plenty of liquor inside, he said. He went in without us. My father tried to call him back. Booze is cheaper down the street, he said. But Uncle Stephen had disappeared.

My father glanced at an empty bench next to the door. I think I'll sit here for minute, he said. You feeling sick? I asked. I took a step toward him. Not at all, he said. You go ahead. The show'll go on without me.

I didn't understand his reluctance. And it made no difference to me whether or not he saw the performance. I turned back toward the door and ran into Uncle Stephen. He saw my father on the bench and asked him if he planned to sit there all night. My father made no reply. She'll ask about you, said Uncle Stephen. What should I say? My father looked up at his brother. You'll think of something, he said.

Uncle Stephen kicked a small stone against the building. He suddenly became angry. You son-of-a-bitch, he said. I'll pull your ass off that bench if I have to. Again my father made no reply. Several people were approaching the club. Uncle Stephen lowered his voice. Then stay here and choke on exhaust, he said. I don't give a damn.

I followed Uncle Stephen inside and the hostess gave us a good table. I asked for 7UP. Uncle Stephen ordered a vodka and tonic. You should go out and get your father, he said. Maybe you'd have more luck than me. I looked toward the entrance. What's going on? I asked. What's the big deal? Uncle Stephen pinched the bridge of his nose. He's your father, he said. Do I have to spell it out?

The whole situation was perfectly obvious and yet it confused me. I felt foolish, like a boy searching for the door in a dark room.

He's usually like this when he drinks, I said. But he didn't drink today. Uncle Stephen asked me again to go outside and reason with him. I went.

I worked my way out, moving against a steady stream of people. A man smoking a cigar held me to one side so as not to obstruct the flow of traffic. Over hats and hairdos I saw my father still sitting on the bench. At length a bus pulled up at the curb. A circle of piano keys, the Baker's Keyboard logo, had been painted on the side of the bus. Inside this circle in bold letters was *Katherine Lennox*. At that, as if it had been the signal he waited for, my father got up and walked slowly in the direction of Wharton's Bar.

AFTER THE SHOW I wanted to find Paul and tell him what he had missed: a woman with a fiery, mobile face; a middle-aged beauty whose shoulders and breasts glistened in the smoky light. She moved with the music, her long, black hair falling forward when she hunkered down close to the keys.

Then there were the parts I couldn't tell. How the music was often complicated and difficult to understand. How it sometimes made me frustrated and tired. I didn't recognize many of the compositions. At one point the music disappeared completely. Then it returned with a vengeance, as if angry for being ignored. And then she played a melody that I swore was Beethoven's, though I couldn't be sure, and the growing intensity of her variations made me jealous, almost resentful. I remember thinking that I must somehow learn to listen. I felt the need, though I had no idea how to begin.

When it was over Uncle Stephen went backstage. I stayed at the table. The crowd cleared out quickly. I could see people at the door waiting for the second show. Busboys moved through the room, clearing and wiping tables. The hostess finally came over and informed me that I had to leave. I'm waiting for someone, I said. She suggested, in a pleasant voice, that I wait outside. I took a last look around and then headed out, taking a seat on the bench where I'd last seen my father. The crowd for the second show had already gone in by the time Uncle Stephen found me.

She must have been happy to see you, I said. Uncle Stephen nodded. He looked up the street toward Wharton's Bar. We should go look for him, he said. The blue Corvette suddenly materialized. The valet parked it at the curb. Fuck it, said Uncle Stephen. He can call a cab.

I DIDN'T SEE Paul again until Uncle Stephen had gone back to Cleveland, until Denny McLain had won his thirty-first game for the Tigers. It was a Thursday. The local branch of the Selective Service had granted Paul a hearing. He said he had to represent himself, offer his own arguments, make a speech if necessary. I skipped school so that I could go with him.

Paul had filed for a hearing with the help of Students for a Democratic Society, a tired organization that occupied a small office at Macomb College. Paul had spoken twice to the director, Mr. Albert Friend. The first meeting involved the filling out of necessary forms. Mr. Friend assured my brother that there would be no problem. When Paul went back to inquire about the status of his application, Mr. Friend was unavailable. The secretary said that he would be unavailable for several days. The second meeting was brief and took place the day before the hearing. Hardship cases are a breeze, said Mr. Friend. Don't worry about a thing. Then Mr. Friend invested my brother with the full weight of his authority. If things don't seem to be going your way, he said, tell them the SDS will intervene on your behalf.

The Office of Selective Service was appropriately austere.

Once inside we didn't speak. We sat like truant students in straight-back chairs. A man in uniform walked out from behind a long counter. Paul Tollman, he called. My brother shot up and so did I. Are the two of you Paul Tollman? My brother stepped forward. The man in uniform was expressionless. You can both follow me, he said.

We were ushered into a small office. Resting like an enormous Buddha behind a tidy desk was Shirley Lipton, a caseworker for the Selective Service. Which one of you is Paul? she asked. I am, said Paul. Lipton looked at me. That makes you his brother or his best friend. I think I smiled. I'm his brother, I said. She gestured for me to take a seat. Paul stayed standing.

Lipton opened the folder on her desk. You're asking to be absolved from duty based on your status as a student, she said. You also claim family hardship. That's right, said Paul. She wrote something down. Are you now full-time? she asked. Yes, said Paul, cracking his knuckles. She examined a small slip of paper in the file. The Registrar at Macomb College informs me that your standing was part-time at the beginning of the semester.

Paul was prepared for this. When I registered last spring, he said, I was closed out of two classes. I was told to wait until places opened up. Shirley Lipton again scrutinized the file. I'd believe your story, she said, if you'd started a full schedule of classes during the first or second week of school. But the record shows that you only began a full-time load last week. You would also have me believe that Psychology 101 and the History of Popular Music were the two classes closed to you. It seems clear that your decision to become a full-time student was motivated by a desire to avoid military service. Paul denied the accusation, but Lipton maintained that my brother did not meet the appropriate criteria for a student deferment.

You've also claimed hardship, she said. Paul changed his expression from disconcerted to dejected. We were married less than two weeks ago, he said. I'm her only means of support. Lipton made a clicking sound with her tongue. Her fleshy arms jiggled. But your wife is not pregnant, she said. I also see that she is capable of working and that her parents are still alive. In any case, the army often proves lucrative for the family breadwinner. You can send home at least half your pay each month. You'll probably make more in Vietnam than you can make in Detroit. Lipton raised a large rubber stamp and brought it down firmly on the first page of Paul's file. Request denied, she said.

My brother took a deep breath. I should tell you, he said, that the SDS is prepared to intervene on my behalf. Shirley Lipton looked squarely at my brother for the first time. Let's see, she said. You're from Macomb. That would be Mr. Albert Friend. Let me tell you something Mr. Tollman, the last time your sponsor, Mr. Friend, was in this office — I threw him out on his ear.

Back in the parking lot, Paul was more embarrassed than angry. I knew it wouldn't work, he said. That asshole Friend is full of shit. We pulled out of the driveway. Let's go somewhere, I said. I can't go back to school. Let's drive up to Metropolitan Beach. My brother turned down the radio. I gotta get home, he said. I have to oil and bag my tools. I thought he was kidding. Oil your tools, I said. What the fuck is that? My brother adjusted the rearview mirror. So they won't rust, he said.

THE REST I remember in fragments. I talked to Paul on the phone. Once or twice we went out to dinner with Char and Maria. We made no plans beyond the next day or two. We didn't mention next week or next month or next year. We pretended that nothing mattered.

My mother spent those days planning a party for Paul. She complained about doing it, but she said it wouldn't look right if he left without one. She asked me to call his friends. She wanted music, but she wanted something quieter than a band. I thought of Selena. My mother suggested that I invite her and ask her to play. Selena liked the idea. It'll be my first gig, she said. My mother rented an upright piano for the occasion.

The first week of October was unseasonably warm. Weathermen called it Indian summer. The St. Louis Cardinals won the first game of the World Series with machine-like precision. Bob Gibson struck out seventeen Tigers and set a new record. The Tigers came back in the second game. Mickey Lolich, a fine pitcher overshadowed by Denny McLain, caught the Cardinals off guard. Then he surprised everyone by hitting the first home run of his career. By Friday the World Series was tied. It was the main topic of conversation at Paul's party.

Everyone invited was there by eight o'clock. Except for sports talk, the group was somber. No one wanted to think about Vietnam. It sounded absurd to me when friends wished my brother good luck. A farewell dinner would have been better, I thought. The passing of bowls and platters and the tapping of coffee spoons would have helped. As it was, Selena filled the gaps with music. People paused in conversation and looked in the direction of the piano. I managed to talk and listen at the same time.

Maria helped my mother in the kitchen, and after most of the food had been carried downstairs and arranged on card tables, Maria pulled me aside. Your father's giving me the creeps, she said. He keeps staring at me. I saw my father behind the bar. He pounded down a shot and opened a beer. He's probably drunk, I said. Maria looked askance. Of course he's drunk, she said. But tonight it's different. I've talked to him when he's smashed. I've sat next to him. And always it's like he never sees me. Like I'm invisible. But tonight I'm not invisible. He keeps staring.

I buried my face in Maria's black hair and drew in the scent. It's Moondrops, she said. My eyes followed the slope of her breasts before they disappeared beneath her blouse. I wanted to take her away. I wanted to tell her that I wasn't so modern after all. That seeing anyone other than her struck me now as stupid. Just forget about 'im, I said.

Maria and I moved around the basement together. Paul and Char were standing with a group of old friends reminiscing about high school. They talked mostly about *Shenanigans,* the annual talent show, laughing about the backstage chaos. Then someone brought up our first band and told the story of how Paul and I broke into the sacristy at St. Veronica's and stole a Fender amplifier. A week later, I said, another thief took the speaker. I mean *just* the speaker. He took out sixteen screws and opened the back. He left the cabinet. He even left the screws. The folk mass crew showed up and found nothing in the closet but an empty box. Then Paul remembered the time that he and some of his pals put Bogich's desk in the boy's lavatory. Everyone laughed. Then the laughter suddenly stopped. I listened for Selena but she was between pieces.

Maria tapped me on the shoulder and said she was going upstairs to see if my mother needed anything. I watched her go. I watched my father go up after her. I thought nothing of it at that moment. I waited for Maria to reappear. She'd been gone for a minute or two when I saw my mother behind the bar pouring soft drinks.

I climbed the steps and turned the corner on the landing. The kitchen was thick with the smell of food and coffee. Maria stood stiffly at the sink as if she were looking out the window. My father stood behind her, leaning against her, rubbing her hair between his fingers. He heard my footfalls before I could say or do anything. He wheeled around and dropped his eyes on my face. He didn't seem to know me. It ain't right, he sniped. Then he slammed me against the wall as he pushed through the doorway.

Maria was frozen in place. Her shoulders were trembling. A thin line of water ran down her cheek. Get me out of here, she said. Let's just get out.

I went to find Maria's purse, and when I returned, I discovered a commotion on the stairs. Paul shouted, Let's go, you son-of-a-bitch. And then I heard a thumping on the steps. Paul's voice was strained. This is what you always wanted, he said. Then I heard my father breathing, yelling at my brother. It's never been that, he said. Never what I wanted. My mother screamed at both of them to stop, but it was no good.

I handed Maria her purse and stepped down to the landing. I saw my father dragging Paul up the steps. The old man swayed and grabbed the railing and Paul brought his fist down on my father's hand. You little prick, said my father, and he grabbed a handful of Paul's hair. I hooked my arm around my father's chest when he reached the top, but Paul waved me off. I followed them out onto the side drive. So did most of the party.

Paul landed a punch just above my father's kidney. The blow dropped my father to his knees. Paul stepped back and snatched a bottle out of someone's hand. I need one more, he said. Another bottle suddenly appeared. Paul broke both on the pavement and laid the neck with its jagged edge in front of my father. Then the old man did something that no one expected. He began to talk.

I'm the only one, he said. The only one . . . who has the right. He pulled himself up and kicked aside the broken bottle. C'mon. Don't back down. Don't think you'll get away. Paul lunged at my father. The two men locked arms and pushed against each other until Paul's twisted wrist gave up and bits of glass skittered across the concrete. This is your chance, said my father. Sooner or later there'll be nothing left. He swung at my brother and missed. Paul's fist connected with my father's cheek. I could hear the liquid sound of broken flesh. It ain't right, said my father. You go out stupid.

My mother screamed again, imploring them to stop. Char stood off to the side with her arms around Maria. I kept looking at Paul, waiting for a signal, but he wanted no help. Fuck your stupid life, said Paul. I'll kill you. He went after the old man, swinging wildly.

My father crouched down and protected his head. Then he staggered Paul with an uppercut to the chin. There's no killing me, he said. All these years and you're still stupid. He took hold of Paul at that moment and squeezed him to his chest. Paul's body went limp. You won't believe it, said my father. I could snap your spine between my arms. I could crush your skull with my hands. There's no killing me. There's only you.

Paul found his feet and tried to shake himself free. My father refused to let go. Your legs'll carry a dead trunk for twenty years, he said. Or maybe it starts with your fingers. Moves up to your elbow. Until your arms feel like concrete. You can try to beat me down. But there's no killing me. He loosened his grip and Paul stepped back. My father spat out blood. Go and die, he said. It's easier.

My father pushed through the crowd and stumbled into the house. Char ran to Paul and cradled his swollen jaw. I tried to move but my feet and legs were frozen.

PAUL DIDN'T speak to my father before he shipped out. My father made no attempt to reach Paul. My mother, assuming a familiar role, positioned herself in the middle. She waited until Monday.

I'm going over to the Kingsly house to say good-bye, she said. If you were any kind of a father, you'd come with me. He stared at the television set. What if something happens? she asked. What will you do then? She kept trying to turn his head, but he wouldn't look at her. If something happens, she said, he'll never forgive you. He kept his eyes on the TV. That's right, he said.

LATER THAT week a fresh group of boys filed through the gate at Fort Wayne. Paul, however, wasn't among them. He was holding out for the true end of summer, for the season's emphatic end. My brother had decided to wait for a Tiger victory in the World Series.

We had watched the Cardinals win three of the first four games. We had watched the less devoted among us turn away. But those who had gone to the ballpark each week during the regular season nodded with confidence when Detroit, refusing to roll over, defeated St. Louis in game five.

On Wednesday, October ninth, the Tigers won the sixth game and again tied the World Series. Even the most faithful were thunderstruck. Schools and banks and small businesses locked their doors in anticipation of the seventh contest. That's when my brother put Uncle Sam on hold. I'll be AWOL, he said. I'll say I got lost. With any luck, they'll shoot me.

On Thursday, the last game of the World Series was played at Busch Memorial Stadium in St. Louis. We watched some of it on television and listened to the rest of it on radio. It went scoreless for six innings. The sportscasters called it a defensive battle, a pitchers' duel. I remember the waiting, the long stretches of silence.

We were told at the end as we were told in the beginning that St. Louis was the younger team, stronger and faster with steely nerves. But then two Tigers crossed the plate after one Cardinal misjudged a deep fly. Detroit needed no more.

PAUL DROVE the Mercury Comet into downtown Detroit after dark. We joined a traffic jam of horns blowing, radios blaring, and beer spraying. Passersby shot shaving cream across windshields. Strings of firecrackers exploded on the sidewalks. A blizzard of confetti fell from office windows.

On every corner people were laughing and embracing. Old-timers and young punks walked arm in arm, singing the same songs. The poor were surrounded by friends. The air was empty of fear. No other news mattered.

Music came from all directions. Loudspeakers sat in doorways or on windowsills, flooding the streets. Musicians and bands played on courthouse steps and café patios and flatbed trucks. Char and Maria danced in the middle of Woodward Avenue. A tall man with the blackest skin I'd ever seen took hold of me and kissed me on both cheeks.

Detroit was filled with light. It softened the hard edges of glass and cinder block. It made every movement more graceful. I looked for the moon and stars but found nothing. It was the glow of old street lamps, the gleam of headlights and brake lights, the light streaming down from towering skyscrapers. It flattered old storefronts and tired faces. All the cracks and bruises for a moment disappeared.

We deserted the Mercury Comet after midnight, leaving it in a jam of abandoned cars on Jefferson Avenue. We walked a good distance. There seemed no end to the revelry.

In the night I feel free, I thought. The air is cool and it's easy to breathe. I can keep my eyes open.

We kept going until we found a street running with traffic. A bus stopped at the curb. It made a hissing sound when the doors opened.

I took in the bus driver's blank expression when we stepped off. No one said a word about Paul reporting for duty. We talked like two couples who would probably see each other on the weekend. Then Paul and Char started walking. Come back to Mom and Dad's with us, I said. We can give you a lift. Paul looked at Char. We're in no hurry, he said. Then I thought of the Mercury Comet. What about your car? I asked. Just leave it, said Paul. And then my brother was gone.

BOOK FOUR

Stephen

c h a p t e r   t h i r t e e n

THE SUMMER of 1974 was a hard, dry season. Without rain the earth became fallow, and my Polish neighbor, a retired farmer, a man famous for his beefsteak tomatoes, turned his garden under, a course of action devoid of sentimentality or spite. "The soil is useless," he said. "Like the bones of old men."

During those sweltering days, television announcers reported an increase in cases of sunstroke; they interviewed concerned health officials who outlined the dangers of working outdoors. Those of us who worked indoors put up with nosebleeds and an occasional outbreak of prickly heat. My brother, avoiding these lesser complications, fractured his wrist while arguing with his wife, slapping the bathroom tile with his open hand; and despite the swelling and the obvious immobility, he insisted that nothing was wrong. He refused to see a doctor for more than a week. When he finally broke down, he accused the doctor, an orthopedist, of aggravating his condition. He maintained that the examination was careless, that the X-ray was vague, that he'd do better with a sling and good whiskey.

My brother did not mend easily. He cracked the first cast and scratched and beat up the second, wearing it longer than should've been necessary. It was still on his arm when I saw him in Detroit for his birthday. He sat in the shade and griped about the itch, cursing at the sun and shaking his good fist at the cloudless sky. He kept pointing at the lawn and apologizing for its sorry state. "Let it go brown," I said. "It'll come back in the fall." I could've told him that Lake Erie was down several inches from last year, and that all along the turnpike between Cleveland and Detroit old trees stooped in the arid haze, their mottled leaves curling at the edges like peeling skin. I could've mentioned these things. He might have felt better about the grass.

I saw Phil three times that summer, a Sunday in June for cake and ice cream, a Monday in August to bury our mother, and a Saturday night in early September to pay his bond, to walk with him past an indifferent guard and out of the city jail.

MY BROTHER turned fifty-nine on a weekend of oppressive heat. I started early for Detroit, but the humidity was already up and sweat glued me to the seat before I'd gone far. I closed the windows and turned on the air.

My car is my home, I said to myself. Nothing's better than the road, nothing exists here except concrete and the passing landscape. An old but familiar voice tells me to pull over, to step out and stay put—but my car refuses. It follows the road to its birthplace. The way is easy.

The car kept going, my brain in high gear all the while, and before long I found myself in Detroit. Things were bad in Cleveland, but Detroit looked like a cursed city. I took Gratiot Avenue up to the east side through a mute landscape of burned out storefronts and abandoned homes. I passed churches with open doors, but I never saw more than a handful of parishioners. No one was out for a Sunday walk. Even diners and neighborhood bars were closed. Phil said that everyone here, rich and poor alike, locked their doors and kept their windows nailed shut. I assumed that Cleveland would soon be the same.

Detroit, for me, had never been an attractive place. Even in its glory days it seemed cold and unforgiving. But in the fifties, swollen with prosperity, its threat had more to do with competition than death. Now the city looked hollow, stultified by the monotony of making cars, dispossessed of its future, dispossessed of its dreams, like gray-haired men working the line.

My brother blamed black people for everything that happened in Detroit. "This city's a toilet," he was fond of saying. "Give niggers ground and all they do is squat." He believed that black men all by themselves accounted for poverty, robbery, and drugs—not to mention defective American cars.

When Phil's words were ugly enough, I could taste the bigotry, the bitterness, like bile in the mouth. I lived close to his rage. He escaped the factory, working at the suburban Tech Center, but he couldn't escape the beliefs of a factory town. Nor did he escape the grating routine, all the deadening repetition that too soon showed itself in his hands and face. Like me and like the men who worked with me at the assembly plant, my brother's hands grew coarse. Wear and tear on the face came with more time, but my brother, scowling over his work and then boozing at night and on weekends, accelerated the process. He wore no lines or wrinkles, but still his face became old. His eyes were sunken, rimmed with black rings, and his mouth turned down at the edges. His chin was no longer firm.

In his fifty-ninth year, Philip Tollman, in the opinion of those who knew him, lived alone. It was true that he and Carrie Ann still shared the house on Lincoln Street, but there was very little in the way they resided that suggested a partnership. My brother worked forty hours a week, read the paper after dinner, watched television from dusk until bedtime, and drank, especially on weekends, until he was comfortably unaware.

With the boys gone, Carrie Ann took a second job selling

women's apparel at an upscale department store. She continued her secretarial work at the parish rectory, but she added book-keeping to her list of duties, and with that came additional hours. Her "situations," as she liked to call them, offered not much more than minimum wage, but I never once heard her complain about small paychecks. Perhaps she fancied herself a career woman. She'd been surprised, so had Phil, when the department store hired her without sales experience, but she soon ingratiated herself with the management, accepting evening and weekend assignments without protest. "I've learned to cook," said my brother, a quiet pride in his voice. "I have the radio and the whole kitchen to myself."

On Friday or Saturday evenings, in the interest of variety, Phil and Carrie Ann went out to dinner. On Sunday, they went to church. These outings were similar in that both were silent affairs.

My brother and his wife kept to their weekly routines and, for the most part, saw no one. Whenever we talked, I asked about my nephews.

"Paul's fixing cars," said Phil.

"I know," I said. "He looked at mine. Last time I was up."

"On his driveway?"

"His garage."

"Not much room in there."

"Talk with Jim?"

"He's in Buffalo."

"I know."

I'd seen Paul on the day he came back from Vietnam. He was holding Kimberly, whom he'd just met. She was already more than a year old. He seemed to be in a hurry, shifting his weight from one leg to the other while he talked. He told me that he hadn't received a single letter from his father during his entire tour of duty. I told him I was sorry. "Don't apologize," he said.

Paul, Charlene, and the baby lived in the neighborhood, and they were invited to the house on Lincoln Street for the usual holidays, but as I understood it, they visited only on Christmas. This came as no surprise. Paul had told me, when I stopped to see him about my car, that his mother treated Charlene like a chambermaid. "It's no different than it's ever been," he said. "When I got back from 'Nam, we took Kimberly over for visits. Still do sometimes. But the old man just sits there, camping out behind his newspaper."

I assumed that Carrie Ann, despite her disregard for Charlene, visited Kimberly on a regular basis. Paul shook his head. "My mother says she won't move to Florida when the old man retires because she wants to be close to her grandchildren. But she never calls." Paul adjusted the carburetor and then listened to the idle. "So I stopped calling her. She came over once. And when she was here she criticized Char's housekeeping."

It occurred to me that Phil and Carrie Ann's reclusive habits were intentional. Maybe they were preparing themselves for a long and wintry dotage. Perhaps the plan was to conserve energy and resources by eliminating all human relationships. I'd seen this pattern before. One of the old widowers who worked at the plant, in the year before his retirement, stopped accepting invitations for dinner. He made no apologies for letters and bills that fell by the wayside, for the telephone that went unanswered, and then, after a time, he gave up his regular trips to Dayton to visit his children. A few of his friends began to worry. They looked in his locker expecting to find a gun or, at the very least, a fresh package of razor blades. Instead, they found girlie magazines and an onion sandwich wrapped in wax paper. Finally, on his last day of work, someone asked the old widower why he never came around any-more. "Dying is a helpless and undignified thing," he said. "It's better to get on with it out of sight."

I remember thinking at the time that his words sounded like something my brother would say. I thought of Phil as a retiree, liv-ing alone with a wife and preparing for death. There'd always been a strange resignation in the pattern of his life. Now he seemed immutable. His job and his television and his booze offered no satisfaction, but still he embraced these habits like a man eager to surrender.

Phil's garden, after a few plentiful years, became too much trouble; Carrie Ann's crafts, an assembly line of decorated baskets and hand-painted Christmas ornaments, became, in her own words, "too much." As a couple, they took less and less interest in each other's lives, even less in the lives of their children, and less again in the daily possibilities of living. They did not follow the ups and downs of Paul and his family, and they made no serious attempt to understand what Jim was doing in graduate school.

"He's already got one degree in English," Phil had said. "Why does he need another one?" My brother didn't want or expect an answer. "The kid was barely out of high school—still sitting at my dinner table—when he tells me he's picked his major. 'English,' he says, as if that's something to be proud of. I told him, 'You'll never have more than two dimes to rub together.' But he didn't lis-ten. What a rumdumb."

After that, my brother stopped following his son's progress, and Jim, I realize now, turned to me, writing or calling with news of his life. When he went to Buffalo to pursue his graduate degree, I was jealous. I wanted someone to give me the opportunity to read and discuss literature for four or five years. I tried to imagine the life of an intellectual, the work of an academic. I tried to picture myself as a college professor, but I could only get as far as the beard and the tweed sport coat.

Unlike his brother's, Jim's college career went forward without the interruption of Vietnam. His physical uncovered a rare cardiac anomaly, and so the government refused him, and he legally escaped the war. He stayed home and objected to the military escalation, but he never involved himself in a demonstration or protest march. His girlfriend, Maria, called him politically passive. She threw herself into every cause like a firebrand and tried to make Jim an activist. Her efforts were not rewarded.

Jim wrote me letters about their doomed relationship. He went on about the incomprehensible nature of women, about the fact that Maria despised him for the person he was. These diatribes were soon followed by calmer reflections, a short note suggesting that he and Maria were on the verge of patching up their differences, that love was confounding but resilient. After years of separations and reconciliations, Maria finally broke it off. "She dropped everything and moved to Colorado," said Jim, "to live in an ashram."

He decided much later that he drove her away, that her going left him broken, without any resolution. Whenever he wrote or called from Buffalo, I heard a well-rehearsed fatalism in his words. He began to see his loss as irrevocable, to view his situation as somehow privileged, as mythic in proportion. He became a spectator to his condition, summing up his youth as "... a botched life of squandered affection." He blamed himself for the ruin of a pure and devoted love, for unspeakable rifts brought on by conceit and the pursuit of grandiose dreams.

I don't want to give the impression that these were my insights or judgments; Jim said most of these things about himself. In two or three years of correspondence, he spoke repeatedly about

Maria and lost love. Sometimes we talked about books, and I speculated, based on his favorite stories, that he saw himself as a tragic figure, a man caught up in a maelstrom of forces beyond his control. I knew from my own experience that he savored the sad beauty of his childhood romance. He looked for Maria in other women and repeated certain key scenes in each new relationship—he became, quite naturally, a poet.

A musician, I think, would've been better. There'd been no music in the Tollman family until Paul and Jim came along. I enjoyed seeing them up on a bandstand, and sometimes my brother did too, though he was loath to admit it. It was never clear to me why my nephews gave it up. Their father's displeasure gave them reason enough to continue. They could've fueled their musical ambitions with rebellion, adopted the pose of misunderstood artists, turned their patricidal fantasies into teenage anthems. When I asked Jim why the band broke up, he muttered something about disagreements and a blown amplifier. "And we lost our drummer," he said. "Pounded a back-beat like a jackhammer. His fiancée made him quit." I told him to replace the drummer. "Paul's a family man now," said Jim. "And I've got to get on with my studies." I tried to tell him that school and work could wait, but it was no use.

In those days I imposed my point of view on just about anyone who would listen. I argued and cajoled, reserving my best efforts for my intractable brother, who listened—or gave the appearance of listening—and then dismissed what I had to say. Some people considered me arrogant and presumptuous, and their opinions were no doubt justified. I tried to tell a woman who once loved my brother that her affection had been misplaced. And more than once I tried to convince my brother to quit his job, to forget about his pension and his benefits, to work for himself as a general carpenter or a cabinetmaker or an expert in furniture restoration. I told my brother not to vote for Nixon in 1968, and when he voted for Nixon again in 1972, I threw a drink in his face. And for years I argued with myself, wanting to believe that my father was alive somewhere and thinking about his children and waiting to be found. And now, after all the indignation and the disappointment, I've stopped arguing. I've begun to leave things alone.

I remembered Jim's call earlier in the week. He'd been out of touch, and so I was happy to hear from him. I asked him about his classes, but the spring term had already ended and school wasn't on his mind. "This bachelor shit gives me too much time to think," he said.

"That's never been my problem," I said.

"Do you like living alone?"

"I've gotten used to it."

"Do you eat in front of the TV?"

"Sometimes."

"Do you listen to your neighbors fighting?"

"Is this the reason you called?"

"But there have been women?"

"Yes."

"It just never worked out."

"No."

"Any regrets?"

"I suppose you think you're the only one?"

"The only one with regrets?"

"No. The only one with a bum heart."

He didn't acknowledge the remark. "I'm painting houses for the summer," he said. "But I spend most of my time scraping and sanding . . . and listening to music."

"Hard work," I said. "Even with music."

"We take it down to the bare wood."

"The whole house?"

"Most of it. It's all in the preparation."

"How far can you go with old siding?"

"According to my boss, it's like seducing a woman. You have to make all the right moves and then recognize when she's ready."

"Your boss is a philosopher."

"He enjoys his work."

"You'd never get me up there. I'd go too far. And I hate the way a long ladder shakes."

"It's your legs," said Jim. "Not the ladder."

That was a good one, I thought. That business about the legs. I punched the accelerator, eager to get off the road, dying to un-buckle my seat belt and stretch. I drove with the windows closed and the radio off, the air conditioner making the only discernible sound, and I began to notice the closeness of the car and the hyp-notic white noise of the engine, and I wondered when it was that I stopped listening to music. It was before Berry Gordy packed his bags and left Detroit; it was before the Beatles showed up on the Ed Sullivan Show. I'd read somewhere that popular music took a wrong turn after Elvis, but I knew it wasn't that exactly. I thought about it for a while, and then, without warning, it came to me.

TWO DECADES earlier, my radio blaring, I rolled through Detroit and made the turn for Chicago, heading west to see Katherine. I was thirty-seven and fresh from ending a short but gloomy affair. On the night of the breakup, I'd uncorked a bottle of wine and telephoned Katherine in New York, a celebration of sorts, and she mentioned a gig in Chicago at the Drake Hotel. Something in her voice invited me.

We met in the hotel restaurant. Katherine was talking to the headwaiter when I came up behind her. She turned and threw her arms around me and I kissed her. We took a table near a window. Katherine pulled back the heavy curtains, widening our view of Lincoln Park and the endless blue water of Lake Michigan.

"Has it been forever?" She squeezed my hand and smiled. "It seems absolutely like forever."

"Let's not think about it," I said.

"Why Chicago? What's wrong with New York?"

"I don't like New York. Never did."

"You didn't see it."

"I saw enough."

She laughed and seemed exactly like the girl she'd been in Cleveland.

"How's Phil? And what about your mother? Oh, I have a thousand questions."

"Let's save the questions for later. I didn't drive ten hours for that."

She looked at the menu. "Are you hungry?"

"Not really," I said.

"Neither am I." Katherine folded her hands on the table. I thought she wanted a cigarette, but she didn't reach for her purse. "How long will you be here?"

"Just tonight."

"Where are you staying?"

"I don't have a place yet."

She looked out the window. "It's so calm," she said. "Bluer than Lake Erie."

Sometime after that the waitress brought the coffee. Katherine asked for sugar and cream.

I wanted to start gracefully, but I didn't know how to begin. "Phil's still married to Carrie Ann," I said. "Almost ten years now."

"I thought we were saving that for later."

"I'd like to. But there's no other way."

Katherine's smile disappeared. "I don't know what you mean."

"I mean to explain."

"Explain what?"

"Phil's committed. He'll stay married for the rest of his life."

"I never doubted that," she said. "And your point?"

"He's involved," I said. "Now we can figure things out."

Katherine leaned forward, both elbows on the table.

"We were confused when it started," I said. "You loved me first, and then you had feelings for Phil. But they weren't the same feelings."

"No," she said. "They weren't the same."

"That's what I mean. Now that we're older and understand things—"

"I'm sorry. Is there something here I don't understand?"

"Maybe we can start over—"

She raised her hand. "I won't do this again. Not today. Not after all this time."

I had rehearsed the whole thing carefully but now it was coming out wrong.

"None of us understood," I said.

"Oh, Stephen," she said. "Don't make me do this."

Everything in the room seemed to shift. "If you and Phil had really loved each other, you'd be together."

Katherine leveled me with her eyes. "Do you believe that? Do you really? Because if you do and if it's true, then it's also true for us." She picked up her coffee cup and then set it back down without drinking. "Is this why you came to Chicago? To tell me I was confused."

"No."

"Then why are you here?"

"I want you to marry me."

This time everything in the room froze. My legs trembled and sweat trickled down my spine. I imagined my fingers undoing the buttons on Katherine's dress.

She was crying now. "I can't marry you," she said. "You know that."

I don't remember what I thought or felt. The only thing that registered was the look of total surprise on Katherine's face when I cleared the table—spoons and half-filled cups, sugar and cream—with one sweep of my arm.

After that the hotel detective escorted me to the door. Katherine stood on the curb and I kissed her. She asked me if I was going to be all right. The valet brought my car around. Music was coming from the radio when I got in. I turned it off and drove east into the cooling twilight.

As EARLY as that, I thought, staring at the brake lights of a Sunday driver. I had no exposure to music as a child, no ability to sing or play, but Katherine had taught me to listen. I often caught myself humming old tunes and felt grateful when Paul and Jim slipped in a standard or two to slow things down. But by then most of the old songs had lost their charm. Nothing moved me, not even Jelly Roll or Django or Lester Young. It felt strange, as if a sense or nerve that resonated with music had atrophied.

I suddenly remembered a sad-faced commentator saying that Nixon never listened to music. I looked at myself in the rearview mirror but saw no resemblance to the chief executive. I knew that Nixon had his own collection of tapes, and I knew that the Supreme Court would soon decide whether or not he'd be forced to give them up. One of the guys at the plant worried himself sick over Nixon's possible impeachment. He said it was a bad idea. He said he didn't want to live in a fatherless country. I told him that Nixon had jumped ship a long time ago. "He should go quietly," I said. "He should slip out the side door of the White House. Tell everyone he's going for a quart of milk or a box of Cheerios. Walk out through the garden and disappear." My worried friend turned his attention to me. "You been working in the sun?" he asked. "Not today," I said.

But my friend was probably right. Perhaps I'd stayed out too long. And so, arriving for my brother's birthday, I found Detroit sweating beneath the light of too many suns, my eyes squinting against the glare and searching for shade, for the consolation of nightfall. And feeling drugged by the steady drone of my wheels, I yearned for a fresh sound to wash over me, to fill my ears and move me, make me forget the throb of the factory, the dull thump of the road. But I found no music on the radio, at least none that I could listen to, and the absence of it left me alone with thoughts of Katherine.

I made a left turn onto Lincoln Street and saw my brother sitting on the front porch, watching for me like a stone sentinel, waiting for me as he'd waited so often. I felt haunted, possessed by a woman I did not know, by the ghost of a woman that I created and embellished all the nights of my life, burnishing each gesture and movement, revising each word until it suited my purpose, storing the knowledge of her perfection in my mournful heart.

"How's THE drive?" Phil swayed a little when he stood up, but then he caught himself in the next moment.

"Same as always," I said.

"No traffic on Sunday."

"No. No traffic."

"Carrie Ann is making spaghetti."

"Sounds good."

"Too hot for spaghetti."

"It'll be fine."

"We'll have to eat in the yard."

"How's the wrist?"

"Useless."

"Looks clumsy."

"I can't wipe my own ass."

"That's appetizing."

"Want a drink?"

"Yeah. Something cold."

I could smell the sauce before my brother opened the screen door. We walked through the living room and into the kitchen, where Carrie Ann stirred a steaming pot. The walls glistened with sweat and the ceiling seemed to sag; the smell of wine and garlic hung in the air.

"Good drive?" asked Carrie Ann.

"Fine."

"How's Myron?"

"He's doing well," I said. "But his dog's been sick."

"What now?"

"Some kind of intestinal parasite."

"Myron keeps his vet in business," said Phil.

"Max would have been enough for me," said Carrie Ann. "I never understood why he wanted another dog."

I saw the cake with chocolate frosting on the counter. "Looks like you made my favorite."

"We're getting too old for cake," she said.

My brother opened the freezer and a white cloud poured out over his arms. He handed me a bottle of beer and grabbed another for himself.

"And how's Jessica?"

"Save the gay banter for dinner," said Phil. "If I stand here much longer, I'll boil."

We left Carrie Ann in the kitchen and walked out onto the back porch. All the fruit trees had disappeared and the yard seemed tiny in the unbroken light. A white stump, about three or four feet high, stood near a wilted strawberry patch; shorn of its bark and bulging at the top, it looked like a giant mushroom. This stub, prominent and peculiar by itself, served as a pedestal for a birdhouse, a weather vane and a pinwheel.

"She wants to see you."

Phil pointed at the lawn. "Look at that god-forsaken crap. I water it every day and it still looks like shit."

"Don't take it personally."

"Wasted effort. That's what it is."

"She's worse."

"You've said that before."

"It's shingles this time."

My brother stepped off the porch, kicked off his sandals, and planted his bare feet in the dry grass. "We're planning a trip."

"When?"

"Next month."

I upended my bottle and took a long drink. "She may not last."

"We'll get there." He dragged his toes across a patch of brown stubble. "Jesus. Feels like straw."

"Have you seen Paul?"

"Talked to him last week on the telephone."

"How's business?"

"He says it's okay." My brother slipped back into his sandals and returned to the porch. He looked at me. Then he said, "Can I ask you something?"

"Feel free."

"What makes you come here for my birthday?"

I laughed. "It's the cake. I come for the cake."

"I don't think you've missed a single one."

"Yes I have. I've missed a lot more than one."

"I never remember your birthday. I don't even know what month you were born."

"So—"

"So why do you still come?"

"I'm an optimist."

He guffawed. "Funny. I never pegged you for one."

"No?"

"I thought you were like me. A pessimist."

"You're the 'Prophet of Doom.'"

"I'm the prophet of dead grass."

"Let's not talk about the grass."

"Whatever you like."

I thought hard for a moment but nothing of interest came to mind. "Did you make the birdhouse?"

"Made it at work."

"So you're that busy."

"About as busy as a supervisor."

He was right. I spent a few hours each day checking my zones and the rest of the time sitting at my desk. "It's nice."

"What is?"

"The birdhouse."

Carrie Ann appeared at the back door. "Pick up your plates," she said. She pointed at the picnic table that had been set for dinner. I picked up two plates, one for her and one for myself, and followed her inside. She forked a huge pile of noodles onto my dish and then smothered it with sauce. "There's salad outside," she said. "Just take off the foil and help yourself. You'll find bread and cheese, too."

Phil held his pasta at arm's length. "Too damn hot for spaghetti."

"And it's too hot to barbecue," said Carrie Ann. "And it's too hot to use the oven. What would *you* like for dinner? A salami sandwich?"

My brother did not answer. He grabbed another beer as he passed the refrigerator and the three of us went out and sat down.

Dinner wasn't so much a trio of conversation as it was a trio of rhythmic chewing; it was the occasional sucking of noodles and the crunch of salad or bread that saved us all from a lethal dose of monotony. I should've brought a good bottle of Chianti, I thought. But then I remembered that it was Sunday and that every liquor store between Cleveland and Detroit was closed. Carrie Ann asked again about Jessica, and I described the shingles and the severe palsy and the almost transparent skin of my mother's hands. "The doctor says she weighs less than ninety pounds."

"The poor thing," said Carrie Ann.

Phil moved between his salad and spaghetti with the ferocity of a man eating his last meal. "Is that old battle-ax of a nurse still there?" he asked.

"She won't go until they tear the place down," I said. "And she won't let Mom get away with anything."

"I suppose not," said Phil.

"Your mother didn't send a birthday card," said Carrie Ann.

Phil swallowed a mouthful of noodles. "So what?"

"So nothing. Except that she always sends a card."

"I'll get by."

"That's not the point."

"What is then? You worried about Hallmark?"

"She can't manage it anymore," I said.

"That's all I'm saying," said Carrie Ann.

I swabbed my plate with a piece of bread and Carrie Ann cleared the table.

"Let's go for a drink," said my brother. "I owe you one."

"Right now?"

"When we're finished."

"Whatever you want. It's your birthday."

"Maybe we can find a place with air conditioning."

"It's cooling off now."

"Do you wanna go?"

"Sure. But I'll buy the drinks. Call it your present."

"A useful gift."

"What else did you get?"

"Nothing."

"Same as last year."

"I don't want—"

I cut him off. "I know. You don't want any presents."

He brushed bread crumbs and grated cheese off the table. "That's right."

Carrie Ann brought out the chocolate cake and ice cream and placed them in front of Phil. The frosting was brown and plain. She hadn't bothered with lettering or candles or fanciful decorations. She poured three cups of coffee and waited for Phil to cut the cake. "Hurry up," she said. "Before the ants come and carry it off."

My brother served up two slices with runny ice cream but took nothing for himself. "Wait a minute," I said. "What about you?"

"None for me," said Phil. "Too sweet."

"It's your birthday cake," I said.

"I know that. I don't want any."

Carrie Ann ignored her husband's reluctance. She ate her dessert and sipped her coffee and seemed to lose herself in her own thoughts.

"It's moist," I said.

"About the only thing around here that is," said Phil. He looked at Carrie Ann. "What about the room upstairs? Is there a clean sheet on the bed?"

"Of course," said Carrie Ann.

"Thanks," I said. "I have a place."

"Save yourself the money," said Phil.

"I'll sleep better at the motel," I said.

My brother nodded and nearly winked at me, as if to say he understood the reason for my preference.

"Suit yourself," said Carrie Ann.

"Let's go," said Phil.

Carrie Ann put her hands on the table. "Where are we going?"

"Steve and I are going out for a drink."

"On Sunday night?"

"I know a lot of bars that are open on Sunday."

"You'll be sorry tomorrow."

"I hope so."

"I should stop at the motel and check in," I said.

My brother stood up and jingled his keys. "I'll drive."

I WATCHED for obvious signs of drunkenness as we made our way through the house and out the side door. I saw nothing unusual, but I distrusted his enthusiasm, his need to get away, and I decided that any sobriety test would find him well beyond the legal limit. "We can take my car," I said.

"You drive too much," he said.

"It'll be easier. I can drop you and then go."

"Same difference. Either way, we have to come back."

"All right," I said. "I've never been in the Buick."

"Let's do the Tempest," he said, opening the door.

"I'll drive the Buick if you're drunk."

"Blow it out your ass."

"But the deuce and a quarter has air, doesn't it?"

He hesitated and ran his hand through his damp hair. "We'll take the Tempest," he said, slipping in behind the wheel. "It's more fun."

"Since when is an old Pontiac more fun than a deuce and a quarter?"

He ignored my question and started the engine. *Fun,* I thought. It must be the booze. "Don't forget to stop at the Parkcrest," I said. He drove to the motel and then to the bar like a man being followed by the police.

At Pat O'Grady's we ordered Manhattans. My brother asked for the bartender's special, a double served in a glass pitcher with extra cherries. We took a table and sat across from each other but didn't speak, at least not in the manner of two friends or two brothers out for a birthday libation. We spent our time watching other customers and listening to strange music and trying to read unfamiliar labels on bottles behind the bar. We flirted with the waitress, a girl who indulged our bantering because we were older and proud of our bulging wallets. "She likes us," said Phil. I crushed a cherry between my teeth. "What she likes," I said, "is the possibility of a big tip."

We sat and drank through the early evening rush, through the ebb and flow of voices and laughter, through the closing of the kitchen and the arrival of neighborhood regulars. My brother, as if challenging me to keep up, swilled two or three pitchers, and then he made a show of plugging the jukebox and walking to the bathroom, navigating the disarray of tables and chairs with the precision of a sober man.

While Phil was away, an older guy and a young woman sat down at the next table. I imagined the couple as illicit lovers who lied to their respective partners and drove over from the west side, flushed with the risk of discovery, to rendezvous at O'Grady's and indulge in the foreplay of passionate conversation. He wore khakis and a polo shirt and looked to be in his mid-forties; she wore jeans and a tube top and was somewhere around thirty. I watched them out of the corner of my eye and waited for their first words. He asked her if they needed dog food. "I picked up a bag this afternoon," she said. She extended her arm and brushed a piece of lint from his eyebrow. I noticed a gold band next to her diamond and saw the same ring on his finger. My fantasy crumbled.

Phil noticed the woman even before he sat down. Her face wasn't extraordinary, and yet it was difficult to look at anything else in the room. Maybe it was her bare shoulders or the way her dark hair fell to the middle of her back. The bartender turned on the television and someone dropped a bottle, but my brother and I kept glancing in her direction. We didn't acknowledge our shared interest, but we did very little to hide it.

Our friendly waitress stopped and asked us if we wanted another round. Phil ordered bourbon and water. I declined. She cleared our empties and then turned to the other table; the man wanted a pint of Guinness and the woman asked for a vodka gimlet. Phil leaned over and tapped the waitress's serving tray. "Bring my brother a gimlet," he said.

"I don't drink vodka gimlets."

Phil looked at the woman with dark hair. "It's not for you."

I tried to ignore it. "Was there anything on the jukebox worth playing?"

"Patsy Cline."

"Which songs?"

"'Crazy.' And something else."

"That's it?"

"Oh, what's his name . . ." Phil's eyes wandered to the television. ". . . Pat Boone."

"Playing something familiar is one thing. Stinking up the place is another."

"What's wrong with Pat Boone?"

"Nothing that a good enema wouldn't fix."

"I played him."

"You're not serious?"

"I am."

"Why?"

"Because he's a milksop. Because listening to him should make any man shit thin gruel."

I would have laughed, but I heard something ugly in his voice. "I see. So you've decided to punish everyone within earshot."

"Something like that," said Phil.

We watched the activity of the bar and said nothing for a long time. Then the waitress returned with our drinks; I paid the tab and gave her a hefty tip. She thanked me and smiled at Phil, but he was no longer interested.

"We should've left it open," I said. I pushed the vodka gimlet toward my brother, but he left it on the table between us. I said, "If I hear Pat Boone, I'll need another double."

"That's a fine way to talk."

"About what?"

"About milksops."

"Fuck off."

"I hear about milksops all the time. Old Dick Daub was up from Cleveland last month, and he was asking about Myron and you. Said he runs into Myron every now and then. And you, too. 'Strange,' he says. 'Your brothers are always alone. So I'm wondering,' he says. 'Is Myron a homo? Is Stephen . . . ?'"

"We can leave now," I said, rising from my chair. Phil grabbed my arm and pulled me down.

"'No,' I say. 'My bachelor brothers go for girls. They've just been laying off for a while.'"

"That's right," I whispered. "Just like you. When was the last time you buried the bone? I mean, what year was it?"

My brother flinched. "And I defended your reputation. I told Dick that you and I once shared the same girl. I even told him that you were there first — but like a gentleman you walked away."

"At least I didn't run."

Phil pushed back from the table and picked up the gimlet. He reached over and offered it to the woman next to us. "It's for you," he said, putting it down in front of her. The man in khakis waved it off.

"I already have one," said the woman.

"You might want it later," said Phil. Then he stood up and headed for the door.

I caught up with him in the parking lot. I insisted that he give me the keys. He refused. "Just walk," he said. He jumped into the car and started the engine before I could stop him. I didn't want him to drive alone. I got in.

He handled the streets reasonably well, or so it seemed, until he turned onto Eight Mile Road. Multiple lanes meant more traffic and more speed. Even so, he kept to the middle and let drivers pass on both sides, their headlights slitting the darkness like white knives.

We were halfway home when a Chevy Malibu filled with teenagers cut us off and left us standing at a red light. My brother stared at the signal, watching and waiting without saying a word, but when red slipped to green, he slammed the gas and warned me not to puke. We swung out from behind drowsing cars and flew past a stinking bus, and when we came up alongside those kids, we slowed down. And then, by degrees that were almost imperceptible, our Tempest drifted across the broken white line until the flare of the rear bumper ground against the Malibu's fender. The kids screamed, not knowing that anyone was after them, and when the driver looked over, terror on his face, my brother flipped him off and bumped him again. After that, we sped away.

At the next light, I pulled the keys out of the ignition and by right of possession forced my brother into the passenger seat. "You're a pathetic asshole," I said. Phil rolled his head toward the window and started to shake. I heard a sound that I thought was laughter, but it soon turned edgy and bitter, and after a while it became something desperate.

He was quiet by the time I pulled the Tempest into the driveway. Most of the houses on Lincoln were dark.

"You should check these brakes," I said. "There's too much fade."

"What in the fuck are you talking about?"

"Your goddamn brakes. They're spongy." I got out of the car and looked at the firewall under the steering column. I pointed at the dark stain. "You've got brake fluid coming in. You need a new master cylinder." Then I shut the door and said goodnight.

Phil slid across the bench seat and turned the key. "There's nothing wrong." He backed down the driveway and pumped the brakes. The car stopped. He did the same thing going up the driveway. He repeated this test several times.

"Your head's the thing that's spongy," he said. "And I'll prove it." Again he shot the Tempest toward the house and again he came to a lurching stop. Then he dropped the transmission into reverse and nudged the gas. This time the brakes gave out. The Tempest rolled backward, gathering speed, until it struck the rear quarter of a pickup truck parked across the street. On the side of the truck was a phone number for *Leo A. Furnari Home Improvement.*

My brother got out and surveyed the damage. I walked over and took a good look myself. "Happy birthday," I said. He was still standing in the road when I drove away.

chapter fourteen

PHIL FAILED to visit his mother in July. He stayed in Detroit while she became a figure of crossed bones, a bedridden scarecrow, shooing Death away from her door, daring Death to step over her threshold, demanding that Death come back another day when all her business was in order. She endured bedsores and a bladder infection and survived the first sweltering weeks of August, and she put up with all this because she wanted to touch her first-born for the last time, because she wanted to hear his voice. She did not ask for him. She did not speak his name. She simply waited, her thin hands clinging to those final days with whatever strength she could muster.

My brother stayed away. I called to say that Mother had stopped eating, that she'd requested a minister, and still he made excuses. He put off his trip to Cleveland until the day of her funeral, stumbling up the aisle, leaning on Carrie Ann, his face swollen and his eyes red, stubble on his face.

The Lutheran Church in North Olmstead was austere, so much so that my brother's disarray appeared garish, mildly grotesque. Many of the assembled mourners had no idea that the awkward man squeezing into the first pew was Jessica Tollman's son. Some people pointed and stared at him as if he were a stranger, a derelict from skid row who had wandered in hoping to rest his feet. He brought with him a cloud of barroom smells: cigarettes and beer and sour whiskey.

Myron moved down the pew, making room. Carrie Ann smoothed her dress and fumbled the car keys still in her hand. They fell like coins on the wooden bench and the clatter echoed and intensified through the hollow church. In the next pew, Paul, Charlene, and Jim, having predicted a scene, showed no obvious discomfort about the odor or the noise. I tried to catch my brother's eye, but he sat down and fixed his gaze on the minister and squeezed a tattered hymnal.

The minister struck me as detached, a man going through the motions of a familiar and monotonous ceremony, as if my mother's coffin had come to him for inspection at the end of a long line of coffins, as if the unfailing repetition of his job rendered him indifferent. He didn't acknowledge my brothers or me and mentioned more than once that he was a stranger to our family. He reflected on whether or not my mother had been a regular parishioner. If so, how had he missed her? He recounted a few facts about her life, a short list of interests.

It occurred to me that one of us should speak for her instead. One of us should say something in honor of her life. Phil, if asked, would refuse, and Myron had retreated long ago into a forced silence. The responsibility was undoubtedly mine. But this minister invited no one to speak. He made it his job, his duty, to give voice to our grief, but he did it with the mechanical attitude of a traffic cop. Even in his best moments he reminded me of a bored guest at a dinner party, a man forever looking at his watch, a man anxious for fresh air and unfamiliar faces.

I stopped listening to the minister and became acutely aware of people breathing and praying and clearing their throats. Candle wax spotted the floor and everywhere was a thin layer of dust. I thought of Margie and tried to remember her face, but her features would not take shape, not fully, and after a long struggle, my mind was left with a shadowy and dissatisfying image. Katherine came to me then, as if to make up for Margie's sudden obscurity; I pictured her smooth hands and capable arms, the perfect face that had lived with me since boyhood. I wanted this woman beside me, and I felt that Mother would want her here because she often asked about Katherine, a nicety that deepened near the end when the only matters she cared to talk about were time and distance.

I closed my eyes and replayed old scenes with Katherine: a conversation from before the War, her profile when she looked out the window of a train, and finally her moon-white face, her astonished face, floating on a mirror edged with lights. She wiped away a heavy layer of cold cream. She looked older, though no less beautiful, without the flattery of make-up. My sudden appearance had surprised her, so much so that she said nothing at first. Her silence made me impatient. The cramped dressing room was bright and uncomfortably warm.

"I have no flowers," I said.

Katherine smiled. "Just as well. The poor things never last."

I felt the urge to lie, to invent a new life for myself. "Good to see you," I said.

"Yes," she said. "I mean —"

There was nothing she needed to explain. "The show's different," I said.

"Of course it's different. If you play the same songs again and again, they die."

"Do they?"

She brushed her hair. "Did you come up just to see me?"

I shook my head. "A wedding. Phil's eldest."

"And was it a lovely affair?"

"Lovely enough."

"I've given up weddings. I've attended too many. It's unhealthy. Too many weddings . . . and too many christenings." She said this with an absolute authority, as if everyone she knew would eventually make the same resolution.

"What about your own?" I asked.

"My christening or my wedding?"

"Your wedding."

"I've decided against it." She put down her brush and turned to face me. "We've had this conversation, haven't we?"

"Yes. I think it was Chicago. But that was a long time ago. Things change."

"Only the show." She lit a cigarette and leaned forward. "And you? Have you changed?"

"Not a bit."

"That's grand. I should like to count on that. You should always be the same Stephen." She inhaled deeply. "Let me buy you a drink."

"I'm with my nephew. The unmarried one."

"Someone told me that the drinking age is eighteen. Is he?"

"No."

"Then I'll buy him a soda."

"He's a musician."

"Really?!" She looked askance. "Who'd have thought?"

"In fact, both boys play."

"Then where's the other one?"

"On his honeymoon."

"That's right."

She considered the situation. "Then I'll satisfy myself with one admirer."

"Two."

She smiled again and stood up and stepped behind a dressing

screen. I wanted to stay inside that tiny room. Even with beads of sweat running down my back, I wanted more time.

"There should be three of us," I said. "Phil made it to the door, but he wouldn't come in."

"Phil's with you?"

"Not anymore. He made the drive over, but then he wandered off."

Katherine came out from behind the screen. She turned around. She asked me to zip her summer dress as she lifted her bare arms and gathered her hair into a ponytail. Then she picked up her handbag. "I'm ready," she said.

We stepped out into the hall and Katherine signed autographs for a small huddle of fans, most of them soft-spoken, until a statuesque woman, shrieking about the show and Katherine's sublime talent, broke up the party. "You must let me take you away," said this dowager, waving her cigarette. "I must have you all to myself." Katherine whispered something to the woman and she graciously retreated. The others, seeing their idol preoccupied, also disappeared.

"I'm sorry, Stephen. I forgot about Mata Hari."

"You mean you really have to go?"

"She's a producer." Katherine looked in the woman's direction. "My agent made me promise."

"How will I explain it to Jim?"

"Another time, maybe."

"Or another life."

"You're not the same," she said. "You say you are, but I don't think it's true." She fiddled with the lapel of my sport coat. "Anyway, it's just as well."

"Why?"

"Your brother's waiting."

Katherine opened and closed the clasp on her handbag. She did it repeatedly. She leaned her bare shoulder against the tile wall.

"I don't want to go," I said.

"Neither do I," she said.

"Will you write?"

"Of course, silly. As much as ever."

"I'll answer as much as ever."

"And I won't forget," Katherine said.

I couldn't touch her. I wanted very much to touch her, but my hands felt heavy and cold.

"We should go, Stephen. People are waiting."

"All right. You go first."

WHEN THE service ended, a man from the funeral parlor came forward and repositioned the shroud that covered my mother's coffin. Then he bent down and released the brake on the dolly. This was the same man who thought pallbearers were a bad idea. "Very dangerous," he said. "For the bones of the dead and backs of the living." He pushed my mother toward the door with the minister leading the way. The congregation followed.

We emerged into bright daylight, and I had to shade my eyes against the glaring chrome of the hearse. From somewhere behind the church came the sound of a piano, a stark and poignant melody that seemed to be at odds with the sunshine. I imagined it was Katherine playing. I felt disloyal, not thinking of my mother, but the guilt I felt—even the sadness—wasn't enough to sway me. I could only think of Katherine.

I'd seen her last in Cleveland, an October of muted grays, over-cast and cold and two years gone, at a café not far from the building where my father worked on radios. The waitress wore a Nixon/Agnew button. Katherine wore blue.

"I've always known where you were," I said. "I might have turned up at your door and refused to leave."

"I very much doubt it," said Katherine. "You're romantic but not impractical."

"I might surprise you. I heard somewhere that it's never too late."

"You don't believe that. It's a pleasant thing to say, but you don't believe it."

"Fine. Have it your way."

"It's not my way. It has very little to do with me."

"Is that what you believe?"

Katherine stirred her coffee. She tapped the spoon on the rim of the cup. "Except for the very lucky—or the very wicked—it's always too late."

"I count myself among the lucky," I said.

"And I count myself among the wicked," said Katherine. "But neither of us is very much one or the other."

"So we lose by degree?"

"Something like that."

Her indifference made me feel reckless. "In those first days, when we—"

She shook her head and spoke quickly. "You always talk about the past as if it were yesterday. As if your version of history is the only one that matters."

"I remember how I felt. That's all."

"Is that what you've been thinking about all this time? How you felt? Is that why you live alone?"

"I see no ring on your finger," I said.

"I never felt the need," she said.

"And I remember that, too."

"What?"

"Feeling the need."

"So what did you do about it? You're still in Cleveland. You stayed the course." She dug in her purse for a cigarette, and not finding one, she called the waitress and ordered more coffee. "And now, at long last, you want to get away."

"Why not? Maybe another state. Another city."

"And where is that city?" she asked. "I know too many people who've tried to find it; and, believe me, they all got out by mistake at wayside stations, at places like Miami, or New Orleans, or Los Angeles — and it wasn't at all different from the city they'd left, but only rather bigger and dingier and less forgiving."

She made me feel stupid. That much was still the same. "I'm sorry," I said. "I can't always stop myself."

We sat for a long time in silence drinking our coffee. I wanted to start all over again, but I gave it up. I didn't have the energy. Finally, the waitress brought the check.

"I do remember things," said Katherine. "I remember days when each new object and each new experience struck me as wondrous. And I remember that you were there." She took out a ten-dollar bill and put it on the table. "That's why I see you. You remind me that it must have been so."

WE ACCOMPANIED the coffin to the gravesite, and the minister led the family in a final prayer. A cluster of maple trees shaded my mother's plot making it a serene and friendly place, a shelter from the midday sun. A light breeze moved the thin stems of flowers.

There was nothing I wanted to say to my mother. I'd said everything while she was alive. She'd been as good a woman as she had to be in a life that was hard and even. Now the gathering of her children and grandchildren felt to me like a formality, an obligation rather than a celebration, something she would have disliked.

I thought I saw a tear on my brother's face when it was over and we started for the cars, but then I realized that his eyes were swollen with booze, and I wondered if he was showing grief or the late stages of a hangover. I walked with Jim and Paul and Charlene, and then I hung back and waited for Phil.

"You might have showered for the occasion," I said.

"Don't do this," said Carrie Ann.

Phil shaded his eyes. "Let 'im say what he wants."

"Thanks for the permission," I said.

Myron joined us and we all walked for a while without speaking. "You should have a drink," I said.

"Let's just leave," said Phil.

"You ought to have a drink to keep your strength up."

Myron caught my arm. "Can't you wait? Mmm-Mom's not . . . she's not even in the g-g-ground yet."

I shook loose and kept walking. I felt an unexpected anger roiling in my gut.

"You're both selfish," said Myron, without stuttering. He pulled at his tie. "Too fond of your own crap. Both of you." He began to walk faster and went on ahead by himself.

"You could've buttoned it for Myron's sake," said Phil.

I thought about punching him. "What gives you the right?"

"What now?" asked Phil, dropping his shoulders.

"Telling me to shut-up for Myron's sake."

Carrie Ann frowned. "Can't you argue about this some other time?"

"This may be our last family get-together," I said. "Unless you're planning a reunion."

Phil stopped and faced me. "What do you want? An apology."

I pushed past him. "No."

Back at the cars, I said good-bye to Jim. He took me by surprise, throwing his arms around me and kissing me on the cheek. "I learned this from my Italian uncles," he said.

Paul and I shook hands. "Come visit us," said Charlene. "Kimberly's talking up a storm."

"I won't promise," I said. "But I'll call if I'm up there."

Myron was already in his car and starting the engine. I walked over and he rolled down the window. "I'll call you later," I said. "I'll make dinner—or we can go out." He offered me his hand. "G-Give it some time," he said. Then the window went up and he drove away.

Parked in the shade of a horse-chestnut tree, Phil and Carrie Ann sat like statues listening to an old song on the radio. I pulled out and turned around. I fixed my eyes on the road and forced myself, as I drove past, not to glance in their direction. I didn't look back.

Six days before my mother died Nixon resigned the presidency. The Watergate cover-up had dominated the news for two years—even the end of the Vietnam war failed to divert its inexorable course—and I waited eagerly for impeachment procedures to begin, for a momentous upheaval that would scour the landscape and make it ready for redemption. Nixon, quite naturally, was the only one absolved, an executive pardon from his successor. His forgiveness came a few short days after his farewell to the White House staff, after his vainglorious gesture of victory against the backdrop of a military helicopter. The dark blades whirled, startling the air and lifting the President, a ruined but unvanquished man, into the August night.

The fall of the President and the death of my mother demanded a third event, something of equal consequence, something large and incomprehensible. I felt a need to take action, to change the established course of my life, but no immediate direction made itself clear. I went back to work. I cleaned my apartment and did some reading. I played poker with friends.

A week after the funeral I phoned Myron. "Drinks and dinner on me," I said. "You name the place." He said he'd take a "rain check," that he needed to get out of Cleveland for a while and would call once he was back in town. I said I could pick up his mail and keep his dog at my place, but Myron declined the offer, said he'd made other arrangements. After work that day I stopped at a newspaper kiosk and bought a copy of the *New York Times*. I went home and showered, put on a clean shirt, and set out for a restaurant with the *Times* as my companion.

I made my way without thinking to Ernie's Bar & Grill. I saw people with children and dogs sitting at sidewalk tables beneath the generous green awning. I went inside and the hostess recognized me.

"Good evening, sir," she said. "Table for one?"

"Yes," I said.

"Inside or out?"

"Inside," I said. "I'd like 'Automatic Anthole.' If it's available."

The young woman turned and her breasts brushed the menu. "That shouldn't be a problem."

The walls at Ernie's were a collage of limericks and comic poems. Some were framed and signed, others were written on napkins and hung with thumbtacks or tape. My favorite, in a corner booth, was "Automatic Anthole."

The hostess led me to the table and I slid into the bench seat. Before opening the paper, I looked up at the poem. The streaked glass was cracked at the edge. My lips moved as I read:

AUTOMATIC ANTHOLE
Driven by hunger, I had another
forced bachelor dinner tonight.
I had a lot of trouble making
up my mind whether to eat Chinese
food or have a hamburger. God,
I hate eating dinner alone. It's
like being dead.

I smiled when I finished reading and felt relieved that the poem always amused me. I looked at the menu for the sake of ritual and then ordered my usual meal, Ernie's specialty, grilled Lake Superior whitefish with steamed asparagus tips and garlic mashed potatoes. I ordered a bottle of wine and drank half of it and read most of the first- and second-page stories before the food was ready. I ate slowly and drank the rest of the wine and decided that the wine was better company than the newspaper. I raised my glass in honor of the fine poet who wrote "Automatic Anthole." I decided that death wasn't such a bad thing after all. Afterward I had coffee and a small snifter of brandy.

I wanted to stay and drink coffee and read, but I could see a line of people waiting for tables. I asked the waiter if there was any room at the bar. He secured a seat for me and I paid for dinner and gave up my booth. The bar was crowded and not an easy place to unfold the paper. The owner of the establishment, presumably Ernie, fancied himself a great hunter, and the space above the cash register was filled with bird decoys and photographs of men with dead pheasants.

I'd hunted only once in my life, a last-minute adventure just before my brother's nuptials. I trudged after the groom and his soon to be father-in-law in borrowed boots, carrying a borrowed shotgun. After an hour or two in the woods, we came upon an old buck with a respectable set of antlers. Phil had the best shot and he took it. I saw the legs wobble and the knees buckle and the head roll skyward before the huge body crashed down. Phil marked the animal and took a compass reading. Then we continued. The idea was that each of us would bring home a good kill. We walked for the rest of the day on abandoned trails, the ground sprinkled with mottled light, but no more deer came our way. We circled back and found the place where we'd left the buck.

I knew that there were too many deer in the woods and that some of them were starving and that it would be better if hunters thinned out the population. I understood these things. I tried to think about the good in what we had done, and I tried not to think about the sickness in my belly, but I had seen how the buck lost all dignity as soon as his eyes ceased to be alive, and how, by the end of the day, the stomach had begun to swell. The buck's antlers had been splattered with blood, and I scraped some of it off with my thumbnail and held it like a dried piece of sealing wax in my hand. I squeezed the dried blood between my fingers. Now it seemed strange to sit in a bar, in the presence of wooden ducks and stuffed owls, remembering the blood and the unfilled eyes and my feeling in that moment of being completely and irrevocably alone.

The bartender put down a fresh napkin and my second whiskey and water. I studied the pictures of upended birds in the gloved hands of hunters. I watched the faces of beautiful women in the long mirror behind the bar. I tried to read, but there was too much talk all around and the newcomer next to me insisted on striking up a conversation. I acquiesced without a struggle.

"Name's Jake," he said. "Come here often?"

I nodded. "I'm a regular."

"I've never seen you before," he said.

"I've never seen you," I said.

"Maybe we should report ourselves as missing persons." He laughed. "Then again, I may not answer to my own description." He looked hard at his face in the mirror.

"I'll vouch for you," I said. "What do you do?"

"I sell carpet," said Jake. "You?"

"I work for General Motors. Chevrolet division."

"Now that's a real job. You a big shot executive?"

I laughed. "Supervisor. Assembly line."

Jake looked to be in his late forties, maybe his early fifties. I saw the ring on his finger and asked him if he was married.

"Divorced," he said. "Final about three months ago, but I can't seem to get rid of the ring."

"It wasn't your idea?"

"No. It was my fault."

I didn't think I should ask. The bartender came around and Jake said he was fine for now. I ordered coffee.

"Tell me, . . ." Jake snapped his fingers.

"Stephen," I said.

"Tell me, Stephen. What's the greatest talent of women in general?"

"I don't know."

"It's the capacity to spend endless amounts of time with dull men. To spend it without being bored, or at least without minding that they are."

I looked at Jake's face in the mirror. "But she minded."

"That's right," said Jake. "She wasn't talented enough."

Jake excused himself and headed in the direction of the bathroom. I drank my coffee and asked for a refill. I bought Jake another drink. It came and the bartender set it beside Jake's cigarettes and matches. A woman asked me about the empty chair and I told her it was taken. I watched for Jake in the mirror. I waited until the ice in his drink had melted, until an old man came in and took Jake's seat for himself.

Sometime just before or after the old man appeared, the thing I needed to do, the large, incomprehensible thing, came to me. Jake had made it clear. I left a good tip and my newspaper on the bar.

THE NEXT morning I got up for work at the usual time. I brewed a strong pot of coffee and washed my face and shaved. I skipped the morning paper and left early, listening to talk radio for a while but then running the dial up and down until I found a station that played music. I drove the speed limit and made all but one traffic signal and pulled into the plant parking lot long before the rest of the guys on my shift.

I punched the clock and checked the board for messages, and after settling in at my desk, I dug into a pile of long overdue paperwork. I filled out forms, completed work schedules, and reviewed injury reports. I checked and double-checked my zones until I felt satisfied that there were no operational problems. After lunch, I handed my resignation to the area manager.

"This is a hot one," he said. "Come back when you're sober."

"I'm serious," I said.

"For fuck's sake," he said. "You can't be fuckin' serious. How long you got before you bail?"

"Eight years."

"Five. If you go early."

"So what."

"So fuckin' what? I'll tell you so fuckin' what. You're flushin' your pension down the crapper."

"Today's my last day."

"You need to see the nurse. Go down there right now and get some pills or somethin'."

"I'm not coming in tomorrow."

"Of course you are," he said. "I need at least two weeks' notice. And you need two weeks to change your fucked-up mind."

"I can't give you two weeks."

"What is this?" He stepped toward me and for a second looked ready to hit me. "You runnin' off with a rich widow?"

"I'll clear out my desk at the end of the day."

"I'm kickin' this upstairs. You can't piss on twenty-five years."

"It's my twenty-five years."

"Steve . . . for God's sake."

I had no explanation that would satisfy him. "Thanks for everything," I said.

"You can't be serious," he said. "What's a matter? You sicka chassis? I can give you trim?"

"No. It's nothing like that," I said.

"Then what?"

"I quit. That's all. I just quit."

Most of the guys came by that afternoon to express their disbelief or to try and convince themselves that my resignation was some sort of elaborate practical joke. Some of them went away laughing; one or two stomped off angry. Not a single man, not even my friends, could slap me on the back for what I was doing. I wanted someone to wish me well but only Ray, the sweeper, came close. "Good luck," he said. "I imagine you'll need it." The procession stopped toward the end of the day without any parting gifts or kind words from the plant brass. There wasn't much in my desk that I wanted to keep. I managed to fit most of it into a cardboard box.

THAT EVENING I called hotels in San Francisco and reserved a room at the Washington Square Inn in North Beach. The voice on the phone said that my timing was very good, that the place was booked solid, like other establishments in the city, except for a cancellation only ten minutes old. I packed two suitcases with books and magazines and as much clothing as I could carry. I post-dated a check for the September rent and delivered it to the building manager, who asked me if I planned to move to California. He wanted to know because he had a friend who needed an apartment. I told him that I had no specific plans at the moment but that I would honor the terms of the lease if I decided to leave. I gave him the address and telephone number of the Washington Square Inn, and I put a forwarding notice in my mailbox. I canceled the newspaper and cleaned out the refrigerator—wrinkled peaches and an old container of cottage cheese—and I sacked the houseplants that looked a bit peaked, giving the healthy ones to the old woman who lived down the hall.

The next morning I went to the airport without a ticket and put my name in for stand-by on several flights. I got out on a plane to Denver with a connection to San Francisco. I knew only two things about my destination: that North Beach wasn't a beach, and that a place called Russian Hill was Katherine's home.

I took a cab from the airport to the hotel, and they gave me a quiet room with a window that looked out at Washington Square, at its playground, its park benches and poplars, at the back of a statue that I later identified as Ben Franklin. I unpacked my bags, stacked my books and magazines on the table beside the bed, put out my toiletries, hung up some clothes in the antique armoire, and called the concierge about ice and a bottle of whiskey. Then I took a long shower. I was still wrapped in a towel when the concierge knocked. I tipped him and thanked him for his trouble and poured myself a weak drink. I put on khaki pants and a white cotton shirt and went out into the city for a late lunch.

The weather was surprisingly warm that afternoon, but I soon discovered that San Francisco enjoys a certain early evening quality at all times of day. The air is fresh and the narrow streets without trees are shaded by tall Victorian homes. On every corner in North Beach is a bar or café with small tables that allow a person to be alone without feeling out of place.

After lunch I went back to the hotel and read for several hours. I felt the urge to go out and see the city at night, but the journey and the events of the day before had left me exhausted. I stayed in, wanting to savor the newness of the place for as long a time as possible. I opened my window and stretched out on the bed listening to the sound of traffic.

Tomorrow I'll look for Katherine's street, I thought. I'll find the door to her apartment and I'll walk past it without ringing the bell. I wondered how many times I would go to Katherine's street without stopping. I wondered if she would be happy to see me or if, being caught off guard, she'd think me absurd for calling her bluff. I fell asleep wondering if I had the courage to see her.

In the morning I walked from my hotel to the Golden Gate Bridge. The route I chose followed the marina, keeping me well away from Russian Hill. I decided it was too soon to go there; I'd save that for another day. I walked out onto the bridge and felt the wind against my body. The headland on the other side looked as though it had just been sprinkled with water; it appeared to be an uninhabited place, a sparkling shoulder of green earth. I leaned into the wind and kept walking. When I reached the northern end of the bridge the blowing diminished, and from there I climbed a narrow road that led to a blustery ridge. I looked out across the sea to the Farallon Islands.

I returned to the road, my face tingling, and followed it down in the direction I had come, passing under the bridge and descending toward the bay, until I found myself in Sausalito. It was mid-afternoon by that time and my stomach felt empty. I bought cheese and fruit at an expensive deli and found a bench facing the water.

Behind me and across the street was a tavern that seemed unpretentious and friendly. I stopped for a beer and heard from the bartender that I could catch a ferry from the Sausalito pier back to Fisherman's Wharf. I drank a second beer and watched one or two innings of a baseball game on television. Then I headed straight for the ferry. It was late by the time I reached my hotel. I showered and shaved and rubbed my feet. Luckily there was no dearth of Italian restaurants in North Beach; I would not have to go far for dinner.

On the third day I rented a car and drove north along the Pacific Coast Highway to Stinson Beach. The desk captain at the hotel had recommended the trip, encouraging me to take advantage of the warm temperatures. The fog that morning was very thick, but it took time to rent the car and consult the map and make the drive, and when I finally dug my toes into the sand, the fog had retreated.

I decided to hike down the beach, away from the parking lot, where I could swim in the slow breakers without the distraction of dogs and children. The wet sand felt smooth and firm, and when the water rushed in around my ankles, I could feel myself slipping toward the sea. When I had gone far enough, I spread my towel on the sand and took off my hat and T-shirt. I ran into the water knowing that it was cold and knowing that if I went slowly I might not get in all the way. I dove into a whitecap, swam out underwater, and broke the surface feeling the chill. I floated on my back and let the waves cradle me, my body moving back and forth between the shore and the sea, and then I attempted all the swimming strokes I could remember. I felt tired before very long, and I floated on my back again to catch my breath. I let the slow rollers nudge me toward the beach. I came out of the water and sprawled on my towel listening to the steady rhythm of the surf.

I walked into town when I was hungry and after lunch bought lemonade from an enterprising youngster who touted his product as the freshest in California. I bought sandals from a sidewalk vendor and browsed in a used bookstore. Then I went back to the beach and swam and rested and swam again. At the public bathhouse, I rinsed myself with fresh water and put on the extra shirt and pants I'd brought with me. My body felt cool and clean in the dry clothes, and I drove back to the city in my rented car with all the windows open.

I didn't leave San Francisco in the days that followed. I spent my time at City Lights Bookstore and drank coffee and apéritifs at Vesuvio's. I rode the cable cars to Union Square and rubbed elbows with the well-heeled. I visited art galleries, asking questions like a serious buyer, and almost every night I took a table near the piano at the Sir Francis Drake Hotel.

I walked the streets of Russian Hill many times but never saw Katherine coming or going, and I never saw shadows in the third floor window, and I convinced myself that the time just after a tour wasn't a good time to drop in unannounced, that Katherine would be weary from travel, and seeing her then, I thought, would prove to be unlucky.

I tried to extend my stay at the Washington Square Inn, and in an effort to accommodate me, the desk captain changed my room twice. I moved cheerily enough, giving the impression that I might stay there indefinitely, playing the role of a wealthy and sophisticated playboy. But reality wasn't so glamorous. Needing to conserve money, I planned to start looking for an efficiency apartment where I could do my own cooking and live a more normal, if less sumptuous, life. I decided to look for a job.

I'd gone so far as to buy a Sunday paper, and I spent the next morning in my room reading the classifieds, circling a few possibilities, and then the telephone rang. Hearing it ring at that moment seemed a novelty. I'd received no calls during my stay, only mail. No one but the manager in my apartment building knew where I was. I let the phone ring several times, savoring the sound.

The words that came through the line were harsh and frantic. "It'll kill me . . . too much worry . . . you'll come, I know." I finally recognized Carrie Ann's voice.

"Slow down," I said.

"Is this California? Are you really in California?"

"Yes. Where are you?"

"I'm home. I told him I'd drive to Cleveland. But there's no time."

"Why would you drive to Cleveland?"

"I kept calling all night for two nights. Maybe an accident. Maybe a heart attack. I didn't know. I called the police and they went over. A man there had your number."

"I'm fine," I said.

"Good. Then you'll come?"

"For what?"

"By then he'll be arrested. I know it. He'll be arrested." Except for a low hum, the line went silent.

"Carrie Ann?"

"Yes."

"What's he done?"

"It's the neighbors."

"Is that it? You want me to come there because he's fighting with the neighbors?"

"No. I mean—yes. He's already done it."

"Done what?"

"He's signing a complaint."

"Who is?"

"Knute."

I kept her on the phone and asked questions, trying to calm her down and make her explain. She would only say that Phil was in trouble, that the police would be there soon and put the handcuffs on him in front of the whole neighborhood.

"Let me talk to my brother," I said.

"He's sleeping."

"He's drunk," I said.

"All the time."

I told her I'd go straight to the airport and take the first available flight to Detroit. "He'll be arrested by then," she said. "I know it."

I packed one suitcase and asked the concierge to ship the rest. "It's not common practice," he said. I gave him more money than was necessary. "If it's too much trouble," I said, "then give the stuff away." He wrote down my Cleveland address and agreed to take care of everything. I settled my bill with the desk captain and then stood at the curb in Washington Square waiting for my cab.

I called Carrie Ann before I got on the plane. "Just tell me the whole story," I said. "From the beginning."

"You'll understand when you get here," she said. She sounded calmer, perhaps exhausted.

"Did you try to call Myron?" I asked.

"No," she said. "I have a postcard from Myron. He's in Maine."

"Okay," I said. "Is there anything you can tell me?"

"I don't know the whole story," she said.

I realized later that Carrie Ann was right. She knew very little. Knute and Selena knew some of the story, and so did the policeman who took the complaint. Those present at the arraignment heard only the smallest part; the court-appointed defender knew nothing. It was the hospital psychologist who knew the most, but her version didn't include my brother's past. For the people who lived on Lincoln Street, the ones who came out of their houses to watch, the story began with two peace officers and my brother in handcuffs.

But this was not the beginning.

MY BROTHER had heard the music for a long time, longer than he could remember, the notes floating through open windows, through doors flung wide, visiting him in summers of ripe strawberries and sudden storms. He paid no attention to it at first, but as the years piled up and smothered all other sounds, the music by necessity became more pronounced. My brother came to depend on it, listening in his most private moments, recognizing over time that the music was growing, becoming more and more complex, until finally he heard recognizable songs, melodies that stirred the far reaches of his body, those parts that he had abandoned long ago.

The moment must have seemed to him like a waking dream,

when he stood in the back yard of his mortgaged home, a man of fifty-nine, and looked through the open French doors of his neighbor's house to discover that the little girl playing was no longer a child. She had become seventeen. Her black hair had grown, touching the piano bench when she raised her head.

He often worked in the yard after that, finding more to do than was necessary, and he drank whiskey to kill the feeling, drank through his mother's death and funeral, drank when he returned home and found Knute and his family away on vacation.

Phil waited for the music's return, looking for a car in the driveway, watching for an open window or door. And when the girl came back and the music began, he could not drink enough.

Two evenings later, when Knute and his wife drove away, my brother climbed the fence in the back yard, slicing his hand on a rusty post, and he walked across the patio and through the French doors and stood behind Selena, who did not hear him, absorbed as she was in her playing, and my brother in his haze of pain and memory bent over and kissed her, a damp and trembling kiss, on the neck.

Her screams frightened him until he saw his blood pooling on the floor. Then he backed away through the French doors and threw himself over the fence that had cut his palm. Carrie Ann heard the outcry. She rushed into the yard and found her husband kneeling between his roses, trying to cover his bleeding hand with dirt.

Days passed before Knute and his wife decided to file a complaint. Phil stayed inside, pacing from room to room like a condemned man, looking much older with his gray, unshaved stubble, and despite the still warm weather of early September, he closed all the windows and doors. Then the squad car came at dusk and my brother surrendered himself without a word or a struggle.

I arrived that night, miring myself in the strange dissolution of my brother's life, promising myself that this was the last time. I went to the arraignment, arranged the money, and collected the prisoner from the city jail. He didn't speak either to me or to Carrie Ann, but we stayed nearby as he drank and paced the house, refusing to prepare for his day in court, until Knute and his family suddenly and inexplicably dropped the charges.

Here the story should've ended. But my brother, enraged by Knute's change of heart, was not satisfied. He demanded more. He wanted his last confrontation, his last climb into forces beyond his control, living only for the struggle and the clarity that follows, the decisive blade of judgment. It must have felt unfair—he had settled for so little for so many years—or entirely senseless, even cruel, when the law dropped the question, when the law insisted that there was nothing now, nothing to be expiated or punished.

So Phil took matters into his own hands. He bought a fifth of Jack Daniels and drank all of it in an hour. His body couldn't tolerate or transform the poison, and so for the second time in two weeks, much to the satisfaction of his neighbors, uniformed men and flashing lights returned to Lincoln Street to rush my brother away. The paramedic pushed the gurney, said it looked to him like alcohol-induced coma, and then the ambulance was gone.

The doctors made no promises, but after the stomach pump and the IV and the hours of shallow breathing, my brother opened his eyes. He made no response to our greetings or to the nurse's questions and so, for a while, seemed entirely himself, and then we discovered that not a single sound disturbed him, that my brother was deaf, stone deaf, as a result of his body's shock.

There was no precise explanation for the deafness, even the specialist they called in admitted that he was baffled. He tapped his tuning fork on his open hand. "I really can't say," he said. Then the tuning fork disappeared into his pocket.

WHEN THE hospital released my brother and he returned to the house on Lincoln Street, a deaf but sober man, he sat down in his armchair in front of the television set and did not move. He took his meals in that chair. He slept in it. He left it only when he needed the toilet or a bath.

Carrie Ann did her best to keep things going, but as the trees in the neighborhood turned, a rain of red leaves disappearing on the wind, her husband's flowerbeds and green lawn went without care. The front porch settled after a hard freeze and the roof began to sag. "The place is a mess," said Carrie Ann. "When you walk out onto the porch at night, you can't see the moon or stars. It's that bad."

I SAW PHIL occasionally, after he took early retirement, after the gossip and the slow wagging of heads. His eyes looking at me or in the direction of Carrie Ann were entirely empty, his body awkward and stiff. Too see him was unbearably sad. When he did venture outside, to haul out garbage or close the garage door, the neighbors looked away, and the children, those who were not frightened by his face, pointed and laughed and yelled names.

Time ran fast, losing its hard edges. Selena went off to boarding school and Knute sold his house, moving himself and his wife to a more hospitable climate, a place where the sun is warmer. Paul and Jim, treated like spectators during the jailing and the illness, went to visit their father at Thanksgiving. After that they chose to avoid him—forever. Myron heard the whole story from me and drove up to Detroit once, but Phil would not see him. And after a while, a short while, Phil would not see me.

Winter moved permanently into his face; it refused to budge. It scored deep and unforgiving ruts into his forehead and cheeks. And he did nothing to protect himself. He gave himself over to the cold.

I WENT BACK to Cleveland. I kept my apartment and found a job setting type for a small press—limited editions printed on fine paper with hand-sewn spines. I started with slim volumes. Now I do longer works and broadsides. Myron walks his dog down to the shop and the three of us go out for lunch. My brother's sons call me when they can. We exchange cards at Christmas.

I live in the city where my brother and I grew up, where we made our choices, and choices were made for us. I think of Margie and Katherine and my mother. I go to the old places to make peace with what happened there, but then memories take hold of me and I twist and turn my body, trying to keep the past at arm's length, trying to shake it off, feeling a grip that is strong and absolute. And in such moments I think of Phil and his surrender to the past, his sacrifice, and I am drawn to the silence of his world. I understand its power.

I think of my brother. What I have of him is memory. And sometimes when I walk away from the old places, going home through the streets of Cleveland, I look to the West and wish that my brother and I were not so much the same. I try not to remember, hoping that his absence will change me or allow me a second life. But then the night sky goes blank. Beyond the dark silhouettes of trees there is nothing. Memory is all.